Praise for *The Serbian Dane:*

'Brilliant! More, more! I believed every word of it — the danger, the action, the politics of power and fear. Davidsen writes like an assassin'
— Fay Weldon

'An absolutely gripping thriller, with insights into the horrors of the Bosnian war and the problems of being a writer in a world where words are dangerous' — Joan Smith

'Resonates because one can't dismiss its frightening truth'
— Paul Binding, *Independent*

'This pacy political thriller takes us into a world of endangered writers and global intrigues ... the cast of characters and the plot have an uncanny sense of the all-too-real. I couldn't put it down' — Lisa Appignanesi

'A fast-paced action thriller, worth reading for its unusual setting and vivid characterisation' — Peter Millar, *The Times*

'An unusually intelligent and thoughtful thriller — and beautifully translated by Barbara J. Haveland with scarcely a false note'
— Bob Cornwall, *Tangled Web*

The Serbian Dane

Leif Davidsen is a Danish journalist and the author of a number of best-selling suspense novels. He has worked for many years for Danish radio and television as a foreign correspondent and editor of foreign news, specialising in Russian, East and Central European affairs.

Barbara J. Haveland was born in Scotland, and now lives in Denmark with her Norwegian husband and teenage son. She has translated works by several leading Danish and Norwegian authors, including Peter Høeg, Linn Ullmann and Jan Kjærstad.

Leif Davidsen

The Serbian Dane

Translated from the Danish by
Barbara J. Haveland

ARCADIA BOOKS

Arcadia Books Ltd
15-16 Nassau Street
London W1W 7AB

www.arcadiabooks.co.uk

First published in the United Kingdom by Arcadia Books, 2007
This B format edition printed May 2007
Originally published by Lindhardt og Ringhof, 1996
Copyright © Leif Davidsen, 1996

The English translation from the Danish, *Den serbiske dansker*
Copyright © Barbara J. Haveland, 2007

A catalogue record for this book is available from the British Library

ISBN 1-905147-67-8

Typeset in Bembo by Basement Press
Printed in Finland by WS Bookwell

Arcadia Books Ltd gratefully acknowledges the financial support of The Arts Council of
England. This book is supported by the Danish Art Council's Committee for Literature.

Arcadia Books supports English PEN, the fellowship of writers who work together to promote
literature and its understanding. English PEN upholds writers' freedoms in Britain and around
the world, challenging political and cultural limits on free expression. To find out more, visit
www.englishpen.org or contact
English PEN, 6-8 Amwell Street, London EC1R 1UQ

Arcadia Books distributors are as follows:

in the UK and elsewhere in Europe:
Turnaround Publishers Services
Unit 3, Olympia Trading Estate
Coburg Road
London N22 6TZ

in the US and Canada:
Independent Publishers Group
814 N. Franklin Street Chicago, IL 60610

in Australia:
Tower Books
PO Box 213 Brookvale, NSW 2100

in New Zealand:
Addenda
PO Box 78224 Grey Lynn Auckland

in South Africa:
Quartet Sales and Marketing
PO Box 1218 Northcliffe Johannesburg 2115

Arcadia Books is the *Sunday Times* Small Publisher of the Year

Chapter 1

Franji Draskuvic, writer and philosopher, was a happy man. He was well-pleased with himself and his carefully tended beard, with the late summer sunshine, in which his fine city of Zagreb looked as lovely as a young maiden, and with the fact that the powerful new Croatian army had finally driven the fucking Serbs out of Krajina. But above all, Draskuvic was pleased with the broadcast he had just made on Croatian national radio, from a studio watched over by a picture of the president. As was his wont, he had made his address in a voice that was soft, not much more than a whisper really, yet firm. Introduced just the right note of huskiness into his voice, a rasp that sent a cold but delicious shiver running down the spines of his devoted listeners. The grand, flowery, patriotic sentences had flowed from the little mouth buried within the bushy grey beard and been swallowed up by the microphone, to be recorded on tape for broadcasting in the afternoon to all the good citizens of a strong free Croatia.

Draskuvic was a Balkan intellectual and proud of it. In pointed yet lofty terms his broadcast had once again made it quite clear who had the right to Krajina. It had exposed the lies of the Serbs and the international mafia who claimed that this was old Serbian territory. But Draskuvic was here to tell them that the Serbs had been put there three hundred years earlier by those lily-livered Austro-Hungarians to form an outpost against the heathen Turks. In exchange for land, these Serbian barons were to defend the outermost frontier of the empire. The Serbs were nothing but colonists. Now Krajina had been liberated. At long last. In the face of international boycotts and Russo-Serb conspiracies, and with the help of the Germans and the Americans, Croatia had rebuilt its glorious army. Its troops had fought like true patriots and proved that a new balance of power now prevailed in the Balkans. After four

1

years of mortification, Croatia was ready to defend its sacred soil. For the first time the Serbians were on the run. Now they were being given a taste of their own medicine. When it came to the crunch they had turned and fled like mangy dogs, while the UN troops, those scurrilous lackeys of the traitorous international community, cowered in their pathetic little foxholes.

'Spit on them, true patriots! They deserve nothing but your contempt!' he had urged. Television footage of Serbian refugees with their ridiculous belongings packed into ancient farm carts gave him great satisfaction. The only thing that annoyed him was that they were allowed to drive off on tractors that were doubtless stolen. They should be made to walk. To crawl on their bleeding knees. They had much to feel sorry for. He had briefly considered going to Krajina to see the fleeing curs with his own eyes and perhaps speed them on their way with a few well-chosen words. It would be reported in the press, of course. For a moment he saw the picture in his mind: a distinguished European intellectual who was not afraid to join the brave sons of the people. But no, he must restrain himself. His life was too important. He was a great poet and an old man, and so he stayed in Zagreb. He fought on his own front. The intellectual front. It was every bit as vital as the other fronts. The soldiers could not fight without spiritual nourishment. Did they not want to know why they were fighting? Would they not need moral and spiritual strength? He had closed his broadcast by saying:

'Fellow countrymen! Go with God to Krajina and make that liberated soil fertile once more!'

Draskuvic was a happy man. Despite the heat, he was wearing a suit. Under his arm he carried a Croatian magazine to which he had contributed an article on the need to purge liberated areas of impure elements. Draskuvic regarded himself as a thinker and a patriot. He wrote of valour and patriotic justice in exactly the same way as Serbian intellectuals wrote about bravery and honour. Intellectuals who never saw the blood and the suffering. He penned his venomous commentaries as a counterweight to the malicious spoutings of the Serbs. From other safe offices and comfortable apartments the intellectuals disseminated the words that generated and nurtured hate.

Slowly he made his way through the crowd to his favourite café. He nodded distantly to people who recognized him and eyed with disgust a couple of tipsy UN soldiers who were attempting to chat up two young girls. The soldiers were from the Ukraine, so the girls were unlikely to be interested in them, unless the men had made enough deutschmarks from their smuggling activities to win them over. He made a mental note for his next radio broadcast. About the necessity of keeping oneself pure in the dark hour of conflict. It would provide yet another moral boost to those fighting at the front, he thought with satisfaction.

Vuk watched him from a distance.

Vuk was sitting astride a battered motorbike, the number plate of which was caked with mud. He was wearing a helmet with the visor down. In his blue jeans and worn, brown leather jacket he looked like any other young guy in the capital of independent Croatia.

Vuk observed Draskuvic closely. The rolling gait that lent an almost feminine sway to his fat arse, and the belly that ploughed the air ahead of him like a heavy-laden, flat-bottomed barge on the Danube. This was the fifth day Vuk had waited for him at the café. On the first Vuk had worn a suit and sat at one of the tables set out on the pavement. On the second day he had walked past dressed in the uniform of the Danish UN contingent. On the third day he was back in his suit. On the fourth he wore a short-sleeved shirt with a pair of beige chinos and the kind of padded gilet that the foreign correspondents loved to swan around in.

Draskuvic's routine never varied. He arrived at the radio station at 9.00 am; at 10.30 am he strolled down to the café to have coffee and read the newspapers. To Vuk it seemed quite crazy that he was not more security-conscious. The country was at war, and Draskuvic was one of the bastards who, with his propaganda, had whipped up hatred against the Serbs. Didn't he realize he was a possible target? Was he really that stupid? Or that arrogant?

Vuk was perspiring heavily. He could feel the beads of sweat running down the back of his neck and over his cheeks. His T-shirt clung to his back and stomach. It was hot inside the close-fitting helmet and the leather jacket, but it wasn't just that. He had a tendency to break out into a sweat before a hit. People talked about the sweat of fear, but that they described as cold. So maybe it wasn't fear or nervousness that caused it, but simply an excess of adrenalin. His hands were steady enough. His senses became ultra-sharp, registering details so accurately and so clearly that they seemed almost to be etched on his mind: a woman's shapely cupid's bow, the almost black eyes of a child, the Ukrainian soldier's pimply cheek, the yellow paint flaking off a wall, the grating cough of a broken exhaust silencer, the reek of low-grade petrol and an unwashed body passing close by his motorbike. Draskuvic, his vulnerable belly and unsuspecting, almost child-like, smooth-skinned face.

Draskuvic sat down at an empty table in the second row from the front but still in the shade of the canopy. He was well known to the waiters, they brought him his coffee and a newspaper. Draskuvic lit his cigar, and Vuk started his motorbike. It purred into life. The engine revved, revealing to anyone who cared to notice that beneath the dirty battered exterior lay a relatively new engine. He pulled the zip of the leather jacket halfway down, stuck his right hand inside and curled his fingers around the butt of the Russian-made Markarov. It held eight 9 mm bullets. It was a pretty clumsy pistol, but Vuk found it reliable: like most old Soviet equipment, it was simply made and worked well in tricky situations. The Markarov had quite a hefty butt, but that was no big problem. In any case, he was wearing a pair of fine leather gloves. At this distance it wasn't accuracy he needed, but penetration. Two tables away from Draskuvic a young couple were talking quietly. They sat with their faces close together, the way lovers do. Farther back in the café some elderly men were playing cards. To Draskuvic's right was a group that might pose a threat: three Croatian soldiers, but they weren't wearing any visible weapons and were obviously drunk. They had probably been drinking all night and would carry on drinking all day. They were having an incoherent argument about whose turn it was to buy the next bottle of slivovitz. They had spent the past fifteen minutes bragging about their exploits during the Krajina campaign. The Serbian dogs had dropped like flies under their fire.

Traffic was light on the narrow side street. An old, grey-streaked Mercedes drove slowly past, leaving a trail of uncombusted diesel in its wake. An elderly couple carrying an empty string shopping bag hirpled past in the gutter. A mother scolded her child and hauled it away howling in protest.

Vuk took three deep breaths and thought of the Commandant's words: no dramatics, not ever. Leave that to actors in the movies. Quick in. Quick out. Don't think about anything except survival.

He dismounted from the bike. The rubber soles of his Reeboks made no sound as he walked the few steps across the narrow thoroughfare towards Draskuvic while pulling the pistol out of its shoulder holster and cocking it in one long, controlled movement. Draskuvic looked up. He may have glimpsed Vuk's face behind the smoked visor, although there's no way of knowing. Vuk shot him twice in the face and once in the chest. Draskuvic toppled backwards. The cigar dropped from his lips onto his jacket. Before Drascuvic had hit the ground Vuk was walking calmly, but with long strides, back to the motorbike. He didn't hold on to the pistol, instead he let it slide down onto the tarmac as he swung his leg back over the bike. There was no shortage of guns in this country. He gained a second by dropping it instead of returning it to the shoulder holster. Those few people who managed to react were looking at Draskuvic, not at Vuk. Their eyes stayed riveted on the blood that was spurting over the table and gushing onto the café floor before, war-hardened as they were, they threw themselves to the ground and started shrieking. The first screams broke out as Vuk put the motorbike into first gear and sped off around the corner.

A brown, leather-clad back and a pair of blue jeans astride a motorbike. Probably a Japanese make. It looked old, but that might have been mainly due to the dirt and mud. That was all that witnesses could remember.

The bike was in fact quite new, stolen a couple of days earlier from a notorious smuggler who hung out down by the harbour in Split and was still considering whether to report the theft, seeing that he had brought the bike over the border without the knowledge of the relevant authorities.

Vuk turned onto the main road and drove on, fast but not recklessly, for a few hundred yards. He parked outside a supermarket and took off the helmet. He hung it over the handlebar, pulled a small, snub-nosed Smith &Wesson revolver out of the motorbike pannier, stuffed it into the pocket of his leather jacket and walked off down the pavement without a backward glance, slipping the jacket off as he did so and slinging it nonchalantly over his shoulder, one finger hooked through the loop at the collar. He had tucked the gloves into the jacket's other pocket. His hair was black. Passers-by saw a young man like so many others, with black hair and a dark bushy moustache. He was well built. A pair of bright blue eyes did, however, mark him out from other young

5

men and prompted a few women to look twice at him. He turned down a side street, unlocked the door of a tan-coloured Lada and drove away.

Here the Croatian police lost track of him. No one could remember the registration number of the car, and descriptions of the hit man varied so much that an Identikit picture was out of the question. The killer had vanished into thin air. Or into the chaos of war.

The young man who called himself Vuk drove south-east, towards Slovenia. He took it nice and easy. Traffic was light. The little villages were bathed in the golden glow of late summer. Red-tile roofs were pocked with black shell-holes. A breeze tugged at white curtains and sent them billowing out of broken windowpanes. Very few people were about, even though the war had moved on. After driving for a couple of hours Vuk stopped on a hilltop and looked down onto a broad highway. Dust swirled up around a convoy: hay-wagons towed by tractors, and small carts, each drawn by a single horse. Blue diesel fumes hung in the air. The carts were laden with clothes, old furniture, pots and pans and mattresses. The children were vacant-eyed, the men unshaven. The women's colourful headscarves were coated with fine dust. He followed his countrymen with his eyes. Now they too were tasting the dust of flight. He smoked a cigarette and watched them for a while, then climbed back into the car. He drove a couple of hundred yards down a dirt road and parked the Lada on the fringe of a clump of trees. He took a well-worn rucksack from the boot and placed it on the ground; removed an explosive device from the rucksack, set the detonator to go off in five minutes then threw the device into the front seat of the car. He pulled on the leather jacket, slung the rucksack onto his back and strode briskly, but not too hastily, away from the car, heading downhill towards the River Sava, which divided Croatia from Bosnia-Herzegovina. He did not look back when he heard the dull boom and the crackling sound of the Lada burning. Then the petrol tank exploded and a black cloud of smoke rose into the air. It was a long time since anyone had paid much heed to a bomb in the Balkans. But somewhere in that blue sky an inquisitive NATO plane might wheel lazily around and fly down to see what was burning. The pilot would see a car in flames and a tiny dot walking down a track. A shepherd, minding his own business. Yet another lone refugee in a land of refugees.

Evening was drawing on when Vuk came to a little house on the outskirts of the village. He was dog-tired and his shoulders ached. White smoke rose from the house's one chimney. Roof and walls were intact. The war had not knocked at this door. Vuk scanned his surroundings carefully. A solitary dog came running along the side of the house, its tail between its legs. It was yellow and scrawny, but it didn't bark. He was raising his hand to knock when the door opened.

'Hello, Vuk, I've been expecting you,' said the woman who had opened it. She was very young, with long black hair and beautiful dark eyes that seemed somehow lifeless.

'Hello, Emma,' he said and kissed her on the lips.

'I was watching for you,' she said. 'It's been on the news already.'

Vuk made no response.

'About the Croatian writer,' she went on.

'It's best that you know nothing.'

'Come in, Vuk. Are you staying the night?'

'I'll cross the river later tonight.'

'That's a pity. But...he sent a message, the Commandant. He needs to speak to you as soon as possible.'

For the first time Vuk smiled. His face lit up. The tense lines seemed to melt away, and he became the boy he was beneath that stony face.

'Come on in, Vuk. Let me wash your hair,' Emma said, and she too smiled.

The living room was simply and tastefully furnished with a dining table and a bookcase full of hardbound books. There were pictures of the Bosnian mountains on the walls, and in one corner a lamp shed a warm light over an armchair and a small table decked with a crocheted mat. A book and some sewing lay on the table. It was a very neat feminine room. Beyond it a tiny kitchenette was visible. A pot of water steamed on the hob. A short hallway led to a bedroom containing a double bed. Over the bed hung an Orthodox crucifix.

Vuk's eyes followed the movement of Emma's slender legs under the thin stuff of her dress, as he took off his leather jacket and his shirt. His body was slim but muscular. A scar ran across his left shoulder; it looked like an old knife wound. Emma took one of the chairs from around the dining table and set it on some sheets of newspaper spread out in the middle of the kitchenette's tiled floor.

'Sit down, Vuk,' she said.

She picked up a ladle and poured the hot water from the pot into a bowl on the kitchen bench. She added cold water and tested it gingerly with her elbow before dipping a sponge into the warm water and wetting his black hair.

He sat with his eyes closed while she gently soaped his hair. He savoured the feel of the strong soft hands slowly massaging the soap into his scalp. The suds turned black and ran down onto the newspapers as she rinsed his hair, then lathered it again. By the third rinsing his hair was a light blond. Very carefully she dampened his moustache. He sat perfectly still. Then, with one quick tug she ripped it off, like a mother removing a plaster from a child's knee. Vuk opened his eyes. Emma's face was very close to his. He smiled.

'Hello, lover,' she said.

He kissed her.

'Stand up,' she said.

He stood up. Emma undid his belt and pulled down his trousers. He had closed his eyes again, merely lifted one leg, then the other. She ran her hand down the back of his boxer shorts and pulled them off too. He stood quietly with his eyes shut. Another scar from yet another knife wound undulated across his hip like a little snake. She touched it lightly, and his skin broke out in goosebumps as he recalled the pain of the Croatian's knife. She poured the water down the sink and ladled more warm water from the pot into the bowl, before dipping the sponge into it again and slowly washing him down. She started at his shoulders and ended with his feet. He stood there naked and perfectly still. His fair skin reddened easily, and she could see that she was having an effect on his penis, but she could also sense his self-control. She wiped off the soap with a freshly rinsed sponge. Then she pulled her dress over her head and lifted a clean towel that she had left lying on the kitchen bench next to the bowl.

Vuk opened his eyes when he heard her pulling her dress over her head. He smiled, and the smile spread to his blue eyes. She dried him all over, slowly and sensually. Rubbed him down gently but firmly. Again beginning with his face and shoulders and working her way down. When at last she softly stroked his balls, his cock rapidly swelled, she pushed him back onto the chair and settled herself on top of him.

They stayed quite still. She tipped her head back slightly. He cupped his hands around her buttocks.

'Stay with me tonight, Vuk,' she said.

'I'll stay with you.'

'What about him?'

'He can wait. The war's lost anyway. The treachery has begun. One day more or less won't make any difference.'

'Stay tonight and keep the demons away,' she said.

'I'll stay with you tonight,' he said and held her close.

The demons would visit her anyway, he knew. They came in the mornings, in the cruel grey dawn, before the light broke through. Ghosts, skeletons, spirits and ethnic purgers. Shadows from the land of the dead that had visited her family and wiped it out in the first year of the war four years earlier, when she was only fifteen. Now they returned every night in her dreams, but the nightmares were more real to her than her waking life.

Vuk envied her. Emma could feel pain and guilt. Vuk could feel her body.

The rest was coldness.

Chapter 2

These days, when Lise Carlsen woke, it was always with the shade of some stupid dream on the fringes of her still more or less slumbering consciousness. She woke up panic-stricken, feeling somehow outside of herself. As if she were hovering over the double bed in the light of a late August morning, looking down on herself and her husband, who lay there curled up in a ball or on his back, his lips straining, as though he were struggling to say something. She never remembered her dreams. They faded as soon as she heard the sound of the radio. Music or voices. It woke her just before the news: she had no wish to wake up to death and destruction; better to start the day with pop music or the latest traffic update. For thirty-four years she had taken sleep and the waking from it for granted. As far as she could remember, at any rate. She had been such an easy baby too. Slept soundly at night and woke up cooing and smiling, content to lie there on her own for a while, playing with her fingers or toes. Or so her mum said. But this summer sleep did not come easy, and she woke up with the flat taste of unresolved dreams lingering at the back of her mind.

Lise Carlsen rolled onto her back and gazed at the ceiling while listening to the closing strains of the Take That number that was being played constantly on Radio P3 that summer. It was going to be another scorcher, she could tell. The curtain barely moved in the soft breeze. Ole groaned and turned over onto his side with his back to her. Time was when he would have slipped his hand into hers and snuggled up to her. Or she to him. Her heart sank still further at the thought that the only memory she had of their lovemaking the night before was a stickiness between her legs, there was no recollection of pleasure. They were both naked. There was nothing else for it

11

in this heat. She longed for rain and cool air. The hot weather generated sweat and lust and moved one to reach for the nearest body. And it didn't really matter if one's feelings were lying dormant. The heat craved release. It caused the hormones to run riot. She slid the duvet down to her waist, folded her hands behind her head on the damp pillow and listened to the radio that had woken her. She could not really have said why she greeted the coming of each new morning by listening to the seven o'clock news. She didn't remember a word of it afterwards. Not until she heard it all repeated an hour later. But she derived a certain comfort from being reminded that her own troubles were as nothing compared to the horrors with which the smooth neutral tones of the newsreader brought her back to reality each morning. Maybe it was because Ole hated being woken by music and chatter. Could it be that what she was really trying to do here was to drive him out of the marriage bed? Or out of the marriage? She was a journalist, earned her own living, could buy her own clock radio, *had* bought it, plugged it in and used it. So there! Was that what she'd said? Was it perhaps also a sign of her own lack of resolve that she had turned the volume down so low that she could hardly hear it herself? It would have taken a bomb to wake Ole, so it really didn't bother him at all. While the slightest sound could wake her. These days, at any rate, when every nerve ending seemed to have been dusted with itching powder.

There were all the usual stories: an incipient stage battle over the forthcoming budget, the never-ending war in Yugoslavia and the continuing drought. She wasn't listening; instead she was trying to figure out why she felt so miserable and why she always seemed able to shake off this feeling once she'd had her shower. Then she heard Santanda's name mentioned. She pictured the writer: a pleasant little woman with a round face, brown eyes and the ability to speak about difficult, life-and-death issues without making one feel uncomfortable. She didn't catch what it was all about. Only the mention of both Sara Santanda and Iran. And the Danish foreign minister, speaking on a sluggish phone link, deploring the fact that the crucial dialogue with the clerical government in Teheran had not given the expected result. Well, she would catch the story again at eight o'clock. If it was big enough. Otherwise she would just have to wait until she got to the newsroom.

She nudged Ole and got out of bed. He sighed, but she noticed that he opened his eyes before she disappeared into the bathroom. He smelled faintly of stale alcohol.

'Turn off that radio, for Christ's sake,' she heard before she shut the door.

As always, a shower helped. First the hot water then the cold. Once out in the spacious open-plan kitchen, with the light cascading through the window and the faint hum of the Østerbro morning traffic in the background, what she herself would have called her black waking thoughts disappeared. Then she no longer longed for rain and cold. They would return soon enough to Denmark, where grey seemed to be the most constant hue. She loved the warmth and sunshine. She poured water into the coffee machine, set the table, boiled eggs and sliced bread for toasting, while making up her mind yet again that she would speak to Ole about *it*. I mean, if you couldn't talk to your husband about a little bout of the morning blues, who could you talk to? And he was a psychologist. He was paid to listen to people with serious psychological problems. Maybe that was why he was so bad at listening to her? Maybe she didn't conform to his textbook theories? Maybe the problem was that she only ever told him half of what she was thinking and feeling.

Lise collected the newspapers from the hall. Her own paper, *Politiken*, and *Berlingske Tidende*, so that she could check out the competition's arts pages. She opened *Politiken* straight away and found that her piece on the new gallery had been given quite a decent space under a three-column headline, but *Berlingske Tidende* had used a picture as well. And those dummies at Rådhuspladsen wondered why circulation was dropping! She turned to the foreign news and ran a quick eye over the headlines. She would read each report in depth after she had had her breakfast, or once she got to the office. She preferred to get out of the apartment quickly at this time of day. Somehow she found it hard to concentrate here. She dumped the papers onto the big, scrubbed-oak table that dominated the kitchen-cum-living room. The coffee machine gave a little hiss. Outside a bird was singing half-heartedly.

Ole came in and kissed her on the cheek before settling himself with the main section of *Berlingske Tidende*. Once he had been a radical socialist, now he had his own practice.

'D'you think you could switch off that radio or at least turn it down?' he said.

'I want to hear the news. It'll be on in a minute.'

'Surely it can't make any bloody difference whether you hear it now or in an hour's time.'

'I'm a journalist.'

'So?'

'So I need to know what's going on, Ole.'

'You can do that at work.'

'We have this same conversation every single morning.'

'Well, there's a reason for everything...'

'What's that supposed to mean?'

He looked up from his paper. The two slices of bread popped out of the toaster. Instinctively she turned to take them.

'That we seem to put all our energy into arguing about little things instead of having a serious talk about why our marriage appears to be in trouble.'

For a moment she stood there saying nothing, holding the hot slices of bread. Then they burned her fingers, and she almost threw them onto the table, wafted her fingers and said 'Ow'. She really did not want to talk about this right now. *She* wanted to be the one to say when the time was right.

'There's no need to exaggerate. Are you going to tell me you didn't have a good time last night? Just because I like listening to the radio in the morning.'

He turned back to his newspaper.

'I've got a long day ahead of me,' he said.

'Well, didn't you?'

'You've always been hot-blooded, Lise. I'm here, aren't I?'

'God, you're a hard nut.'

'It was meant as a compliment.'

'It didn't sound like one,' she said, and he looked back down at his newspaper.

'Maybe I could book an appointment with you?' she added. She didn't mean to say it; it just came out.

He glanced up again. Regarded her with those wise, weary eyes that watched all the folly of mankind pass in review while his secretary wrote out the bills. Depression measured in kroner and øre. Solutions on the National Health. Help doled out in carefully measured doses. Why had she fallen for him? He was good-looking, even if he was ten years older than her. Intelligent, articulate, a good listener, well read, an idealist, good in bed, funny, a keen traveller. Can a person change so much in eight years? Or was it her?

'You can have all the time you want, Lise,' he said. 'If that's what you want.'

'I just want to hear the news,' she said, placing butter and cheese on the table before picking up *Politiken* and proceeding to flick through it to see what sort of treatment her friends' – and her enemies' – pieces had received.

'Good morning, Lise,' he said, making her smile in spite of herself. And then they were able to eat in silence until she heard the jingle announcing the news, followed by the mellifluous tones of the newsreader:

Good morning. Fierce fighting in central Bosnia again last night. And the Serbian flight from Krajina continues. At home, the government risks being outvoted on the question of funding for exports to Iran. Yesterday Iran reaffirmed the sentence of death on the writer Sara Santanda and raised the price on her head to four million dollars. It will be another warm sunny day.

Lise felt the usual sense of helplessness like a sharp pang in her stomach. How could they? How could such fanaticism exist in a modern world? How could her own government be so weak? How could they sentence a writer to death simply for writing a novel that described the way in which women in Iran were oppressed by those bloody ayatollahs? First Rushdie, now Santanda. Who would be next? The western nations had never taken the defence of Rushdie seriously. So the oppressors were left to pursue their ruthless policies. She was seething inside but couldn't bring herself to share her thoughts with Ole. They had been through all this so many times. He listened with interest, but he had no time for politics these days. Whether on the international scale or closer to home.

She looked across at him. He was reading his *Berlingske Tidende*, absorbed in the latest Danish tittle-tattle. What had become of the dedicated campaigner whom she had married? What had happened to them over the years? Could love, desire, joy die without you being aware of it? She felt depression creeping over her again. She feared it, fought it. She was afraid that one day she might succumb and embrace it. She refused to give in to it. She had to pull herself together.

There must be some bond between them still, because he looked up as if picking up vibrations from her.

'Is something the matter, Lise?' he said.

'No. It's just this thing with Santanda. It's so appalling.'

'Yeah, you're right there.'

She sighed and stood up.

'Is that all you have to say? Didn't you hear what they said on the news?'

He glanced over at the radio, as if only noticing it now.

'You know I hate listening to the radio in the morning. You insist on having background noise, so I've learned to switch off. Block it out… I simply don't hear what they say, or the ghastly music they play. It's just a lot of gibberish to me. I prefer to read my paper. I can't do two things at once.'

'Okay.'

'Is that all you have to say?'

'I'm off, Ole. Have a good day!'

She tried to sound sarcastic, but either he didn't hear it or chose to ignore it.

'You too, love,' was all he said.

The sunshine made her feel a bit better. It had been such a long hot summer. Just one glorious day after another, and Copenhagen had sizzled and simmered like some Mediterranean harbour town. Lise loved her city as only an incomer can do. She had joined *Politiken* as a cub reporter, and they would have to carry her out of the apartment in Østerbro. She was never going to move back to a small town again or even to the suburbs. She zoomed along with her head held high on the snazzy scarlet bike with masses of gears that she had treated herself to in the spring. She was well aware that she drew a few glances. She knew that she and the bike were a good match. Not bad, she thought to herself, getting looks like that from young guys when you're in your mid-thirties. It's the summer weather that does it. People simply feel better when the sun shines. With every turn of the pedals her mood lightened. Her spirits rose with every flutter of her skirt. It would all work out all right. For Ole and her too. If not, then they would have to try living apart. That needn't be such a bad thing either: a bit of a breathing space. And maybe he would discover that he couldn't do without her. Or she him. She wasn't going to think any more about it. But at some point they really would have to sit down and talk things through.

She took a roundabout route to Rådhuspladsen, across Fælledparken and Sankt Hans Torv, which she loved now that it had been done up. Then along the lakes. She wanted to put off having to face the mess in Rådhuspladsen. This time the council had made a real job of digging it up. They did the same thing every summer, but this year the whole square was being repaved and a hideous, new black bus terminal had been erected at one end of it. Inept politicians, rotten architects, burger joints and ugly shop fronts, exhaust fumes and litter – none of this would be allowed to kill her delight in her city. Not today anyway, with the sun shining from a clear blue sky. Oh, the Danish summer, how I love you. And this year you haven't let me down!

'Tagesen wants to see you right away,' the receptionist told her as she was picking up her mail.

She stepped into the corner office. Tagesen, the paper's editor-in-chief, turned to face her. His office was even more of a shambles than her own. Books, letters, papers and clippings scattered all over the place. He had been gazing down at the chaos and dust in Rådhuspladsen. The sound of chugging machinery and grinding car engines penetrated the windows. Tagesen had only recently taken over the corner office. Lise liked him. And so she should. He had brought her and a number of other journalists with him from his old paper. That had given rise to some muttering in corners among the old hands at *Politiken*. But Tagesen didn't care, nor did Lise for that matter. The staff of *Politiken* were no different from journalists anywhere else in Denmark. Generally speaking, they constituted the most conservative section of the Danish workforce. They hated change, and they hated new bosses.

'Hi, Lise,' Tagesen said. 'D'you think that tip down there'll ever look like a square again?' He was a burly man in his forties with a bushy moustache that he tugged at when agitated, which was almost always. There were those who called him a hothead. But Lise thought he was a real live wire. He had leaned pretty far to the right in his younger days, a product of America's Ivy league, but had now settled somewhere in the grey centre of Danish politics, where people from right and left tended to wind up meeting when they got a bit older and their careers mattered more than ideology. That, at least, was one way of putting it. Lise preferred, except where Ole was concerned, to say that we all grow older and wiser.

17

'What do you say, Lise? Couldn't we do a piece in the paper? You could write one of those scathing articles of yours. Nail the architect. Hang the Town Hall out to dry. Eh, Lise?' Tagesen talked fast, in quick-fire bursts. He needed only a few hours' sleep, he was an early riser, at the office before anyone else, his head buzzing with a thousand ideas.

'Good morning, Tagesen. Up and at it before the rest of us had even had breakfast, were you?' she said.

Tagesen tugged his moustache and grinned. The wry smile passing over his face made him look very young. Lise thought there was something very attractive about him, and she was glad that she was on his side. In a newspaper office alliances are vital. And she had been right to hook up with Tagesen. She had left *Politiken* to work with him when he was chief-sub with the rival broadsheet and followed him back to her old paper without a second thought. In so doing, though, she had in a way also yoked her career to his.

'Have a seat, Lise,' he said.

Lise removed a pile of newspapers from a chair and sat down. Tagesen seated himself behind his desk and toyed with a pen. He had given up smoking. So instead he was always fiddling with things: paper knives, pencils, pens, the dog-eared corners of papers.

'Now, wait till you hear what I've got for you! The biggest story of your career. Sara Santanda wants to break out of the murk of barbarism. Out into the public eye. Out into the light!'

Lise felt a flutter of excitement in the pit of her stomach, a thrill that told her this was something big. She knew what was coming.

'That's right, Lise. She's coming to Denmark. At our invitation. She'll be presented by us. Escorted by us. Reported on and applauded, all thanks to us!'

'But this morning…on the radio…I heard…Iran has just…'

'The death sentence. They've raised the price on her head. I know, but Sara's no longer prepared to put up with being forced to live in hiding. She wants to come out into the open.'

Lise could not sit still. She got to her feet, crossed to the window and looked down into the square. People edged their way past heaps of paving stones, lots of bare brown arms and legs: the T-shirt-and-shorts brigade was out in force again today.

'But why us? Why Denmark?' she said at length.

Tagesen began ripping a sheet of paper into tiny pieces.

'Denmark's a peaceable country. No terrorists here.'

'But it's not exactly big.'

'This story will be reported worldwide.'

'But why *Politiken*?'

'Well, I don't mean to boast, but we've done our share in support of Rushdie. And the Kurds. I have. This is an activist newspaper. And I've met Sara Santanda a couple of times through different acquaintances...you've interviewed her yourself a couple of times. She remembered you. Then there's the fact that you're chair of Danish PEN. Her visit will be organized jointly by PEN and us. But mostly us, right? She's looking forward to seeing you again.'

'Where is she now? Has she left England?'

'She's still holed up somewhere in London. But she's tired of being a prisoner. She wants her freedom. And she has a thing or two to say about the so-called critical dialogue with Iran that our government is pushing for down in Brussels.'

'Don't get on your soapbox now, Tagesen,' she said.

'No, no. There'll be plenty of time for that later,' he said cheerfully.

'When is she coming?'

'In just under a month from now.'

Lise sat down again. It was a tricky one; she could see that. And they didn't have much time to prepare. There were two main points to be considered. Tagesen, and no doubt Sara too, would want her visit to be as high profile as possible. That was, after all, the whole point of her decision to come out in the open. The security guys at PET and the Copenhagen police would insist on maximum secrecy and maximum isolation. It would make their job easier. She remembered them from Rushdie's visit. They were a hardnosed lot but very professional. And they took no chances. Took their work very seriously. They used the weirdest terminology. Instead of checking out an apartment to see whether it would make a good safe house, they said that they were looking the area over. They would want to boss around the representatives from PEN as well as any other writers or reporters involved in the visit, and that would lead to arguments. But Lise had to admit, albeit reluctantly, that they had the whip hand here. It was hard to argue with the fact that whatever they said could mean the difference between life and death, it was just that she didn't like the way they said it.

'Have you spoken with PET?' she said.

'It's pronounced P-E-T,' Tagesen said.

'Well, have you?'

'Yes. They want us to keep the whole thing under our hats until she gives her first press conference. Then we drop the bombshell…'

'Have you agreed to that?'

'I think it's fair enough. We still get an exclusive.'

'Okay.'

'I've made an appointment for you this afternoon with the special branch guy who'll be in charge of the visit. His name's Per Toftlund. A good man, by all accounts. About your age. Have a word with him. Work something out! It's your story.'

'Yes, sir,' she said with mock deference.

'I've also informed Svendsen at the prime minister's office, otherwise this is just between you and me, right, Lise?'

'Absolutely.'

'Good…oh, and say hello to Ole for me, will you?'

'Will do,' she said, but she knew that Tagesen had already moved on to the next matter on his mind. There would be no point in trying to tell him how things were with her and Ole. Tagesen wasn't really all that interested anyway. He was interested in ideas and in the paper, not people. That was maybe a bit harsh, she told herself. But his eyes tended to glaze over if you got too personal. And yet she supposed in a sort of a way they were friends. But now Tagesen had put her onto a story. He would expect her to run with it and only to come to him if she had problems. He trusted her. That was the kind of boss she liked, while others wanted to be nursed through the whole process of producing a story. She preferred to do things herself.

Chapter 3

Detective Inspector Per Toftlund had a hangover. The back of his head was the worst. That and his throat, which was as scratched as an old 78. Everything was a bit blurred, and he felt as though two steely fingers were boring into the nape of his neck. He didn't really have anything against hangovers. It seemed a fair price to pay for abusing one's body. He did not, however, like having a hangover when he had to go to work. He would never have agreed to going on a stag night had he known he would be getting a call from Vuldom the following morning. Even if Jens *was* the last of the gang to get married. Apart from himself of course. So they'd really made a night of it, knocking them back as only a bunch of former frogmen know how. Soon they'd all be settled down with kids and mortgages, and he'd be the funny old bachelor at their get-togethers. There was no point in bemoaning the fact. It was his own choice, and the domesticating of his mates had been a gradual process. He had grown used to the fact that he wasn't as young as he used to be. Maybe someday he too would start hankering after a wife and kids and a cosy little nest. But by then it would probably too late.

He drank a pint of cola and forced himself to do twenty-five press-ups before a scalding hot, then ice-cold, shower. He shaved. It made his head ache, and the whine of the shaver grated on his ear. He dropped two soluble painkillers into a glass of water. Then he ate a bowl of cornflakes with lots of milk and drank a whole bucketful of black coffee. The radio was playing in the background. The kitchen was small and modern. It contained a table with room for two, a dishwasher, a microwave and an array of gleaming copper pots and pans suspended on metal hooks above the kitchen bench. Everything was spotless. He took care of the place himself. He had tried having someone

21

come in to clean, but they hadn't done a good enough job. As an old navy man he liked things shipshape and Bristol fashion. He set store by a tidy apartment, ironed shirts, knife-edge creases and well-polished shoes, and the navy had taught him how to fend for himself. He slipped into a pair of freshly pressed Levis, a cream button-down shirt, a blue tie and a lightweight jacket to cover the gun in the holster at his hip.

The rest of the apartment consisted of a comfortable living room, a bedroom and a box room in which Toftlund kept his books and a computer. The furniture was of pale wood and functional. There was a good view of the low housing in Albertslund and of Vestskoven. The wood was a hazy green in the morning sunlight. A band of smog and mist hung on the horizon.

He took the car. He knew he shouldn't. The alcohol was by no means out of his system yet, but he was running late and couldn't face taking the train or the bus. Any fellow officer who might stop him would have to be incredibly dumb to breathalyse him once he'd shown his badge. Or rather: the new ID card that had replaced the old police badge. It just wasn't done, not unless he was actually involved in an accident. And he was too good a driver for that. Besides which, he loved his blue BMW. It was his one indulgence. A nippy little number, which might have gobbled up all his savings but made driving a sheer delight every day. Cars were few and far between on the road out to Bellahøj Police Station, where a modern concrete building is home to G division, the Danish Security Intelligence Service.

Why had Vuldom's secretary called him in, he wondered. He had put in for these two days' leave ages ago, and he had loads of time off owing to him. He hoped he wasn't going to have to baby sit the Crown Prince. He simply couldn't face that again. He'd done his fair share: sitting nursing a mineral water and watching those kids whooping it up. Not that there was anything wrong with that, really. He'd been no saint either as a teenager. And it was a different story now. The Crown Prince was a frogman himself. He was one of the gang. Per took his hat off to him for that. He had gone through the same admission and training process as the rest of them, the hardest thing he had ever done. But looking after Frederik would be a pretty boring assignment, even if it was also a damned important one. For one thing, because he was the Crown Prince, but also because of all the flaming reporters who were always on his tail.

But he didn't like having to face Vuldom when he had a hangover. Despite the shower and deodorant, he knew the stale reek of the pub was seeping out of every pore. He had hardly slept at all. Now he was sweating out the rest of the booze. Vuldom was a formidable boss, a formidable woman. Per had nothing against female bosses. He had no time for the canteen game in which the guys had fun playing with her name. Calling the boss 'Vulva' was not his idea of a joke. As long as a boss was competent and fair, he didn't care whether they were male or female, gay or lesbian. That was their own bloody business. And besides, he belonged to a generation that had spent its entire childhood and youth being cared for by women. The men had been strangely invisible until he joined the navy. Women had run the crèche, kindergarten, school and youth club, and he had never really known his father, who had remarried and moved to Jutland when Per was three. Per had been brought up by his mother. A succession of different men had shared their apartment, but his mother had always worn the trousers.

Maybe that was why he couldn't face being tied down to one woman, he thought, as he eased the BMW into a parking space next to the long low building. For most of his life women had been deciding things for him. Now he wanted to make his own decisions. But there was no getting away from it: within a few years, the majority of judges would be women, the majority of prosecutors and lawyers, the majority of civil service chiefs, the majority of...yeah, you name it. That's just how it was.

He waved hello to one of the guys from Traffic, all dressed in his motorbike gear and looking as if he couldn't wait to hit the road on such a beautiful morning. Per's headache was gone, and although his throat was still as dry as that of the ale-hound in the old music-hall song, he was actually feeling not too bad. He was ready for anything. Or anybody.

Jytte Vuldom had him shown straight in. Per saw that she was in a good mood, she made no comment about his rather bloodshot eyes. Merely said she was sorry to call him in on his day off. She was a fine-looking woman, Per thought, even if she wouldn't see fifty again. She had an attractive face, a slim figure, bright brown eyes and a melodious voice. Her only flaw, as far as he was concerned was that she was forever smoking those long menthol cigarettes of hers and never asked whether he minded. She stubbed out her cigarette, offered him coffee. He nodded in assent; she poured him a cup from the white thermos jug that was a permanent fixture on her desk, along with a picture of her husband and her two grown-up children. Strong women like her, Per thought to himself, they've had to fight harder than the men, but they've come a long way, they're hungry for power and they know how to wield it.

She passed him his coffee, then handed him a picture. It was a colour photograph of a youthful-looking, dark-skinned woman with short curly hair. She was staring gravely at the photographer, unsmiling. She had dark eyes, a plump little mouth in a round face framed by a pair of gold earrings. She must have been about forty.

'Recognize her, Per?'

Per studied the picture.

'Yes. She's been in the news quite a bit. Some writer. Sara something or other…'

'Santanda.'

'Yes, that's it…Santanda. Bloody Iranians have a contract out on her. She's in hiding in England. Like Rushdie.'

'Only worse, Per. Because she's a woman.'

'What has she written?'

He wrinkled his nose as she lit another cigarette. She curled her lip at him but said nothing about the look on his face. She was the boss, and in the boss's office she called the shots. The anti-smoking fanatics had soon learned to keep their traps shut.

'Five years ago she published a collection of essays in which she described the way in which women are oppressed by the fundamentalist clerics in Iran. How the ayatollahs misinterpret and misuse the Koran. She smuggled herself and her manuscript out of the country, but it's doing the rounds in Iran on tape and in print. She's becoming a political animal. She's western in her thinking, like Tansu Çiller in Turkey. The daughter of an English businessman and an Iranian woman. But she's an Iranian citizen. Sentenced to death *in absentia* for high treason. In her latest novel she tells the story of a corrupt mullah, his pathological lust for power and his abuse of his mistresses. If they don't do what he says, he punishes them – by making them eat pork, for example. The Iranians want her out of the way, although that's not the official line, of course.'

Per smiled and said:

'Kind of ironic, isn't it?'

'What's ironic about this business, Per?'

'That's how Khomeini undermined the Shah. Had tapes of his speeches put into circulation. A highly effective ploy in a country where so many people are illiterate.'

'Sara Santanda will be coming to Copenhagen in a month's time. It will be your job to protect her and take care of the security arrangements for her visit.'

'Who has invited her? The government?'

'*Politiken.* Your contact there is Lise Carlsen.'

'Who's she?'

'Don't you read the arts pages, Toftlund?'

'Nope.'

Vuldom shook her head, as if he was a child who hadn't done his homework, but Per didn't care. He read the political and economic news, crime reports and the sports pages. He wasn't interested in the arts. Most Danish artists did nothing but whine about money and only appeared to be interested in sticking their trunks into the state coffers and siphoning off as much as they could. When he did read a book, it was usually an international thriller in English, but he'd really rather see a film.

'Lise Carlsen is chair of Danish PEN. One of the youngest chairs in the organization and one of only a handful of women in the world to hold that post. She's very bright. She also happens to be a reporter on the staff of *Politiken.* And in this matter she will be playing the hostess.'

'But the host is in charge, right?'

'Host and hostess have to work together to ensure that their guests feel welcome. Is that clear, Toftlund?'

'Yes, quite clear.'

She leaned across the desk between the two neat little piles of green files. Lowered her voice. Per loved that voice. It was deep, husky from the cigarettes and reminded him of Lauren Bacall in *The Big Sleep.*

'It's a complex surveillance operation, Per. I know that. For one thing, our resources are limited. We've got this summit meeting in the autumn. Preparations for that are already eating into what we have…and for another, you'll have to be prepared for the fact that Danish PEN, the writer and the newspaper will be looking for as much publicity as possible. That's the whole point of the exercise. As far as they're concerned, that is. We, on the other hand, want maximum security. So keep Sara Santanda under wraps, Toftlund.'

'Maximum security and maximum publicity. The two don't equate.'

'Well, it's your job, along with Lise Carlsen's, to make them equate. But we don't want to lose her. Is that understood? Safety first. Then the press.'

'There's also another side to this,' Per said.

He took a sip of his coffee. Vuldom waited. This was one of her good points. She gave an order, presented you with an assignment and expected it to be carried out, but she also gave people time to think before answering. She liked good answers, not smart ones. Per took another sip and continued:

'The politicians will be up in arms. There'll be a helluva row…'

'And…?'

'Well, Denmark makes somewhere in the region of a couple of billion kroner a year from exports to Iran. There have been reports in the paper about a company in Randers receiving an order for railway rolling stock. From Iran. And this is a company that's in financial difficulties. So…'

'So that particular matter is of no political relevance,' Vuldom said, glancing pointedly at her watch. Per let this pass. But he knew this was not true. With both journalists and politicians involved, he knew there was no chance of keeping anything secret. These people lived by leaking information and foisting things onto one another. Most politicians would sell their grandmother for a two-minute spot on the evening news. He suddenly realized what a real bugger of a job Vuldom had so elegantly dropped into his lap. He raised his head, but she beat him to it.

'Well, I'm sure you've plenty to be getting on with,' she said, concluding their meeting.

Toftlund hung his jacket on a hanger in his office and called John Nikolajsen. John and he had worked together before on a number of big cases, and both had acted as bodyguards for the royal family and visiting VIPs. They trusted one another, and trust is one of the most essential elements of police teamwork the world over. Fortunately, John had not been assigned to the summit meeting. They would be allowed two more officers for the planning phase, so Per asked John to round them up for a meeting in one hour in the second-floor office they had been given as a temporary operations room. He called *Politiken* and made an appointment with Lise Carlsen. Her voice was soft and pleasant. Was there a trace of a Jutland accent there? Would she be kind enough to meet him at Café Norden at three o'clock?

Then he started preparing for the meeting. They had a month. He had a feeling that was going to fly by all too fast.

A little over an hour later he surveyed his team. It wasn't big, but he liked what he saw. Besides John, there was Frands Petersen – maybe not the brightest spark on earth but a methodical and thorough sort who didn't mind the long slow process of investigative and surveillance work – and Bente Carlsen: in her mid-thirties and a fine policewoman by all accounts. Per hadn't worked with Bente before but had heard only good things about her. He liked policewomen. They tended to keep a cool head in a crisis and usually put everything they had into the job. Possibly because they had to fight that bit harder than the men to get promotion. What did he know? At any rate, there seemed to be more and more of them.

It was a small team, but it would have to do for now. When the subject herself came to town he would have to get help from the Copenhagen Police Department's surveillance unit. The room was a good-sized one, with two double windows through which the glorious August sunshine streamed onto some worn desks, a couple of computers, telephones and an overhead projector, by which Per was sitting. There was also a whiteboard. On the board, in red, Per had written: SIMBA. A coffee machine hissed in the corner, and steam was already rising from four paper cups. They were all in plain clothes: jeans and shirts, almost a uniform for anyone who had done their stint with the undercover squad.

'Right then,' said Per. He set down his paper cup of black coffee, stood up and placed an overhead on the projector. His hangover had diminished to a faint rumbling in his stomach.

On the overhead was an *en face* picture of Sara Santanda: the round face, the little, lopsided smile, the short, black curly hair and a striking pair of earrings.

'Here, my friends, is our subject,' Per went on. 'The writer Sara Santanda, whom I'm sure none of you philistines has ever heard of. But she has written a couple of books for which the mad mullahs in Iran have sentenced her to death. From now on the subject will be known as "Simba". That is how we will refer to her amongst ourselves, in reports, memos and computer files. *Comprende?*'

They nodded and smiled. They knew Per. He liked to show off a bit and pepper his speech with Spanish words and phrases. Some people found it pretentious, but John went along with it because he knew that this was Per's way of bringing some structure to an assignment. It was as if he had to put his thoughts into words in order to sort them out and remember them later. He also had a thing about Spain and South America.

'Where the hell do you get those codenames from, Per?' John said with a laugh. 'Simba! What's next? Mowgli?'

The others laughed too. Bente's teeth were slightly crooked, and she brayed a little too loudly when she laughed, but it was probably just nerves. That would go once they found a way of working together.

'It's the name of a dog I had as a boy,' Per said. This elicited more laughter. He let them laugh. There was nothing wrong with starting their first operational meeting with a good laugh. They would make a fine team.

Per raised a hand.

'Settle down now. Simba will be arriving here in just under a month. She has chosen to show her pretty little face in Copenhagen after a year in hiding. The police in London are guarding her round the clock. She's a writer, which means she's probably mad as a hatter. She's going to be surrounded by Danish writers and reporters – who are, as you know, a pain in the arse and don't know the first bloody thing about security.'

Bente cleared her throat. Per broke off and eyed her encouragingly:

'Yes, Bente?'

'We don't have that many Muslim extremists here in Denmark. We're keeping a careful eye on the Egyptian's cells. We know the people he associates with. And I'm sure the majority of Muslims in this country would be only happy to help, so if we just keep the handful of extremists under surveillance…'

'It's not just the fanatics we're up against.' Per picked up a marker and tossed it from hand to hand. 'Any true believer who bumps her off will go to paradise and sit at Allah's right hand. That's their drug. But the state of Iran is also allowing us infidels a crack at the whip. The reward for taking out Simba now stands at four million US dollars.'

He enjoyed his colleagues' reaction to this. They exchanged glances, whistled through their teeth. The mention of the sum involved would bring it home to them that this was a big job and an important one.

'I know. Tempting, isn't it?' he said. 'To the professional hit men and the amateurs. To anyone who can get close to little Simba.'

Per turned to the board and went on talking while he wrote up a few keywords:

'We have to look over some safe houses. We have to work out a route from the airport to the safe house as well as an alternative route and transport from the safe house to the press conference. We also need to find a nice secure venue for the press conference. And whether the reporters like it or not, there has to be strict monitoring of everyone who wants to meet Simba. *Comprende*?'

'What have we got in the way of resources?' Bente again, wanting to make sure that she was seen to be contributing right from the start.

'Not enough. Not what we'd have for a state visit,' Per said. 'So what it boils down to is: keep Simba's visit a secret. Into the country with the woman. Press conference. Out again. End of operation.'

'Right,' said Bente.

'Way to go, Per!' said Frands. He was a burly character who had trouble holding his stomach in. He looked like a man who was soon going to give up the fight and let his belly hang over his belt.

Per laughed, straightened his shoulders and intoned with affected solemnity:

'The Secret Service lost Kennedy. Reagan got hit. We've never lost anyone yet. And Simba's not going to be the first.'

John and Frands cheered and stamped their feet. Bente looked as if she found it hard to see what was so funny.

'Yes, but remember, this *is* Denmark,' she said.

Per looked at her.

'Exactly, Bente, and from a purely statistical point of view our luck's bound to run out some time. So…*vamos*!'

Per Toftlund found a parking space for his blue BMW down by the canal on Gammel Strand. He popped some coins into the parking meter and walked along the canalside. People were sitting with their legs dangling over the edge, drinking beer and cola. He was early on purpose. The heavy fug of summer hung over the city, a blend of exhaust fumes, sunshine and the smells of food and drink emanating from pavement cafés and kitchen doors. The arms and legs of people cycling past were every shade of red and brown. He strolled to the café through the hot afternoon and found himself a table inside, in the far corner, from which he could keep an eye on the door. He fetched a cup of coffee from the bar and sat down with a copy of *Ekstra Bladet* in front of him, as arranged.

He spotted her right away. She was obviously looking for someone, but he would have noticed her anyway. She had a pretty face and a nice body, but then so do a lot of women. No, it wasn't just that. He liked the way she lifted her head and tossed back her fair hair, and her light springy step on the paving stones. She had good legs too under her filmy summer skirt, and she wasn't wearing much make-up. He guessed she must be about thirty, maybe a couple of years older. She would probably still look like that at forty. If she wasn't the stroppy type, it would be a pleasure working with her.

He noticed a certain hesitancy about her when she entered the café. Although she seemed like a typical café-goer, used to frequenting the hot spots of the moment in Copenhagen. Yet here she was, glancing round about as if unhappy about having to stand and wait for a total stranger. As if she wasn't used to waiting at all. She looked like a rotten actor in a bad B-movie, he thought to himself. He let her sweat for a minute, then raised his *Ekstra Bladet* and gave the ghost of a smile. She smiled back, which did her face no harm at all. Then she walked smartly over to him and sat down. Per immediately started talking. He saw the look on her face turn to one of confusion, then of anger. In his experience, you had to take the lead from the word go. Show who was boss. It was always easier to work with someone once the pecking order had been established. Intellectuals always thought they had the right to call the tune, but that wasn't on, not when he was in charge of security.

'You're late,' he said.

'I just had to finish something first.' Her voice was warm and musical, and there was definitely a hint of a Jutland accent.

'I don't like it when people don't turn up on time. It's sloppy. *Comprende?*'

She stared at him as if he had fallen down from the moon. He was about to defuse the situation with a joke, but her reply stopped him short.

'*Entiendo, coño,*' said Lise Carlsen quite coolly.

Per leaned back in his chair with a laugh that sounded more supercilious than he had intended it to be:

'Well, I never,' he said.

'Yes, thanks. I *would* like a coffee.'

'Anything in it?'

'Black.'

He got up and went over to the bar. Lise followed him with her eyes. He was a rude son-of-a-bitch, that much she had discovered. And first impressions were usually right. Which was a load of crap, of course, but that was how she liked to put it. He wasn't bad looking, though, if you went for the athletic type with designer stubble. He was a nice dresser. A bit on the classic, conservative side perhaps, but neat and clean. She didn't know much about policemen or the life they led, but she guessed it wasn't exactly the biggest brains in the country who chose a career that bore more resemblance to the army than to civilian life. But perhaps the air of confidence he had about him came from carrying a gun and having physical power over people. If she could hold onto that thought, she might actually have the germ of an article. Well, at least she had got them onto an equal footing right at the start. He'd given her all that Spanish crap, but she'd thrown it straight back in his face: 'Understood, arsehole.'

Toftlund reappeared and placed a cup of coffee in front of Lise with a 'There you go'. Lise held out her hand, and Per almost knocked over his own half-full cup as he made to shake it. She introduced herself: 'Lise Carlsen,' she said. And Per responded, somewhat flustered:

'Per Toftlund…arsehole. Me, I mean. Not you. As you said.'

She laughed with him. He had a nice smile. Even white teeth and a dimple. A strong chin, brown eyes and dark hair that was thinning a little at the temples, although this he was making no effort to conceal. She liked that, she thought to herself involuntarily and suddenly felt a little shy.

'So you speak Spanish,' she said, lifting her cup.

'Like Hemingway.'

'Ah, yes. I bet he's just the writer for you.'

'I can even spell if I put my mind to it.'

'Really?'

He drank the rest of his coffee and regarded her. She forced herself to put down her cup, rummaged in her bag and pulled out her cigarettes.

'D'you mind?'

'Just keep it away from me.'

'A hardliner, eh?'

'Just sensible,' he said.

She lit up and blew the smoke away from him.

'Now, where were we?' she said.

Per leaned across the table and spoke softly, as if they were lovers having a tête-à-tête.

'We're here to talk about a character by the name of Simba.'

'Who?'

'Sara S. Who from now on will be known as Simba. When speaking of her, we will refer to her as Simba. We two have to find a way to work together, so that you can present Simba to the public and I can keep Simba alive. All right?'

'All right! But I do have a mind of my own, you know. And you giving the orders while I and the rest of PEN click our heels and say "Yessir!" like so many raw recruits is not my idea of working together.'

He looked at her.

'Who knows about Simba's visit?' was all he said.

'Tagesen – my editor-in-chief, that is. Me. The prime minister and his permanent undersecretary. Tagesen knows the prime minister personally and informed him, in order to get your lot involved.'

'Right. Let's confine this to as small a group as possible.'

'You can't keep Santanda under wraps…'

'Simba.'

'What a lot of nonsense! She has to get out and meet people. That's the whole point, don't you see…?'

'No, that is not the point.'

'Oh, and what is the point, then?'

'To keep her alive,' said Per.

Chapter 4

The Foreign Policy Committee is the Danish parliamentary body responsible for monitoring the government's activities on the foreign policy and security policy fronts. It meets once a week and is presided over by a chairman responsible for drawing up the agenda. The prime minister, foreign minister and minister for defence can all be requested to appear before the committee to account for their actions. Or they may ask to attend a meeting in order to advise the committee of existing situations. The heads of Military Intelligence – FET – and Security Intelligence – PET – may also keep the MPs on the Foreign Policy Committee up to date on threats to national security and ongoing matters. The matters discussed by the committee are private and confidential, and its members are forbidden to divulge any of the information to which they are made privy behind the closed doors of the committee room, most of which has been gathered by Denmark's two intelligence services or is based on top-secret reports from the country's foreign ambassadors.

Johannes Jørgensen MP knew all of this, but he was angry, so angry that he had decided that somehow this matter had to be made public. And if it meant breaking the Official Secrets Act in order to save good jobs in Jutland, then he knew where his duty lay, and to whom he owed loyalty. The voters, that's who. Not some foreign heathen. He was the elected representative of the people, he had been for fifteen years, and he was in his element at Christiansborg. He was familiar with all the political and practical shortcuts through the corridors and recesses of the House. He had no wish to return to his dull law practice in Central Jutland. His brother was managing that just fine. Johannes Jørgensen was fifty-six years old. He was an accomplished spokesman and felt that he would soon be ready for an actual government post. But for that he needed to be re-elected, and in this country you could never tell when an election might be called. The slightest and most unexpected thing could cause the veneer of peace and stability between the centre parties to crack.

So this matter had to be made public. It was his duty; it was as simple as that.

In any case, it wouldn't be the first time that a committee member had made discreet use of information that he or she had acquired at its meetings. It wasn't as if you had to advertise where you'd got your information from. But first he had to try to make the prime minister see reason.

Jørgensen was a slim, broad-shouldered man. In his youth he had done a bit of boxing, and this had left him with a nose that was slightly off-kilter. At one point he had considered getting it fixed, but the voters seemed to kind of like the rather tough masculine look the nose gave him. He never made any secret of the fact that he was an ex-boxer and often used boxing metaphors when interviewed on TV. He had read law in Copenhagen and spoke perfect *rigsdansk*, but on television he auto-matically modified his speech, lacing it with a healthy dash of his original Jutland brogue. Not too thick, of course. But a grain of Jutland credibility tended to work like a charm these days.

He let the other committee members leave the room ahead him. Most of them hurried off, intent solely on avoiding the little clutch of reporters waiting outside. A couple of the less well-known MPs seemed more inclined to dawdle, in hopes that the reporters might ask them for a word. But the television guys were only interested in the prime minister and his feelings about the latest developments in Bosnia: the reason for this extraor-dinary meeting of the Foreign Policy Committee during the summer recess. Everyone was talking about the Danish troops that were to be sent to the region under NATO command. And if the television people were interested in that, then you could bet your boots the papers would be too. Less experienced members of the committee would never dream of passing on the confidential information which the country's prime minister had asked them to keep to themselves, after presenting them with it under AOB. Although they might drop a discreet hint or two in a couple of days, to a spouse, a lover or a mistress. To show that they knew something nobody else knew.

These were the thoughts that were running through Jørgensen's mind as he stood there waiting. He knew his fellow MPs, knew their burning ambitions. Once politics got into your blood, you were hooked for life. Politics and power were more addictive than the worst narcotic. If you gave it up too abruptly or were dumped by the voters, you could slide into the depths of depression. He thought of Jens Otto Krag, who had left politics of his own free will. He had expected to enjoy life, unburdened by power, but his final years had been a dismal tragedy because, when it came to the point, he could not live without politics, without the sweet taste of power. He knew other people too who had been consigned to obscurity by the fickle electorate and lapsed into alcoholism and self-loathing if they didn't make a political comeback very quickly.

Not a fate Johannes Jørgensen wished for himself. He wanted to stay where he was and to one day belong to the inner circle.

Jørgensen said a friendly hello to a couple of reporters, nodded to a cameraman who, he remembered, had been behind the lens on several occasions when he had been interviewed on TV2, then moved a little further down the corridor. He could see that the prime minister was preparing to leave and would shortly be shaking off the journalists with his characteristic, long brisk stride as he made for the glass doors leading to the safe haven of his office.

Prime Minister Carl Bang was a tall, slightly stooped man. Like most prime ministers of Denmark, his existence depended on his ability to unite the many different camps within parliament and persuade them to bow to one another in order to ensure the survival of yet another minority government. He was a good card player and adept at playing people and parties off against one another. But he was also a man of his word and scored well in the Gallup polls, so his position was as secure as that of any Danish government can ever hope to be. He had learned early on that in Danish politics it is better to take one year at a time and push through whatever compromises the reigning majority at any given moment would allow. That, more or less, had been the practice in Denmark since the war, and that, so it seemed, was how the Danes liked it. The government was enjoying a period of stability, and Carl Bang himself really did feel that everything needful was being done and that things were going well.

Johannes Jørgensen fell into step beside him. He could see Svendsen, the permanent undersecretary, whispering something in Bang's ear, but he didn't care. If he asked for a formal meeting it could be days before the prime minister could squeeze him into his schedule.

'Prime Minister! Hello! Could I have a moment?'

Carl Bang stopped and switched on his famous smile.

'I don't really have the time right now,' he said, looking at his watch. Jørgensen glanced round about. They were alone. Svendsen stepped discreetly back a pace. Although he could just as well listen in, since he would get it all from Bang anyway.

'Well, you'll just have to make time. Because I won't bloody well stand for this.'

'Okay, Jørgensen.' Carl Bang was no longer smiling. He inclined his head, motioning for them to move over to the window. Svendsen would screen them. Jørgensen and Bang were much of a height, wearing similar dark suits and ties patterned with tiny squares of a design that everyone seemed to be sporting that year. The halls of Christiansborg were cool, despite the heat outside. A summertime hush hung over the House, and the air smelled of varnish and paint. 'I refuse to go along with this,' Jørgensen hissed. 'I have no intention of seeing three billion good honest kroner in exports thrown out the window.'

Carl Bang eyed Jørgensen: all this, over such a piddling little matter. But he concealed his irritation:

'I was merely passing on the information. This is not a government undertaking, you know.'

'Now you listen to me, Bang! I helped put you where you are today. And if you think I'm going to stand by and see a major employer…'

Bang couldn't resist it:

'A dairy firm in your constituency…' he said with a smile, but Jørgensen chose to ignore this jibe and continued:

'…go under because of a stupid, empty little gesture, then you don't know me very well.'

The look Carl Bang gave him said that unfortunately he knew the populist politician all too well. As the sort who didn't give a toss about objectivity and would happily send up a couple of political balloons during the summer recess just to get his face on TV.

'It's not a government undertaking, Jørgensen. There's nothing we can do.'

'It's not just the feta cheese, you know. Trade with the Middle East is booming. It's a market with enormous potential. I don't see why we have to be the boy scouts of Europe.'

'You know we're keen to pursue a critical dialogue. And, as I say, it's a private visit. The government has nothing to do with it.'

'So she won't be meeting anyone from the government?'

Carl Bang was quiet for a moment.

'It's a private affair. There's nothing we can do. One way or the other. That is not our job,' he said.

'Well, think of something, Bang. This is a matter very close to my heart.'

'I'll see what I can do. But now I really have to run.'

Johannes Jørgensen nodded stiffly and watched the prime minister and Svendsen stride off down the corridor.

Carl Bang took care of the most urgent matters with Svendsen and then, alone at last in his office, he picked up the phone and himself dialled Tagesen's direct number at *Politiken*. They were old friends from their student days in Århus. Well, 'friends' was probably too strong a word, but they met socially from time to time and always enjoyed talking to one another about politics and books. Each was glad to see that the other had done well for himself, even though one of them had chosen a career in the media, and the other in politics. And although it was never said in so many words, there was also a tacit understanding between them that they were not on opposite sides: that the symbiosis formed by a responsible media and responsible politicians in Christiansborg constituted the very cornerstone of Danish democracy. That they needed one another. Denmark was a very small country, so it was inevitable that top people in the press and television, the civil service and the political arena all had at least a nodding acquaintance with one another.

He had called Tagesen's private number, and it was the newspaperman himself who picked up the phone. They chatted politely about the summer and the hot weather, asked after each other's wives and children and groused a bit about the fact that busy men like them had to slog away at their desks while everyone else was basking on the beach.

Then Bang said:

'There's a little matter I'd like to discuss with you.'

'Feel free, Carl.'

'The visit by this author. Any chance of cancelling it? Or at least postponing it until later in the year?'

Tagesen was instantly on his guard; the warmth disappeared from his voice:

'Why on earth would we do that?'

'There are those who feel it's bad timing. And what with the political situation as it is, I need to…particularly when we think about Bosnia and the fact of the Danish troops who are being sent down there. This has to be our top priority, and it will have the support of a wide majority. Party politics shouldn't enter into it. You said the very same thing in one of your leaders, didn't you?'

'You brought it up with the committee!' There was anger in Tagesen's voice. He had told Svendsen about the visit in strictest confidence and made it quite clear that it was not something that need go any further. Parliament was on summer recess, so there was every chance that the whole thing could pass off without any great debate. But Bang had got cold feet. There had been too many cases in which parliament had accused the government of not keeping them well enough informed, so he had covered himself and mentioned Santanda's visit, seeing that the Foreign Policy Committee had convened and called him in for a meeting anyway…

'It's just a friendly piece of advice,' Carl Bang said. He wished he hadn't called Tagesen. You never knew where you were with journalists. One minute they could be bought for a helping of roast pork with parsley sauce. The next they were taking their independence so all-fired seriously.

'And one which I will do you the favour of forgetting that you ever offered,' Tagesen said coldly, and they bade each other a curt goodbye without the ritual assurances that the four of them really should get together soon.

Johannes Jørgensen usually chose the lunch restaurant Gitte Kik as the place for a confidential chat with a fellow MP or a reporter. As a young district councillor in Jutland, he had learned the importance of keeping on the right side of the press. And the difference between establishing a good relationship with a reporter from a small provincial paper and one from the television news,

Ritzau Bureau or one of the leading Copenhagen papers was really not that great. The trick was to treat them decently, answer their questions and every now and again give them a good story over lunch. A story they could use. One that held water – at least for a while. Politicians and journalists were heavily dependent on one another, and it didn't pay to badmouth the press. Denmark has the press it has, and it's a waste of time moaning about it, as he always said. Use the reporters. They use you. This was the advice he usually gave to green, newly elected MPs as they crept diffidently up and down the corridors of Christiansborg looking like little kids who had lost their mummies.

As always, Gitte Kik was packed to the gunnels. The restaurant lay only a stone's throw from the seat of power, and civil servants, politicians, journalists and business people met here to partake of good solid *smørbrød*. The health and fitness tidal wave had not swept through these low-ceilinged premises. On the menu here were pork dripping and jellied stock, liver pâté and salami, herring and mature cheese, beer and schnapps, and ashtrays adorned every table.

There were a couple of women in the place, but this was primarily a male preserve. Johannes Jørgensen sat at a table for two at the very back, from which he could keep an eye on the door and the two steps down to the basement restaurant. He saw the journalist come in and look about him. He was a tall, middle-aged man, thinning on top. His shirt was a bit crumpled and his tie askew. The top button of his shirt was undone. There were beads of sweat on his brow. A band of low pressure had moved in across the North Sea, bringing some cooler air, but it was still very close, as if the Almighty had spread a duvet over Denmark.

Johannes Jørgensen waved to Torsten Hansen, who waved back. He dumped his bag on the floor next to the table and shook Jørgensen's hand. They ordered *smørbrød*: one apiece with herring, one with smoked eel and one with cheese, along with beer and a shot of aquavit. They chatted first about the political situation and about the Danish troops who would be joining the NATO forces in the former Yugoslavia. Jørgensen assured Hansen that there was a broad political consensus on this question. And he could quote him as saying that parliament would not be summoned back from summer recess. The government's decision was backed by a good solid majority.

Torsten Hansen made a note and ate his *smørbrød*. It was very warm in the restaurant, and all the men had taken off their jackets. The cigarette smoke stung the eyes. Hansen didn't smoke and often longed for the USA's restrictive smoking regulations. It might have rendered it difficult for the smoking minority to enjoy a cig, but it made offices and restaurants pure heaven for the non-smoker. In Denmark, however, he was wise enough not to say anything. It wasn't worth the hassle.

Johannes Jørgensen laid down his knife and fork and knocked back the last of his aquavit.

'This here is off the record, Torsten,' he said, leaning across the table.

'I'm all ears!' Hansen said, demonstratively laying down his pen.

'You know that writer who's been sentenced to death, Sara Santanda?'

Torsten Hansen nodded and took a swig of his beer.

'She's coming to Denmark.'

'But she's in hiding somewhere in London, isn't she?'

'Right. But now it's to be our turn. It beats me why Denmark, of all places, should be used for the making of such an empty gesture.'

Torsten Hansen cut a slice of his cheese. He knew there was a great story here and was experienced enough to keep quiet and let Jørgensen do the talking. The latter had given him a good tip-off before, and even though it had been off the record it had been solid enough. Jørgensen was a reliable source: a somewhat frustrated politician who did have a degree of influence certainly but who also felt that he had been passed over by Bang in the last cabinet reshuffle. Such people were the lifeblood of a newspaper, which relied on there always being someone with something they wanted made public. Torsten guessed that this must have come up at yesterday's meeting of the Foreign Policy Committee, but Jørgensen wasn't going to come right out and say that. He would expect Torsten to work that out for himself and realize, therefore, that the information was rock solid.

Johannes Jørgensen took another sip of his beer before continuing in a hushed voice:

'I don't think it's wise. Trade figures aren't as healthy as they have been. Why go upsetting a foreign country that has been a good trading partner and has the potential to become an even better one? And all because of some foreigner who has written a book of, from what I hear, somewhat dubious literary merit. A book which, by the way, nobody seems to have read!'

'When is she expected?'

'Quite soon. I don't know exactly. It's *Politiken* who's invited her. But it's the taxpayers who'll have to foot the bill for the security arrangements, of course. It's always the same. But everyone involved is trying to keep it a secret. And in a democratic society that, in itself, is all wrong. Which is why I'm telling you all this.'

Johannes Jørgensen sat back in his chair.

'And then there's the question of the feta cheese exports, isn't there?' Hansen said. 'Isn't there some dairy in your constituency which is totally dependent on them?'

Jørgensen leaned forward again and said without lowering his voice: 'All religions must be respected. Including the Muslim religion. And Muslims have the right to defend themselves against blasphemy. Just as we Christians have. But obviously I condemn this death sentence. That goes without saying. Would you like some more cheese? Another beer?'

Torsten Hansen shook his head.

'How about an official comment? On camera?'

It was Jørgensen's turn to shake his head.

'Not today. I'm giving you the story today. If you can have it confirmed, then I'll make myself available...but...'

'But then everyone else gets it too?'

'Right.'

'Tomorrow?'

'Naturally, as a member of the Foreign Policy Committee, I will have something to say on this matter, if you should wish to pursue it.'

To be honest, Torsten Hansen thought this was fair enough. He had an exclusive for this evening, as a pure news item, and he could contact the various parties concerned tomorrow, when he was on the early shift anyway. If he started making calls now, the other reporters would soon get wind of it. Better to run it as a pure news item on the six-thirty broadcast and then see if he could turn it into a bigger feature with a couple of comments for the nine o'clock news. It was a good story, at any rate. Santanda had never appeared in public before. Reuter's and CNN would be on it like a shot. But he would be first with it. And no matter how long he had been in the business, an exclusive like this always gave him a nice warm feeling inside.

In just a few hours, the world would learn that Sara Santanda had chosen Denmark as the place where she would defy the mad mullahs and their barbaric death sentence. If the disclosure of this fact meant that she had to go somewhere else instead, then he could live with that. He was well aware that this was what Jørgensen was angling for. But he hadn't become a journalist in order to keep things secret. It was a good story, and it was all his.

Chapter 5

Vuk sat alone at a table on the hilltop overlooking Pale. Four plastic chairs were set around the maroon laminated table. The door of the small café hung loose on its hinges. A grimy curtain graced the one window that still had glass in it. The other had been smashed by a stray bullet on a day long ago by a couple of drunken militiamen with a petty score to settle. They had been fighting over a woman. Their anger had been greater than their marksmanship. Vuk was drinking slivovitz. It was a bad habit. There had been a time when he hadn't needed alcohol to get through the days, but now it did him good sometimes. He never got drunk, but it had a wonderfully soothing, numbing effect. It blanked out the images that were prone to come into his mind without warning. He had survived longer than most, and statistics said his number should be flashing up on the board any time now. He had a feeling too that the past was about to catch up on them. Those acts that, in the euphoria of victory had, in some bizarre way, seemed perfectly natural, were now turning into horrific memories that presented themselves when least expected.

He drained his glass in one gulp. He could see the proprietor sitting inside behind the curtain. He was watching football on some German channel. The satellite dish fixed to his tumbledown premises still worked perfectly. But it looked out of place against the white concrete walls and the grey roof. Possibly it had been installed back in the days when there was still some hope that the odd tourist might wander all the way to the top of the hill. But the last tourist had left for home long ago. Vuk filled his glass again. The sun hung low over the green mountain slopes, and the air was heavy with the scents of high summer. Scents that always made him think of his father and little Katarina, but he didn't want to do that. Pale, and beyond it Sarajevo, lay shrouded in mist. All was quiet down there. The war was drawing towards an end, and it was not a good end. He knew that many of the others would not accept it, but they had lost. The first round, at any rate. Now they would have to wait and see what happened once another winter had gone by. It would not be long before the cool air, and after it the cold, breathed its white breath over those same slopes which now lay drenched in a golden light that danced with insects.

Vuk heard the car before he saw it. His hand slid down to the Kalashnikov at his feet, then curled once more around his glass. It was the Commandant's old Mercedes. He recognized the laboured growl of the engine and the snarl of the rear axle.

The Commandant was not alone. With him was a middle-aged man dressed in a dark, well-cut suit, white shirt, dark tie and black shoes. As usual, the Commandant was wearing his green uniform, with his gun at his belt. Vuk had always thought he looked like a younger version of Fidel Castro. *El jefe*. Yes, that was him. Vuk was well aware that the Commandant was a father substitute, but it didn't matter. The Commandant had taught him all he knew at the best military academy in the world: the Yugoslavian Federal Army's Special Forces school, where the toughest young men were schooled in sabotage, infiltration techniques, sniping, communi-cation, self-defence, swimming underwater and survival in the field. It had been Tito's own idea: to train up a force capable of operating as guerrillas should the bloody Russians try to invade the country, as the Germans had done. Instead the Commandant had had to employ his expensive education and his best pupils against traitorous Muslims and Croatian fascists. Tito had probably never thought it would come to that.

'Another two glasses,' Vuk said.

The owner of the café looked up, and Vuk raised two fingers. The man brought out two glasses and placed them on the table without a word. Then he returned to his football match.

The Commandant and the man in the suit were standing talking next to the dirty black Mercedes, which was parked at the foot of the low hill. A flight of steps, several of them crumbling away, led up to the café. Vuk saw Radovan get out and light a cigarette. He waved to Vuk, who waved back at him. Radovan acted as both driver and bodyguard for the Commandant, although they were safe enough here. It had taken Vuk two days to reach this spot after crossing the river late that night. As so often before, after a mission, he had stayed an extra day with Emma. Made love to her in the morning, slept most of the day, made love to her again in the evening and then crossed the river at night in his little collapsible raft. The journey had been totally without incident. He had heard gunfire to the east and south of him, but it had come from small-calibre weapons and been so far away that he hadn't taken cover, just walked on alone through the night.

The Commandant and the man in the suit climbed the steps towards Vuk. Radovan stayed where he was. He drove the car and guarded the Commandant's life, but it was his belief that the less he knew about whatever deals were struck the better. The day of reckoning would come eventually, and when it did you wanted to have seen, heard and done as little as possible.

The man in the suit was compact and muscular, although starting to put on a bit of weight around the waist. The sweat was running off him, but he kept on his jacket. Vuk was wearing a pair of faded blue jeans and a white T-shirt. His brown leather jacket was draped over the back of his chair. Vuk could tell that the man in the suit was a Russian. He could spot them easily. Americans likewise. They could change their dress, try to alter their appearance, but it made no difference. It had to do with the way they walked, the way they held their heads, their whole body language. The same went for the Danes. Vuk knew a fair bit about disguise. He also knew that it was their way of walking, of holding themselves, their mannerisms that gave people away, and he kept his eye in by always studying others closely.

The Russian might be wearing a smart western suit, but he was either an old soldier or an ex-KGB man, it stood out a mile; possibly one who was now making use of his talents to smuggle weapons to the various warring factions in the Yugoslavian civil war. He had broad Slavic features and dark eyes. His short black hair was thick and neatly parted. In fact he reeked to high heaven of the Mafia.

Vuk got to his feet and waited expectantly. The Commandant strode forward and put out his hand to Vuk. When Vuk took it, the Commandant pulled the younger man to him and gave him a quick hug, and they thumped one another on the back.

'Another job well done. I'm proud of you, my lad,' the Commandant said in Serbo-Croatian, in a voice roughened by black Balkan tobacco.

'It was nothing,' Vuk said, stepping back a pace.

'You like killing, Vuk,' the Commandant said.

'That's what you always say.'

'But don't you?'

'No,' Vuk said.

'You're good at it.'

'Who's he?' Vuk asked.

The Commandant turned to the Russian and said in English, although both he and Vuk knew enough Russian to carry on a conversation in the language:

'This is my boy. The one I think might be able to help you. The Serbian Dane. Vuk.'

His English was heavily accented, but it had an American twang to it. He had attended a number of courses run by the Green Berets in Texas, all strictly hush-hush. That was during the Cold War, when Yugoslavia, for all that it was neutral, feared the Russian Bear more than the imperialists in Washington. The Americans had taken great pleasure in training anyone who could, however temporarily, be regarded as an ally. Be it an Iraqi officer opposed to Iran, or a Serbian soldier who hated the Soviet Union. The Yanks had no sense of history and no talent for strategic thinking, the Commandant had told him. The Commandant was proud of his American English and loved to show it off.

The Russian offered his hand, and Vuk shook it. The Russian had a firm handshake, and he looked you straight in the eye.

'Pleased to meet you, Vuk,' he said in beautiful English. Had to be an old KGB agent who had worked undercover as a diplomat in London and possibly other European cities. 'I've heard a lot about you. And all good.'

'Do you have a name?'

'Kravtjov.'

'Sit down, Mr Kravtjov. Have a drink.'

Kravtjov pulled a handkerchief from his trouser pocket and carefully wiped the dusty, scuffed plastic slats before sitting down. Vuk filled the three small glasses and raised his own:

'A toast?'

'To mutual understanding,' the Russian said.

'To victory,' said Vuk.

Kravtjov glanced at the Commandant and drained his glass in one long swallow.

'Shit!' he said. 'That's good, very good, but it's not a civilized drink without pickled gherkins.'

The Commandant laughed:

'I'll have to remember that for next time.'

'What does Mr Kravtjov want with us?' Vuk asked.

He refilled their glasses. He could both see and sense that Kravtjov and the Commandant had been discussing something. He had the impression that some sort of business deal had already been struck. Something that involved him and his unique gifts. That went without saying. But it irked him that the Commandant took him so much for granted. There was a time when he could have done so, but not now, or not in quite the same way.

The Commandant fiddled with his glass and lit a cigarette. Kravtjov did likewise. The Russian held out his pack of Marlboros to Vuk, who took one.

The Commandant excused himself to Kravtjov and switched to Serbo-Croat. But the Russian probably understood a good bit of it, Vuk thought to himself, as he listened without interrupting.

'Vuk. Before the collapse of the Soviet Union, Kravtjov worked for the KGB. He still has friends in high places. He can get us the information we need. He can also provide us with arms.'

Vuk said nothing, but he gazed intently at the Russian. The Commandant went on:

'He will pay us four million American dollars for a hit.'

Vuk said in English:

'I don't kill for money.'

Kravtjov leaned forward and said in the same language:

'That's a lot of fucking money, Vuk!'

'I don't kill for money.'

'It's not for you. It's not for me. It's for the cause,' the Commandant said.

'I don't kill for money,' Vuk repeated.

Still with his arms folded on the table, Kravtjov said softly:

'I understand how you feel, Vuk. Believe me, I do understand. But think about it. The war will soon be over. Your lot haven't exactly won the first round. You need money. You're pariahs. You need money to buy arms. To safeguard your future.'

'Listen to what he has to offer,' the Commandant said.

Vuk made no reply, simply waited. Again Kravtjov exchanged a glance with the Commandant before going on.

'I can't go into detail until I know whether you're in. You do see that, don't you? You know how these things work, right? But I am acting as middle-man for a nation which is willing to pay four million dollars for the liquidation of a target who has trod on rather too many toes.'

'Why me?' Vuk asked.

'The target will be making an appearance in Denmark. You're the perfect man for the job,' the Commandant said.

Vuk emptied his glass.

'The perfect man,' said Kravtjov.

'The target is not an enemy as such,' the Commandant said. 'But innocent civilians lose their lives in every war. You know that better than anyone, Vuk. Kravtjov has a plan, a good one. We pin the blame on someone else, a Muslim. One of our enemies. We'll get the money. They'll get the blame.'

Vuk stood up and walked away from the table. The Commandant kept his eyes on him.

'What's all this about?' Vuk said.

The Commandant dropped his cigarette and ground it under the sole of his American army boot.

'At the end of the day, a ticket out of here,' he said wryly.

'I thought as much.'

'We're done for, Vuk. Soon NATO and the Americans will be charging all over the place. They mean it this time. And this time it won't be blue-capped Mamma's boys from the UN with light arms. This time they'll have tanks and heavy artillery, and the right and the will to use them. They might start digging. In the wrong places, Vuk. Think about that. Think hard.'

But that was the one thing Vuk did not want to think about. The murky, grey spring afternoon in that Muslim village when all sense of humanity had evaporated, and the air was heavy with the sickly smell of blood. When not even the earth that was shovelled over them afterwards, or the smoke from the burning houses, could expunge that smell. It would be there in his nostrils for the rest of his life. They had been seized by bloodlust and behaved like the berserkers he had learned about in school in another country.

'I don't trust the Russian,' Vuk said.

'Do you trust me?'

Vuk regarded him.

'You're all I've got. You and Emma, maybe, but I'm not sure,' Vuk said.

'Vuk! Listen to me. Milosovic is selling us down the river. As sure as a whore spreads her legs. He wants to have the embargo lifted and stay in power. He's selling out the Bosnian Serbs. We'll be allowed to stay with him, but the Muslims will get our old land. We're done for. Slobodan has sold us for thirty pieces of silver. And he'll turn us in too, if the Americans insist. Vuk! I know the Americans. They don't appreciate the nuances of the situation, they don't know the first thing about politics, they don't know the first thing about the Balkans, but they know all about making deals.'

'So it's you and me?'

'That's the essence of it, yes,' the Commandant said. He rummaged around for his cigarettes. It was the first time Vuk had ever seen him look ruffled — no, panic-stricken almost. Beneath the uniform and those impassive features was a frightened man.

'The essence?'

'Of whom you and I can trust.'

'I don't understand,' Vuk said, although in fact he did.

'The Russian's money will give us freedom. We can stay here. Carry on the fight. We could move to Serbia. Or South America. Start a new life. This is our chance. You can be the one to take that chance for your comrades.'

'For you,' Vuk said.

'For you and me. And perhaps for Emma.'

'So this is not about the cause?'

'The cause is dead, Vuk. We've got to look out for ourselves now. You owe me that. I made you who you are. I took you in when you were nothing but a kid, shaking in your shoes and weeping in horror at what they had done to your parents…'

'Enough.' Vuk did not raise his voice, but he saw fear flicker in the Commandant's eyes. It was the first time Vuk had ever known the Commandant to show fear of him. He was right of course. He was who he was because the Commandant had licked him into shape and given him a mission. Taught him the sweetness of revenge and given him the tools with which to wreak such vengeance. But then he had had the cause. Now there was only the money.

The Commandant put a hand on his arm:

'Do you still trust me, Vuk?'

'Yes,' Vuk lied.

'Then prove it,' the Commandant said.

Vuk walked back to the table and sat down. He emptied his glass again. His hands were steady, but his throat was still dry. There seemed to be a spot there that could never be slaked. The Commandant also took a seat, raised his glass, drained it and nodded to Kravtjov.

'Do you have anything against killing a woman, Vuk?' Kravtjov asked.

'As long as it's understood that I don't kill for money,' said Vuk.

'Of course.'

'Who and when?'

The Russian leaned forward again and lowered his voice, as if they were on intimate terms. Vuk looked at the Commandant. His face was beaded with sweat. He lit another cigarette, and for the first time since he had known him Vuk felt no sense of awe, respect or love. He felt only contempt. The Commandant had sold him out, but Vuk would make sure that he never got to cash in. He did not hear what the Russian had said, so he asked him to repeat it.

'I said, we'll meet in three days' time in Berlin. I live in Berlin. It makes a good base. All right?'

'All right.'

'How will you get there?' the Russian asked.

'That's none of your business.'

'No, of course not.'

Kravtjov raised his glass in a silent toast and knocked back his drink.

'Who's the target?' Vuk asked.

Kravtjov produced a picture from his inside pocket and pushed it across the table to Vuk. The face meant nothing to him: it was that of an attractive woman of around forty who obviously had a penchant for large gold earrings. She had a round face and curly hair. She had a rather sweet gentle look about her, but there was also something about that face which spoke of a determined and forceful personality.

'Does she have a name?'

'Sara Santanda.'

Vuk sat back in his chair and gave a sudden laugh, a quiet laugh, deep in his chest, but it made the Commandant and Kravtjov sit bolt upright in their seats.

'What's so funny, Vuk?'

'You want me to take out a woman on whom those fucking ayatollahs in Teheran have put out a contract because she has insulted the Prophet and a religion that I hate more than anything else in the world.'

At this the Commandant laughed too, a loud bark that rapidly degenerated into a bout of coughing.

'Exactly, my lad, exactly,' he said between coughs. 'That's the beauty of it. You take her out, some fucking Muslim gets the blame, and we get four million dollars.

Vuk looked at him, then at Kravtjov.

'I'll see you in Berlin, Mr Kravtjov. Till then, you keep this to yourself. This is between you and me. Is that understood?'

'And your commandant?'

'And my commandant.'

'Agreed,' said Kravtjov, putting out his hand. But instead of shaking it, Vuk reached for the bottle and filled his glass again. He drained it in one gulp, got up and walked away.

Chapter 6

Vuk left that same evening. He packed his rucksack with a couple of spare shirts, a pair of beige chinos, a blue tie, underwear, camouflage paint, a black polo-neck sweater and black jeans. His apartment in Pale consisted of just two rooms. The bed was unmade, and in the kitchen stood a pan containing the remains of a meal: baked beans with a couple of fried eggs on top. There was a table with three high-backed chairs set round it and an empty bookcase. The floor was bare and dusty.

He stayed off the bottle, drank black coffee instead. Not that it mattered so much tonight, but in a couple of days he would need to be in command of all his faculties. He felt hollow inside but at the same time relieved. He had made a decision, and there was no going back. He felt his own treachery like a solid lump in the pit of his stomach, but he had come to the conclusion that there was no other way. A card had been dealt. Now it was up to him to play his ace. He knew he would miss the light and the scent of these green hills, but he also knew in his heart that he had had his day. And so had the Commandant.

Vuk assembled the bomb. It was a simple device. A few grams of Semtex and a detonator pencil. Once the pencil was snapped it would take an hour for the acid thus released to burn through to the Semtex. The Commandant was a creature of habit. He visited his mistress every day between seven and nine pm, then went home to his wife and two children. Radovan would be sitting in a nearby café, having a coffee and a short, while the Commandant was enjoying himself. Vuk no longer trusted the Commandant. He had sold him once. He would do it again. The first time was always the hardest. Betrayal came easier the second time, and the third. He pressed the pencil detonator gently into the soft plastic explosive and stuck the magnet to the other side. He held it close to the pan on the top of the cooker and it snapped onto the metal. He wrenched it free and wound some dark-grey tape around the little clump to hold everything in place, then slipped his Smith & Wesson into the pocket of his leather jacket along with a small carton of bullets.

He opened the door of the broom cupboard built in alongside the old gas cooker and removed a brush, a bucket and a dustpan. He opened his Swiss Army knife and carefully prised up two of the floorboards. They were already loose. He fished a brown leather pouch out of the space underneath the rest of the floorboards inside the cupboard and took from it three passports: one Danish, one Swedish and one Russian, all well worn. In the Russian passport photo Vuk had black hair and a moustache. In the Swedish and Danish ones he was fair-haired and clean-shaven. Each passport contained a number of stamps. Also in the bag were two Eurocards, an American Express card and a Swedish press card. The man pictured on this last was somewhat younger. The resemblance wasn't too good, but it might do at a pinch. Vuk tucked the whole lot into the inside pocket of his jacket. He groped around under the floor again and came up with another pouch. He undid the strings and pulled out two bundles of banknotes. A fat roll of American dollars with an elastic band around them and a bundle of deutschmarks held by a money clip. He popped the deutschmarks into his trouser pocket and the dollar bills into the jacket's inside pocket.

He was quite calm. The alcohol had gradually been sweated out of his system, and he always had his nerves well under control when preparing for or carrying out a mission. His mind was taken up solely with calculating, assessing and predicting what his enemies might do. It was as if there was no room for those demons and unforeseen thoughts to elbow their way to the fore.

Getting out of the country had become easier. Planes were flying out of Belgrade again now that the embargo had been partially lifted. Milosovic had sold them for a couple of plane tickets. Although of course, he thought, that was only the down payment. But it spelled the beginning of the end for the Bosnian Serbs.

It took a few moments, but eventually he got through to Belgrade.

'Vuk here,' he said.

'Yes, Vuk,' the voice on the other end said.

'Warsaw tomorrow.'

'One thousand deutschmarks, plus the ticket.'

'Okay.'

'Let me have the name you'll be using.'

'Sven Ericson, Swedish citizen.'

'Spell it!' came the distant sound of the black marketeer's voice from his little apartment in Belgrade. The international embargo and sanctions had given rise to a whole new class of business people in Belgrade. Anything could be obtained. Anything could be fixed. You just had to know the right people. Vuk spelled out the name and hung up. It was getting dark outside. He shouldered his rucksack, switched off the light and locked the door behind him.

There was no point in looking back. There was nothing in the apartment to say who had lived there. If anyone in the Bosnian Serbs' self-appointed capital ever took it into their heads to search the place they would find no leads there. Vuk might as well never have existed. Only one person knew his address, and he would never be able to tell anyone. Emma had no idea where he lived. His heart sank briefly, but he fought back this little surge of longing.

Vuk walked down the stairs and across to the car, a Russian Niva with Belgrade plates. It was parked in a side street, covered by a tarpaulin. He had been holding the little four-wheel drive in reserve for a month. It had a full tank and could handle the narrow roads that would take him that night into Serbia and to Belgrade. He had bought it on the black market, but the dealer had assured him that it was clean. New plates. The Ukrainian officer had returned to Kiev long since. He had reported it as being a write-off and been well paid to do so. So everybody had been happy.

Vuk hauled off the tarpaulin, folded it and laid it on the back seat. He took out the bomb and placed it on the passenger seat. The car started at the third attempt. The engine sounded good. It made a hell of a racket, but that was a Niva for you. He had done a thorough check of the powerful little car himself. Vuk had learned very early on that it was always wise to have a set of wheels handy. The day was still warm, but there weren't many people around. A couple of soldiers were sauntering along the street as Vuk drove up to the commandant's Mercedes, which was parked, as usual, in a side street fifty yards from his mistress's house. Vuk got out, but left the Niva's engine running. He looked about him. The soldiers were gone. He was alone. Radovan would be sitting in the café round the corner. It was a shame about him, but in every war people are killed simply because they happen to be in the wrong place at the wrong time. There was not a soul to be seen. He checked his watch. Six-thirty. Half an hour from now Radovan would drive the Commandant home. He had commandeered a mansion in the hills, once the property of a wealthy Slovenian. It would take him forty-five minutes to get there. Vuk glanced up and down the quiet side street one more time, then dropped swiftly to the ground and attached the magnet to the underside of the car just below the fuel tank. The dark-grey tape made the bomb almost invisible, and Vuk knew that the Commandant tended to be a bit slack about security when he was in Pale, particularly after a couple of hours with his mistress. He would come out smelling of brandy and get into the back seat, puffing on his cigar. On the mountain roads up to the mansion it would all be over. The burn-through time on the detonator had a margin of two minutes either way.

Vuk drove through the night. He kept to the minor roads and met no one. In this, the final phase of the war, most people stayed indoors. The negotiations that had now begun were being described as 'peace talks', but as far as Vuk was concerned they were 'capitulation talks'. His people were going to be sold down the river. It was only a matter of months before they would be placed under Muslim and Croatian control. A couple of years back the situation had been very different. They had been all set to conquer almost the whole of Bosnia-Herzegovina, but they had not been sure enough of their hand and had faltered at the crucial moment. Now Bosnia would build up a powerful government army, and those traitorous Serbs in Belgrade would sell them for the price of international recognition and the lifting of the blockade. They would also hand over one or two so-called war criminals to the ravening wolves in the west, to get themselves off the hook. He had made the right decision. It was time to get out.

The border loomed out of the gloom just after Screbrenica. It was patrolled by a sleepy-looking border guard. Vuk reduced speed and rolled his window right down. The guard was little more than a kid. They were on Serbian territory; he could not see any Bosnian guards. Vuk put a hand to his brow in a sketchy salute and handed the guard his military pass signed by the

Commandant, which could usually open any door. But to be on the safe side he had slipped a fifty-deutschmark note inside it. You never could tell these days, but it didn't look as if security had been stepped up. He hoped, though, that by now the Commandant was in no position to verify his own signature. The guard took the money and gave back the pass with a limp, nonchalant hand before raising the barrier and allowing Vuk to drive into Serbia. Vuk put his foot down and headed for Belgrade.

He reached Belgrade airport in the early hours. It lay still and ghostly in the soft, hazy, morning light. Time was when this had been a busy modern airport with connections to almost all of the world's major cities, but in recent years the international embargo had reduced the number of daily departures and arrivals to a minimum. Now air traffic was slowly returning to normal, and Vuk could see several of the old Yugoslavian Airlines planes sitting on the tarmac, ready for take-off. There were only a few cars in the car park. Vuk drove the Niva in and parked it. He took the gun from his inside pocket, emptied the bullets out of it and pushed them and the gun under the passenger seat. He didn't relish the thought of being unarmed, but he knew it was far too risky to carry a gun in an airport.

He leaned up against the Niva with his rucksack at his feet and lit a cigarette. He felt a little groggy from lack of sleep, but that would soon pass. He had gone for several days before without more than a couple of hours' sleep here and there, and he knew he could do it again. He heard a car door slam and saw a small, dark-suited man in his thirties walking towards him from a grey Ford Scorpio. Vuk straightened up and waited. He knew this man. He was known as the Snake, because he was said to have a cobra tattooed on his right buttock: a souvenir from prison.

The Snake came up to Vuk and clasped his hand.

'Any problems?'

'No.'

'They're saying your commandant had a bit of an accident?'

'These are dangerous times we're living in,' Vuk said.

'They are indeed,' said the Snake, handing Vuk a ticket. 'With Yugoslavian to Vienna, then Lot to Warsaw. That'll be two thousand exactly. You wanted them in a hurry, right?'

Vuk slipped the ticket into his inside pocket. He knew it would be okay. It was a lot of money, but you were paying for quality, and the Snake had only survived as long as he had because he knew that the best way of securing future custom was to let it be known that the last transaction was always forgotten as soon as it was completed. Vuk gave the Snake the two thousand marks. The Snake didn't count them, merely slipped the neatly folded notes into his inside pocket.

'Do what you like with the car,' Vuk said.

'Is it hot?'

'On the lukewarm side, maybe.'

'Okay.'

'There's a hot piece under the seat.'

'Right. I'll have that collected.'

Vuk handed him the keys and hoisted the rucksack onto his right shoulder.

'*Bon voyage*,' said the Snake.

'*Merci*,' said Vuk and stepped inside the terminal.

Vuk slept on the plane to Vienna and had time for a quick shower and shave at the busy airport terminal before boarding a half-full flight to Warsaw. He ate some cheese and a roll, then slept again. Passport control at Warsaw was more thorough than he had expected, but his plane had landed at the same time as an SAS flight from Copenhagen. He left the queue he was in and joined the line of Swedish and Danish business people. It was strange but nice to hear Swedish and Danish spoken again. Particularly Danish. It brought back a lot of memories, but he quashed them and concentrated on gauging how carefully passports were being checked. When a Scandinavian passport was presented it was given only a cursory glance. When his turn came the female passport controller took only one look at his passport and at him. He gave her a big smile, and she couldn't help but smile back.

'Have a nice stay in Poland, Mr Ericson,' she said.

'I'll do my best, ma'am,' he said, took his passport and entered Poland.

Vuk went to the gents. He found a vacant cubicle, placed his rucksack on the floor. He got out his make-up box and a small mirror, blackened his hair with a powder dye. This done, he very carefully glued on his moustache and popped a baseball cap on his head. He returned the make-up box to the rucksack and got out the Russian passport. He waited until he was sure that all the people with whom he had arrived would be safely through baggage reclaim and on their way into the Polish capital. Then he emerged from the gents and made for the bank, where he exchanged some deutschmarks for Polish zloty.

At the Avis desk he slapped his red Russian passport down on the counter along with his Russian driving licence. The Polish girl behind the counter gave him a sour look, but then her training gained the upper hand and he was treated to a bright Avis smile. He knew she was well aware that, as a Russian, he would be paying cash. Car-hire firms weren't happy about taking anything but credit cards, but the business in both legitimate and somewhat shadier Russians travelling around Eastern and Western Europe was too good to pass up. So the odd car might go missing, but that was what you had insurance for. Both the passport and the driving licence looked all right, so the assistant decided not to call a superior. In any case the Russian had only asked for a medium-class car. When they meant to strip them down they always went for the luxury models.

Nonetheless: 'Cash or credit?' she asked.

'Cash,' Vuk said and lit a cigarette while the girl was entering his passport and driving licence details on the rental form. Being Polish she had no trouble reading the Cyrillic script, and she probably remembered a fair bit of Russian from compulsory lessons at school but would never speak it. Vuk could well understand her. He said that, yes, he would pay for insurance. And he would want the car for two days. In true Russian fashion he pulled a roll of hundred-dollar bills from his pocket and counted out the appropriate amount. He was given the keys to a Ford Fiesta and within a matter of minutes he was on the road, heading south-west towards Wroclaw. Mr Ericson had arrived in Poland and then vanished into thin air. Mr Jenikov had hired a car, although no passport authority had registered his entry into the Polish Republic. Although this was actually less unusual than one might think. There was a lot of toing and froing of Russians and Ukrainians across the Polish–Ukrainian border. And the formalities were not always observed in the new, galloping market economy that had taken over from the planned economy to the east of the old Iron Curtain.

Vuk stopped at a supermarket in a small town. He bought bread, sausage, cheese, some apples and two large bottles of mineral water before continuing westwards along a good highway as twilight descended on the flat Polish countryside. He bought a couple of bottles of cola when he stopped for petrol. He paid cash. In the middle of the night he stopped at a lay-by, ate his bread and sausage and drank one of the bottles of mineral water. He locked the car doors and slept for four hours. He was woken twice by the hiss of hydraulic brakes as a couple of big Polish trucks pulled in.

It was another beautiful morning. The light shifted from rosy to pale blue, and dew sparkled on the meadows. There was no sign of movement in the two trucks. The drivers were obviously sleeping. Vuk brushed his teeth with mineral water, ate the last of the bread and cheese. He was dying for a cup of coffee. He brushed most of the black powder out of his hair, leaving it more of a mousy-brown colour. He was stiff all over, so he did some stretching exercises and twenty press-ups.

Before driving on he changed into his black jeans and swapped the pale-grey Reeboks for a pair of plain black sneakers. But he kept on the red checked shirt. He didn't want to show up in a border town dressed all in black. He stopped at a modern-looking fast-food joint, had a coffee and a cheese roll. He gave his order in German and used a foul-smelling, antiquated toilet, where he managed to brush some more of the black dye out of his hair and washed his face. His eyes were a bit bloodshot, and he had a faint headache, but otherwise he was feeling pretty good. He was running on adrenalin. Traffic was light. Mostly old Polish cars and the occasional farm vehicle. The fields had been harvested and in a few places ploughing had already begun. He saw horses pulling a plough and one or twice he overtook a flat-bottomed cart drawn by a single sturdy horse. The day was warm with a light scattering of cloud. In a small town not far from Wroclaw he called in at the local post office and obtained the number for a hotel booking service in Berlin. He called the number and was given the names of several small family hotels in the centre of the city. The first two were fully booked, but the third could fit him in. He said that he was calling from Denmark and would like to book a room for two, or possibly three, nights in the name of Per Larsen. He spoke English to the receptionist.

He munched apples as he drove, and listened to a Polish channel playing pop music. By the time it was really dark the first German FM stations were coming through loud and clear on the car radio. He listened to the news. It was the usual stuff: isolated skirmishes in Bosnia, negotiations, political infighting in Germany, hold-ups on the motorway. There were more and more juggernauts driving in both directions. It wouldn't be too long before he hit the start of the long queue of trucks waiting to enter the EU at Görlitz, so he turned off and drove into the centre of the Polish border town, Zgorzelec, and parked in a small square. It was a dusty, run-down place, but there were signs here and there that the work of rebuilding and renovating the old houses had begun.

He made sure the car was securely locked. It would have to sit here for at least a couple of days, if it didn't get stolen that very night. But that wasn't his problem. He shouldered his rucksack and walked off. He noticed groups of gaudily dressed gypsies or Romanians hanging around one corner of the square. A Polish patrol car cruised past them, and they huddled together like a flock of startled chickens.

With his dark hair, cap, jeans and leather jacket, Vuk looked like a Polish farm labourer on his way into town, like so many others, to have a beer or two. And maybe a chat about all the weird, raggle-taggle foreigners who were streaming into their town in the hope of finding a way over the border into the EU's land of milk and honey. He dropped the car keys through a grating and strolled back out of the town. On the outskirts he drew a small compass from his pocket and took his bearings: south-west. It should be just under five miles to the border and the Oder-Niesse line – the narrow shallow river course which separated the affluent west from the poor, newly liberated part of Europe. It wasn't the ideal evening: a three-quarters full moon lit up the flat terrain from time to time, but he noted with satisfaction that heavy black clouds occasionally blocked out its pale light and plunged the stubble-fields into darkness. In any case, he had no choice. And he did not expect to be the only one out there that night. He ripped up his Russian passport and driving licence and let the fragments fly out behind him like confetti. A light west wind caught the fragments and swept them off across the fields. The route he had chosen had been a long and tortuous one, but Vuk had learned that all tracks had to be thoroughly erased, in an age when anyone travelling across the continent invariably left an electronic trail behind them, in the form of passports and credit cards, automatic ticket registration and online booking systems.

He smelled the river before he saw it. He cut across the field and into a little copse. Then he heard voices. Talking in whispers. These people didn't realize how far a whisper could carry at night. He also spotted the red glow of a cigarette. It was a good way off, but he shut his eyes anyway to preserve his night vision. They were Romanian voices. He heard a loud shushing sound, and when he opened one eye a peek the glow from the cigarette was gone. A child's voice said something, then whimpered. As an adult hand clenched round a childish arm, no doubt. Vuk drew back a little from the Romanians, although still staying close enough to keep track of them. They were too inexperienced and too scared to keep perfectly quiet.

He hunkered down, gently eased off his leather jacket and folded it. He pulled on the black polo-neck and packed his jacket into his rucksack. In the dark he smeared his face and hands with camouflage paint. He could do it with his eyes shut. This had been one of the main principles of the Commandant's special training programme: any action that could be carried out in daylight ought also to be performed as surely and swiftly in total darkness. And in this case the darkness wasn't even total. Now and again the moon cast a faint glow over the few solitary trees and the flat meadows. The scent of the water was in his nostrils. Before too long the Germans on the other side would be erecting fences topped by barbed wire. It was only a matter of time. A new wall would go up. It would have moved further east and would no longer be there to keep people in, but to keep them out. A new Welfare Wall, Vuk thought to himself. The world was still divided into the haves and the have-nots. And if you wanted something, you just had to grab it.

He settled down to wait. Emptied his mind of all thoughts and concentrated on listening, smelling and accustoming his eyes to the darkness. A bird flitted soundlessly down, landed only three feet away from him then took off again with a tiny mouse in its grip. The grass was damp with dew, and the air was cool but not really cold.

Around midnight, after a ninety-minute wait during which he had seen yet another owl bag its prey, he heard the Romanians. He counted ten shadows: seven adults and three half-grown children. They were led by a burly man in black who chivvied them along in a hushed voice. This was their guide, to whom they had paid a lot of money, all they had left, and who had promised them that he knew the German border guards' patrolling routine. The group passed only ten yards from Vuk, but they did not see him. They were not worried about the authorities on the Polish side: they were too few and underpaid, and it was no longer illegal to leave the Free Republic of Poland. The men all carried suitcases; each of the three women held a child by the hand and had a rolled-up bundle under her other arm.

Vuk allowed the bunch of terrified refugees to pass. Then started after them. Even though the Romanians' minds were on what lay ahead, Vuk trod warily, bringing down the soles of his feet first, to feel for loose stones or dried twigs. Suddenly the shallow river hove into view fifty yards ahead of them. He saw the guide point to it, and to the moon that had broken free of the clouds once more. Then he pointed to the ground. The band of refugees crouched down. The guide turned and headed back towards Vuk, who stepped slowly but smoothly first one, then two, then three steps to the left, glided down onto his haunches and from there onto his stomach. It is the quick movements that are noticeable in the dark. The guide stopped short, as if he had seen something. Or heard something. Then the owl swooped low over the meadow again, pounced and flew up and away. The mouse gave a little squeak, a faint sound, but one which carried clearly through the night. The guide shook his head and marched on. Vuk let him pass then raised himself back onto his haunches. He could hear the Romanians arguing among themselves.

The moon disappeared behind a cloud. It wasn't big enough, but one of the Romanian men got to his feet anyway and waded out into the shallow river, which was no wider than the average road. The other men followed him and the women brought up the rear, holding the children by the hand. They balanced the suitcases and bundles on their heads. In midstream the adults were almost waist-high in the water, and the children had to crane their necks as the water crept up over their chests. Oddly enough they did not cry. Vuk stole after them. He slipped off his rucksack and crouched down again only yards from the riverbank. Near him was a small bush; he crept behind it. He heard a dog bark and shut his eyes when he saw the dancing beams of light and heard the swish of boots on damp grass. He slid all the way down onto his stomach and lay there with his eyes closed. He could hear what was going on.

The four German border guards waited patiently until all of the refugees were back on dry land. They were carrying blankets, which they wrapped around the soaked, fearful and bedraggled Romanians. The dog sat quietly. The Romanians blinked in the glare of the powerful torches. One of the border guards pointed and the group set off across the field. Even in the dark Vuk was conscious of the German border guard's torch beam sweeping across the Polish bank. He heard a radio crackle and an indistinct German voice receiving a message and reporting back that a group of refugees had been caught. The beam of light swept across the pitch-black riverbank yet again.

'No more here, Hans,' the German voice said. 'That's it for tonight. Come on! We've got to get this lot sent back tomorrow.'

Vuk heard the sound of footsteps receding. He waited only a moment before getting up and hastening down to the riverbank. Rumour had it that the German border authorities had installed sensors. If that were true, the Romanians and the German guards would confuse them. The water was cold when he waded out with his rucksack on his head, like an African woman going to fetch water. Once over on the German side he slung his rucksack onto his back and set off at a quick march into the German Federal Republic.

He was not much over a hundred miles from Berlin. He walked across the fields for an hour, until he came to a main road. Next to it sat a service station. It looked new and modern. Things were moving fast in the former GDR, Vuk thought to himself. Every time he came back he found more changes. The service station was lit up, and there were four or five private cars and a lot of trucks in the forecourt. Vuk had wiped off most of the camouflage paint with a handkerchief, but he couldn't be sure he'd got rid of it all. On the other hand, you get a lot of funny-looking people wandering about in the early hours of the morning. Vuk found a toilet at the side of the service building, splashed his face with water and pressed his moustache back into place. It was the best he could do, and it wasn't bad. He hung about beside a truck with Polish plates. The driver emerged from the shop: a short, stocky man with a five o'clock shadow.

Vuk stepped into the light with his rucksack in his hand. He gave the driver a big smile and said in German: 'Any chance of a lift?'

The driver stopped in his tracks. He saw a young man, unshaven, but with a nice friendly smile. It was three in the morning, the driver was tired and he still had a good few hours' driving ahead of him.

'I'm headed for Berlin,' he said with a heavy accent.

'Me too.'

'My boss wouldn't like it.'

'Your boss doesn't need to know.'

'I'm not sure.'

'I could pay something towards the petrol,' Vuk said, holding out a fifty-deutschmark note.

'Aw, hop in,' the driver said. 'What he doesn't know won't hurt him. The name's Karol.'

'Werner,' said Vuk.

They chatted about football as they bowled along. Listened to German pop music and, later, traffic reports on the morning rush hour in Berlin. Queues were building up on a number of roads. Berlin appeared out of the morning haze. There were construction cranes everywhere, towering over the grey suburbs of old East Berlin. Karol was carrying a load of textiles from Kraków. He dropped Vuk not far from Alexanderplatz. Vuk found a cafeteria where three middle-aged men appeared to be tending their hangovers with coffee and schnapps. Vuk paid for a coffee, then visited the gents. When he reappeared he was wearing the beige chinos, a clean striped shirt and a pale-blue tie. The moustache was gone and his hair slicked back. On his feet were a pair of brown loafers. If the three men noticed anything, then they gave no sign of it: it seemed that in this part of town people minded their own business. Vuk drank his coffee and left.

He spotted a sign for the U-bahn, purchased a single ticket and took a westbound train. The Hotel Heidelberg was situated in Knesebechstrasse, off the Kurfürstendamm in West Berlin. It was a small family hotel with a restaurant just inside the main door. The reception desk was situated at the rear of the restaurant. Three sales reps were in the midst of a late breakfast.

At reception Vuk put his rucksack on the floor and presented the young woman behind the desk with the Danish passport.

'You have a room for Mr Per Larsen,' he said in English.

She checked on the computer, found his name. She pushed a yellow registration form across the desk, leaving him to fill in the details himself. She did not so much as glance at the passport. He was Danish and hence a member of the EU.

She handed him an old-style key.

'Number sixty-seven,' she said.

'Thanks,' Vuk said and climbed the stairs. All of a sudden he felt dog-tired. And he could have done with a good hot meal. But the main thing was that now he could safely rest.

The room was quite big, with a double bed. He put down his rucksack and called the number Kravtjov had given him in Bosnia.

'It's me,' Vuk said in English.

'Welcome to Berlin,' Kravtjov said. 'He wants to see you as soon as possible.'

'I need to get some sleep first,' Vuk said. The tiredness had suddenly hit him. He had been on the move for three days and had used up all his last reserves of strength and adrenalin. Even during the few hours when he had managed to grab some sleep his body had been on the alert. What rest he had got had been of the most superficial sort.

'I understand,' said Kravtjov.

'I'll call you in a few hours' time.'

'Fine. Where are you?'

'You'll find out, all in good time.'

'Sleep tight,' Kravtjov said with a chuckle.

Vuk hung the '*Nicht Stören*' sign on the door and locked it. No one knew where he was, but he called reception anyway, from the bedside, and said he did not wish to be disturbed. His teeth needed brushing, but he lay down just for a moment and promptly fell fast asleep.

Chapter 7

Looking back on the last few days, Lise Carlsen could well understand why she was tired. What she found harder to comprehend was why she should be so strangely exhilarated. She couldn't explain how she felt. And she had given up trying to talk to Ole about it. She didn't know what was the matter with him. He came home late every evening, reeking of booze and the pub, then he would take a beer from the fridge or a bottle from the wine rack and just sit there drinking. She'd been avoiding him; she didn't like the thought of him touching her. She knew it was wrong, but she couldn't help it: if he tried to give her a cuddle, if his hand so much as brushed hers at the dinner table she instinctively shrank away. Nonetheless, she endeavoured to keep up the pretence, kissing him hello and goodbye. She hated herself for it, detecting as she did an incipient repugnance inside herself to which she did not dare give full rein.

The nights were still hot. And she dreamed of Per Toftlund. Weird, never-ending dreams. In one of these he was riding a motorbike, in another hauling a net out of an ocean. The net was full of silvery fish with little monkey faces, and the muscles of his tanned back bulged as he pulled in the fine-meshed, green net. The fish flopped and floundered, their scales glinting like silver coins in the pale, gold light. On the horizon was a reef beset by masses of birds. They were yellow and big as gulls. She wanted to warn Per, because she was afraid that the yellow birds would eat the dancing silver fish. But she couldn't make him hear her.

She woke up bathed in sweat. Ole was asleep beside her. He stank of tobacco and alcohol. Lise got up. She was naked, and she shivered in the cool night air. She pulled on her dressing gown, padded through to the kitchen and got herself a glass of milk. It was a few minutes to four. Soon the first light would appear as a bright band on the horizon. She was tired and yet wide-awake: a clear sign of stress. She ought to know that.

Maybe it was because things had been so hectic, after the announcement on the evening news of Sara Santanda's visit to Denmark.

Tagesen had been furious. Although she wasn't sure whether he was mad because the word had got out, thus increasing the threat to Sara's life, or because Danmarks Radio, and not *Politiken*, had been first with the news. She had been given something approaching a bawling out. As if it were her fault. When it was so obvious that the information had been leaked from Christiansborg. Toftlund wanted the visit cancelled or postponed indefinitely, but neither Lise or Tagesen would agree to that. Nor, thank goodness, would Sara Santanda. She remained adamant. She was a brave woman. They might be able to put the visit off for a couple of weeks. Most news stories were soon forgotten, although this one had, of course, made the headlines in all the papers. Lise herself had reported on it for her own paper and written a portrait of the writer. She had also been interviewed on the radio and on both national TV channels. She had appeared on talk shows morning, noon and night: Fax, Stax, Pax – whatever they were called, all those radio programmes. A record and then a chat about some weighty issue. Ole hated that sort of thing. In fact, he loathed all electronic media, so more often than not she watched the television news on her own. All things considered, she might as well have been living alone: they no longer seemed to have anything in common. They couldn't even be bothered arguing about things anymore. Their differences stretched like a barren desert between them.

Lise got herself another glass of milk. Then there was Per Toftlund: a pain in the neck but a very attractive one. Handsome in a rugged sort of a way. He wasn't really her type at all. What she looked for in a man was depth. He was bossy too and a right know-it-all, always harping on about the arrangements for Santanda's visit: the press conference, safe houses, escape routes, security corridors and the easiest ways in and out of the airport, not to mention angles of elevation and the life stories of the best known snipers and contract killers. He had a fund of horrendous stories about the Iranian security service's liquidation of political rivals. She had learned that its people were more ruthless and every bit as professional as the hit men of the old KGB. She had also discovered that PET kept detailed files on both Danish citizens and foreign nationals. And although she could see that these were bound to be of great help in this particular situation, she was also shocked. The sheer extent of it!

But Per was also fun to be with.

The other day he had treated her to a hotdog, and they had sat on a bench overlooking the Sound, munching companionably. It was as if he already knew that she loved to eat. The weather was still glorious, the air not quite as close. Sweden was hidden by a heat haze, and she had the sudden urge to go off somewhere. It didn't matter where. All she wanted was to be on the move. To just get into a car and drive south, head for Spain. To drive and drive, for so long that the car wrapped itself around you and you became a part of it, came to smell of it, and your scent rubbed off on it. To climb out and stretch, feast your eyes on the red soil of Spain and decide to drive inland to where the country was vast and deserted.

'Hey, where did you go?' Per Toftlund asked. He was wearing a thin windcheater over a short-sleeved, open-necked shirt. She was slowly getting used to the gun at his belt, but it still made her feel a mite uneasy. She had never spent hours in the company of a man who wore a gun as if it was the most natural thing in the world. She knew nothing about his world.

'Out travelling.'

'Sounds good. Where to?'

'Spain,' she said and took a bite of her hotdog. 'Umm...this is so disgustingly delicious.'

'*España sea muy buena*,' he said.

She carried on chewing. They seemed to be warming to one another. Sitting on a bench, eating hotdogs and talking with your mouth full: that's the sort of thing you only do when you feel comfortable with someone, she thought.

'Where did you learn to speak Spanish?' she asked.

'In South America. I spent some time hitchhiking around out there after I left the service – I'd made good money there. And at evening classes. And in Spain.'

Toftlund's jaws were working too.

'Macho man,' she said, with no note of disparagement in her voice. 'I bet you were in the commandos or something daft like that.'

'Nearly right. I was a frogman.'

'Ooh, like the Crown Prince. Not bad.'

'Hm, well I was there first. What about you? And Spain, I mean.'

'Where I learned to speak Spanish? In Spain. A long, long time ago.'

'It's a great country, isn't it?'

He got up, turned to face her and did a little sashay. He looked a bit silly, and a couple of passers-by stared at him. A big man doing a really quite elegant imitation of a bullfighter, dodging the bull with a flourish of an imaginary red cape. It would have been very effective, if he hadn't been clutching a half-eaten hotdog in one hand. He let the bull pass to his right and then to his left, crying out in Spanish as he did so: '*Andalucia. Estremadura. Euskadi. Madrid. Valencia. Sol y sombra. Toros. Vino. Señoritas. Olé!*' He would never have made an actor.

She laughed at his clowning and choked on her hotdog. He plonked himself down on the bench and thumped her gently on the back.

'Do you go there often?' she said, once she'd got her breath back.

'At least once a year. What about you?'

'Oh, it's a few years since I was there.'

He had looked at her. He had the kindest blue eyes.

'Ole's kind of gone off Spain,' she had said, a little more dolefully than she had intended. But Per had handled it perfectly. He had pulled a napkin from his jacket pocket, lightly dabbed her lips and then shown her the little red spot.

'Ketchup,' he had said, and she had started to laugh again.

She was stressed out. That had to be the explanation, she told herself, standing there by the scrubbed deal kitchen bench. For the fact that she was acting like a giggly schoolgirl.

No wonder she was tired and tense. She hadn't really been home at all in the past week. Imagine if they'd had kids. If they'd been able to have them. How would she and Ole have fitted *them* into in their busy lives? She supposed that was one positive aspect of their childlessness: they weren't tied down. As always, though, it hurt to think about it and feel the emptiness inside; the longing, like a hollowness that could never be filled. Maybe a baby would have added a new dimension to their relationship, lent it meaning, forged a bond between them. They had actually talked about this. They had talked it through and agreed that nature's perverse logic had simply dictated that she couldn't get pregnant and they were not going to try to change that by resorting to artificial means of any sort. They didn't want to adopt. They had each other and that would have to do. That is what they had said, back then. So why did it still hurt?

She sensed rather than heard Ole standing in the doorway of the open-plan kitchen. She turned round. He was tousle-headed, and she noticed that the hair on his chest was starting to turn grey. In the morning light he actually looked quite old. She'd never thought of him that way before. She felt a little sorry for him, was struck by a wave of sympathy that promptly turned to self-loathing. Why couldn't she just love him the way she used to do?

He stood in the doorway, leaning against the jamb.

'Trouble sleeping?' he said.

'Looks that way, doesn't it?'

He said nothing for a moment. Then:

'Is there someone else, Lise?' he said.

She ventured a little laugh, but it didn't ring true.

'No. For God's sake, of course there isn't.'

'But you're hardly ever home. Out most of the night.'

'Read the paper and you'll see what I'm doing.'

'Maybe you ought to invest some time in us as well.'

She looked away from him.

'Well, Lise?' he said.

'This isn't going to go on for ever,' she said.

'So how long *is* it going to go on for?'

She turned to face him again:

'I've promised not to say anything. Per says…'

'He says a lot of things, this Per.'

'Oh, do me a favour, Ole.'

'Get some sleep,' he muttered.

She knew she ought to, but she sat where she was for a while longer. She could have kicked herself. Ole had reached out a hand to her, so why hadn't she grasped it? There was no one else, but did she have a sneaking suspicion that there soon would be?

Her black mood had lifted by the time she climbed into Per Toftlund's BMW later that day. She had merely been suffering from a slightly longer bout of the morning blues than usual. Who could possibly be downhearted when it was another beautiful sunny day, with people strolling along Langelinie eating ice cream, and Japanese tourists frantically filming the unimposing figure of the Little Mermaid? They listened to P3 on the car radio. A nice sentimental ballad. Toftlund sang along with it for a while, but basically he felt the same as she did: it was just nice to have the radio playing. As always he seemed calm and contented. As if the world were still fresh and young and it was wonderful to begin upon a brand new day.

'Are you always in such a good mood?' she said.

'Usually. I've got no complaints.'

'There are those who would interpret that as a sign of stupidity. Life isn't that great. In fact, it's pretty awful. Only someone with no imagination can go through life without ever getting depressed.'

'I'm smarter than most, and I have a job I like,' he said with not a hint of irony. He didn't go in much for irony. While she spent her days surrounded by press and TV folk who wore irony like a medieval suit of armour.

She could have made some retort but hadn't the heart. It was too nice a day.

'Do you really like your job?' she asked instead.

'Yeah, it's fantastic.'

They weren't really driving anywhere in particular. They had to look at a couple of apartments she had been offered the loan of. They also had to check out a hotel. Or look it over, as Per said. But he wasn't very keen on hotels. They were too public, too easy to get in and out of. He was more in favour of a discreet private apartment. But nothing they had looked at had been good enough. There was always some fault to find. Either there was no rear entrance. Or there was a rear entrance, which made the apartment difficult to guard. Either a place wasn't easy to get to and from. Or the very problem was that it was easy to get to and from. She had given up trying to figure out what he was really looking for.

He drove slowly along the quay, then stopped.

'Smoke if you want. As long as you roll down the window,' he said.

'My, aren't we tolerant today?' she said, thankfully lighting a cigarette and blowing the smoke out of the open window.

'What about your work?' he said.

'It's all right.'

'Poking your nose into people's business to keep other people entertained.'

She felt rather offended by this remark and could not hide it.

'I'm an arts journalist!' The minute the words left her mouth she wished she hadn't said it. It sounded so pompous, but Per merely said:

'Even worse. Arrogant asinine artists sucking money out of the state coffers.'

'Oh, come *on*...'

'They spend all their time moaning that nobody wants to buy their rotten books or see their lousy films.'

'I knew you were a reactionary.' Her dander was really up now. She could not stand that sort of facile comment. She found stupidity and ignorance infuriating and narrow-minded. Denmark was a prosperous country with a fine educational system. There was no excuse for ignorance. For not making the most of all the cultural experiences on offer. As far as she was concerned, art and culture were, by definition, good.

'Clint Eastwood doesn't need any bloody grants.'

Lise flung open the car door demonstratively and got out. A soft cool breeze was blowing in from Sweden, and the Sound looked like a picture postcard: the blue water dotted by gaily-coloured sails and sedate ferries. And oh, the glorious scent of sea air and sunshine. She saw a cutter heading out of the harbour. The quarterdeck was packed with people.

'Wait, Per!' she cried.

Toftlund also got out and stood by the door. She tossed her cigarette over the edge of the quay.

'You're right. There's no bloody point in arguing about art,' he said placidly.

She walked up to him and took his arm.

'It's not that, stupid. I've just had an idea. You're really worried about the press conference, right?'

Per nodded. She shook his arm vigorously, as if he were a little kid. She could feel his muscles. His arm was soft and yet solid. Totally different from Ole's, she felt a surge of warmth in her breast.

'There!' she said, pointing beyond the harbour mouth, out into the Sound.

'Sweden?' Per said.

'No. On an island in the middle of the Sound.'

Toftlund stood for a moment scanning the waves, looked down at her, then back at the water.

'Christ,' he said. 'Christ-all-bloody-Mighty. Flakfortet. Easy to monitor. Easy to guard. Easy to block off. It's bloody perfect, *chica*. God, you're smart.'

She felt like a schoolgirl who had been praised for writing a good essay. It was a great idea, and she couldn't help doing a little hop, skip and jump before having almost all the breath squeezed out of her as he gave her a big hug and pounded her gently but firmly on the back, sending a warm thrill all the way down her spine, from the nape of her neck to the soles of her feet.

Chapter 8

Vuk had a dream in the hotel room in Berlin. As usual it began well. He saw his parents far in the distance, standing on a green hill under a pale-blue sky. They were waving to him. The light was golden, peaceful, but not for long. Suddenly the sun altered character. It turned a fiery red, even though it was high in the sky. It looked like a child's drawing, with a glimmer of a smile and long tongues of flame shooting out from it. But there was laughter hidden within the sun-reddened landscape, and faint music. He was both in the picture and watching from the outside. Then a deep rumbling sounded in the distance, and he knew the blood-roller was on its way. The thunderous rumble grew louder, and at the same time the picture in his dream was filled with people. At first they were waving, then they started screaming. But their screams were soundless. He could only hear his parents. They were calling plaintively for his sister, but he could not see her. All he knew was that she was somewhere in the crowd. Soon the blood-roller would appear and he knew that he would be driving it and would, therefore, be three people at the same time. Three shadows in a bloodshot landscape.

Vuk struggled to wake up, and this time he managed it before the blood-roller came into full view on the horizon. He sat bolt upright in bed, trembling and drenched in sweat. The sheet was soaked through. The room was in darkness, and the furniture was nothing but flickering shadows. He had slept the whole day away. He switched on the light and helped himself to two miniatures of vodka from the minibar. He knocked back one bottle then went into the bathroom, poured the contents of the second into his tooth-glass and drank this too. Gradually his breathing calmed down. He looked at himself in the mirror: a young frightened face with narrowed eyes. He was having this

75

dream more and more often. He could control what happened in his life when he was awake, but it was becoming harder and harder to keep the demons at bay when he was asleep. Which was why he tried to sleep as little as possible. He dreaded sleep as others dread the calamities of waking life. But this time his body had triumphed over his mind. It had simply had need of all those hours. He tasted the sleep, like a greasy coating in his mouth. His head was heavy, but his body felt well rested.

Vuk showered. He called Kravtjov and was given the name of a café near Alexanderplatz. He was to be there at midnight. He stuck his Swiss Army knife in the pocket of his leather jacket and went out.

From the side street Vuk turned onto the Kurfürstendamm. He bought that day's edition of the *Herald Tribune* and repaired to a café for a quick cup of coffee and a mineral water. He skimmed through the paper: things were not going well in Bosnia. There was a brief note on the back page announcing that the writer Sara Santanda would be visiting a number of European countries, including Denmark. There was also a piece about the CIA, which had been granted sixteen billion dollars to undermine the clerical government in Iran. Vuk didn't understand the Americans. How could they let it be known that their intelligence agency had instigated such a project? Vuk hoped the CIA would succeed in their undertaking. He hated the Iranians. He had seen them in action in Bosnia, where these holy warriors had fought on the side of the government army. They were fanatics, ruthless killers. But they were also careless where their own safety was concerned. They probably imagined that the hand of Allah would protect them, but he had managed to bring down a few of them with his rifle while they were ordering about their Bosnian Muslim recruits. So much for Allah.

He was ready for anything again. He felt safe in the big anonymous city, where he was just one young man among many in his blue jeans, checked shirt and shabby, brown leather jacket. The Berlin evening was cool but not cold. There were lots of people in the streets. He walked up the Kurfürstendamm to Brandenburger Tor. Construction cranes pierced the night sky like the church spires of a new age. The din of the traffic throbbed in his ears, making his nerve-endings vibrate. It was a long time since he had strolled around a city that was not in the grip of war or blockades. The city soon came to feel to him like a welcoming glove into which he could crawl and disappear. He was on his guard, but he felt secure. No one knew where he was. Nonetheless, he took no chances. He crossed the street a couple of times. Walked back the way he had come. Walked quickly in and out of a café. Stayed in one spot for a long time, using a shop window as a mirror. He was alone in the crowd.

He stood for a while watching a couple of Romanians trying to hoodwink two East Germans. The trick was as old as the hills, but apparently it still worked: three small eggcups and a tiny pea set out on a speedily erected table. The pea disappears under one of the eggcups, and all three cups are shuffled around at lightning speed. Punters have to bet on which cup the pea is under. But maybe the trick was too old after all. The Romanians spent most of their time playing together, endeavouring to attract custom, and the man with the cups always lost. But Vuk knew that he could have won any time he wanted to. The few bystanders gathered around the table looked as if they had seen it all before.

Vuk walked on until he came to a steakhouse. There was a table by a window. He ate a steak and drank a bottle of mineral water followed by a coffee before moving on. He crossed the old sector boundary. There was no sign of the Wall. It might never have existed except in nightmares. No one had considered preserving it as a historic monument. Where the Wall had stood was a broad band of upturned earth, tufts of grass and disintegrating chunks of stone, punctuated by cranes and half-finished buildings. But Vuk knew right away that he was now in East Berlin. He found himself surrounded by Soviet-style concrete buildings. He could have been in Belgrade or Minsk. But there were more neon signs and western cars here than previously, and the shop windows cast a golden glow over the pavement which ran past ranks of identical concrete tower blocks, like giant soldiers in a petrified army.

Vuk reached Alexanderplatz. There were only a handful of people about. Marx and Engels stood alone on the square in the shadow of the television tower, looking lost and forlorn. They seemed so small. As if the regime had not thought them worth expending too much granite on. Vuk walked over to the statue and lit a cigarette. He pulled his map of Berlin from his inside pocket and checked the location of the café: down a side street only a few hundred yards away.

It was on the ground floor of the building and looked like an old East-German *kneipe*, but Vuk noted that the proprietor seemed to have splashed out on a new sign and a lick of paint for the facade when the place had been privatised. It had the look of a place frequented by Russians. Vuk positioned himself in a doorway opposite the café. He zipped his jacket up to the neck and waited.

It was close on midnight when Kravtjov showed up. With him was a slim, very short man with black hair. They could have passed for a couple of businessmen in their navy suits and blue coats. Kravtjov let the Iranian precede him into the bar. Vuk stayed where he was. He waited fifteen minutes more, but no one else appeared. He took a walk up one side of the street and back down the other. There were only a few late-night wanderers around. The two men had been on their own.

The café was bigger than Vuk had expected. It stretched a long way back. It was simply furnished with a bar and some wooden tables and chairs. There were about a score of people in the place, drinking beer and schnapps. A couple of them glanced his way, then promptly turned back to their talk and their beer. Vuk peered through the smoke that obscured the blue lighting in the dim room. The Russian and the Iranian were sitting alone at a table right at the far end of the café. Kravtjov sat facing the door, while the Iranian had his back to it. The latter had short black hair that was plastered down with gel. Kravtjov had an almost empty glass of draught beer in front of him. The Iranian appeared to be drinking coffee. Two extra cups stood on the table next to the coffee jug.

Kravtjov caught sight of Vuk and lifted a hand ever so slightly. Vuk crossed the floor silently in his trainers. The Iranian turned to look at him. Vuk could see he was surprised that he was so young. He had been expecting a more experienced man. As if experience comes only with age. It has as much to do with the chances that come your way. Vuk had learned more in four years than most people would learn in a lifetime. And he had survived. He took a seat at the end of the table with his back to the wall, Kravtjov on his right and the Iranian on his left.

Kravtjov smiled. The smile did not reach his eyes. The Iranian looked long and hard at Vuk. He had close-set, dark eyes. He was toying with his teaspoon.

'Coffee?' he said in English.

Vuk nodded.

The Iranian picked up the jug on the table and poured him a cup.

'Vuk, meet Mr Rezi. Mr Rezi, this is Vuk.'

Vuk nodded again and raised his coffee cup. His hand was steady as a rock. Kravtjov shrugged and said:

'Right, then. Mr Rezi is authorized to speak for his government.'

'Then let him speak,' said Vuk wryly. The Iranian looked at him, and Vuk looked straight back at him. Kravtjov felt the frostiness of the atmosphere between them. He'd been expecting that. These days, seating a Serb and a Muslim at the same table was possibly not the wisest move, but Kravtjov had learned from long experience that big business makes for the most unlikely bedfellows. Even though Rezi must know that Vuk had hunted and killed his countrymen in Bosnia. But this was business. These former enemies now had a common interest. There was no room here for ideology or idealism.

Rezi raised his own coffee cup, took a sip and set the cup down again without a chink. He lit a cigarette and leaned across the table. His voice was hushed. He spoke exquisite English. BBC English, Vuk thought. He had to be about forty, seemed well educated and urbane, but Vuk knew that Rezi would kill a man as dispassionately as he sipped his coffee. Whether he was pulling the trigger himself or dispatching someone else to do it. The Iranian security police showed their enemies no mercy.

'We want that infidel whore dead,' he said in his smooth, dry voice. 'We are willing to pay you and Mr Kravtjov's organization four million dollars to do the job. The contract stands for six months.'

It was Vuk's turn to lean across the table.

'I don't kill for money,' he said.

'I realize that. You can do what you like with the money.'

Again Vuk took his time. Drank some more coffee. It was lukewarm. The pleasant low hum of voices filled the room. The bartender had switched on the television and was watching football highlights. Vuk fixed his eyes on Rezi as the latter spoke again:

'Officially, Iran does not send out hit squads. It would not be politic at the moment. It is important for our economy that we collaborate with the infidels. But we want that whore done away with. A fatwa is final. No politician can rescind what Allah has decreed. No matter what our official line may be. Do you understand me?'

'Perfectly,' Vuk said.

'So Mr…'

'Just Vuk…'

'So, Mr Vuk. Where do you stand?'

Vuk had had enough of his smooth diplomatic mouthings.

'I hate all fucking Muslims,' he said.

Vuk saw Rezi blink, with eyes that turned black as pitch. The businessman and the diplomat seemed suddenly to have disappeared. The blue suit no longer appeared to sit right on him. The security agent, the torturer from Tehran could no longer conceal his true self.

'Take it easy, Vuk. Please.' Kravtjov fiddled anxiously with his teaspoon.

Rezi smiled and raised his hands deprecatingly.

'It's all right. It's all right,' he said. 'He is young. I understand. Perhaps his family has suffered. War is a terrible thing. We know. We fought for eight years against the godless Iraqis. I myself fought in the swamps of Basra. War leaves its mark on a man, although the scars are not always visible.'

Kravtjov smiled, but there was sweat on his brow. He drained the last of his beer and said:

'Tell him about the plan, Mr Rezi. The beauty of it.'

'Ah, but it's your plan. I think…'

Kravtjov laid a hand on Vuk's arm but removed it again hastily when he caught the look on the young man's face. Instead he began to talk very fast:

'Listen, Vuk, Mr Rezi will put the finger on a Bosnian Muslim. And you hate those people, right? A good, dead Bosnian Muslim. He'll get the blame. He'll be proclaimed a martyr in Tehran. They can always rustle up a mob down there. All those stupid bleeding hearts in the West will be outraged! And you Serbs could do with a little sympathy. Think about it! What does some woman writer matter to you? Fuck-all. And some dumb Bosnian Muslim and all his kind will get the blame It's beautiful. Can't you see that?'

For the first time Vuk smiled. The atmosphere around the table had improved. Yes, he could see that. He saw it better than Kravtjov, because the old KGB bastard didn't know what Vuk's actual plan was.

'Your old organization has trained you well,' Vuk said. 'But what do you get out of it? And don't say "money". The money's ours.'

'That really is none of your business,' Kravtjov said.

'It could turn out to be.'

Rezi leaned over the table again. He poured coffee, first for Vuk then for himself, and passed round a pack of Marlboros. The others both took one, and he lit their cigarettes for them before saying:

'Gentlemen, let's be businesslike. Mr Vuk! My government will give Mr Kravtjov and his – how shall I put it? – his business associates access to some bank accounts. Legal bank accounts. Clean bank accounts.'

Kravtjov hunched forward:

'Vuk, listen to me! Nowadays, it's easy to make money. But it's not so easy to spend it. We need channels. Legal channels.'

At this Vuk's face broke in a broad grin.

'So your government is going to be laundering money for the Russian Mafia?'

Rezi was grinning now too. But his eyes weren't smiling as he spread his hands in a gesture that said that was about the size of it.

'It's perfect,' Kravtjov said. 'It's perfect, Vuk. No one loses out.'

'Except Sara Santanda,' Vuk said.

'Just silence that infidel bitch,' Rezi snarled. 'Send her to hell. She deserves to lie there and rot until the end of time.'

'Okay,' Vuk said, getting to his feet.

Kravtjov looked up.

'From now on it's between you and me,' Vuk said.

He strode quickly away without shaking Rezi's hand. Kravtjov rose and went after him. They stopped by the door.

'Meet me at the Tiergarten tomorrow. At the Goethe Memorial. Twelve o'clock,' Vuk said.

'Right,' said Kravtjov.

'Watch out for Rezi. The Germans are bound to be keeping an eye on him.'

'He only got here yesterday.'

'Even so.'

'Okay, Vuk. It's a good deal.'

'We'll see.'

Vuk placed his hand on the door handle. Kravtjov whispered in his ear:

'I heard your friend in Pale had an accident.'

Vuk turned and looked him straight in the eye:

'It's a dangerous world we're living in. Remember that, Kravtjov,' he said.

Kravtjov nodded. He felt a chill in the pit of his stomach. Vuk was so young, but he had the same effect on other people as a venomous snake. He had a nice smile but teeth of steel, Kravtjov thought to himself.

'Until tomorrow, Vuk,' was all he said and left Vuk to vanish into the Berlin night while he returned to Rezi to finalize the details concerning a down payment, the channelling of the money, weapons and other equipment which he wanted the Iranian government to deliver by diplomatic bag. Best to get everything sorted out tonight. Kravtjov was like Vuk in that respect. As an old KGB man he had great respect for the German security service and did not want to be seen in the company of an Iranian agent any more than was absolutely necessary. Besides, you never could tell with the Iranians. He didn't have many old friends from his halcyon days in Teheran. Moscow had been on the other side in the war between Iran and Iraq, but that hadn't stopped Kravtjov from keeping up with his contacts there. That was in the days when he was serving a state that commanded respect. He was better off financially now, but given the chance he would happily turn back the clock in order to work once again for a major power whose influence extended to every corner of the globe. There was nothing quite like the feeling of belonging to the nation's elite. So deep inside him Kravtjov also felt a little thrill of pleasure. This reminded him of the old days when he pulled the strings and sent agents out into hostile territory. Nothing could compare to an undercover operation. Not even sex, he thought.

This same thought struck him again the next morning as he was walking through the Tiergarten. The trees in the park were a dusty-green, and the first yellow leaves lay scattered around his feet as he strolled along the gravel paths, making for the Goethe Memorial. Every now and again a bike would pass him. Mothers pushed babies in prams. He could hear the distant drone of the city traffic. Lovers walked by, closely entwined. A squirrel scampered nimbly up a tree. The whole scene put him in mind of the parks in Moscow and his youth. He wandered on, lost in his own thoughts. A smartly dressed middle-aged man taking a morning stroll. Anyone watching him could have been forgiven for mistaking him for a businessman who had done so well for himself that he had been able to take early retirement.

Kravtjov did not notice the young man in the blue tracksuit stretching out by a tree twenty yards or so behind him. He was just one of many joggers in the park. A cyclist pulled up next to the guy in the tracksuit. He had a camera slung round his neck and a book on the birds in the Tiergarten in the carrier. He stopped, and the jogger gave a faint nod. The birdwatcher lifted his camera and took a series of quick shots of Kravtjov. This done, he climbed back onto his bike and cycled past the strolling Russian. A little further on he stopped, got out his book and looked at it. He propped the bike up on its foot stand and sauntered across to the grassy bank beside the path. He raised his camera and took some pictures of a tree in the distance. Then he whipped it round, aimed it at Kravtjov walking along the path and took two rapid shots of the Russian's face before consulting his bird book once again.

Kravtjov had in fact noticed the photographer and immediately been on his guard but only for a moment, then he saw the book, the man's checked baseball cap and the ecstatic look on his face – that of a birdwatcher who has spotted some rare feathered creature – and he lapsed back into his reverie. He was thinking about his youth and his career with the KGB. In the greater scheme of things maybe it had all been in vain, but he had memories of successful operations and good comradeship that no one could take away from him. He thought of Vuk. A strange, young man. Unbelievably intelligent. Charming, when he had a mind to be. With nerves of steel and iced water in his veins. And those remarkable blue eyes: so cold looking, but harbouring some terrible hurt. He had come across young men like him in Afghanistan, in Angola and, of course, in Bosnia. They gave nothing away, and yet they gave away everything. They were good to have on one's side. And they made lethal enemies. If they had any scruples, they did not let them show. Had he not been the same? Once. In the days when he had not baulked at throwing himself out of a plane flying at ten thousand feet and swooping towards the dark earth below, waiting until the very last minute before releasing his parachute. When, instead of inducing paralysis, that fear which all men feel acted like a propellant, sharpening every sense and causing all one's muscles to work together and do their utmost. He had been in the field himself, so he knew that he had become a good commander. Demanding, hard-headed and tough but always loyal and sympathetic. And all to no avail. Or...? He had all the money he needed now, but he knew in his heart that this was not the only reason why he was now employing his skills in the service of another secret organization. It gave him a buzz that he could not do without. And he knew too much for them simply to let him pack it in now and enjoy his retirement. The organization was his family. That was how it had always been. It went by another name these days; that was all. It did not serve one country, it served Mammon, but like the KGB in the old days, the Mafia also considered itself to be above all laws except its own.

Kravtjov caught sight of Vuk. He was standing next to the statue of Goethe, smoking a cigarette. He was clad in his usual blue jeans and leather jacket. But he had had his hair cut this morning, quite short with a side parting. Kravtjov saw Vuk follow a jogger with his eyes and, moments later, the bird lover, cycling past him on his tall gent's bike. He was a cautious one, this Vuk. What was his real name, he wondered. What was his story? Perhaps he would tell him one day. These young agents often had need of a father figure. Personal bonds were frequently forged. Doing something for your country was a strangely abstract concept. Doing something difficult and often terrible for a friend, a comrade, was much easier. That was how he had always run his network. Taken time to listen, to have a drink, get them to open up to him. It inspired loyalty. Unfortunately it looked as though Vuk did not need this. It was as if there was a block of ice inside him. But perhaps...when all this was over, he would invite Vuk to Moscow. When the winter had really set in and they could sit by the fire in his new dacha and drink vodka and tell stories.

'Good morning, Vuk,' he said.

'Let's keep this short, Kravtjov,' Vuk said.

'No one knows I'm here. I am retired, you know.'

'Short, Kravtjov,' Vuk said. 'Let's walk.'

They walked side by side along the gravel path.

'I want a Danish passport. Clean. Not stolen.'

'No problem. Two days. When were you born?'

'Nineteen sixty-nine.'

A Danish passport was the easiest in the world to forge or alter. Kravtjov could not understand why the Danes had produced a passport in which the two most important pages were so easy to remove and the photograph wasn't even laminated. Mind you, this did make it easier for people like him, so the longer this style of passport was in circulation the better he liked it.

'Okay. What else?' he asked.

'A British passport. Also clean. A driving licence in the same name and a credit card. They have to be good for a week.'

'No problem.' This was more difficult but still doable.

Vuk handed him two passport photos. He was wearing a tie in the picture, which had probably been taken in a booth that morning. In the photograph Vuk looked like a high-flying young businessman, candidly and confidently looking the observer in the eye.

'No more meetings. We'll keep in touch by post. Poste restante, Købmagergade Post Office, Købmagergade 33, 1000 Copenhagen K.' He handed Kravtjov a slip of paper containing the Danish address and went on: 'I'll write care of the Central Post Office here. To Mr John Smith, if necessary. You will send me the key to a left-luggage locker when the guns have been organized. It'll be up to you to get them into Denmark.'

'Okay. What type?'

'Dragunov rifle with both day and night sights. Beretta 92. Two extra magazines. Ammunition, naturally.'

Just what I would have expected him to choose, Kravtjov thought. The Dragunov sniper rifle was manufactured in Russia, and the Yugoslavian Army had produced a copy of it. The Beretta 92 was a modern, mass-produced pistol holding fifteen cartridges. Not the world's most sophisticated weapon, perhaps, but solid, reliable and readily come by. A good choice.

'Right. Anything else?' he said easily, although he was feeling anything but easy in his mind. Behind that calm exterior, Vuk was on edge. It suddenly struck Kravtjov that underneath the veneer of self-confidence, the kid was cracking up. But his eyes and hands were steady.

Vuk stopped in his tracks, handed him a slip of paper with some figures on it. Kravtjov studied the figures briefly then stuffed the slip into his pocket. Neither of them noticed the birdwatcher. He had parked his bike by the grass verge and was lying behind a tree. He had the telephoto lens trained on Kravtjov's face. The back of the young man's head was in the way, but it was the best shot he had had so far. He held down the shutter release button and took several pictures in rapid succession. Then he pulled back the camera and his head. He had been warned that Kravtjov was an old pro, and been told to tread carefully. So that would have to do.

Vuk looked Kravtjov in the eye and said:

'Have your Iranian friend deposit one million dollars in this account on the Cayman Islands. That's the first instalment. I'll be transferring it straight away, so don't try anything clever!'

'Vuk! What do you take me for? We're partners. You can trust me.'

'Not in a month of Sundays. And I want fifty thousand Danish kroner. In cash.'

'That'll take a couple of days. Where do you want it sent?'

'Put the two passports, the credit card, the driving licence and the money in a locked bag and leave the bag at the left luggage office at the Central Station in West Berlin. Post the receipt and the key to Per Larsen, poste restante, Central Post Office, Berlin. Okay?'

Kravtjov passed him a piece of paper inscribed with an eight-digit number.

'If there should be anything…call this mobile number. You'll always get me or someone else…at this number. Just say "Vuk", give us your number and we'll call you back. Look upon it as a kind of insurance. And don't let anyone else get their hands on it.'

Vuk hesitated for a moment, then slipped the paper into his pocket. He would memorize it later.

'And the rest of the money?' said Kravtjov.

'You'll receive the number of another account in the Caymans.'

'When?'

'Oh, you'll know when. Just read the papers,' Vuk said, with no trace of sarcasm.

'Right,' said Kravtjov. Vuk knew that payment would be forthcoming. This sort of money was peanuts to the Russian Mafia, and Kravtjov certainly had no wish to spend the rest of his life looking over his shoulder for Vuk. Cheating in matters of this nature was bad for business and for customer relations. And besides, they might have need of him again some time. They didn't know that once this business was dealt with he would never be seen in Europe again.

'Right,' said Vuk. 'That's all.'

He looked around him. Peace reigned in the park. Some distance away a couple of children were playing while their mothers sat on a bench chatting, and a man was walking his dog. He threw a stick for it to fetch: a peaceable activity which made Vuk long, suddenly, for another time, but he forced himself to banish such thoughts. The commandant had taught him to focus on the job in hand, rid his mind of anything that might distract him and never let himself be consumed by a longing for things he could never have.

Kravtjov extended his hand, and Vuk shook it briefly.

'Well...break a leg,' Kravtjov said.

'Yeah,' said Vuk.

'This is just like the old days. When I sent agents into the field. Thrilling and, at the same time, terrifying. They were good times.'

Vuk nodded and turned to leave. Kravtjov called after him:

'Does it bother you, going back to Denmark?'

Vuk looked back and said, almost dreamily, Kravtjov thought:

'Not at all. Killing someone in Denmark is very easy.'

Chapter 9

V_{uk} had to stay another five nights in Berlin. He spent most of the time sleeping and watching CNN or dubbed American movies on German satellite channels: Cary Grant, John Wayne, Tom Cruise and Sean Connery talking in deep voices that didn't fit. He ran six miles every morning and evening in the Tiergarten and did a stiff half-hour workout on the floor of his hotel room: press-ups, sit-ups and backstretches. The physical activity kept him away from the bottles in the minibar. The TV helped keep his gnawing demons at bay; he had only had the blood-roller dream once, and he had managed to wake up before it appeared over the horizon under the flaming sun.

He bought a medium-size suitcase, a sports holdall and a navy-blue suit, a pale-blue shirt and a tie patterned with tiny red and purple squares. This, he had observed, was what was being worn by most of the businessmen he had seen charging up and down the streets of Berlin, briefcase in one hand and mobile phone in the other.

The hotel staff were quietly solicitous and clearly regarded him as just another harmless tourist taking in the sights of the newly reunified Berlin. Breakfast was the one meal he ate at the hotel; each evening he found a new and anonymous steakhouse close to the crowds on the Kurfürstendamm. The weather was still warm, although the odd shower of rain had fallen on the city, soaking him to the skin on the second morning when he was out running under the Tiergarten's tall trees. Summer was preparing to pass into autumn, and the bigger leaves on the trees were already yellowing at the edges. It made him feel good to run in the soft rain, with the faint rumble of the traffic on June Seventeenth Street in his ears. These runs reminded him of the happy days with the band of specially selected men at the elite academy, when they ran five miles at the crack of dawn every day, and his body sang for the sheer joy of being used.

He bought a map of Denmark and of Copenhagen and studied them in the evening, while the television played in the background with the sound turned down. He shut his eyes and called up the memory of those familiar streets. He had no trouble converting the flat lines of the city map into roads, buildings, lanes, railway lines and suburbs. In his mind's eye he saw houses and blocks of apartments. He populated the Town Hall Square, Nørrebrogade, Valby Langgade and Strøget with Danish faces and tried to call up the sound of the language in his head. He placed a hotdog stall on a street corner and picked up a paper in a newsagent's where the Pakistani shopkeeper's Danish was even worse than his father's. He remembered everything, let the memories come and go as they pleased. Most of them were good. His life could have been very different, had his family not moved back to Bosnia. He might have studied maths or engineering, had a steady girlfriend and lived in a student residence like everyone else. He might have had a wife and kids by now. Told them about the old country and tried to make them understand why it was necessary to fight. And yet. Would he have understood? If he hadn't gone there but had stayed in that safe little land nestling so snugly in its small corner, sheltered both from stormy weather and from cataclysmic man-made disasters and upheaval. Who could say? In any case, it was a waste of time wondering what might have been. He had been born the person he was, with the nationality he had, on the inside at least, although you wouldn't have known it to look at him. His features were not the least bit Slavic, but unmistakably Nordic. He didn't know why this should be, but his mother's family hailed from Slovenia originally, and there was German blood there too. Maybe that was where he got his blond good looks, his fair hair and his mother's blue eyes. There wasn't much of his father about him. He had been a dark, powerfully built man with broad shoulders and big hands. But had he not perhaps inherited his father's sure hand and cold-blooded nature? Thoughts of his family were not permitted to encroach. It would hurt too much to pursue them.

In a newsagent's he found a Danish newspaper, no more than a day old. But only the foreign news meant anything to him. He could make nothing of the Danish stories. What he did see, though, was that Denmark was still a country where minor problems were blown up into major issues, simply because there really wasn't that much to write about. He read aloud to himself, and the words flowed easily. From the newspaper reports he picked up the name of the current prime minister and an idea of what people in Denmark were talking about. The television programmes now took up a whole page. There were two evening news broadcasts, at quite different times from what he remembered. TV2 was showing more, or at least as many, programmes as the old Danmarks Radio channel, which apparently now called itself TV1. There were also lots of foreign channels, which the Danes could seemingly receive, since they were listed on the TV page. People in Denmark could watch the same programmes as he was watching in Berlin. Everybody in Europe could, so it seemed, watch the same programme at the same time, if they so desired.

Each day he called in at the Central Post Office and presented his Per Larsen passport at the poste restante desk. The day after his meeting with Kravtjov he called the bank in the Cayman Islands that guarded his banking secrets more closely than the Swiss. He phoned from a box where he could pay in cash after making his call. He gave the bank his code number, enquired as to whether the money had been paid in, was told that it had and asked them to transfer the full amount, minus a small handling charge, to a bank in Leichtenstein into which Vuk had been paying his salary and bonuses for the past four years. It was a discreet establishment, would never divulge information regarding a customer's identity or sums held in foreign accounts to the local or national tax authorities. Access to an account might possibly be gained by court order but as far as the bank knew such a thing had never happened. No one in the tiny principality saw any reason to kill the goose that laid such lovely, labour-free golden eggs. Vuk had opened an account there under the name of Peter Nielsen and could make withdrawals from this simply by quoting his code number.

On the fourth day he was presented with a padded envelope, the sole contents of which were a suitcase key and a left-luggage ticket from the Central Station in West Berlin. He found the right U-bahn line on his map of Berlin and took it to the station. Young people from all over the world were milling around the left-luggage office, checking their rucksacks in and out, comparing notes on accommodation, cheap eating places and spots you just had to visit where you could stay for next to nothing. Vuk got the impression that the whole point of backpacking was to spend as little as possible and consort only with other like-minded souls. They travelled in order to learn about themselves and other people, but in their search for security they ended up sticking with kids who spoke, thought and dressed exactly the same as themselves. In his blue jeans, trainers and brown leather jacket he blended in easily with the young backpackers. He mingled with them and scanned his surroundings carefully but discreetly. The railway station exuded an air of bustling normality.

He handed over the left-luggage ticket.

'*Ein Moment,*' said the beefy elderly man who took it from him.

Vuk glanced round about. His unease made itself felt as a tremor in the small of his back. What if he was being watched? What if Kravtjov wasn't who he said he was? Or – if he had betrayed Vuk – then this was the moment when the German police were liable to pounce. He was in Germany illegally, and on CNN he had seen that they had now started arresting Bosnian Serbs, to hand them over to the War Crimes Tribunal in the Hague. But Vuk knew that he had always covered his tracks well. He was known only to a very few. On the one occasion when, with the Commandant, he had gone too far, they had left no witnesses. He had been a soldier in a dirty war, but he knew that he had merely done his duty as a soldier. Only the blood-roller told him that he might never forget that afternoon when he had lost his head and they had gone on killing until not a single soul was left alive in the village.

The elderly man reappeared, carrying a small, grey Samsonite suitcase. Vuk took it, paid and walked off quickly. No one took any notice of him. Hundreds of bags, rucksacks and suitcases passed over the left-luggage counter every day.

He took a taxi but asked to be set down at the corner of Knesebechsstrasse and the Ku'damm. He stood for a moment or two with the case at his feet, surveying the crowd on the street, before picking up the suitcase and walking the few hundred yards to his hotel. The case was very light. Back in his room, with the door locked, he opened it with the key he had received in the padded envelope. Inside, as agreed, were the Danish passport, the British passport, the British driving licence and a Eurocard/Mastercard – issued in

London – together with bundles of Danish kroner, two thousand in each, all in one hundred- and five hundred-kroner notes. Vuk unwrapped a couple of the bundles. It was all there. Kravtjov was a pro. He could, of course, still draw on his contacts from the old days, when the KGB operated over the whole of Central and Eastern Europe. The rapid growth of the Russian Mafia and its ability to function had much to do with its close links with the old regime's security system and party *apparat*. Such were the subtle but influential workings of the old boys' network.

The passports were relatively new but showed signs of normal wear and tear. He signed them in two different hands. Kravtjov had come up with good sound names: Carsten Petersen in the Danish passport and John Thatcher in the British one. It could be that Kravtjov still had access to forgery departments in Moscow, or perhaps he had been far-sighted enough to pocket a bundle of passports when the system collapsed? Or did the Russian Mafia have such enormous clout that it could in fact ask favours of the new Russian security service? Vuk knew that these two passports would be fine for travelling within the EU. Airport computer systems were always a problem, but he wasn't planning on flying to Denmark anyway. Kravtjov had promised that they were clean and not reported missing, and Vuk had no choice but to trust him. With all boundaries within the EU now open, he was expecting any checks to be of the most cursory nature. Vuk didn't like playing with too many blind cards, but he had nothing against taking a well-calculated risk.

Vuk stuffed his old rucksack into Kravtjov's suitcase and returned to the Central Station. On the way there he threw the suitcase into a rubbish skip on a building site. After long and careful scrutiny of the railway timetable he bought a second-class single on the early morning train to Hamburg, paying with cash. This done, he settled down in his room to watch a football match on TV. Afterwards, he ran his six miles around the Tiergarten, then showered and went out to a restaurant where he ordered his usual steak and baked potato. He drank the lion's share of a bottle of wine with his steak. He wanted to get a good night's sleep. Back at the hotel he packed his old clothes, the leather jacket, trainers and most of the money into his new suitcase. Then he sat back in the armchair and watched CNN until the stream of news reports and endlessly repeated advertisements was just a blur and he felt that he could sleep.

He woke rested the next morning. He felt fighting fit, felt nothing could touch him, though he knew that would not make him any the less cautious. He did twenty-five quick push-ups before showering and putting on the pale-blue shirt, the navy suit and the red and purple patterned tie. He slipped his feet into a pair of new, black lace-up shoes and picked up his suitcase. He paid for the hotel room in cash with Deutschmarks and thanked the receptionist in English for a pleasant stay. He had enough marks to cover any last outgoings, so he wouldn't need to exchange any dollars or Danish kroner.

Vuk hailed a taxi on the Ku'damm and took it to the Central Station where he settled himself in a café with a cup of coffee and the *Herald Tribune* until it was time for his train.

The rush hour was more or less over when the train pulled slowly out of Berlin, bound for Hamburg. Vuk had a compartment to himself. He gazed out of the window, watched the city give way to suburbs, then open country. There were building sites and construction cranes everywhere, and when the train ran alongside the autobahn he saw dense streams of traffic flowing in both directions. The old GDR was falling apart before his very eyes. In a few years the Wall would be nothing but a memory, and all other traces of a divided Germany would have been erased. Vuk remembered how, back in 1989, they had cried 'We are one people'. He had been just a kid then, and like other young people he had regarded the collapse of the Eastern Bloc as a just punishment for the old men. Their regimes had fallen like so many houses of cards, and they had not lifted a finger. He still did not understand how the Soviet leaders could have given up without a fight. They had taken power by force, they hung on to it by dint of terror tactics and oppression, then willingly relinquished it. How come? He had no idea. He just didn't get it. He had believed that the fall of the Wall heralded a new beginning. But that conviction had been short-lived. We are one people, they had cried in the East. So are we, had been the speedy response from the West when the collapse of the old order began to tug at the purse-strings of wealthy Western Europe, which had grown affluent at the other side's expense. The people had brought about the revolution. But their new leaders had soon taken it for their own.

The German Federal Railway train had departed on the dot and arrived in Hamburg bang on time. Vuk paid cash again for a single to Århus on the new German regional service. He just had time to eat a hotdog and buy a couple of German newspapers before the train left for Denmark at 12.30 pm. It was the middle of the week, so there weren't very many people on the train: a German businessman and a young Danish couple talking softly to one another; a good-looking woman with her teenage son, who was playing his Walkman so loudly that the hiss of it penetrated the railway carriage. She asked him in Danish to turn it down: it was bad for his ears. He grumbled but did as she asked. Vuk sat behind his newspaper, listening to the lilt of the Danish. The German ticket inspector checked his ticket without looking at him twice. His eyes were on the ticket, not the man. Vuk thanked him with a *danke* and put down his paper. The flat north-German countryside slipped past the window. The houses looked well kept, the fields had been harvested, and the sky was clear over the woods in the background. He was filled with a sense of expectation, a feeling of being on holiday, of rediscovering a normality that he had left behind long ago. Did he not also feel a kind of inverted homesickness? Because, although the country that lay ahead was not his native land, it was a country which he had once found it natural to called home. Home sweet home: *hyggeligt hjemme* – the Danish words ran through his mind, strange and yet so familiar.

They were approaching the border. The train stopped at Padborg on the German side, then moved off again. A Danish passport controller passed through the train. He merely glanced at most of the green and red German passports, Vuk noted, watching him work his way through the carriage. But occasionally he opened a passport and took a closer look at it. Then it was Vuk's turn.

'*Pas, bitte,*' the passport controller said.

'Hi. Doing a bit of a check today, then, are you?' Vuk said. His Danish was totally without accent. He handed the passport controller his beetroot-red passport in the name of Carsten Petersen. The controller opened it, then promptly closed it again and handed it back to him.

'Yes. We do a spot check every now and again,' the man said. He spoke with a Jutland accent. Then, as he moved on: 'Enjoy the rest of your day.'

'Thanks,' Vuk said, somewhat puzzled by the man's choice of words. Enjoy the rest of your day: *Kan du fortsat ha' en god dag* – they never used to say that.

It must be something they had borrowed from English. The Danish language snapped up foreign words and phrases and made them its own like no other language Vuk knew.

They trundled into Denmark and headed north through Jutland. The place hadn't changed a bit. It looked so neat and trim, so innocent; lying there bathed in sunlight under a clear blue sky, smiling at Vuk, who settled back in his seat. The cars were newer, the houses bigger and the farms better kept than he remembered. But that might be because his own country consisted of nothing but ruins and streams of refugees. The contrast was so great simply because he did not feel there were any contrasts in the Danish countryside, only countless subtle nuances which, to a Dane, seemed like enormous differences but which, to a foreigner were like a piece of music, constantly repeating variations on the same theme. The train stopped at almost every station and he recited their names in the voice inside his head: Vojens, Røde Kro, Fredericia, Kolding, Vejle. The Danes didn't look any different either. Dressed in jeans, which they called 'cowboy trousers', and sensible jackets. The few children he saw were well dressed and well fed. The land was bursting with health and plenty. All the way to Århus he feasted his eyes and ears on the landscape and the steady lilt of the Danish voices around him in the train. He felt as if he had divested himself of his Balkan cloak in order, instead, to garb himself in his Danish identity. He didn't find it difficult. On the contrary, it came so naturally to him that for a moment he wasn't sure who he really was and why he had come back here.

When he arrived in Århus at 17.28 pm he was just another face in the crowd.

Chapter 10

More than once Lise Carlsen had to check herself, but it was no use: she couldn't take her eyes off Per, he was so hard to ignore, blast him: perched there so nonchalantly on the edge of a desk. He didn't say much, left most of the talking to his boss. He had, however, run through the schedule as it now stood. Explained simply and matter-of-factly where they were thinking of holding the press conference and that they were still trying to find secure overnight accommodation. He seemed so self-assured, in a way that was new to Lise, used as she was to a world where a gift of the gab was the mark of a person's worth; while Per, with his sparing use of words, showed that he knew he was good at his job and that they would listen to him. Had he nothing to prove? Was he simply perfectly content with his own capabilities? Was that his secret? Per had told them the word on the street was that a contract on the subject had been signed and sealed. This came as a surprise to Lise: he had never said anything to her about it, even though they spent hours of each day in each other's company.

Lise had also taken a back seat, letting Tagesen speak for their newspaper, and for the press in general. As chair of Danish PEN, she had every right to speak up and say what she thought. She might be young and relatively new to the post, which she had only held for a year, but she was a well-respected arts journalist and social commentator. And she had done her stint on various committees working for persecuted writers and imprisoned intellectuals around the world. She had been a member of PEN for almost ten years. She had travelled abroad for the organization and had been elected chair because she was good at what she did and because the large majority of members had felt that an injection of younger blood would be no bad thing. But she had to confess that she was feeling slightly unsure of herself. It wasn't like her, but she was rather thrown by the fact that her marriage was in trouble. She had never been in such a situation before. And she had never had responsibility for such an important matter as this before either. One which could be a matter of life and death. Besides, it was Tagesen who had requested and been granted this meeting. And the powers that be did not want to get on the wrong side of the press: a media storm could rise up as suddenly as a dust storm in Texas, and if everybody was playing the same tune, it could sweep the country and clear a foodstuff off the market in a day, ruin the career of a bureaucrat or a politician in a week. Once the whole orchestra struck up, the facts were of little consequence. From then on, emotions governed events. Ole said folk must be scared to death of the life they were leading, to be so easily influenced. People no longer had any sort of an anchor, no firm belief in anything whatsoever, so it was the easiest thing in the world for the mass media to sway them and scare them. It wasn't a thought Lise relished, but he was probably right.

She tried to concentrate, but her thoughts kept returning to Per and from there to Ole: she felt she never saw him anymore. He was asleep when she left in the mornings and never at home when she got back. He would roll in late at night, reeking of booze, and crawl into bed beside her without a word, while she lay with her eyes closed, pretending to be asleep. Things seemed to have been going on like this for years, but it must only be a few months since their relationship began to fall apart. She did not know whether it had already fallen over the edge of a precipice or whether it could still be salvaged. And whether she or he was prepared to rock the boat. They were going to have to have a talk. But now she had to concentrate on the matter in hand.

She brought her thoughts back to the meeting. The man from the prime minister's office, who had introduced himself as Stig something-or-other, had a grating, high-pitched voice. He was one of those real high-flying, little political-science graduates, the same age as herself: already a department head and a man who loved playing the part of armchair politician and string-puller. Like her he was a child of the seventies, but he had distanced himself totally from that mixed-up era. Everything about him was perfectly tailored: both suit and opinions.

The meeting was being held in an anonymous office at Police Headquarters, and it was such an important one that Jytte Vuldom, Per's boss, had even made the journey from Bellahøj for it. She, unlike Stig whatsisname, Lise found impressive. She had a good powerful voice, and she did not have to raise it to get men to listen. Lise could tell by the glance Per sent his boss when he spoke of the possible contract that this announcement had been cleared with her beforehand. It struck her that there was talk here of scare tactics. She saw where it was leading.

'I would like to emphasize that the prime minister also considers it deplorable that this matter should have been made public. The information did not, of course, come from our office. Just for the record,' said Stig Thor Kasper Nielsen, to give him his full name. He had assured them again and again that he had not leaked the story, but this had only had the opposite effect. Everyone now believed Stig Nielsen to be the source. But it was evidently important to him to scotch this rumour, so much so that he was protesting too much; or perhaps the fact of the matter was that he didn't really have anything to say, or didn't dare come to the point.

'There's no need to go on about it,' said Tagesen. 'I'm sure our excellent police force will arrange for the necessary protection.'

'Naturally,' said Vuldom, lighting another cigarette. 'But, like everyone else, we have to get our priorities right. We have a big state visit in the offing, as well as a summit meeting, and both of these are going to stretch our resources to the limit.'

'And what's that supposed to mean?' Tagesen asked.

'Exactly what I say,' said Vuldom. 'No more and no less.'

Lise could tell that Per was about to say something, but she also noticed how one look from Vuldom and he bit it back.

'Well, let me just say this,' Tagesen said, and Lise could tell that he was starting to lose his temper. He started fiddling with the buttons on his jacket. He tugged at his moustache. 'You're saying that you can't commit all your resources to protecting Sara, because there are other things which are more important.'

'I don't think that's what the chief superintendent is saying,' said Stig Thor Kasper Nielsen. 'I think the chief superintendent is saying that the timing is not of the best, coinciding as it does with a couple of state occasions.'

Lise knew exactly what he was getting at, and so did Tagesen:

'No way,' Tagesen said.

'No way what?' said Stig Nielsen.

'We are not cancelling or postponing this visit. Because that's what you're telling us to do. That's the message you're saying the prime minister has asked you to pass on, isn't it? Well we won't hear of it, and neither will Sara Santanda. I spoke to her only yesterday.'

'Well, if that's how you wish to interpret it,' said the man from the prime minister's office, but Lise could tell that Tagesen had hit the nail on the head.

Per was about to butt in again, and again he received a warning look from his boss.

'But I'm right, aren't I?' Tagesen said.

'We wouldn't dream of interfering with a private visit,' said Stig Thor Kasper Nielsen, deliberately stressing the word 'private'. '*Politiken* has every right to do whatever *Politiken* likes.'

'Yeah, right,' said Tagesen. 'We get the picture. So what about the invitation to Bang?'

The man from the ministry stood up, straightened his back and looked pointedly at his watch.

'Look, it all comes down to the same thing, Tagesen. We've got a very tight schedule over the next couple of months, what with the state visit, the prime minister's tour of the Jutland constituencies and, as you know, some very delicate budget talks. There simply is not a free slot in his diary. However much the government would like to show that we will not let ourselves be browbeaten.'

'But that's exactly what you're *doing*. You know as well as I do how vital it is, for Sara and for us, that she should meet a member of the government. That we show that Denmark will not, in fact, be browbeaten by a gang of criminals.'

'It is the government's policy to pursue a critical dialogue with Iran. We believe that at the end of the day this will give the best outcome. We didn't set the date. Our diary is completely full for the next year. It is not a question of politics but of practicalities.'

Stig Thor Kasper Nielsen ran his eye round the room. And as he did so, Lise realized how it felt when, as the saying goes, someone walks over your grave. That phoney word 'practicalities' hung in the air. A phoney word but so wonderfully sweeping, so useful. One of the main objects of the whole exercise was for a western government to publicly meet and embrace an intellectual who had been sentenced to death by a state that flouted all the international conventions. Such a demonstration would be reported on by newspapers all over the world. And the Danish government had said no. They would call it *realpolitik*, but Lise knew it had more to do with export figures and the government's narrow majority in the house. A government which, her colleagues on the political desk said, was plagued by internal unrest and seemed to have run out of steam.

She couldn't keep quiet any longer.

'What a copout!' she said, her voice almost breaking. The others stared at her in astonishment. Even Tagesen looked as though he thought this outburst was a bit much. She stopped before she could say any more. She was afraid she might burst into tears of rage, and that would, of course, be regarded by the others as typical feminine frailty. But she felt disgust and fury writhing like a viper in her bosom.

'It'll be okay, Lise,' Tagesen said. 'I'm assuming that we'll get all the help we need from the police at any rate.'

'Of course you will,' Vuldom said. 'Per Toftlund is one of my most experienced officers. We will do all we can with the means at our disposal, if the visit cannot be postponed.'

She let these last words hang in the air, but Tagesen was not about to help her out. Instead he said his goodbyes, shaking hands with Vuldom and Toftlund and vouchsafing merely a nod to the man from the prime minister's office. Toftlund also got to his feet, but Vuldom asked him to stay behind for a moment.

'Would you mind waiting outside, Lise?' he said.

Vuldom waited until everyone had gone, then closed the door.

'Well, that didn't work, did it?' she said.

'Nope, I didn't think it would.'

'But…both we and the foreign ministry have been asking around, and those buggers in Teheran won't get upset as long as it isn't treated as an official state visit. All this talk of a fatwa is mainly for internal use. I don't think we need to worry. And anyway…the Swedes and the Norwegians are in much the same situation. So: quick in and quick out, and there's little chance of anything going wrong, is there?'

'Some world we're living in,' Per said.

'I've received a subtle hint to the effect that certain people would prefer it if the visit were cancelled completely. But if there's no way round it, then I'm expecting you to make sure we're not left to carry the can.'

Per couldn't help smiling. It sounded so funny coming from Vuldom, this expression common throughout the central administration for the way in which, whenever anything went wrong, the politicians would make sure that the responsibility was offloaded onto some civil servant, high-ranking or low.

'I'm going to need more people,' he said.

'The bit about our resources is true enough. We're still coping with people taking time off in lieu after the social summit meeting. But we'll let you have as many people as we can spare from surveillance duties – on the day itself. Otherwise you'll have to make do with what you've got. And who's to say that a definite contract has been taken out on the subject?'

'I've got a gut feeling about it.'

'Is there anything you want?'

'Yes.'

'Within reason.'

'The safe house on Nygårdsvej.'

'You've got it, Per.'

Stig Thor Kasper Nielsen caught Prime Minister Carl Bang between two meetings and put him in the picture. He could see that Bang was not happy with the outcome of the Santanda meeting, but he would have to go along with it: Stig had the impression that the prime minister felt he had handled the situation as well as was possible under the prevailing circumstances. And that was, after all, the main thing. That same afternoon, Bang sought out Johannes Jørgensen in the long gallery of the Parliament building. The Defence Committee was in session, and the Foreign Policy Committee was scheduled to meet the following day, so there was some activity at Christiansborg, and it was only natural for the pair to exchange a few words. They walked along side-by-side, smoking and speaking – as custom dictated – in hushed voices. They chatted briefly about the Budget, turned on their heels and slowly retraced their steps. As so often before, Bang brought the conversation round to what was really on his mind by first going through the ritual of saying that what he was about to say was in strictest confidence, and Jørgensen played his part in the ritual by saying that, of course, he quite understood, but he knew right away that what he was about to hear would be good news, so there would be no need to tell anyone else.

'No one from the government will be meeting…her,' Bang said. 'It will be a completely private visit. Arranged by a daily newspaper. I was wondering if you could see to it that no – how should I put it? – prominent member of the opposition will be able to spare the time…to see her.'

Jørgensen regarded the prime minister with open admiration. Bang was known for being an excellent tactician. In Danish politics you had to be, if you wanted to survive for any length of time as a minority government. It was a neat piece of work. The decision would not be his alone; instead he would get the big guns of the opposition roped into the affair. Thus spreading the responsibility. Jørgensen's party had been in power last time round, and its members still had a big say in things. Bang knew that Jørgensen kept up with all his old contacts. In Danish politics you can easily be in government one year and in opposition the next. It was not a matter of politics but of practical necessity.

'I think that can be arranged,' Jørgensen said, 'but there are always going to be a couple from the lower ranks desperate for a mention in the press.'

'That doesn't matter. Not from what I hear.'

Jørgensen broke stride momentarily, then fell into step again.

'So you've been in touch with…?'

Bang cut him off sharply:

'Unofficially, we have been given to understand that as long as no official representative meets with the person concerned, the relationship between our two countries will not be affected.'

'It's good to know that common sense has prevailed,' Jørgensen said with a satisfied smile, but Prime Minister Carl Bang did not smile. With a curt nod he strode away, as if intent on washing his hands of the conversation.

Lise Carlsen let rip in the car. Per had to pull into the side until she had got all of the anger and frustration out of her system and was left, instead, feeling absolutely ravenous. It was always the same, whenever she lost her temper or got upset about something. She simply had to eat something.

'You must have a really good metabolism,' Per said with a smile that stirred something inside her.

'He has a nice smile but teeth of steel,' she said.

'What?'

'It's a quotation. I don't remember where from.'

'Gromyko,' he said. 'In his speech nominating Gorbachov as the new general secretary of the Soviet Communist Party. Back in the good old days.'

'I doubt if one could call them that,' she said, thinking of the dreary bureaucrats whom she had met in the east, the canny writers balancing on a knife-edge in their efforts to get round the censor and, not least, the persecuted authors who had been driven into exile – if, that is, they hadn't ended up in the Gulags. 'Good' was not a word she would ever have used of those days.

'It was easier to tell your friends from your enemies,' he said.

'I feel like pasta.' All of a sudden she couldn't face talking about anything at all. It wasn't just Santanda's visit; it was her relationship with Ole. Why couldn't she say the word? Her marriage. It wasn't working. She kept telling herself that they would have to talk, but if the truth were told, she really didn't want that. It was over, but she couldn't bring herself to say it out loud, to herself or to Ole. And it couldn't have happened at a worse time: her biggest story, her first major undertaking as chair of PEN, and now her marriage was on the rocks. And on top of all that, there was Per. But what was he? A catalyst or a lightning conductor? Or an excuse. If nothing else, she was grateful for his silence. He had his antennae out, she was sure, and knew when to hold his peace. Instead of talking, he drove to Nørrebro and drew up in a side street, in front of an Italian restaurant.

There were only three other people in the restaurant, which was furnished with the traditional red-and-white checked tablecloths and low lamps. Both ordered fettucine, along with a carafe of the house wine and two citrus mineral waters. The light fell softly through the little windows. There was autumn in its greyish cast, as if the light were being filtered through a fine blue cloth to strike the right note of melancholy. He broke off a piece of bread and made no comment when she lit a cigarette. That was his one, really annoying trait: that he always let her know, implicitly or directly, that he thought it was a dirty habit. Instead he started talking about safe houses, security scans, the press conference and the contract on Santanda.

'How did you find out about that?' she asked.

'We have our sources, just as you reporters have yours,' he said and was about to go on when she interrupted:

'Can't we talk about something else? Can't we just forget all that for a while? Can't we just pretend you invited me out to lunch because you fancy me? And not because it's work?'

His eyes changed colour, or so it seemed to her. They became very soft.

'We don't need to pretend,' he said.

Just for a second she thought she was going to blush. She had done that all the time until she was well into her twenties, and she still didn't have it totally under control. So to distract herself she played with the tablecloth, stubbed out her cigarette and ran her fingers through her hair. He just looked at her, and she couldn't help giggling and then they were both laughing out loud. Afterwards, while they ate, she regaled him with wryly amusing stories from her visits to Spain. It made a lovely break from reality. She recounted anecdotes from the paper and the arts world about egocentric writers and pompous critics.

She even allowed him to pay the bill then, a little light-headed from the wine of which she had drunk most, she got back into his car and let herself be driven.

'Where are we going?' she asked, however, when she realized they were heading towards Østerbro. He never told her what he had planned for them. He merely drove her around, expecting her to blithely follow his lead. Suddenly she was afraid that he was going to drive her home. She didn't want to go home. She wanted to stay here with him and hold onto this easy bantering mood. If she went home, she knew the darkness would descend on her; it would envelop her like a thick black cape, making her fear that she would never be able to pull it off again.

'I'm going to show you Simba's kennel,' he said, making her laugh.

She rolled her window down and barked 'woof-woof' at a young man walking along the pavement with a big black Rotweiler. The young man didn't hear a thing, but to her great satisfaction the dog pricked up its ears, and Per chuckled.

They turned off the main road into Sejrøgade. The large Irma supermarket with its distinctive blue sign still sat on the corner. He drove across Sankt Kjelds Plads and down Nygårdsvej. She didn't come out this way very often now. From the apartment on Trianglen her route always took her into the city centre or over to the new trendy cafés in Nørrebro. Partly because of work. She wrote columns for the paper on life in the city. Articles which she endeavoured to endow with a light, almost dreamy quality. She frequently used a café as the backdrop to her fictional tête-à-têtes. These articles were written from a personal point of view, but much of what she wrote really reflected how she would like it − life, that is − to be, rather than how it actually was.

'I used to live around here,' she said.

Per parked outside a red-brick building. A gate led into a courtyard. The courtyard had been recently done up: there were benches, a children's playground and lots of green bushes and trees. It was like a huge, walled town garden, encircled by blocks of yellow and red.

'It was actually right here!' she said. She pointed to the other side of the courtyard. 'Over there! I shared an apartment with a girlfriend for a couple of years while we were both at university. It really is a small world. There was a factory next door. I think they made artificial limbs. But there are apartments there now.'

Per made no reply. Instead, he entered the first door they came to and walked up three flights. He unlocked a brown front door on which stood the name 'Per Hansen' in small white letters.

The apartment was small but spacious enough. There was a small spare room to the right and a bedroom straight ahead, a living room, a kitchen and a tiny bathroom. The place smelled clean, if a little stuffy. Like a summerhouse that has been opened up after having stood empty for some time. The furniture was of light wood and classic design. The parquet flooring was clean, and there was a radio, a television and video machine and lots of books.

Per seemed very much at home here. The light that fell through the beige curtains covering the living-room windows was grey and already fading. Lise ran an eye over the book spines. There were titles in English, Danish and what looked like Russian. Thrillers and Danish classics. She pulled out one book but could not read the Cyrillic writing.

'This is Russian, isn't it?' she said.

Per eyed her. He tossed the key to the apartment up into the air a couple of times. There was something odd about the way he looked at her, she thought. She still felt light-hearted and a little giddy from the wine. She felt so carefree, and she didn't want to lose that feeling.

'That's correct,' he said.

'And so are you,' she said.

'Okay, *chica*. This apartment is kind of special. We don't normally show it to strangers.'

'Oh, so I'm a stranger now? What's so special about it? That there are Russian novels on the shelves?'

'It's an old safe house,' he said.

'What exactly *is* a safe house?' she said.

He took the book from her and put it back on the shelf. She felt his hand brush hers, and the moment suddenly stretched out, until he took a step back and said:

'You ought to read more thrillers instead of all your highfalutin' literary novels. You might learn something.'

'Why, Per?'

'Why should you read more thrillers?' The bantering note was back in his voice. It sounded good.

Lise pulled out the book again and held it up in front of his face.

'No, *hombre*! What is a safe house? Why Russian novels?'

'It's an apartment which we pay for, but which no one knows anything about.'

She took a step towards him. She caught the scent of him. He smelled of Italian herbs and an aftershave that was tangy but nice. Sounds like an advert, she thought, feeling rather foolish.

'Come on, Per! We're partners!'

Again he took the book from her and put it back. Again that feather-light touch of his hand on hers.

'It's an apartment where we used to house Russian defectors…or people we wanted to talk to in private. You know. During the Cold War. And today too.'

'So my income-tax money also helps pay PET's rent? I've been living next door to a bloody listening post. This is like something straight out of John le Carré.'

He gripped her arms gently. It felt good.

'Listen, Lise. A defector turns up in Copenhagen. Or an agent. We need time alone with him. We need to talk to him. He stays here, snug and safe. It's easy to guard. We know this patch inside out. There's a clear view of the whole courtyard. The neighbourhood is perfectly ordinary. We've scanned the whole of the surrounding area. There are hidden alarms. We can keep an eye on it from the apartment opposite. It's perfect for Simba. Because it doesn't exist. This is not a listening post. It's just a safe place to stay.'

'I see,' was all she said.

He let go of one of her arms but held onto the other.

'Come with me. I want to show you something,' He drew her with him, his hand sliding down her arm until it was clasped round hers as he led her around the apartment, like an estate agent trying to convince yet another fussy client that it was worth buying. He led her into the kitchen and, awkward though it was, kept a hold of her hand while he opened the fridge, drawers and cupboard doors, showing her all the banal paraphernalia of everyday life as if they were rare antiques. She couldn't help smiling at the stream of estate-agent patter that accompanied his presentation of cutlery, plates, coffee and teabags, pots and pans, powdered soups and dry goods. Cold meats and cheese in plastic packaging, juice and water, and in the freezer a neat pile of frozen dinners to pop into the brand-new microwave oven.

'I'll take it,' Lise joked, but he wasn't listening. He dragged her off again, to show her the perfectly unexceptional bathroom with its white tiles, white loo and a shower cabinet that could have done with a new curtain.

'A perfectly charming abode,' she said.

'Yeah. *Perfecto*, isn't it?' he said without a grain of irony.

'*Perfecto, hombre*. Every woman's dream.'

He didn't hear her, drew her with him again. She felt the warmth of his hand in hers gradually spreading to the rest of her body. He led her into the bedroom. It wasn't very big. A double bed and a wardrobe took up most of the space. The curtains were almost fully drawn. A single shaft of light fell on the bed, which was made up hotel-style. The bed linen was a pristine white.

'What more could one ask for?' he said at last.

Lise stood there, holding his hand. Suddenly it felt awkward and all wrong. The silence swelled and lengthened, the way it does when there is a technical hitch on the radio and every second of silence feels like a minute. Lise pulled her hand away. She was conscious of a slight resistance, then he let go.

'Yes, well, everything seems to be…um, I don't know,' she said when the silence seemed in danger of choking her.

'Hm, we're getting there,' he said.

There was another prolonged silence. She looked up at him, a sidelong glance meant to be brief, but she saw that he was looking down at her. Her stomach gave an agonizing, but delicious, lurch as she thought to herself: that's enough now. I've gone way too far already. Now it's up to him. If he reaches out for me it'll be too late to back out, too late to think better of it. I'll be stepping over a line I've never crossed before and a new phase of my life will have begun.

Per took one of her hands and then the other. She saw the way his eyes left hers for a moment and slid towards the bed then back at her and felt her own eyes following his. He drew her to him.

'Okay. Okay. It's okay, I think…' she murmured, letting go of his hands and wrapping her arms around his neck.

Chapter 11

Vuk got hold of a copy of the Yellow Pages for Copenhagen and ran an eye down the list of hotels before buying a ticket for the overnight Intercity train to the Danish capital. Train number 590 was scheduled to depart at 1.06 am and arrive at 7.00 am. He paid for a whole couchette to himself, boarding from 10.30 pm. He called the hotel from a phone box and booked a room. It all seemed a little unreal. Århus station was suffused with a yellowish light, and only a handful of silent people with tired eyes were wandering about. A bunch of young immigrants gave him the once-over, but they must have sensed some latent menace in him, because they left him in peace with his morning papers. He remembered the crowd of Turks who used to haunt Copenhagen Central Station when he was a boy. They had hung around in dispirited huddles, looking as though they were apologizing for living. But this lot were second-generation immigrants, cocky and aggressive-looking. They drew strength, he could tell, from being part of an ethnic brotherhood. They were no longer prepared to put up with racism or the claustrophobic Danish mentality that demanded that anyone taking up residence in the country had to behave like every other Dane. These boys didn't want to be turned into welfare cases. They channelled their anger outwards. To some extent he sympathized with them, but their war was not his, and he turned back to his paper. He wasn't reading it; he was keeping a weather eye on his surroundings. The wastepaper bins were overflowing with the remains of hamburgers, bits of paper, french-fry trays and orange peel, but no bottles. Vuk had noticed some seedy-looking characters trawling the station, rummaging in the bins for them. Denmark had grown both richer and poorer in his absence. There were more new cars and more beggars. The contrasts were greater. Pasty-faced figures flitted like shadows around the station concourse. Three drunk men were knocking back bottles of Carlsberg Gold and arguing about a football match. Cracks were clearly beginning to appear in the welfare idyll. Could it be that the majority had finally decided to turn its back on the outcast minority?

At midnight he made his way down the stairs to the platform and located his carriage. The train appeared to be half-empty. Alone at last, he gradually began to relax. Both bunks were made up, and there was a washbasin in the couchette. He washed and put on his smart clothes. It had been a long journey, but he was sure that he had covered all his tracks.

He had taken a long road for a shortcut, and not only so as to merge with the crowd in Denmark and become indistinguishable from everyone else. He also wanted to make absolutely certain that he was not being tailed by Kravtjov or his Iranians. They might not have been following him, but Vuk had not survived four years of war by taking unnecessary risks. Playing safe was a time-consuming business, but it paid to be careful and thorough. So he still did not allow himself to sleep. That would have to wait until he got to the hotel. He gazed out of the window and watched the darkness hurtling past. The roads were deserted. Only occasionally did the long beam of a lone car's headlights sweep an inky road. Denmark seemed deserted at night. All alone in the railway compartment, he pressed his forehead against the cool windowpane.

On the ferry across the Big Belt he drank a cup of coffee and ate a cheese sandwich. The few other passengers in the cafeteria kept themselves to themselves. He went out on deck and was met by the glorious scent of sea air and diesel. It was chilly now, and low clouds were drifting over a half-moon. The island of Füne disappeared from view, and he gazed in amazement at the long low bridge that stretched out from its shoreline. The bridge was strung with lights, and on the tiny islet of Sprogø majestic floodlit pylons reared into the air. Work on the bridge had really progressed while he'd been away. When he left it had still been on the drawing board. He had never imagined it would be so huge. He could see boats around the feet of the pylons and lights winking on their tops. He found bridges more awe-inspiring than cathedrals. They were the churches and temples of today, the largest constructions built by modern man. He smoked a cigarette and drank in the sight. He couldn't get enough of it. This was probably the last time he would take a ferry across the Big Belt. And it was unlikely that he would ever drive over the completed bridge. He was impressed by the fact that a nation as small as Denmark could build such a construction across this stretch of water. Along with a tunnel dug under the seabed. He felt sorry and a little sad when the voice over the Tannoy summoned him below decks to the train. He could have done with more time to just sit there looking at that view. Here was something permanent, something that would outlive him and the senseless war he had left behind. He was grateful for the sight and took it as an encouraging sign – a good omen. Confirmation that he had chosen the right route.

The hotel lay in a side street off Istedgade. He knew the Vesterbro area well and had picked it deliberately. People in Vesterbro didn't ask too many questions and were suspicious of most forms of officialdom. They asked only to be left alone, as they left others alone. An east wind was blowing, bringing with it the taste of autumn: an edge that almost moved people to button up their jackets. But the sun still had the upper hand. The street was already teeming with life. Life of another sort than that on the Kurfürstendamm in Berlin. The buildings here were shabbier, the cars smaller, and the abundantly stocked shops seemed poky and cramped. Turkish, or possibly Arabian, women walked by with their heads veiled, and the porno shops were closed. But the main difference was the bikes. Vuk loved the sight of all the bikes, and best of all were the women: so easy on the eye with their strong brown legs, transporting everything from shopping to children on their shiny new cycles. To Vuk, the bikes represented the very essence of Copenhagen. He stood for a while, just watching them. A young man went by carrying a bottle of beer. The bottle had a gold top. What was it called again? Elephant Beer, that was it. The young man drank the beer down, tipped the foaming dregs into the gutter and belched. He hung onto the bottle.

Vuk walked on, with his suitcase in one hand and his holdall in the other. He was wearing beige chinos, a dark-blue shirt and a new brown leather jacket. On his feet he had a pair of sensible, brown lace-up shoes. A scruffy-looking young man with long greasy hair tried to stop him with an outstretched palm, but Vuk didn't so much as look at him. He walked through the hotel door and one flight up. The reception desk was to the left. Behind it stood a youngish man in a short-sleeved shirt teamed with a blue and red checked tie. It was a good, reasonably priced hotel and as a result was much favoured by executives from small but flourishing businesses in Jutland.

Vuk put down his bags.

'You have a room for me. Carsten Petersen, Jutland Technoplast,' he said.

'One moment,' the desk clerk said. He had a computer sitting on the desk but referred instead to a ledger in front of him.

'Yes, that's right,' he said. 'Booked yesterday evening.'

'It was a bit of a last-minute thing,' Vuk said.

'Well, these days sometimes there's just no way round it,' the clerk said. 'How long were you thinking of staying?' He handed Vuk a key.

'A couple of days. Maybe closer to a week. It depends how quickly I get things sorted out.'

'Room 311. Up the stairs and to your right.'

'Thanks,' Vuk said, lifted his bags and made his way up the stairs without a backward glance. The Danes were such a naïve nation. They recognized one another by their language, and if you spoke it without an accent they would not dream of asking you for your passport or ID. Vuk had guessed that in this respect things would not have changed, and fortunately he had been proved right. Otherwise he would have made some excuse to leave, found another hotel and checked in for a couple of days as a British citizen, but he didn't want to do that just yet. He had no desire to leave an electronic paper trail behind him if he could help it. His plan was to switch to another small hotel after three nights at most, so that he could pay in cash without anyone thinking too much of it.

His room was small, but comfortable, with a double bed, a bedside table, a little desk and a television. He dumped his bags on the floor, locked the door and stripped off. Then he took a hot shower. His head was buzzing, and suddenly the tiredness hit him full on. He lay down on the bed and instantly fell fast asleep.

Vuk slept for six hours, then spent the rest of the afternoon strolling around the city. In his blue jeans, light-coloured shirt and leather jacket he passed largely unremarked, although he couldn't help noticing the long looks sent his way by some of the girls. He had forgotten how direct Danish girls could be. He bought a scout knife and a whetstone in a shop specializing in outdoor pursuits. In a toyshop he purchased an old-style skipping-rope with wooden handles, and in an ironmonger's a small roll of fine steel wire. He carried his purchases home in a carrier bag from the ironmonger's. A good-looking young man on his way home from the shops.

Copenhagen looked just the same. The city, blue and golden in the late afternoon light, wrapped itself around him like a favourite old sweater. The Town Hall Square alone was almost unrecognisable. They seemed to be in the midst of clearing up after some really serious road works. At one end reared a long, black rectangular box. It looked like an outsized anti-tank barrier, behind which the inhabitants of a besieged city could take cover from snipers. But behind it sat the familiar yellow buses: these too he always associated with Copenhagen, bowling gently along its streets. They always seemed to be half-empty, except for that one hour in the morning and in the afternoon. Also new were the green-clad bicycle messengers, zooming this way and that, jinking in and out of the traffic. He walked down Strøget. The long pedestrianised shopping drag was, he would have said, busy but not crowded. The pavement was littered with paper and takeaway leftovers, and a lot of people were eating as they walked. No one paid him any heed. He had been a bit worried as to whether he would still be able to fall in with the distinctive rhythm of this city, but it felt like only yesterday that he had walked these streets. He blended with the crowd and, like them, was soon able to pick out the foreigners in their midst, be it an American businessman or a group of Swedish tourists.

But when he got to Kultorvet he received a shock. The building was still there, but where was the library? He could see the bookshop, but the Central Library and its reading room were gone. Two young girls happened to bump into him as he stood there, momentarily distracted.

'Sorry,' one of them said when she saw his face. It was an ice-cold mask. He was not used to being touched suddenly and without warning. The war had left its mark on him, causing him to instantly sense the presence of an enemy, but he promptly pulled himself together and gave them a big smile that lit up his face and made them smile too.

'I was standing dreaming,' he said.

'No, we should have looked where we were going.'

'I was on my way to the library…'

'Oh, then you'll have to go down to Krystalgade,' they said both at once and laughed.

'Oh right, of course. Force of habit…you know…'

'Yeah, God knows why they have to keep moving things around,' the girls said, and they both giggled.

'Thanks a lot.'

'No problem.'

They linked arms and waltzed off.

'*Kan du ha' en god dag,*' they called back to him. Have a nice day.

He must remember that expression. Everybody seemed to be saying it nowadays.

He found himself a seat among the other browsers in the new Central Library reading room. He asked to see all copies of *Politiken* for the past month and proceeded to work his way systematically through them as the afternoon passed into evening. He found the article on Sara Santanda, studied the picture of her and that of Lise Carlsen. The caption underneath the latter said that Lise Carlsen, a staff reporter with *Politiken* and the chair of Danish PEN, would be Santanda's host during her visit, the schedule for which was, for the moment, being kept secret. The date for the arrival of the condemned writer was also a secret. But *Politiken* expected the visit to go ahead as planned, despite the imprudent leak. He looked at the picture of Lise. He saw an attractive, young-looking woman smiling softly at the camera.

Vuk left the library, carrying his plastic bag, and found a phone box, but it did not accept coins. There was a sign saying you had to use a phone card. What was a phone card? He walked on. In the next phone box he came to he could use his coins. He called directory enquiries and was given Lise Carlsen's telephone number and her Østerbro address. He walked down to Nørreport station, bought a phone card and a bus ticket and scanned the row of bus stops till he found the one for buses to Østerbro.

The apartment lay on the third floor. Next to the call-porter button for the third floor right were the names Ole Carlsen and Lise Carlsen. Across the road from the building lay an old-fashioned pub, one that had not yet been converted into a café or fast food joint. Tables and chairs had been set out on the pavement, even though the weather was wavering between summer and autumn, but that side of the street got the afternoon sun. Vuk sat down, put his carrier bag at his feet. He ordered a draught beer and lit a cigarette while considering the tenement from behind his dark sunglasses. It was a big building and well looked after, with new windows throughout. Its residents arrived home, one after another. Vuk contemplated this scene not with envy, but with a certain wistfulness. He liked other people's everyday lives. It was nice to see Danes returning home with their carrier bags from the local supermarkets: Irma and Super Brugsen. That life would never be his, but regretting that fact was just a waste of time. Although, of course, there were moments when he couldn't help wondering what would have happened if he hadn't gone back to Bosnia, but had stayed in this peaceful little country. He drank his beer and thought of his parents and his sister, and of Emma, then pushed these thoughts away. If he gave them free rein, the blood-roller would run that night, and that he could not take. A car pulled into the kerb, and a man in his mid-forties got out. He looked tired and tight-lipped. He locked the car door and walked up to the front door of the tenement with his door key in one hand and his brown briefcase in the other. He was slightly round-shouldered and dragged his feet a little. He let himself in. The waiter came out and emptied the ashtray. Vuk ordered another beer. Moments later he saw the man from before come out of the door and cross the street to the pub. He walked right past Vuk and through the open door.

'Hi, Ole,' the waiter said as he placed a fresh glass on Vuk's table. He was a youngish man with a muscular torso that looked too big for his short legs. A fitness centre body, Vuk thought to himself. It looked strong but wouldn't be so tough if it came to the crunch. He would never be scared of a bodybuilder.

'Hi, Mads,' the man said without stopping. 'I'll have a beer and a chaser.'

'Erna's inside.'

Vuk sat on, sipping his beer.

'Don't you want to move inside? It's getting cold,' the waiter said.

'No, thanks. I'll just finish this out here,' Vuk said.

'Okay.'

He spun out his drink for another quarter of an hour, then decided that he could not sit there any longer. He got up and had just lifted his carrier bag when he saw Lise Carlsen cycling along the street. She parked her bike and locked it. He saw Lise's eye go to the man's car, then across the road to the pub, then up to the apartment on the third floor. Vuk turned his head away and called into the gloom of the pub:

'Can I pay you now?'

'Certainly,' the muscleman called back.

He came out.

'Thirty-eight kroner,' he said, then caught sight of Lise. He took Vuk's hundred-kroner note, but his eyes were still on Lise.

'Just a sec,' he said and took a couple of steps into the road.

'Lise,' he shouted. 'Lise! Ole's in here.'

Lise glanced across at them. Vuk turned his face away and regarded her out of the corner of his eye.

'Okay, Mads. Just tell him I'm home.'

'Right you are, Lise,' Mads said and gave Vuk his change.

Vuk ran over this scene in his mind later that evening as he sat in his room watching television. Or rather: the TV merely provided some pleasant background noise. It was tuned to some Danish talk show featuring a whole lot of women, all of them well dressed and extremely talkative. Vuk had given up trying to figure out what they were talking about and had turned down the sound while he worked.

He cut the wooden handles off the skipping-rope and pulled half a yard of thin, pliant steel wire through them instead. He tied a knot in the wire at the top of each handle to secure it and tucked in the loose ends. He wrapped a towel around a pipe in the bathroom, slung the wire round it with a quick flick of the wrist and tugged hard on both handles. The wire gave a little, but the knots on the handles held. Satisfied, he laid the garrotte on the small bedside table.

He watched television for a couple of hours, thinking about Lise and her husband Ole. He pondered how best to make contact with her while whetting the dull side of the scout knife, turning it into a double-edged blade. He used slow, steady efficient strokes; the action was soothing and helped him to think. The two edges of the knife were now razor-sharp. It was good Solingen steel, which didn't break easily. He was no longer totally unarmed, and this made him feel a shade easier in his mind. Tomorrow or the next day at the latest, he should receive a postcard from Kravtjov telling him where he could pick up the proper weapons. He knew he didn't have much time, and he had a suspicion that the weakest link in the chain was not Lise, but Lise's husband. It was just a hunch, but he had seen from Lise's face that she was disappointed, upset and a little angry. She had had no desire to join her husband for a quick one after work. On the contrary, she had glared at the pub through narrowed eyes before, to Vuk's surprise, giving the front wheel of the car a quick, vicious little kick. Then she had unlocked her bike and cycled off again without a backward glance.

Chapter 12

Lise pedalled so hard that, much to her dismay, she broke out in a sweat. Suddenly she felt very foolish. This wasn't going to solve anything. It would be far better to confront Ole with the fact that she had taken a lover, got herself a boyfriend, was having an affair. Whatever the hell she was supposed to call it, it made her feel warm all over and made her want to be with Per all the time. But she had been so pissed off when she discovered that Ole had gone over to that pub again – the bloody place stank of foul cigars and stale beer. Why couldn't he drink in a café or a decent bar? She knew that he knew she hated pubs. She couldn't stand the thought of him sitting there chewing the fat with a load of great oafs, maybe even discussing her with men who talked about 'the wife' at home. Because that's what the sort of men who frequented such establishments did, she was sure. Grassroots culture was greatly overrated. Give her the arts and civilized, well-educated people any day. She loathed community centres, bingo and old-fashioned pubs, with their billiard tables and the reek of male bodies. He knew how it irritated her when he went to that place, just as she knew how it irritated him when she played the radio in the mornings. Why was it that suddenly they couldn't talk to one another anymore? Why did they go out of their way to hurt one another? Why did love die?

She climbed off her bike when she got to the lakes, took a deep breath and murmured under her breath:

'Where do we come from? Who are we? Where are we? Where are we going and where do we put the empty bottles?'

Then she burst out laughing at herself. An elderly lady walking a small, podgy black-spotted dog gawped at her. She looked so sour-faced that Lise

121

couldn't resist sticking her tongue out at her as she swung her leg over the saddle man-fashion and set off along the path at such a lick that she sent gravel spurting in all directions. Christ, how childish. But she wasn't used to dealing with the sort of situation in which she now found herself.

She rode home. Ole wasn't there. He would probably spend the whole evening across the road. Shooting dice or discussing football and politics with dumb hulks who had been dumped, kicked out or were just plain lonely – or all three at once And just when she finally had a free evening. They could have talked. Really talked. She had taken time off from the paper, from Sara and from Per. On purpose, because she didn't feel she had as much control over her feelings as she would have liked. Although the truth was that Per couldn't see her that evening anyway. He hadn't said what he was doing, and it really wasn't any of her business. But still it bothered her. She ought to make something to eat. She was getting upset again, so now, of course, she was starving. But instead she put on some water for tea and had just poured herself a cup when she heard the front door, and Ole walked into the room, a little red-eyed, but otherwise as composed and distant as always.

'Hello, love! Where have you been? Have you eaten?' she said, hating herself, because she could hear how forced it sounded.

'Hi,' was all he said, then he stood looking at her until she began to feel rather flurried. She rose and crossed to the sink. Even though there was tea in her cup she got herself a glass of water, just to have something to do with her hands. She felt Ole's eyes on her, steeled herself and turned round. The bright, airy kitchen suddenly seemed dank and stuffy. As if the darkness outside had seeped through the walls and smothered the electric lights.

'What's wrong? Why are you staring at me like that?' she snapped.

Ole merely eyed her up and down. She felt like one of his wealthy neurotic patients. Or clients, as he insisted on calling them. Over the past twenty years the number of psychologists in Denmark had doubled, so you would have thought they'd all be fighting for their share of the cake, but Ole had never earned as much as he did now. Your average Dane must be really fucked up and have no one to talk to, she thought, her mind wandering because his searching glance was too much to take. She lit a cigarette and said:

'Ole! What's the matter?'

'I wanted to see if it were possible to detect some physical change. But I don't think it is. Or is it?'

His voice was, in fact, a little slurred. She could hear the beer and schnapps in his vowel sounds.

'I don't know what you're talking about.'

She quailed under his gaze, looked away.

'Oh, you know, the usual story. There's someone else,' Ole said.

She felt the back of her neck flushing. The man was a psychologist, for Christ's sake, he did know a thing or two about the human mind. She pulled herself together, walked over to him and took his hand. It hung limply in hers. He smelled of the pub.

'Ole, stop it now, okay?'

Ole regarded her with eyes that might have been bleary but were also shrewd: eyes she had loved and which she had thought beautiful. He broke free of her hand and took a step back from her.

'There might be certain physical clues one could go by,' he said. 'An inordinate amount of time spent in the bathroom, for example. Or a new perfume. Rather more frequent changes of underwear. These are the classic signs, but then you've always been incredibly fussy about your appearance. Then there are other signs. You blush very easily these days. Most becoming. But a bit odd in a woman of your age. You're fidgety. And you keep running your fingers through your hair.'

He regarded her with those searching eyes, and she realized, to her horror, that she was blushing and running her fingers through her hair. She swivelled away, turned on the tap, dowsed her cigarette in the stream of water, chucked it in the bin under the sink and filled her glass again.

'I've always done that,' she said at length.

'Are you having an affair, Lise?'

She had her back to him. And for that she was thankful. She knew the look on her face would have told him he had guessed right. Why didn't she just tell him the truth? Why didn't she dare? Because she had never been in a situation like this before? She didn't want to have a showdown now. She wanted to be the one to choose the time and the place.

'I'm just a bit uptight. On edge. This whole Santanda thing is starting to get to me.'

'Are you, Lise?'

She turned to face him:

'You of all people ought to know what I'm talking about. Stress. You make a living out of treating people for it. You're a psychologist. Why the hell can't you understand?'

This last came out as a shout, but Ole remained impassive.

'Okay,' was all he said, and this only served to infuriate and exasperate her.

She took a step towards him, then promptly stepped back again, to where she could once more feel the reassuring edge of the bench in the small of her back.

'What do you mean, "okay"?' she said. 'I'm not one of your patients. So spare me your psychoanalytical "okays". All that means is: I'm listening, but I don't give a fuck!'

'Okay.'

'For Christ's sake, Ole. Give me a little time. It's only two weeks until Sara's visit, after that we have to talk. Once it's all over. I'm just rather stressed…'

'Okay.'

'Ole, will you stop saying "okay".'

She took a step towards him again, hesitated for a moment, then said:

'Look, I've got the night off. Why don't we make ourselves something really nice to eat? Go to bed with a film? Like we used to do. I'm a bit uptight, that's all.'

Ole looked at her. The expression on his face altered. It was no longer simply probing, she felt. There was contempt there too. He considered her for a moment, then turned on his heel and made to leave.

'Where are you going?' she said.

'Don't patronize me. *That* I really don't deserve,' he said, walking away.

She called after his retreating back:

'What's that supposed to mean? I wasn't…Where are you going?'

He stopped and looked back at her:

'Into town.'

'Again? Don't you want me to make us some dinner? Ole? Or I could come with you. We can eat out. Please stay. We need to talk.'

His eyes searched her face again:

'I'm not hungry,' he said and walked out without looking back.

'Oh, for fuck's sake!' Lise cried as she heard the front door slam and she was left alone in the room. She called Per's number, let it ring and ring, but he had said he was going to be out.

'Oh, Per,' she said to the ringing tone. 'What am I going to do?'

In the end she made herself an omelette and ate it in front of the television while she watched an old Danish comedy. They had become amazingly popular again. She needed something else to do. Tomorrow she would sit herself down and write an article about this whole phenomenon. About the nostalgic longing which people felt for the secure familiar order of a bygone era. These films spoke of a time when agriculture did not pollute the earth and the roles of the sexes were clearly defined. Watching them, you could forget that the seventies and eighties had ever happened. In them, Denmark was presented as an immutable rustic idyll in which the sun always shone, and tramps broke into song instead of shambling around collecting empties and begging on the street. She tried calling Per again around midnight, but there was still no answer. So she went to bed. Ole did not come home that night.

Early the next morning she settled herself in front of the computer in her bright feminine office in the newspaper building and wrote her article. Her office was lined with books and posters, international magazines and plants. She thought of Ole, then she thought of Per, but she forced herself to be light of word and profound of thought, as Tagesen put it. The end result actually read rather well, so she passed it on to editorial. Then she went into the file on Sara Santanda's visit. She had furnished it with a password. So no one else could open it. She read through it. Things seemed to be shaping up nicely, and Flakfortet would provide a great backdrop for the television shots. She just hoped the weather would be kind to them. It was cooler today, and grey clouds chased across the sky. It looked like there would be rain later on, even though they had said on the radio that it would clear up. The phone rang. She picked it up, gave her name. A pleasant male voice spoke back.

'Hi,' said the voice – Vuk's voice. 'My name's Keld Hansen. I'm a freelance journalist working for a number of Jutland trade journals. I understand you're involved in organizing the visit by Sara Santanda, the writer?'

'I'm sorry, I can't really comment on that,' she said.

'Well, that's what it says in your newspaper,' the voice said.

'Well, yes…that's right,' said Lise, feeling for a moment rather stupid. She had been spending too much time with Per.

The pleasant voice went on:

'Look, I'm a fellow reporter, and this means a helluva lot to me. I'm a freelancer, I could really do with a good story. And the journals I work for would very much like to present their own slant on this story. A staffer like yourself can understand that, can't you?'

She felt a little guilty now.

'Yes, I do understand that. But we don't even know for sure if she's actually coming.'

'I realize you have to be careful, but if…'

'Well you'll have to contact Danish PEN. It's not really *Politiken's*…'

'I understand. But you're their chair. So could you give me PEN's address?'

'It's actually my own address.'

'Okay, so what do I do?'

'You write to me, and I'll add your name to the list for accreditation. Security surrounding the visit will be pretty tight.'

'When is she coming?'

'I'm not at liberty to say, but write today rather than leave it till tomorrow. And I'll put you on the list.'

'Thanks. And thanks for being so helpful. It's good to know that you guys in Copenhagen do actually spare a thought for us poor sods over here.'

'It's always nice to be able to help a fellow reporter,' Lise said and hung up. Might she have said too much? She had certainly more than implied that Sara would be coming, and soon. Well, what possible good did it do to go on being so vague? And he wasn't the first reporter to call either. At some point they would have to call the Press Corps together, and how were they supposed to do that? Maybe Per had some ideas. He had called her here this morning and said he would pick her up around four. She felt giddy as a schoolgirl. Couldn't wait to be with him. To make love in the safe house, because there was no way she could take him home, and he had not asked her back to his place.

There was a knock on her door, and Tagesen breezed in with his usual air of bustling efficiency. She quickly pressed 'F7', then 'YES' and saved the list just as she heard the door swing open.

'You might wait till I say: "come in",' she snapped.

'I hope you've got it well protected,' Tagesen said.

'Of course I have. Password and everything. Sara is Simba. The apartment is a "safe house", no address. And so on. It's not like I'm just going to spell out exactly what it's all about, is it? I'll finish this at home. Then you can see it.'

She told him that another journalist had called. And that they were going to have to come up with some means of calling a press conference in such a way that the reporters would show up without knowing what for. How were they going to do that?

'Do you see the problem, Tagesen? They know she's coming, but they don't know when. I can hardly write: please be here at 1.00 pm for a press conference with Sara Santanda. All any terrorist would have to do then would be to check the Ritzau Bureau daily events list.'

'No, but they'll have to be lured into attending,' Tagesen said, fiddling with a button. An idea suddenly occurred to Lise. Tagesen was famed for his wide network of contacts in the European arts world. She remembered a story on the international pages in that morning's paper, about the German author, Herbert Scheer. Scheer had received death threats from German neo-Nazis who were demanding his head on a platter because he had spoken out in defence of Turks and other members of the immigrant population.

'You're a good friend of Herbert Scheer's, aren't you?' she said.

Tagesen nodded happily. He was proud of his network and made no secret of it.

'What if you could persuade him to come? We could call a press conference for him.'

Tagesen smiled and gave one of his little bounces.

'The very thing! Scheer's a Nobel Prize-winner, his work's known in Denmark. But…'

'But normally no one but the odd culture vulture would be bothered to show up for a press conference with him. And the TV boys certainly wouldn't be interested,' Lise said, relishing the fact that for once she was one step ahead of Tagesen.

'So what's the point?' he said.

'Oh, come on, Tagesen, you're usually a lot quicker on the uptake,' she said, then explained what she had in mind. Scheer had a holiday cottage in Denmark and often spent his summer holidays there. They would let it slip that there had also been threats on his life in Denmark. That would draw the TV stations and the tabloids. The immigrant debate was always lying simmering just under the surface. Stories about racism and neo-Nazism invariably made good copy. Tagesen thought it was an excellent idea.

'Run it by your friend from PET,' he said.

'I'll do that,' she said.

Tagesen stood where he was for a moment, then his restlessness got the better of him again:

'I'd better be getting on. But nice work, Lise. I've been doing my bit too, you know. I spoke to the minister for culture. She'd like to meet Santanda. So she says.'

'Will she, though?'

'I doubt it. Bang will talk her out of it, and she'll find some excuse.'

'Money talks, eh?' Lise said. She felt let down.

'Yep. And no leader in the paper can change that,' Tagesen said in a rare admission of the helplessness he sometimes felt but was very careful never to voice in public. But Lise was right. Money did speak louder than words. The Rushdie and Santanda affairs were proof of that. Although both actually bordered on the banal and had nothing at all to do with the laws governing freedom of speech, basically they were criminal cases. But you can't arrest a whole country and its government, particularly not when that country's actions can have a bearing on the trade balance.

Lise sat for a while. She was thinking about Per. About their affair. He was not the sort of man she usually fell for. He wasn't much of a talker, he wasn't interested in art and culture, he kept his thoughts to himself. He looked good, had a fabulous body and was a great lover, but was that enough? She really didn't know what it was she had fallen in love with. Maybe it was purely physical. Maybe he was simply the excuse to leave Ole she had been waiting for. Maybe this thing with him was not actually a new love affair but merely a comma between one that had worn thin and something new and unknown that was still waiting round the corner. Maybe she had just wanted to discover what it was like to be wanted again – and that she had. He wanted her body and did wonderful things to it. She was already looking forward to this evening and not the least bit ashamed to be so eager.

But whatever the case, things could not go on as they were. At some point she would have to choose, but right now she needed to concentrate on her work instead of sitting there wondering what her secret lover, the secret agent, got up to when he wasn't with her

Chapter 13

Per Toftlund parked his BMW at Vedbæk Harbour, to the north of Copenhagen. The scent of salt and seaweed was borne in on the wind off the white-capped Sound. The sun had come out again, though, and it wasn't at all cold. Igor had had a fondness for meeting at the Hotel Marina in the old days too, whenever they wanted to have a chat. He was a big football fan, and he had once told Per, only half in jest, that he liked the thought of having lunch at the hotel where the Danish team stayed when they got together to train. It was a good place for a businesslike exchange of ideas about matters with which the diplomats and politicians could get no further.

Igor Kammarasov was cultural attaché at the Russian Embassy in Copenhagen. He had occupied that same post when the legend on the embassy nameplate had read 'Embassy of the Union of Soviet Socialist Republics', but his real employee back then had been the KGB. These days his salary was paid by the ministry of security in Moscow. Toftlund had tailed him during his first posting to Denmark to find out which Danish agents he tried to recruit and had had meetings with him later in connection with the security arrangements surrounding visits to the country by high-ranking Russian politicians. Per knew his Igor in more ways than one. PET had been onto him from the very first minute he set foot on Danish soil. Times had changed, though, and the level of surveillance was, of course, lower, but Per held to the belief that it still made sense to keep the Bear on a leash and thus have a chance of learning what was really going on. Igor spoke fluent Danish with the characteristic accent acquired by students taught at the old Institute for Nordic Philology at the University of Leningrad, now St Petersburg. Igor had called Per on his mobile and suggested that they meet at their old spot, and naturally Per had agreed, even though he

131

did not know what it was all about. Strictly speaking, he had enough on his plate with the Santanda visit, but Igor was a contact and as such had to be cultivated.

Per looked round about. Boats bobbed lightly at their moorings. Lines slapped gently against masts in the breeze, but the harbour was pretty much deserted. The thought of Lise flashed through his mind. It was a nice thought, but he was the sort of person who could compartmentalize his life, capable of concentrating on the matter in hand and tucking other thoughts and feelings away in their pigeonholes until he had the time to take them out and analyse them. Lise wasn't that easily shelved, however. She was so damn lovely and so damn nice to be with. He could really fall for her. She wasn't actually his type, but they got on so well together, talking and laughing. It was years since he had been as attracted to a woman as he was to her. The fact that she was married did not worry him. He had had affairs with married women before. It wasn't his problem if they had a husband or were living with someone. If a woman was going out with him, then something clearly wasn't right. It was a free country and it was the woman's own decision, he thought to himself, letting his mind wander in spite of himself. It occurred to him that once the Simba visit was out of the way he could take some of the leave owing to him and go off to Spain with Lise. There weren't many women with whom he would like to share Spain, but Lise was one of them, and he would be disappointed if she said no.

He caught sight of Kammarasov standing at the edge of the jetty. He was a tall, slim man with thick, dark hair brushed back from a narrow face. Igor was clad in the diplomat's uniform of dark suit and navy coat, worn open on such a mild day. As usual, Per was dressed in clean, neatly pressed jeans, a button-down shirt with a tie and a light-coloured windbreaker.

Per waved to Kammarasov, who raised a hand in greeting. Per walked over to him, they shook hands and exchanged a few remarks about this and that. Per asked after Igor's wife and two teenage children: he was delighted to hear that they were all fit and well. Igor's wife was in Moscow at the moment, but the children were attending a Danish high school.

'They'll soon be more Danish than Russian, Per,' Igor said in his excellent Danish, with that faint accent which put Per in mind of the wiretap recordings of not so very long ago. They had, in many ways, been good times. The fronts had been more clearly defined, the rules easier to follow, and Per had loved the games of cat and mouse, even though sometimes it was the mouse who was playing with the cat and not the other way round. Nowadays they were neither friends nor enemies, but partners of a sort in the big, bewildering schizoid world of the post-Cold War era, and spoke to one another almost as old cronies would do. But still, caution and subterfuge were in their blood. The simple fact that Igor had called him on his eminently tappable mobile phone, instead of ringing him at home or at the office, told Per that he was about to repay an old favour, either that or issue a new promissory note, to be redeemed at some later date. Which was fine. Those were still the rules of the game.

'I'm glad the boys are doing well, Igor,' Per said. 'Shall we walk?'

They strolled out onto the jetty. It was a fine day. The line of the Swedish coast stood out in sharp relief on the other side of the narrow strait. It was like a scene from a picture postcard, with a coaster chugging down the Sound and sails, bright-hued and pristine white, catching the fresh breeze. Out there too, Per noted, was one of those flat-bottomed Russian river barges that plied the Danish coastal waters. They undercut the standard freight rates, and Per was sure it was only a matter of time before one of them went down. They were built for the broad quiet rivers of Russia, not for the open sea. In the old days he would have suspected the KGB of using them as a blind for espionage activities, but he knew that these boats carried only hard-up seamen looking to make some ready money – as well as a fair number of smugglers. They belonged to two different types: the Volga-Balt, which carried general cargo, fodder and fertilizer, and Volga-Nefti, transporting oil. The sea was an iridescent band of blues and greens; it smelled good, clean. It was the sort of day that made you want to take off in an old cutter and fish for cod with the lads, Per thought. Then come back to a hearty meal of lobscouse or fried eel and boiled potatoes washed down by beer and aquavit.

Igor took a cigarette and offered the pack to Per out of politeness, although he knew very well that he did not smoke.

'What've you got for me, Igor?'

'A friendly warning.'

Per did a quick mental recap. To the best of his knowledge, Denmark was not currently running any undercover operations in Russia. PET might have something doing in the Baltic States, but they weren't anything near as active as the Swedes in that area. So what had they got wind of, what was it that Igor wanted to warn him about and have quashed before it became common knowledge?

Per could see that Igor was following his train of thought. They had known one another too long it seemed.

'It's not what you think,' the Russian said. 'It's about Sara Santanda.'

Per halted, turned to Igor.

'What's that got to do with Russia?'

'The Russian Mafia has pledged to carry out the contract for the Iranian government. We're sure of it. They've subcontracted a pro to do the job.'

'Who, Igor?' Per said. He didn't need to ask how Igor knew that he was working on the case. Keeping tabs on things, being well informed – it worked both ways.

'That we don't know. But we don't think it's one of their own. He's not a Russian. Ex-Yugoslavian. Probably a Serb, but some Muslim fanatic will get the blame. They've found themselves a fall guy.'

'It's not much to go on,' Per said, although he didn't mean it.

'Come, let us walk,' Igor said, and they strolled on along the jetty, right to the very end.

'It's just a friendly warning,' the Russian said again.

'I think there's something else you're not telling me, Igor.'

'I have no proof, Per.'

Per laughed:

'This isn't a court of law, you know. When the hell did you and I ever need to have proof in our business?'

It was Kammarasov's turn to laugh. He tossed his cigarette butt into the water. The filter tip bobbed on the choppy waves.

'As a favour to me,' Per said. 'I'll owe you one.'

Kammarasov removed a black-and-white photograph from his inside pocket. A six by eight shot of Kravtjov in Berlin. Toftlund studied the sharp clear image of Kravtjov's features. He was talking to another man, but only the back of his companion's head was visible, to the right in the foreground of the picture. It looked like a young head: fair hair, close-cropped. Per looked at Kammarasov, who said:

'It's the face of a man called Kravtjov. Ex-KGB. A rotten apple.'

'Aha, so the Santanda thing was just by the by?'

Igor nodded. Per knew there had to be more to it than that, but there was a fine line between supplying the necessary information and betraying one's operational methods. They must have had Kravtjov under surveillance for some time – using cameras and microphones. Probably at long-range in the outdoor location where this shot had been captured.

'Where was it taken?'

Igor hesitated, then said:

'Berlin.'

'What's your interest in him?'

'We suspect him of working for the Mafia. Bagman. We've been tailing him for a while. Your problem came up as a spin-off from our investigation. Come, I have to be getting back to the office.'

They started back along the jetty. Two friends having a chinwag.

'Whose is the other head?' Per asked.

'Kravtjov has been seen with him a couple of times. We think that's your man. They had a meeting with an Iranian agent. One known to us. Rezi, one of their best men.'

'But who's that there, Igor? That head?'

'We don't know.'

'Haul Kravtjov back to Moscow. For a little chat.'

'It doesn't work that way anymore, Per. We *think* he has links with the Mafia, but he covers his tracks well. He's resident in Germany quite legally. He went to a good school. We have no proof. Yet. Nowadays we can't just lock him up. Russia is a democratic state.'

Per gave a hoot of derision:

'Yeah, and the moon is made of green cheese.'

Igor stopped and gripped his arm lightly.

'Now who's the one who can't forget the old enemy images?'

Per pulled himself free.

'Stop talking like a high-school student. You know damn well we two will never be out of a job.'

Kammarasov stepped back a pace. Per looked him in the eye. Igor met his gaze unblinkingly. The atmosphere between them chilled slightly, but Igor was the first to look away, as he said:

'We're pretty certain he's already here in Denmark. The hit man.'

'So the contract will be carried out?'

'As agreed. We're quite sure of it.'

'It isn't much to go on,' Per said again, although he still did not mean it. The warning was meant to be taken seriously, and there was no doubt that Igor knew more than he was telling, but he had said enough to enable Denmark to take the appropriate action.

'That's all we know,' Igor said.

'Okay,' Per said.

They walked on. Kammarasov had driven out to Vedbæk in a blue Ford Escort with diplomatic plates, so he evidently had nothing against his car being seen down by the harbour. This was not a clandestine rendezvous, but clearly a meeting about which the ambassador would be informed: should problems arise later, he would have it on record that Russia had given Denmark plenty of warning. You never could tell what the new, sensation-hungry Russian press might dig up.

Per accompanied Igor all the way to the latter's car, then shook his hand.

'Thanks, Igor.'

'Don't mention it. We may still be on opposite sides of the fence where some things are concerned, but we're also partners now, you know. And it is our duty to alert a partner to the risk of terrorist attacks.'

'Now don't get started, Igor. Say hello to the wife and kids from me.'

'See you, Per,' the Russian said with a smile before shutting his car door and driving off.

'Too bloody right, you will. You don't get off that easy,' Per muttered under his breath as he pulled out his mobile phone to call his boss and squeeze himself into a slot in that lady's busy schedule.

She would see him right away, he was told, once he had outlined the situation.

He drove down to Bellahøj and was ushered straight in to Jytte Vuldom, who was at her desk, speaking on the phone. She sent him a friendly nod, and he sat down to wait. When she hung up he gave her an account of his conversation with Kammarasov. Vuldom listened quietly and did not interrupt him.

'He knows more than he's saying, of course,' Toftlund said.

'Oh, I'm sure he does, good old Igor,' said Vuldom, lighting yet another cigarette.

'I'm going to need more help. We'll have to get the undercover guys to ask around. Our hit man is bound to have checked into some hotel in the city.'

Vuldom blew the cigarette smoke away from him. She was in a considerate frame of mind today.

'We can't possibly track him down without a description,' she said.

'I need more help.'

Vuldom leaned forward slightly. Her make-up was subtle and discreet, and she spoke evenly, without raising her voice:

'Per. I'll say it again. It is my clear understanding that no official representatives of the Danish government will be meeting Sara Santanda. Her visit is not a government matter.'

'We have a duty to protect her.'

'Indeed we have, but I had a meeting here the other day with the prime minister and the minister of justice, to discuss the security arrangements for the forthcoming EU summit. Now that *is* a government matter, and a very important one, Per. But perhaps this new information could give cause for a rethink? A breathing space?'

'They'll never agree,' Per said, thinking of both Lise and Tagesen. They were determined to go through with the visit, as was Sara Santanda.

'Okay,' said Vuldom. 'Well then, we'll just have to see what we can spare. Because we will of course do all in our power to see that everything goes smoothly.'

'Right. And in the meantime, I've got a little plan of my own.'

'And that is, Per?'

'To get the Russians to give us a hand – with your permission. Igor could find out a whole lot more. If he wanted to…'

Per regarded his boss intently. He could tell by the look in those shrewd eyes that she knew what he was alluding to, but he wanted the suggestion to come from her, in case there should be complications later. You had to cover your back.

'Our old friend Igor,' she said.

'There's something he's not telling us. So I was thinking…'

'I know what you were thinking, Per. All right. Use your sleazy little file if you must. But this is strictly between the two of us.'

'Fine,' Toftlund said, relieved.

She stubbed out her cigarette and sat back in her chair.

'And there'll be no reason to put any of this down on paper, will there?'

'No, let's play it close to our chests,' Per said.

He drove in to the *Politiken* offices. That had gone well, he thought. He could get in touch with Kammarasov again, with her Ladyship's blessing, but without having to file a report. This was not one of those cases on which Vuldom felt bound to brief the parliamentary board of control. If all went well, then that was fine. And if anything did go wrong, then officially the matter did not exist. That was how both Toftlund and Vuldom preferred to work when things looked liable to get dirty.

He spotted Lise. She was standing outside the swing-doors of the *Politiken* building. She looked so good, he thought, with her fair hair and those blue jeans and a brightly coloured shirt under her short jacket. All of a sudden he just couldn't wait to be with her. He made a snap decision, noting as he did so on his mental balance sheet that he was now crossing a threshold and taking a step further in a relationship. He stretched an arm across the passenger seat and opened the door. Lise got in and gave him a long lingering kiss, oblivious of the cars tooting their horns behind them.

'Hola mi amor,' she said.

'Mi amor yourself,' he retorted and put the car into first gear. 'Dinner's on me, so we have to do a bit of shopping.'

'And where are we eating?'

'My place.'

'Is this a special occasion, then?'

'You've no idea how special,' he said and accelerated past a slow-moving bus, so fast that she was pressed back against her seat.

'Hey, easy does it, cop or no cop,' she cried.

She thought about him as she wandered around his small apartment. How did she actually feel about him, if she looked at it objectively? She was attracted to him, possibly even in love with him, but with what exactly? Did she like him for his own sake – or because he was Ole's diametric opposite? Ole was verbal. Per was physical. But that couldn't be the whole explanation. Maybe there was no explanation. And maybe she should stop looking for one and just go with the flow. The apartment was a clear reflection of Per's personality. Albertslund wasn't an area she would have chosen. Although it was nice enough really, for all her preconceived notions about the place. Four-storey blocks of apartments in yellow brick clustered round a neat landscaped courtyard, the province of mothers, prams and young children. There was a nice view: green fields and, in the distance, Vestskoven. Per only rented the apartment. He didn't like being tied down by a lot of stuff, he had said. Well that he certainly wasn't. The walls were white and totally bare, except for two exquisite Samurai swords hung crosswise on one wall and a poster advertising a bullfight at Las Ventas in Madrid on another. At first glance she had taken it for one of those ghastly posters on which tourists could have their own names printed, but it was an original with Paco Camino's name topping the bill. The swords looked like the genuine article too and had probably been bought in Japan. She understood now that Per spent most of his money on travelling abroad. Or had done. There weren't many books on his bookshelves: a handful of detective novels and some English books on police work and intelligence matters. She roamed the room with a glass of wine in her hand, taking it all in. She could hear Per in the kitchen. He was whistling. Her eye fell on a CD player and tape deck. To her surprise most of the tapes were of classical music by Mozart, Beethoven, Bartok and Vivaldi, as well as opera and some Spanish guitar music. The furniture looked as if it came from a good, but not outrageously expensive, furniture shop. He had a twenty-inch television set and a video recorder. An oval dining table in pale wood with six chairs. A leather sofa with a blond wood coffee table in front of it and two leather armchairs filled the living room. The parquet floors were bare, apart from one richly hued Persian rug. She thought it a rather cold room, but she had been struck right away by how spick and span the apartment was. He had given her a quick tour: the bedroom contained a standard-size double bed and a desk in front of the window on which sat a laptop computer and a small printer. The bed was made, and everything was neat and tidy and very masculine. 'Could you give me the name of your cleaner?' she had asked dryly, but he had taken her seriously and replied that he didn't have one. 'And I suppose you iron your own shirts, too,' she had said. 'Naturally,' he had said. 'I was in the Royal Navy for four years.' As if that explained everything.

The kitchen too was spotlessly clean, and here he appeared to have spent a bit of money on equipment, because above the kitchen worktop hung a battery of gleaming copper pots and pans, which she knew for a fact cost an absolute fortune in Illum's department store. Suspended from a hook was a string of garlic, which she could see was being used, and ranged on top of the cupboards were wine racks filled with bottles of red and white wine. Simple and functional, like everything else in his apartment. It wasn't how she and Ole would furnish a home. Had furnished their home, she corrected herself. They bought only the best and were both concerned that their home should look right, and that they should have the right address. There was no way they could live anywhere but in the city – and even then only in a couple of selected areas – or possibly on the coast north of Copenhagen in some really fantastic, architect-designed house. They would never dream of moving to Albertslund or anywhere else west of the city. It just wasn't on. They had rebelled against the conservative attitudes of their parents, but somewhere along the way her and Ole's generation seemed to have created a fresh set of values which were every bit as conservative. There were certain things *one* simply did not do. In a way she rather envied Per. In this apartment lived a man who had exactly what he needed, but no more than that, so that he could, at a moment's notice, pack his bags and go. She and Ole had accumulated so much in the way of material possessions that the idea of upping sticks was too daunting to even contemplate. Or the idea of divorce, she thought, and promptly dismissed the thought. She walked over to the window and gazed out at the green woods. What the hell was she going to do? She felt a little strange, this wasn't at all like the hours they had spent together at the safe house. That had been different, and a bit naughty, as befits a secret affair – like checking into a hotel. But this was something else: to be here, in his apartment. He was on home ground; she wasn't. What would she do once Sara Santanda had been and gone? She couldn't go on like this. Or could she? Wasn't that the meaning implicit in the word 'affair'? That it lasted for a certain length of time, then came to an end? But what if this was more than an affair, for her and for him? What then? Her thoughts kept going round in circles.

Lise walked through to the kitchen. It was filled with the aroma of basil, garlic and tomatoes. Per was wearing a blue apron over his shirt. He chopped salad greens and tomatoes and mixed them in a bowl. A crusty Italian loaf had also been sliced, and in a large pot on the stove the water for the pasta was just coming to the boil. He worked quickly and efficiently. He flashed her a big smile and pointed to the bottle of rioja.

'Dinner will be ready soon,' he said.

She walked up to him, took the spoon out of his hand and kissed him long and hard.

'It can wait,' she said.

'But it's just about there,' he said.

'It only takes a couple of minutes to cook up a fresh batch of pasta. Switch off the heat and come here,' she said.

He looked at her, switched off both the ceramic hotplates and proceeded to unbutton her shirt.

Afterwards they sat at the table and ate the splendid dinner he had made. He was in a pair of shorts and a T-shirt, and she had borrowed one of his shirts. Lise felt warm and contented, and she could tell just by looking at him that he was very happy. It had been better than ever before. They were getting to know each other's bodies and how they responded. He ogled her with bedroom eyes.

'Stop looking at me like that,' she said.

'I can't,' he said.

He broke off a piece of bread and mopped up the last of his pasta sauce.

'Are you staying the night, Lise?'

She wasn't sure. It was dark outside. They sat in the glow from two lamps, and she didn't have the slightest desire to get up and go.

'Oh, I'd better go home,' she said.

'Why?'

'I don't think I'm ready to leave Ole...not yet.'

He eyed her again and his next words surprised her:

'I've never said this to anyone before, but if you want you can bring your toothbrush next time.'

He looked as if this statement had surprised him as much as it did her. Her heart swelled, and with it her sense of confusion. She thought she might be about to cry.

'Oh, dammit Per,' she said. 'You mustn't say things like that.'

'I've said it.'

'Take me back to bed,' she said. Because she couldn't stand the thought of going home to look Ole in the eye and sit with him in their living room while the silence and the coldness grew between them, as if they were in the process of building their very own Berlin Wall.

Chapter 14

V_{uk} switched hotels to avoid arousing suspicion by paying for a longer stay in cash. He called from the one he was in and booked a room in a similar, modest-sized family hotel a couple of streets further up. There were scores of small hotels in the Vesterbro area. Again he was able to check in without showing any form of identification. After breakfast he walked over, as usual, to the post office in Købmagergade. He wore dark glasses and stepped out smartly in the crisp morning air. Summer was gradually giving way to autumn. He wondered what he would do if he happened to meet anyone he knew from the old days. Would he have to kill them? Or would he be able to talk his way out of trouble? He would have to play it by ear. The odds of him bumping into an old acquaintance were slight. He didn't venture out more than was absolutely necessary, but he had to admit that he could feel his old love for Copenhagen blossoming again. He had the urge just to stroll, to soak up the city. It had its own easy tempo, as slow and easy as the traffic. It amused him that the Danes thought the traffic here was so bad and so chaotic. Compared to that of any other big city, it flowed smoothly and steadily. Cars were parked within the bays reserved for them and not simply abandoned any old where, up on pavements and in all sorts of odd corners as they were in other cities. There was possibly a bit more litter than he remembered. There were potholes in the roads and a strange air of immutability about this town, which never seemed to grow up the way. It was clean, though, and well cared for, and the old Nørrebro area was teeming with new cafés and restaurants. Other cities had changed very fast, but Copenhagen still had a provincial, small-town feel to it; it didn't seem like a city at all. In the newspaper he read reports of murders and killings, but he also noted the statistics: in Copenhagen there were fourteen to fifteen murders a year. Where he came from, that many were killed in a village an hour. In another life he could happily have made his home in Copenhagen. The light falling over the city was clear and opalescent, reflected off the sea, and at night, when it rained, the raindrops glittered like crystal beads on the cobbles and tarmac. It was a strangely hushed town, where all sounds were muffled, especially at nightfall – as if the people and buildings were wrapped in cotton wool. The occasional voices one heard seemed to come from a long way off, and the engines of the few cars on the road purred gently and smoothly.

Vuk took a number at the post office in Købmagergade, waited his turn, then asked for poste restante. He spoke English and showed his British passport. He glanced round about, but no one was paying any attention to the handsome young man waiting patiently at the counter. Kravtjov had at long last delivered the goods: the female assistant handed him a white envelope bearing Danish stamps, but no sender's address. The letter was correctly addressed to John Thatcher, poste restante, Købmagergade Post Office, Købmagergade 33, 1000 Copenhagen K. The address had been typed.

Vuk stepped out onto the street. The sun peeped from behind high, light-grey clouds, a cool wind was blowing from the west. He unsealed the envelope. Inside were two pieces of cardboard between which some Iranian diplomat had sellotaped a suitcase key. There too he found a small laminated keycard for a left-luggage locker at Copenhagen Central Station. From the date on the card, printed under an advert for Gourmet Food, Vuk could tell that the suitcase had been deposited there the day before. Three days' storage had been paid for. Vuk assumed the Iranians had had his weapons sent by diplomatic bag to the embassy, thus avoiding all border checks. Vuk hoped they had found some nondescript man or woman to deposit the suitcase in the locker. He had great respect for PET, or any other intelligence service for that matter. He knew they kept a close eye on Iranians, Iraqis, Syrians, Sudanese, Libyans and anybody else whom they suspected of supporting terrorists or Muslim fundamentalists. The moment when he went to pick up the goods from that locker would, without doubt, be the riskiest so far, if PET happened to be keeping an eye on it, or if the drugs squad suspected it was being used as a letter box. Or he could be unlucky enough to walk right into a stakeout – he had no way of knowing. The good thing about the Central Station was that it was so busy, with people coming and going all the time. The downside was that it was often under surveillance by one police unit or another. Vuk had checked out the Central Station and committed its new layout to memory. It had changed a lot. The left-luggage lockers were in the basement now. The area was monitored by closed-circuit TV, but there was also an exit giving onto the platforms, so he wasn't venturing into a complete dead-end. The problem was that it was so easy to oversee and to seal off.

Vuk headed towards the Central Station. He stayed off Strøget and walked along the canal side instead. He thought about Ole. He had finally made contact with him two days before.

It had happened at the pub across from the couple's apartment. Vuk was sitting at a table just inside the door when Ole walked in and shouted:

'Oi, Erna! A beer and a chaser!'

Erna was a stout woman in a blue dress. She had slammed the glasses down in front of Ole as if she were mad at him.

'You'd be better off going home to that lovely wife of yours,' the woman he called Erna had remarked.

'She's never bloody well home,' Ole had said.

Vuk had grinned and said he'd have the same. To begin with Ole had eyed him with sullen suspicion, but eventually they had got chatting. Vuk introduced himself as a sales rep from Jylland, and after a while he bought a round. It was always easy to strike up a conversation in a pub, in surroundings that were both anonymous and cosy. Words were not as binding here as elsewhere.

Vuk sauntered along the canal side, thinking of Ole and his own gift for getting to know people. He had always had it. His mother had told him that even when he was just a little boy he could smile and charm his way to all the ice creams and lemonades he wanted, and that he had looked so sweet that folk just couldn't resist patting him on the head and ruffling his blond curls. She had had him and his little sister late in life and spoiled them both dreadfully, and they had loved her with all their hearts. He saw his mother in his mind's eye, and had to struggle to erase her image and concentrate on Lise's husband.

Ole had opened up quite a bit. He was a psychologist but evidently not so hot when it came to self-analysis. Or maybe it was just his nature to confide in others, to be so frank. Vuk now knew that he and his wife were not getting on, that he was sick of his job and felt that life was passing him by all too fast; that he didn't really have any friends: all the people he knew, he had met through Lise. Although Ole never said so in so many words, it seemed pretty clear to Vuk that he was terrified of losing Lise, and so he skulked in the pub, even though by doing so he was only causing her to drift further and further away from him He couldn't stand being in that empty apartment. If he sat there alone, he kept seeing Lise in bed with someone else. He had blurted this out the other evening when they were having a few drinks together. Maybe he just needed to talk about himself after spending the whole day having to listen to other people's irresolvable problems. Ole had been easy to woo, to prime for recruitment as an agent, Vuk thought to himself. It had been nice to have a drink. It had been quite a while since he'd touched alcohol, and the beer and aquavit had slid down easily, but he had a strong head and a strong body and at no time did he feel drunk, while Ole's speech had become more and more slurred.

The recruiting of agents had been one part of the training at the Special Forces school at which Vuk had really excelled. People found it so easy to open their hearts to him. He was a good listener, and although he never gave away too much about himself, somehow he always left folk feeling that he had also taken them into his confidence. He could turn the charm on and off, like the sun appearing and disappearing behind a cloud. Once it had been only natural to him to be open and friendly, sweet and funny. That was just how he was. A happy and fairly uncomplicated child who grew into a cheeky, cheerful and charming young man, whom all the girls were wild about and all the boys wanted to be mates with. Until he was seventeen his life had been a pretty unproblematic one. Strolling through lovely timeworn Copenhagen he wondered how it might have turned out if the whole family had not moved back to Bosnia. It was his mother who had been so anxious to go home. She had wanted to spend her twilight years surrounded by their good friends in their old village and be buried in her native soil. His father's back was no longer up to the work at the shipyard, and his invalidity pension would stretch so much further in the old country, but Vuk actually believed that his father would have preferred to stay in Denmark. Nonetheless, he followed Lea, just as she had followed him when they were young and he brought her to that far-off capitalist country in the north where they were so wealthy that they had to import foreign hands to do the dirty work. His parents had saved enough to build a little house back home in Bosnia. Vuk could easily have stayed on in Denmark, but he was fed up with high school, couldn't be bothered staying on to take his diploma; the prospect of running off to Yugoslavia appealed to him, even though he knew this would mean having to do his national service there. But that was okay by him, and his father supported his decision. Yugoslavia's sons had to serve the fatherland, to ensure that the Russians or the Germans did not try to invade them again. This was the lesson Comrade Tito had preached to them, and as far as his father was concerned, what Tito said was law.

Then came the civil war. And with it the pain, the horrors and the rage.

On Rådhuspladsen Vuk halted and gazed over at the weird, black outsize anti-tank barrier. All of a sudden he felt ice-cold, as if the temperature had fallen drastically. The square and the people and the pigeons on it swam before his eyes, the hotdog stalls pitched and swayed, his head reeled, he felt his heart skip a beat, and he was gripped by panic.

'Are you okay?' he heard a voice ask, a long way off. 'You'd better sit down for a minute. There's a bench just over there.'

He felt a hand on his elbow. Rådhuspladsen stopped rocking like the deck of a ship. A young woman had him by the arm. She was leading a little boy by the other hand. The child goggled at Vuk, whose face was white as a sheet and covered in a fine layer of perspiration.

'It's all right. I'm all right now,' Vuk said.

'You looked as if you were about to pass out.'

'Yeah, I know. I had a bit of a dizzy turn, but I'm fine now. Thanks.'

She let go of his arm and gave him a slightly embarrassed look.

'It was just…'

'I'm fine now, really. Maybe it was something I ate. Thanks for your help.'

He smiled.

'Okay. We'll be on our way, then,' and she made to walk off with the little boy, who was staring at Vuk with unabashed curiosity, as only a child can do. The mother also took another look at Vuk.

'Haven't we met before?' she said.

147

Vuk had the same feeling. He *had* seen her before. She was a couple of years older than him, the older sister of one of the guys in his class. Jytte, her name was.

'I don't think so. Unless you're from Århus,' he said.

The woman laughed:

'No, definitely not.'

'But I am.'

'Oh, well enjoy your stay... I just thought.'

'No, I don't think so,' Vuk, said more brusquely than he intended to, and saw from her face that it had hit home.

'Right, well I'll be getting on,' she said and led the child away. Vuk watched them go. She turned around once and looked back at him. He raised a hand and waved. He wanted her to forget this meeting. Not to think too much over it, to simply dismiss it as just another ordinary, everyday incident. He did not want to get rid of her, nor could he. He would have to risk it. Maybe if it hadn't been for the child, he would have gone after her. Maybe Copenhagen was having an effect on him.

Vuk stood for a moment, collecting himself. Everything returned to normal. The advertising signs stood chiselled into the facade of the Trade and Industry building. The *Politiken* house lay where it always had, there were queues at the hotdog stalls, and Hans Christian Andersen sat, as always, staring wistfully into space. Vuk hurried on down the street to the Central Station, struggling, as he went, to ward off the dreaded visions by thinking about Emma and the future he hoped they would have together.

At the Central Station he bought a travel card and a copy of *Ekstra Bladet* and seated himself on a bench from which he could watch the streams of people passing to and fro. The station concourse was bustling with activity, but everything looked pretty normal. He spotted no signs of any sort of surveillance operation. From his bench he had a clear view of the stairs down to the left-luggage lockers, which lay at the far end of the station next to the Reventlowsgade exit. It was only a short step from the station to his hotel. Travellers young and old came and went, leaving or collecting holdalls, rucksacks, shopping bags and suitcases, but Vuk could not see anyone else observing movements in the area the way he was.

He got to his feet and wandered about a bit, but even on this round he had no sense of anything untoward. The new shops and cafés were doing a brisk trade. He drank a cola and ate a hamburger in McDonald's, then made another little round. A smartly dressed man came out of the florist's carrying four long-stemmed roses. A party from a kindergarten had found itself a corner where the tots sat dutifully waiting. In another, a class of schoolchildren were gathered round a teacher. Vuk trusted his intuition implicitly: if he had had any sense that something was wrong, if one single detail had been out of place, he would have been out of there on the instant and never gone back. Then they would have had to find some other way of getting the goods to him.

Vuk made one more circuit of the station concourse. A couple of uniformed policemen paced slowly past him, but they didn't so much as glance at the well-dressed young man. Their eyes did, however, dwell on a young girl in a pair of ripped and faded jeans and a grubby denim jacket. She had something that looked like a spear piercing one earlobe and rings through her nose and lips. Her hair was dyed red and green. Under all the self-mutilation she was quite pretty, and Vuk found himself wondering why anyone would willingly inflict pain and suffering on themselves. An extremely fat man with a white Santa Claus beard was sitting on a bench with his legs spread wide the way fat men do, watching the world go by. His great belly rested on his thighs. The place smelled of food and dust, but Vuk caught no whiff of danger.

He sauntered across to the flight of steps above which hung a sign saying 'Reventlowsgade, Left Luggage Office, Lockers', then made his way down the steps and to the left. The walls were grey and cement-like. Vuk descended another flight of steps. He peered through the double doors leading to the left-luggage area. He saw a long room with banks of lockers running down either side. There were lots of people milling around them, mainly kids. With rucksacks and small holdalls. Above each bank of grey steel lockers was a sign with a number on it. Vuk stopped in front of section 22, locker number 02. There was no one at the actual baggage counter, but Vuk noted that the whole area was monitored by closed-circuit cameras. Most of the lockers were taken; he could tell by the red squares in the little windows on their fronts: when a locker was free a green square showed instead. These new-style lockers were worked by means of ticket consoles, he slid his card into the slot on the one nearest to him. He felt his pulse quicken as he stood there with his back turned and unprotected, but there was no hint of that tingling in his spine that had so often alerted him to danger. The sounds behind him fell sharp and clear on his ears. Time seemed to stand still for a moment. The machine swallowed his ticket. He heard it chuntering away for a second or two, then his locker opened with a little click. He lifted out a locked grey, hard-sided Samsonite suitcase and headed for the exit without a backward glance: past another counter, then a bike shop and up the stairs branching off to Reventlowsgade and platforms 1–12.

Suitcase in hand he headed towards the platform for the suburban lines at a normal walking pace, slipped his travel card into the machine on the platform and clipped it once, then hopped onto the first train to pull into the station. He alighted at the next station, stood for a moment looking up and down the train before jumping back on just as the doors were closing. Everything seemed normal. No panic on the platform. Nobody frantically trying to make contact on a walkie-talkie or a mobile phone. He stayed on the train for another two stops then took a taxi back to the hotel. Normally he steered clear of taxis, preferring to use buses and trains. Taxi drivers are given to being alert and observant. They tend to have better memories than most other people.

Back at the hotel he made sure the door was locked before opening the case. Inside were the items he had requested: a Dragunov sniper rifle with telescopic sight and a Beretta 92F pistol, together with ammunition for the two guns, both of which looked new and well-oiled. The rifle was separated into three parts. He proceeded to assemble it with CNN running quietly in the background. Working with this gun that was so familiar to him had a soothing effect on him. He knew he could hit a target bang-on at up to eight hundred yards with the long-barrelled rifle, developed by Soviet weapons technologists as the SVD. It had a relatively short butt, and the magazine could hold ten bullets. Vuk had trained with and used many weapons in his time. The SVD might not be the most sophisticated of weapons, but he found it reliable, pleasant to handle and accurate.

Now all he needed was a time and a place and these he was certain his new agent, Ole, could obtain for him, willingly or otherwise. As he worked, his thoughts went to Emma. He would write to her from wherever he went once the job was done, and ask her to start a new life with him. He had been giving more and more thought to the idea of Australia. Not only was it a new country, it was a new continent too, offering every opportunity for a fresh start. He had had enough of Europe. It was splitting into a rich side and a poor side, but both the rich and the poor sides of the old continent were doomed to disaster. Yugoslavia had been only the beginning, he thought, carefully wiping every single tiny section of the guns with one of the washcloths he had bought a few days earlier. With Emma he could start again. They each bore their own psychological scars, but Australia and Emma would put an end to the nightmare, and the blood-roller could stop running. In Australia he would be able to shut off all the horrors. In Australia he would find it possible to feel again, and the hollow empty sensation inside him would be gone.

While Vuk was cleaning his guns, Per Toftlund was parking his car next to Fælledparken, on the side just behind Rigshospital, close to the Pavilion. He had called Igor and arranged to meet him there. The circular building was closed and deserted. Behind its pale slender columns, the café inside was in darkness. Some teenage boys were playing football on the grass in front of the old bandstand that, in the summer, formed the setting for music, eating and drinking. A couple of tables and chairs still stood outside. Per sat down and watched the boys playing. A woman in shorts jogged past with her dog on a leash, a lone cyclist rode slowly by and a couple strolled arm in arm. A mother and her baby were sitting on a bench. Normality. Everything in Denmark seemed so normal, but Per had a strong suspicion that they had an assassin in the city. The undercover guys were starting to ask around, and Per had had meetings with the uniformed branch and the crime squad. He had informed them of Sara Santanda's visit and told them what he knew. The most critical point would come with the press conference out on Flakfortet. And even though the politicians could have seen her far enough, the top brass at police headquarters were nothing if not professional. On the day itself he would be given all the officers he needed. They would guard the Østerbro apartment, provide an escort and lend assistance at Flakfortet, which Per himself would be making a recce of, along with Lise Carlsen. Everyone was taking seriously the Russians' averred certainty that a contract had been taken out on Santanda and that this contract would be carried out. But they didn't have a helluva lot to go on: the back of a blond head, a Serb – possibly. No name, no nationality, no description. Well, maybe the Russians could help. They would have to.

He saw Igor coming down the road. The Russian stepped onto the grass, prodded it with the toe of his shoe to see if it was wet, discovered that it wasn't and cut across the green to where Per was sitting. Igor was wearing the same dark suit and navy coat as before, but he looked a little nettled. As far as he was concerned, the case was closed, he had not welcomed the idea of another meeting, but Per had insisted.

The policeman stood up, and they shook hands briefly. Per came right to the point. This was not going to be quite so pleasant a meeting as last time, and he saw no reason to pretend otherwise by asking after the wife and kids, indulging in chitchat. When he played his ace, he wanted Igor to know that he had had it up his sleeve all along. He owed the Russian that much at least.

Per said curtly:

'I want you to bring in that guy in the picture, Kravtjov or whatever his name is, for a little talk. And I want it done yesterday!'

Kammarasov would make a good poker player, Per thought. He saw the Russian's eyes narrow, but his face remained impassive.

'It can't be done,' was all he said.

'In Berlin. To tell us who he's talking to in that picture. As soon as possible.'

'It cannot be done, Toftlund.'

Per considered Kammarasov for a second: held his eye while he drew a black-and-white photograph from the inside pocket of his jerkin. He lifted it up to the Russian, who broke free of his gaze and glanced down at the photograph. Per studied Kammarosov intently. God, what a pro, he thought, impressed in spite of himself. The Russian merely blinked once or twice but remained otherwise unmoved. Per turned the picture round to have a look at it himself. It was a good clear shot, showing Igor together with a young boy who could not have been any more than fourteen or fifteen. It had, Per knew, been taken in HC Ørsted Park one spring evening. Igor's features were slightly distorted by the pleasure of what the boy's mouth was doing to his rigid member, but there was no doubt as to who the man in the photograph was.

Per turned the picture round again, to let Igor look at it. He didn't want to, Per could tell, but he couldn't help himself. The boy's name was Lars and he was seventeen now, but he had been just fourteen when the photograph was taken. It was only four months since they had stopped seeing one another. Per had interviewed Lars personally and got him to describe the nature of their relationship. Per could see from the look on Igor's face that he knew this, but Per kept him dangling a while longer before saying:

'Democracy or no, this sort of thing is still a no-no back home, isn't it, Igor?'

Kammarasov made no reply. They could hear the shouts of the boys playing football; other than that, they were alone in the world. They stood facing one another, like old chums getting together for a good old natter. Kammarasov did not seem able to drag his eyes away from the picture. Per thought it filthy and disgusting and felt nothing but contempt for the Russian, not least because he knew from Lars that Igor had honestly loved the bloody little rent boy.

'It's illegal in Denmark too, you know, Igor. Not being queer – screwing minors, I mean.'

A tremor passed across the Russian's features, a fleeting flicker of pain before he regained control of his facial muscles and said, in a voice that shook only very slightly:

'So the age of dirty tricks is not yet over?'

'Like I said, Igor. We'll never be out of a job, you and I. Would you like to have it? A nice little memento?'

Kammarasov took the picture and gave vent to his anger by ripping it to shreds, tearing and tearing at it frenziedly, until the pieces could be no smaller, then he tossed them into the air to be caught by the breeze and blown across the gravel, round the corner of the Pavilion and into the bushes. Then he got a grip on himself again.

'I'll see what I can do,' he croaked.

Per Toftlund was enjoying this situation. He had nothing against having this big man from the superpower to the east dangling like a cod from his hook.

'That's what happens when you start thinking with your dick,' as Vuldom had put it when he had told her about what they had on Igor.

'What was the penalty in the old Soviet Union – five years in the clink, wasn't it? Not to mention the loss of your career, your wife, your reputation and all that crap. I don't suppose the general view on poofters in the new Russia has changed all that much, or has it?'

By now Kammarasov had completely regained his composure; he eyed Toftlund with something approaching disdain:

'That's enough. Do try to be a little professional. I told you, I'll see what I can do.'

'Good, Igor. And make it quick, eh? It's amazing how easy it is to make copies from a negative. *Pravda tavarijs?*'

'I'll call you,' Igor said and walked off.

'Enjoy the rest of your day,' Per called and kept his eyes on the Russian as the latter marched off, cutting diagonally across the grass of the boys' football pitch. He did not look back but walked with his head held high, deaf to the angry shouts from the players. Per felt a little guilty for crowing over him like that. It wasn't professional, even if it had felt good. But Christ, the Russian had balls. Igor would deliver the goods all right. Per preferred not to think about what would happen to Kravtjov now. Igor had been trained in a hard and brutal school, and when it came to saving his own skin he would be every bit as ruthless as those men who had, down through the ages, manned the Russian security services. Tsar, general secretary or democratically elected president, it made no difference to those who worked undercover for the state. They would always believe that they had been specially chosen and were thus above the law.

Igor knew very well that if he could not come up with something within the next forty-eight hours, he might as well just jump into the harbour and get it over with. But he had been in the business a long time and knew exactly who to call in order to have Kravtjov brought in for a little chat about life and death and a hit man hiding out somewhere in the Queen's Copenhagen.

Igor Kammarasov acted fast, and the three heavies whom the former KGB's Berlin HQ had used in the past picked up Kravtjov that same evening as he was taking his usual promenade along Unter den Linden to view all the new restaurants and shops which seemed to spring up every day. He was walking along, lost in thought, when a grey Mercedes drew up alongside the kerb. At that same moment a powerfully built man drew level with Kravtjov, poked a pistol into his ribs and hissed:

'Get in, Comrade! Or I'll blow your balls off.'

Thus began his hours in Hell.

They took him to a basement in the Turkish quarter in Kreutzberg, divested him of his jacket and shirt, placed him on a high-backed chair, tied his ankles tightly to its legs with wire and pinioned his wrists behind his back with the same agonizing stricture by means of handcuffs.

Then they beat him with socks filled with sand until his face swelled, and his arms, back and kidneys were sending such white-hot flashes of pain shooting through his brain that he wanted only to pass out, to die. But these were professional heavies; they stopped when they could see that he was on the brink of losing consciousness. They beat him systematically and unerringly, and only after they had given him a good going over did they start asking questions. The three men, all in their thirties, were muscular and brutal. Had they not been in the pay of a state they would have been doing the same strong-arm stuff for the Mafia or some other bunch of crooks. They didn't really care who was paying. They did what they were told to do and never gave any thought to the rights and wrongs of it. They might not have gone so far as to say that they enjoyed their work, although they certainly did gain some satisfaction from inflicting pain on other people. It wasn't in their nature to wonder about the meaning of life or come up with motives for the things they were told to do. There was just one thing they were good at: acting as the muscle for cooler, more rational minds that did not always care to know the source of the information they procured. Violence was an inextricable part of their lives; they were called upon when someone had to be punished, or when information had to be obtained on the spot. Two of them were married; they loved their children and respected their wives. The third had been an esteemed member of the local wrestling club back in Vladimir. Once the fat elderly man now wallowing in a pool of his own blood, vomit, urine and excrement had told them what they wanted to know, they would chuck him out of the car onto one of Berlin's countless building sites where he would just have to hope that someone found him and got him to hospital. They had been instructed not to kill him. Somewhere along the way he was evidently part of the family and would not, under any circumstances, go telling tales. To do that, he knew, would be tantamount to signing his own death warrant.

When they were done they would take a bath, call a mobile number in Denmark and relay the information, then they would have a few beers before going home.

One of the hoods grabbed Kravtjov by the hair and pulled his head back until the bloody face with its split lips and eyebrows and broken nose was turned to the ceiling. Without raising his voice he said:

'Who is the bastard? Your little sniper. The guy you met in the park. What's his name?'

For an old guy he was a pretty hard nut, but the thug could tell he was on the verge of cracking. All men cracked sooner or later. That you could be sure of. Everybody had their limit, and he was approaching his. The heavy tugged Kravtjov's hair sharply, then let go and slapped him twice in the face. As if on cue the other two thugs brought the sand-filled socks down on Kravtjov's back and arms. Kravtjov gurgled and rolled his head back and forth.

'We've got all the time in the world,' the heavy said. 'But you don't. Get it over with. Come on! Bastard! Who is he?'

The Russian voice reached Kravtjov's ears from a long way off. The language he knew so well did not seem to make any sense. He hurt all over. The pain in his chest was the worst; it felt as though they were squeezing his heart with red-hot tongs. His left arm was almost paralysed with pain. He felt more blows landing on his body and heard the crunch when one of the hoods punched him smack in the face. He couldn't take any more.

'Vuk. Vuk.'

He did not recognize his own voice. It sounded frail and cracked. His arm and his chest were hurting so badly. They musn't hit him anymore. He was dying.

'Stop. Stop. Stop,' said Kravtjov. 'Don't hit me anymore. Vuk. Vuk. The Serbian Dane.'

The thug took a step back.

'Get some water,' he said. 'The bastard's ready to talk.'

Chapter 15

Per Toftlund received the call from Kammarasov early in the morning at his office and arranged to meet him in Fælledparken in half an hour. He got in touch with his team and asked them to be ready for a briefing session around 11.00 am. He told John, his second-in-command, that when he came back he would probably have some information that would give them a solid lead. He hoped he was right. He had a bad feeling about this whole set-up, although he could not have said exactly why, there was nothing he could put his finger on. But he was so used to trusting his instincts that it would never have occurred to him to disregard his misgivings on this occasion.

The day was cloudy, and the wind sighed in the trees in Fælledparken as he got out of his car and made his way over to the Pavilion. Igor Kammarasov was already there, leaning against one of the pillars, smoking a cigarette. He wore an elegantly tailored suit, a navy-blue overcoat and a discreet scarf. All that was wanting was the fedora and he could have been the tragic hero in a movie from the forties, except that there was nothing sorrowful about his face, his expression was one of loathing and contempt. He saw Per coming and straightened up, but he did not wave, nor did he offer his hand when Per walked up. They had the place to themselves.

Kammarasov came straight to the point:

'His name's Vuk. Or at least, that's what he calls himself. An assumed name, no doubt. Surname unknown. Blond, blue eyes, just over six foot in height, 168 pounds, muscular, athletic. Speaks Danish like a native. Trained at the Yugoslavian Federal Army Special Forces School. Parents were Bosnian Serbs, killed in the civil war. Your man is an ace marksman, a sniper with a lot of lives on his conscience from the war down there.'

Igor Kammarasov rattled all of this off as if delivering a report, with deadpan features and an eye that studiously avoided Per's. And not merely out of shame. Something had gone wrong, Per could tell.

'What papers is he travelling on? I suppose Kravtjov must have procured them for him?'

'A Danish passport and a British one. Both clean.'

'Names, Igor?'

'Something ending in "sen". Common name. Our informant couldn't remember the British name. He became a bit vague. Turned out he had a weak heart.'

Kammarasov looked at Per, as if entreating him to ask about the interrogation instead, but the policeman was not to be put off.

'How come he speaks Danish?' he asked.

'Would you like to know how I obtained this information?'

Per shook his head. It wasn't too hard to figure out how Igor had come by these facts so quickly and efficiently.

Kammarasov looked him straight in the eye:

'Your man was born the son of Yugoslavian immigrant workers living somewhere in Copenhagen, probably in '69.'

'Their names?'

'That information was not forthcoming.'

'This is much better, Igor. But there are still a few gaps.'

'There's no more where that came from. My source suddenly dried up. But this Vuk will be hard to track down. He looks just like all the rest of you.'

'What about your informant's contacts?'

'I don't seem to remember that being part of the deal.'

Toftlund weighed up the situation. He could possibly ask Kammarasov to make use of his Russian military connections with the Serbs to get hold of this so-called Vuk's army file. But that would be a slow business, even at best, and they didn't have much time. Besides which, strictly speaking, Igor had paid his dues. Per tried not to imagine how Kravtjov had died and under what circumstances, but it would not be easy to live with. Nor could he share this knowledge with anyone else. He would have to keep it to himself.

'Right, Igor,' Per said. 'You wouldn't happen to have a picture of this man?'

'I'm afraid not.'

Per stood for a moment. They regarded one another, and that which remained unspoken, the fact that a man had lost his life because of them, and that they shared the burden of guilt, was an invisible chain binding them to one another. Per removed the negative from its flimsy little envelope and handed it to Igor. The latter stuffed it into his coat pocket without looking at it.

'There are no copies, Igor.'

Igor eyed Per. Then he said:

'Goodbye, Mr Toftlund. I doubt if we shall meet again.'

He turned and left. Per watched the lean Russian stride off across the dew-spangled grass. No, it was hardly likely. Igor felt very much at home in Denmark, but he would have to seek another posting or return home to Moscow. Knowing what they now had on him, he could no longer operate openly or undercover. In the old days Per would have taken advantage of this situation to try to turn him, get him to spy for Denmark, but he was glad that such a move was not called for in this instance. To be honest, he had always liked Igor. If circumstances had been different, they could have been friends.

Toftlund rounded up his team and filled them in on the new development. It was still going to be extremely difficult to find Vuk in a city the size of Copenhagen with so little to go on; nonetheless, Toftlund wanted them to instigate a systematic check of all small hotels and produce a formal description for distribution to the mobile units, just in case one of them should come across the Danish-speaking Serb. They knew that it was an almost hopeless exercise, that if they did turn him up, it would be more by good luck than anything else. The town was crawling with fair-haired, blue-eyed, athletic men who spoke Danish. But if he were to put a foot wrong, at least now they knew what they were dealing with. Toftlund warned them that Vuk was dangerous. He was a killer; they should on no account try to play the hero by taking him on single-handed in the unlikely event that they ran into him. Things weren't looking too good, and yet somehow the mood in the room had brightened. The case seemed more concrete now. There was an assassin in the city, they had a description to which – while it was by no means perfect – they could relate when it came to guarding Simba. They also had evidence of a definite threat that would, with any luck, prompt *Politiken* and

Simba to cancel the visit and, if nothing else, would make it easier to scrape together the necessary resources for the assignment.

By the end of the meeting everyone was feeling more positive.

'How are your sea legs, John?' Per asked.

'You know very well how they are. Why'd you ask?'

'Because we're taking a trip out to Flakfortet. But first we have to pick up a lovely lady.'

'A-ha! I thought there was something different about you. Christ man, you're in love.'

'I might be.'

'But she's married.'

'That's not my problem,' said Per.

'My God, you're an unprincipled bugger!' cried John, picking up the jacket that hung over the back of his chair. It was the same style as Per's, only in air force blue. John had been married for ten years to a girl he had gone to school with, and they seemed to Per to be as much in love now as when he had seen them being married in church. Part of him was happy that he hadn't been with the same woman for ten years, and yet he was a trifle envious of John's stable relationship, his cosy home and two lovely boys. Maybe he too was about ready for that, to give it a go at least, although the thought of suddenly having to share everything with another person and always feeling under an obligation to someone else also scared him. But he had meant what he said: Lise was a lovely lady.

In her office in the *Politiken* building Lise Carlsen was writing a press release for distribution to the newspapers and television stations. It took the form of an invitation by Danish PEN to a press conference with the German writer Herbert Scheer. Journalists were to meet on the quayside in Nyhavn, next to the old warehouse now housing the Hotel Nyhavn. From there they would be taken by boat to a certain location in the city – although due to threats against the writer's life by German and Danish neo-Nazis this was being kept secret – where Scheer would be waiting to meet them. Only those members of the press who had put their names down in advance would be allowed on board. A light lunch would be served. She would be glad when the Santanda visit was over and she could get back to practising proper journalism again. And turn her attention to all the other work that was piling up on her desk. She was way behind in the correspondence that fell to her lot as chair of Danish PEN. It involved a lot more work than she had envisaged when she had accepted the post, feeling flattered to have been chosen as a respected journalist and a skilled organizer. But she had also wanted the job. It had been time for a generation shift and for a woman to take the chair. Tagesen had relieved her of all other duties during the run-up to Santanda's visit, so she didn't feel she was letting down the paper, but she missed the day-to-day routine. Afterwards she would find the time and energy to sort out her own messed-up life. Talk things through with Ole, figure out what it was she wanted from Per. She hardly saw Ole at all. She had gone home early the day before, but there had been no sign of him. They had had breakfast together but said very little. Her heart had gone out to him. He looked slightly pathetic, a bit tired, older. With none of Per's vigour and robustness. He looked so frail sitting there, with his shoulders drooping. Greyish, porcelain-like pallor. It wasn't fair to compare them, but she did it all the time. She felt so much younger and stronger. She had a lot of laughs with Per. When had she and Ole last had a good laugh together? She felt sorry for him but knew that if she showed the slightest sign of pity, he would hit the roof.

'Should I make dinner this evening?' she had asked in one such fit of compassion, even though she knew very well that when it came to it she would probably cry off and go into the office or home with Per instead.

'I'll be eating out tonight,' he had replied.

She had been surprised to find that he actually had a life outside of her.

'Oh? Who with?'

Ole had studied her with his weary, slightly bloodshot eyes, but there had been a touch of the old Ole sarcasm in his voice when he said:

'A man, Lise. A young man I met, and whom I've spoken to a couple of times. A lonesome Jutlander, all on his own like me.'

Then she had left, calling back over her shoulder that she would be late home, and bang went yet another opportunity for reconciliation or, if nothing else, a chance to talk. The worst of it was that as soon as she walked out of the door she felt on top of the world: she was on her way to a newspaper office where she really enjoyed working, and afterwards she would be meeting a man she was mad about and with whom, with any luck, later that same day she would make love, if he asked her to come home with him. She didn't like being the dependent one, but at the same time she couldn't do without him. It was like being a teenager again. It was dreadful, really, and yet absolutely wonderful. She felt so alive.

She lit a cigarette and brought her mind back to the press release on the computer screen. It would all work out all right, she was sure, and even if the sky was grey, it wasn't raining, and she was looking forward to the sail out to Flakfortet.

The *White Whale* was a lovely, low-hulled, wooden boat. It was tied up alongside the quay in Nyhavn among all the other wooden boats. The pavement cafés at the feet of the old ochre-, red- and brown-painted houses were crowded with people. The sailboats bobbed gently, and the breeze tugged at their pennants. A canal-tour boat was chugging out of the harbour, and a hydrofoil from Sweden was on its way in. The whole scene was like something off a tourist board poster, Lise thought happily. The *White Whale* had a small quarterdeck, with a life raft slung above it in its canister. The boat could be steered from outside on the quarterdeck by means of a large, old-fashioned wheel and an engine telegraph with a lever for controlling the speed.

Hanging in front of the wheel was a fine old bell, but the sleek motorboat was also equipped with both radio and sonar. The skipper was a man in his thirties who gave his name simply as Jon and introduced his deckhand as Lars. They seemed to know Per and John, who both hopped on board. Per helped her down onto the deck and showed her first the wheelhouse, from which Jon could steer the boat in bad weather, and then the cabin, where six to eight people could be fitted around the table. It was very cosy, with curtains at the portholes, and she also noticed a tiny galley. But it was slightly claustrophobic too. The thought of living on a cramped little boat, with sails or without, did not appeal to Lise. She much preferred the idea of being up on deck in the stern, where she could enjoy the view of Copenhagen's lovely harbour as Jon headed the boat out into the Sound with deft finesse. Lise felt the wind in her hair and gazed at the water, which shifted from grey to bluish-green when the sun broke through the high clouds. A glass of home-brewed aquavit was popped into her hand by Jon, who was steering the *White Whale* from the large wheel on the quarterdeck. The aquavit was strong and bitter-tasting, but it was just the thing on such a bracing day. They made good speed past Tre Kroner Fort and on past the second old army fortress, Middelgrund. Beyond this she could now make out a little dark blotch on the waters of the Sound: the outermost fortress, Flakfortet. Jon did not bear straight towards their destination; instead he appeared to come at it in a wide arc. As if reading the puzzlement on her face he proceeded to explain about the waters on their starboard side, which he called the Dirty Sea. It sounded both alarming and poetic. The Dirty Sea was a large stretch of the sea off Flakfortet and the island of Saltholm where the water was no more than a couple of feet deep. For centuries Copenhagen had used this area as a dumping ground. It was full of railway sleepers and concrete blocks, building rubbish and the hulks of old ships. Only a dinghy or a very flat-bottomed boat could cross that patch. That was why they had to cut round it.

'You get some right fat eels out here,' Per said. 'Don't you, Jon?'

'Oh yes. Over the years the local gangsters have sent a few dead rivals to the bottom well wrapped up in nice cement overcoats,' Jon laughed.

Lise gave him a little dig. The three men were flirting with her, but in a nice way; Jon and John were showing that they knew she and Per were an item. Lars the deckhand kept to himself. A rather shy young man, he busied himself with making coffee in the pantry. Per wrapped a demonstrative arm around her and gave her a quick kiss. He had never done that in public before. It made her feel very happy, taking it as she did as a sign that he wanted to show the world they belonged together.

'So where do you know this buccaneer from?' she asked.

Jon laughed. He wasn't a tall man but slim and compact, like a good midfield player. The skin of his face was tanned and covered in lots of fine and very becoming lines. His black beard was neatly trimmed.

'Oh, the *White Whale* and I have been on Her Majesty's Secret Service on quite a few occasions,' he said.

'Meaning?'

'Ah, I'm not sure James Bond here would let me tell you that,' John replied, pointing at Per.

'Hah, what did you ever do except sit on your butt and get paid a packet by the government for doing sweet bugger-all?' Per retorted.

'Easy money, yeah. But if…'

'Yes, I know…'

Lise had no idea what they were talking about, but Per said oh, it was just that the *White Whale* was often pressed into service during visits by foreign heads of state or individuals whose lives had been threatened by madmen or fanatics. On such occasions the *White Whale* lay at the quay next to the Ministry of Foreign Affairs on Asiatisk Plads, thus affording the security service an alternative evacuation route if, as Per put it, the balloon should go up.

'So the *White Whale* will be carrying Sara out to Flakfortet? Right? That is your plan, isn't it?'

'Uh-huh. She may look old, but she can do seventeen knots when she has to.'

'Well, I only hope Sara is a good sailor. Or that we get good weather.'

'Yeah, it wouldn't be very funny if she threw up all over the world's press the first time they got the chance to ask her a couple of questions,' Per said.

The *White Whale* overtook a lumbering flat-bottomed ship with a wheelhouse in the stern. On the bow was a name in indecipherable Cyrillic script, and Lise recognized the Russian flag fluttering abaft, but in style the boat reminded her more of the barges she had seen on French rivers. The barge was flaking with rust and looked as poor and forlorn as the old Russian women she had seen begging on TV.

'It looks like an old barge,' she remarked.

'It's a filthy, rotten old shitheap of a Russian river barge,' Jon said. 'They're an accident just waiting to happen, those things. They were built for quiet river waters, not the open sea. They're flat-bottomed, unstable and don't have enough engine power. They stink to high heaven, they foul the water, and they're destroying the last vestiges of Denmark's small craft traffic.'

'They have to make a living, I suppose,' Lise said.

'So do the Danish seamen,' Jon rejoined, so curtly that she did not pursue the matter. It was too nice a day to argue about anything, especially politics. She looked back at the barge, butting laboriously through the waves, even though there was only the slightest of swells. She shuddered: it would be no joke if one of those were to go down off the Danish coast with its cargo of oil or coal. Actually, there was quite a good story there – she must remember to mention it to one of the other reporters.

Old Flakfort was looking its best when the *White Whale* nosed its way through the gap in the breakwater and into the harbour. The breakwater ran all the way round the fort. From the air, it looked rather like the ramparts encircling a medieval castle. The harbour entrance was the main gate, and the six-foot wide band between the breakwater and the fort was like a moat, protecting the fortress from the sea. A big break in the clouds allowed the sun's rays to turn the water blue and glint off the gleaming surfaces of the two sailboats moored in the harbour. The fort itself rose up into a grassy hillock surrounded by low bushes; Lise spotted a restaurant, a circular pavilion with a pointed roof reminiscent of an old-fashioned Chinese coolie hat and a small souvenir shop. Two men sat on a bench, shivering slightly as they tried to hang on to the last shreds of summer. Alongside the jetty lay a large boat that might have been an old, converted fishing boat. It had an open quarterdeck with a green canopy strung over it. A small group of people, mostly dads with young kids, were making their way on board. Jon eased the *White Whale* gently into the quay. Lise had never been out to Flakfortet before, but living in Copenhagen as she did, she knew of course that it was one of three forts designed as a defence against attack from the sea. But it had never seen battle, not even on the 9th of April 1940 when German bombers and troopships passed over and by it unchallenged. Its cannons had failed to function. The fort had been decommissioned after the war; it had fallen into disrepair and been vandalized by weekend sailors landing on the islet illegally and plundered by people on the hunt for stone or copper, of which there was no shortage out here. But the old fortress was now a listed building and a favourite spot for summer outings. Renovation work was currently being carried out on it, but still intact inside – and out of bounds to the general public – were a lot of the old casemates and ammunition stores.

Per pointed to the fishing boat, the *M/S Langø* it was called:

'We close off Flakfortet for the day of Simba's visit. There aren't so many pleasure boats around at this time of year, and if there should be a couple in the harbour, we'll check them out. We'll go over the fort with a fine-tooth comb the evening before and again the next morning.'

The last passengers had climbed aboard the *M/S Langø*, and Lise could see from the water that the propeller had started turning.

Per carried on:

'We ferry the press across first in that boat there. We simply charter it for the day and close the fort to the general public. Then we bring Simba over in the *White Whale* and hold the press conference in the restaurant…'

'The television people are going to love this,' Lise interjected.

'What do you mean?'

'Well, look at the pictures they can get out here.'

'Yeah, right. Loads,' Per countered dryly. 'Because I'll be putting three or four men with rifles and machine guns on top of the fort. There's a clear view for miles around. Not so much as a rowboat can get anywhere near without them seeing it. And a couple of men down below, outside the restaurant. Also armed, of course. Screeds of pictures. But it'll be as secure as anything can be in this world.'

'Well, well. I'm impressed. You've thought of everything, haven't you?'

'No, that you can never do.'

They went ashore, and Per made the necessary arrangements with the restaurateur, who had not the slightest objection to being closed to the public for a day once he heard that a whole boatload of reporters would have to kick their heels in his restaurant for an hour. He happily provided them with details of his staff: the chef, a waiter, an assistant in the kiosk, a guide and a washer-up. It was off-season, so they didn't need a lot of staff unless they had to cater for a large party, and they had no big bookings at the moment. The staff worked on a rota. One lot came over on the boat on Tuesday and stayed until Saturday, when a fresh team took over until the following Tuesday. The second team was slightly bigger: they were always busier at weekends. The staff lived in small, well-appointed rooms in the renovated section of the casemates. It was rather like being on a ship at sea. They could see the lights of Copenhagen but couldn't simply pop over to the city if they felt like it. It was a somewhat unusual working situation, a bit like being on an oil platform in the North Sea, but you could get hooked on it, and most of the staff had been working out at Flakfortet for years, not least because the pay was good. Yes, the police could have a list of their names. No, he was sure they wouldn't mind. He knew every one of them. There was no strange, Danish-speaking foreigner among them. A boat came over every day with fresh raw ingredients, but it was the same boat as always, and he knew every member of the crew.

Per and Lise walked up onto the top of Flakfortet hand in hand. The Danish and Swedish coastlines stood out sharply in the limpid light. Grass grew over the roof of the fortress. Lise saw that Per was right. From huge container ships to tiny yachts, every craft on the blue waters of the Sound was clearly visible. Nothing would be able to get close to the fort. They wandered past the old gun carriages and down into the bowels of the fortress. Some of the bunker passageways were well lit and clear; others were dank and dark. Some of the casemates lay open; others were blocked off by steel doors or chains and padlocks. It must be pretty cold and damp in the locked rooms, Lise thought. She had visions of rats and all sorts of other creepy-crawlies inhabiting the old ammunition stores – but, Per told her, one thing she certainly wouldn't have to worry about was spiders: with a constant temperature of ten degrees Celsius down there in the dark, flies and other spider fodder could not survive.

As they walked Per gave her the bare bones of what he had been told by his informant. He also broke his usual rule by telling her that, in keeping with the new spirit of the times, it had been friends in the Russian secret service who had assisted Denmark in this matter. But he didn't tell her how the information had been obtained. They now had a description of sorts and confirmation that a contract had been taken out, so there would probably not be as much resistance within the system to according him the necessary resources. The politicians still refused to meet Simba, and nothing seemed likely to change that. Even in the Danish political system the financial considerations outweighed the human.

'They're a bunch of bloody hypocrites,' Lise muttered.

Per did not answer.

'Don't you think so?'

'It makes no difference what I think,' he said and drew her away from the musty gloom into a brightly lit passageway.

She was a little put out by this, but he didn't appear to notice, had already changed tack.

'Actually it's quite comforting to know that the contract has gone to a professional.'

'You don't mean that, surely!'

'Yes, I do. Because there's a chance this man could infiltrate Flakfortet – always assuming he finds out that this is where the press conference is being held. And how is he supposed to do that? I mean, so far everybody seems to be keeping their lips sealed about the actual schedule for the visit. But just suppose he did – there's no way he can get off again. And our man's a pro. Not some crazy Muslim with his heart set on martyrdom, showing up here with ten pounds of explosive under his shirt.'

'So why is he doing it?'

'*Quien sabe*? Who knows? Money probably. Isn't that usually what drives people? That or sex.'

'What a cynical character you are.'

'I am?'

'Yes, you are. There are other people in the world, you know, besides the sort you mix with.'

'They may have a little more polish, but everybody can be bought. You just have to know their price, sweetheart.'

'Don't call me "sweetheart",' she snapped, letting go of his hand and walking ahead of him towards the light at the end of the concrete passageway. She was annoyed with him and with herself, and those dark corridors gave her the willies. But she wasn't going to let him talk down to her as if she were a child. She hated the shallow cynicism that seemed to her to permeate modern society. Through her work for Danish PEN, she had been given detailed insight into the appalling cruelties devised by regimes and, hence, individuals to plague and torment their fellow human beings. She had spoken to lots of authors and journalists who had been imprisoned, tortured and abused. She had learned more than she wanted to know about repression and evil. But she was not going to allow that to discourage her or make her cynical. Because then the torturers would have won. She had to believe in the good, believe that it could win through.

It was good to be back out in the open air. The sky had clouded over again; a sudden shower of rain swept over the Swedish coast, a grey striated curtain masked the horizon, but it rained itself out before it reached the Sound, and only minutes later she beheld a perfect rainbow arching over the mainland. She took it as a good sign and for the first time felt sure that everything would turn out all right in the end. With Ole, with Per, and with Sara.

Like a film with a happy ending.

Chapter 16

Ole Carlsen and Vuk had dinner together in a small French restaurant in the city centre, a place where Ole had dined with Lise a few times when they first met. He had chosen it in a burst of nostalgia, although to be honest he felt the food there was overpriced. But it was highly rated, had become quite trendy again, and he was keen to impress his new young friend. As soon as they stepped through the door Ole noticed one of Danish television's new light-entertainment hosts sitting with a party at a good table in the corner. 'Aha, so Carl Ohmann comes here,' he remarked, but Vuk merely eyed the gentleman in question indifferently, as if he had no idea who his companion was talking about. Although that couldn't possibly be the case, not after all the coverage the man had received. He had devised a totally new form of Saturday-night entertainment that had been the talk of the country over most of the winter and spring. But there were a number of things about Vuk that Ole found odd and not quite in keeping with his job as a plastic-bag salesman. He was interested in the wrong things.

Vuk was smart but casual in a light-coloured shirt, neatly pressed blue flannels and a grey tweed jacket, but no tie. Several times during the course of the day Ole Carlsen had considered getting out of dinner and plucking up his courage to have it out with Lise instead. He had called the newspaper office only to be told that she was out on a job. No, they couldn't say where she was. So he had pulled himself together and attended to his clients, listened to their problems and endeavoured to solve them, although increasingly he had the feeling that there was nothing he could say, nothing he could do to cure the neuroses from which more and more Danes seemed to be suffering. If he had had to find one word to describe his state of mind it would have been 'confused'. Like most of the Danish population apparently.

But he was glad he had kept the date. He enjoyed having dinner with the engaging young Jutlander, who appeared to be quite content with his life and his job selling plastic bags to supermarkets, for people to put their potatoes into and weigh them themselves. The Danish people were now said to be living in a service economy, when the truth was that the one thing of which there was less and less now was service. Back in the days when a petrol station was known as a filling station, it actually provided a service. An attendant filled up your tank, checked your oil, topped up the air in your tyres and washed your windscreen. Then they started calling them 'service stations', and the customer had to do everything himself. Ole could see the paradox and found it funny when Carsten – as he thought Vuk was called – pointed this out over dinner, in the course of all their chat about this and that, everything and nothing. Ole felt so at ease with this young man. They had drunk some excellent wine, were onto their second bottle in fact, and going by the way he felt, Ole realized that he must have consumed the lion's share of it. Although he had to admit that he had had a head start. It was a bad habit, he knew, but he needed a little nip every now and again throughout the day, so he kept a bottle of vodka at the clinic. It was better than pills anyway, and soon, once he had more control over things in his private life, the bottle would be history. But the last few years had been a living hell: following the derout, from the outside as it were; looking on as a marriage crumbled and two people stopped caring about one another. How had this happened? He was a psychologist, but he could not come up with the answer. He could analyse the problem: they did not talk to one another, they meant nothing to one another, they were forever rubbing each other up the wrong way, but he could not put his finger on how or when it had all started to go downhill. When the love they shared had died. Over the past couple of weeks things had gone from bad to worse. He was afraid he was going to lose Lise if he did not get a grip on himself. If he left it any longer, it would be too late. He freely admitted to himself that he was still in love with her and that he would miss her terribly if she left him. But he found it impossible to come out of his shell and talk the whole thing over with her, put his longing and his love for her into words. And this despite the fact that he belonged to a generation which believed implicitly that everything was up for discussion and that there was nothing that couldn't be straightened out by a good heart-to-heart. Now, suddenly, words failed him. He was convinced that Lise had taken a lover. He was insanely jealous, although deep down he considered jealousy to be a destructive, immature emotion, not to say a character flaw, which had a part to play in the breakdown of most relationships. That, at any rate, was what he had often told the couples whom he counselled. Was that why he could not bring himself to simply go down on his knees in front of Lise and beg her to take him back, to talk to him so that together they could try to make a fresh start and see if they could rekindle the flame which had once burned between them and was now dying out? There might still be a spark into which they could breathe life. Why didn't he just beg her to help him? Could it be that he was somehow incapable of begging? Helped along by the wine, he became quite weepy at the thought of a reconciliation.

Vuk filled Ole's glass and raised his own.

'Cheers, mate. Let me get this, will you? It's been a really nice evening. You get tired of always eating alone.'

Ole also raised his full glass.

'No, it's me who should thank you. I needed the company too.'

They put the glasses to their lips. Vuk sipped his wine, Ole gulped down half a glassful. He couldn't really taste it anymore. Vuk noticed that his speech was also becoming a bit slurred. Not much. He carried it well, but he hissed his 's's.

'So…what does your wife say to you being on the road so much with your plastic bags?' Ole asked.

'I'm not married, Ole, remember?'

'Oh, that's right. You're not. Lucky man, eh?'

'Well, I'm not that old, you know. I hope some day I'll find the right girl for me. Have kids. Settle down. Right now, though, I'm happy playing the field. This way of life suits me fine right now.'

'But selling plastic bags for a living.' Ole said. 'What kind of a life is that?'

'Solving other people's problems day in, day out – what kind of a life is that?'

'Well, it's easier than solving one's own,' Ole said.

Vuk flashed him a warm smile. He knew he had a nice sympathetic smile, that he inspired confidence, that he was a good listener. He could play that part to perfection. So Vuk bided his time. Ole drained his glass and allowed Vuk to refill it before saying:

'The thing is that you invest everything you've got in a marriage… And somewhere along the way you lose touch with your mates. The guys who were such an important part of your life when you were younger. And you get scared. Of suddenly finding yourself all alone in the world.'

'You can always make new friends.'

'It's not so easy. As you get older you become more distanced from other people. It creeps up on you like the dark of winter.'

Ole Carlsen smiled wryly at his own metaphor. Vuk smiled too and said:

'I'm still young.'

'Well, I feel very lucky and very happy to have met you, young man.'

Vuk lifted his glass and watched Ole drink.

'Same here,' he said. He wondered briefly whether the time had come to make his play. Ole's eyes were moist, his vision as blurred as his speech, and he was getting maudlin, so Vuk continued:

'I'd really like to invite you back for a drink, but I don't think my hotel room is the ideal place for entertaining…'

'Why don't you come back to my place?'

'What's your wife going to say to that?'

'Lise? She's never bloody there.'

'It's up to you, you know, if you want to talk about it…'

Ole tipped the last of the bottle into his glass.

'Oh, what the hell, let's have a brandy with our coffee. On me. You'll let me do that, at least.'

He beckoned to the waitress. Like the staff of most Copenhagen restaurants she was young and, hence, cheap labour. Ole ordered coffee and two brandies.

'I don't think there's much chance of saving our marriage,' he said once the waitress had gone off with their order. She hadn't asked which make of brandy they wanted, which was typical. She probably didn't drink anything but Coke anyway, but Ole really couldn't have cared one way or the other. He went on: 'But we'd like to have a go at it. I mean, we are grownups, right?'

Vuk nodded. Ole had said more or less the same thing earlier in the evening, but he was starting to repeat himself. Which was good. Vuk let him ramble on:

'We'll have more time together in a week or so. Then we'll have to talk things through. It might even be easier then. Now that I've discussed it with you, Carsten. You're such a good listener. I feel I've managed to get things straight in my head.'

'Thanks. But why should it be easier in a week's time?'

Carlsen regarded him. For a moment Vuk was afraid he had been too direct. The waitress appeared and placed two glasses of brandy, cups and a pot of coffee on their table. Vuk poured coffee for them both and avoided looking at Ole as the latter resumed.

'Why should it be easier? Well, I shouldn't really be telling you this…but honestly, all this secrecy's a bit much. Does the name Sara Santanda mean anything to you?'

Vuk shook his head.

'No, of course not,' Ole corrected himself. 'You're in plastic bags, right? She's this writer whom the Iranians want dead. She's coming to Denmark in a week's time, Lise's in charge of organizing the visit. She's collaborating with PET on the security arrangements and is probably being screwed rigid by some brainless cop *as we speak*.'

Ole lifted his brandy glass and drained it. His voice had been close to breaking by the end of the sentence.

'That's not necessarily the case,' Vuk said.

Ole steadied himself.

'I'm rather afraid that that is *exactly* the case.'

'I'm sorry to hear it.'

'Thanks, Carsten. You're a good man, so you are, but if it hadn't been this one, it would probably have been someone else. In any case, she's not at home, and to tell the truth I don't really feel like sitting there all alone or going on to a pub, so if you would like…'

'I'd love to,' Vuk said, smiling. But Ole did not see the triumph in that smile.

They took a taxi to the Carlsens' apartment. Ole had some trouble with his balance as he unlocked the door. Vuk made a round of the apartment when Ole took himself off to the toilet. The open-plan kitchen was neat and tidy. The living room was furnished with modern pieces in pale soft colours. Books covered the whole of one wall and in a corner a cream-coloured leather sofa and two leather chairs, all nicely worn-in, were arranged round a coffee table. You could sit there and drink coffee or swivel the chairs round to watch TV. On a sideboard which looked as though it might be an antique, stood framed photographs of Ole and Lise: happy snaps in which they had their arms around one another. And pictures of each of them on their own, taken on holidays abroad. A hallway led to the bathroom and toilet, from which Vuk could hear the sound of running water, and beyond them three rooms: the bedroom with its double bed, a room containing a computer and books on psychology, and another room with yet another computer, Vuk noted, when he quickly switched on the light and popped his head round the door, still listening out for the splash of water. The larger of the two rooms was obviously Lise's. There were newspapers, magazines, books and floppy disks scattered all over the place. A telephone and an answering machine stood on a modern desk. Apart from these and a pile of papers, the desk was completely clear. On the wall hung a poster from Expo '92 in Seville and a beautiful picture of a flamenco dancer. Vuk returned to the living room and gazed down at the street below. There was no traffic on the road, only an elderly man walking past with his dog. The glow from the sign on the pub opposite fell softly on a rain puddle.

Ole came in and urged him to take a seat. He fetched a bottle of whisky, two glasses and a bowl of ice and poured two generous measures. It was almost as if he had made up his mind to drink himself out of, or into, oblivion, because in no time flat he had finished his drink and was refilling his glass. Vuk was full of compliments for the apartment, the furniture and all the laden bookshelves. He could see that Ole was very drunk now, so he wasn't surprised by the sudden change of mood when Ole peered at him and said:

'Christ, you're a strange one, Carsten. In some ways, I mean. You know just about everything there is to know about me. I don't know the first thing about you. Who are you, really?'

'A dumb Jutlander,' said Vuk, on his guard now. He didn't want to have to resort to violence unless absolutely necessary. He lit a cigarette and held the pack of Prince out to Ole, but instead the other man took one of his own Kings, from a yellow pack that was new to Vuk.

'Nah! There's a lot more to you than meets the eye,' Ole drawled.

'I suppose the same could be said of anybody.'

'No, I mean…you're Danish, but somehow you're different.'

'How do you mean?' Vuk asked warily.

'I don't know. I can't quite put my finger on it. But take Carl Ohmann, for instance. Most people would have made some comment about him sitting in that corner having dinner. But anyone would have thought you didn't know who he was.'

'And?'

'It's just odd, that's all, when you live in this country. And you do live here, don't you?'

'Of course I do!'

'Maybe you just don't watch much television?'

'No, I don't suppose I do.'

Vuk rose and walked across to the sideboard. He picked up one of the photographs – of Lise, somewhere down south. She was dressed in a little top and shorts, smiling and squinting at the camera. Her skin was tanned, and just visible in the background were some mountains and a patch of blue sea.

'You've got a lovely wife, you know,' Vuk said, but Ole was not about to be sidetracked:

'Where did you go to school? Did you graduate from high school? Do you have a girlfriend?'

Vuk turned to face Ole. The menace crept into his eyes, and the smile on his lips was, he felt, stiff and false. They were venturing onto dangerous ground.

'Father-fixation, unhappy childhood, rotten sex life,' he laughed.

'Exactly.'

Ole was very, very drunk now, Vuk saw. The whisky had gone straight to his head, and he wasn't even pretending to savour it now. It just had to be gulped down. It just had to black everything out.

Ole was still wittering on:

'Exactly. We all have our baggage. There's something inside you that wants out. Something mysterious. And frightening. You're walking along a road, and there are a whole lot of signposts, but you've lost your bearings, can't decide which sign to follow. Or maybe it's actually me who feels like that.'

Vuk put the photograph back in its place.

'Very lovely wife. You shouldn't let her go gallivanting all over the place.'

175

Ole Carlsen laughed again, an affected, drink-sodden hoot. He lifted up the bottle and sloshed more whisky into his own empty glass and into Vuk's, although this was still half-full. He did not add ice this time, just knocked it back again and underwent another abrupt mood shift, as the seriously inebriated are wont to do. He became tearful and sentimental.

'Oh, she's lovely all right. Christ, yeah. C'mere, Carsten. Fuck's sake man, sit down and have another little drink. C'mon, mystery man. Lovely wife! God Almighty. Lovely! I'll say she is. But what bloody good does that do?'

Vuk sat down. He took a drink, and after twenty minutes Ole's head began to nod and his utterances grew more and more incoherent. He had been talking about Lise and his life with her. About how happy they had been, the holidays they had gone on together. About how much he loved her, and how fuckin' wonderful she was, and what a damn shame it was that they couldn't have children, and about that bloody bitch Santanda, who should just stay the hell away from here, and a dumb cop who might have something between his legs but nothing between his ears, and about what a rotten fucking mess his life was in. And how he couldn't take it any longer. At last Vuk was able to ease the lit cigarette from between his fingers and lift his feet up onto the sofa.

Vuk sat for five minutes smoking a cigarette and considering the sleeping man. Ole was breathing deeply and heavily. His cigarette finished, Vuk got to his feet and gave Ole a gentle nudge. He didn't stir. He was miles away.

Vuk walked down the hallway and into Lise's office. Her computer was an IBM model with which he was familiar; he switched it on. Alongside it was a disk case. It was locked. There were three drawers on either side of the desk next to the computer table. While the computer was loading he checked each one in turn. The top drawer on the right-hand side was locked. Vuk took out his pocket-knife and slid it into the crack, located the bolt and unlocked the drawer. Inside were some bank statements and a small key The computer finished loading, and he found himself looking at the well-known layout of Windows 5.1.

Vuk clicked on the icon for Wordperfect, and the bright blues and reds of the word processing programme flashed up onto the screen. It surprised him slightly that a large newspaper concern such as *Politiken* should still be using the 5.1 version, but that wasn't his problem. He sat down on Lise's office chair and systematically set to work.

By pressing 'F5' he gained access to a list of files. He ran an eye over it: Articles, Report, Pen, Pol, Personal, Letters, Notes. Vuk's hands were steady as he proceeded to go into the various files, folders and documents. Not a thing. He hadn't expected Lise to leave a printout of the schedule for Sara Santanda's visit lying about, but nor would she be experienced enough not to have it written down somewhere. What would she do? Plainly she worked at home as much as she did at her office in the *Politiken* building.

He took the small key from the drawer that had been locked. Not surprisingly, it fitted the disk case. In his experience, most people were pretty careless about computer safety or security in general. They never thought that they would be the victims of a break-in.

Inside the disk case were a number of floppy disks with dividers in between. Lise was well organized; behind the divider marked 'Danish PEN' were four floppy disks, each clearly labelled: 'Work in Progress', 'Meetings', 'Minutes', 'Simba'. 'Simba' sounded like a code word. The sort of thing an amateur would write on a disk. Vuk guessed that Lise was not the sort of person to muddy her trail any more than was absolutely necessary. You had to be trained always to remember to cover your tracks. And by writing down an unintelligible codename she had actually only made things easier for him.

He slid the disk into the A-drive, and a document entitled 'Simba' appeared on the screen, the only document on the disk. He pressed 'Enter' to open the document, but instead, at the bottom of the screen, up came the message: 'Error... Access denied'. She had clearly protected the document with a password. She assumed this meant that it could not be opened or copied. And she was quite right, but just because a document is password-protected doesn't mean the whole disk can't be copied.

Vuk helped himself to a disk from behind the divider marked 'Formatted'.

'Right, Lise. Disk copying time,' he murmured to himself.

It took only a moment for him to copy the disk and slip the copy into his pocket. That done, he placed the original back in the case exactly where he had found it and locked the case with the key. He put the key back in the drawer. Then he duly exited Windows and closed down the computer. There would be no sign of his break-in whatsoever, apart from one missing blank disk, and nobody kept an exact count of those.

Vuk switched off the light and went back to the living room.

Ole was still flat out on the sofa. He gave a little grunt, moaned softly in his sleep but seemed to be completely out of it. The ashtray was full; the living room stank of cigarette smoke and whisky. Vuk scanned the room. He knew he had not left anything behind him. It was past one o'clock, all was quiet in the apartment and out on the street, so he had no trouble hearing the sound of a key being inserted in the lock and, seconds later, the front door closing.

For a moment he stood as if turned to stone.

'Hello. It's only me. Hello-o. I'm home. Ole? Are you there?'

Vuk recognized Lise's voice, and that voice spurred him into action. He swiped at Ole's feet with one hand, knocking them down onto the floor, while with the other he slapped him around the ear, not hard enough to make a noise, but with a resounding precision guaranteed to rouse Ole from his stupor. He mussed up his own hair, plastering it down over his forehead, grabbed his half-full glass, splashed some whisky onto his shirt and threw himself into one of the armchairs with his legs sprawled. Ole gave his head a shake, leaned back in the sofa then put his head in his hands and groaned.

Vuk was now a drunken man staring in bewilderment at the woman now entering the living room.

Lise stared at them. With a mixture of anger, disgust and contempt she took in Ole, the almost empty bottle, the overflowing ashtray and the strange man who was goggling at her in bleary-eyed befuddlement. Her anger evaporated, leaving her merely upset. After all, what right did she have to be mad? She, who had come straight from her lover's bed, how could she cast the first stone? If she had found Ole in bed with another woman, then at least they would have been on equal terms. But there was no way she was on equal terms with the man across from her. She could see his belly under his partially unbuttoned shirt, the red eyes, the greasy rumpled hair. She did not see a man, she saw a loser, and she felt both sorry for him and sickened by him. She didn't love him anymore.

'*Jesus,* Ole,' she burst out.

'Aw shit, Ole. It's your wife. I'd better get the fuck outta here,' mumbled Vuk, struggling to string the words together. Ole clutched his head and groaned.

Vuk pulled himself to his feet, tottered drunkenly for a second, then braced himself and with some difficulty found his balance. He took a couple of steps towards Lise, almost fell as he put his glass down on the coffee table with exaggerated care, so forcefully that it tipped over and the amber liquid spilled out.

'Lady. I'm *outta* here' he said, flinging out his arm.

He made towards her. Saw Lise raise a hand as if to stop him and get him to explain himself, or maybe to strike him. He reacted instinctively, grabbed her arm in midair and held it in a vice-like grip while fixing her with eyes that were cold, menacing and stone-cold sober.

'Who are you? What are you doing with my husband?' she hissed.

Vuk sensed her fear, released her arm and lapsed back into the role of drunkard.

'We were just havin' a bloody whisky,' he said.

Lise stepped aside, leaving the way clear for him.

'Get out of here. Get out, damn you.'

'I'm gone,' Vuk cried, arms flailing so wildly that he almost keeled over.

Lise waited until she heard the front door close, then she sat down across from Ole. He straightened up and sat back in the sofa.

'This isn't going to work, Ole,' she said quietly. 'I've had enough.'

'Lise. Just let me get my breath back, then we'll talk about it.'

He was totally plastered, that she could see, but his speech was, in fact, perfectly lucid, as if he were making a great effort, or as if it had finally dawned on him that it was over.

'Who is he?'

'Just a guy I met in town. Carsten something or other. He sells plastic bags.'

This was evidently a big joke, because Ole began to titter. He reached for both cigarettes and glass, then gave this up as a bad job and slumped back in the sofa again.

'Has he been in my office?'

'No. We just sat here having a drink. He was with me the whole time. Oh, *God*, my head!'

'He scared me.'

'Carsten wouldn't hurt a fly. He just sells plastic bags.'

Ole bent forward and this time managed to get hold of the whisky glass. He took a swig, then started retching.

Lise jumped up.

'Oh, for Christ's sake, Ole. Don't start that now!'

She left him spewing his load. It seemed a fitting way to end a marriage. He could clean it up himself or wake up in his own vomit tomorrow morning. That was one sight she could happily live without.

She went through to her office. Nothing seemed to be out of place. She put a hand to the top right-hand drawer, and it slid open. She was sure she had locked it, although sometimes she did forget. She took out the little key and unlocked the disk case. Her heart beat a little faster, but the disk was right where it ought to be. She lifted it out and slipped it into her bag, then dialled Per's number. He answered right away; she could just picture him in his double bed, exactly as she had left him less than an hour ago.

'Hi, it's me. Is it all right if I come back over?' she said.

Chapter 17

Vuk had drunk enough for his demons to surface like monsters in his subconscious, but not enough for the alcohol to blot them out. As always he dreamed of the mountains around Pale, which lay there like a wolf stronghold surrounded by bloodthirsty enemies. They swarmed down on the town, clad in turbans and baggy trousers and brandishing long curving scimitars: men and women, shouting and screaming and mowing down everyone in their way, and the horizon was all ablaze. First his mother, then his father and then his sister were hacked to pieces before his very eyes. He stretched out his arms, but he was rooted to the spot. He stood there, petrified like Lot's wife, wanting to run, to react, to kill, but even though he was alive his muscles refused to respond. He was imprisoned within the armour of his body but saw everything with stark clarity. The colours were a yellowish-green shot with blood-red, he heard the rumble of the heavy bulldozer in the distance and knew that now the screaming would start. His own screaming, when the nightmare reached the point where the massive road roller hove into view, crushing everyone in its path until its huge steel cylinder was stained crimson with the people's blood, not only that of their enemies but also that of his own family who were suddenly standing there, alive again and terror-stricken in the face of its slowly grinding bulk. And he himself was driving the blood-roller.

Vuk was woken, not by his own screams but by the person in the room next door banging loudly on the wall. He switched on the light and lay there, trembling and drenched in sweat, staring at a ceiling, which was blurred and rippling like the surface of a pond broken by a stone. His heart was pounding fit to burst. It was a long time since it had been this bad. He was filled with dread, and he knew the reason why. His life no longer had focus. He no longer had a goal. The nationalistic fervour that had fed his own personal hatred had burned out, and in its place was a gaping void. He forced himself to think of Emma, of her face, her small delicate hands, her slender feet, her ankles, her slim thighs, her navel, her breasts, her face again. As if he were a sculptor fashioning her in his head. And by the time she stood, perfectly formed, before his mind's eye, his pulse rate had begun to slacken. He opened his eyes again. The ceiling and its hideous light fitting were back in focus.

Vuk got out of bed and found his cigarettes. He took a vodka from the minibar, knocked it back and smoked a cig. He picked up the disk that was lying on the bedside table and held it in his palm. He would force himself to focus on the job in hand. He would force himself to carry it through. He would force himself to shut out everything else and once more become the reliable machine he had been when he was fighting for the cause.

He paced the floor. The watch on his wrist said four o'clock. He had screamed out loud. He would have to change hotel again today. He switched on the television, took another miniature of vodka and sat down to watch CNN to keep his mind off things while he waited for it to get light outside. He was far too frightened to sleep.

Vuk had breakfast and read the Danish papers. Then he went back to his room, dismantled and then assembled his pistol, which he had stashed away in a locked suitcase. Every time he left the hotel room he smeared a little talcum powder around the keyholes, but no one had attempted to discover what he had in his case.

By ten o'clock he reckoned that Mikael would be awake. He had got hold of his parents' telephone number through directory enquiries. It turned out that they were still living in the same big house as when Mikael and Vuk were boys. Back then Vuk had been called something else, but Mikael, Vuk and Peter, whom Vuk had once seen on the Danish news, had been the three musketeers. Best pals. Mikael had to a great extent grown up along with the others in Nørrebro, in the inner city, while his extremely wealthy parents spent most of their time in Spain. Mikael had been a bit of an afterthought, and his parents had not wanted to spend any more time in Denmark than absolutely necessary, not once his father sold his firm, so he was left with his mother's sister, who was happy to have his company in her large apartment –

until he got to be big and pale and weird, but by then it didn't matter because he was old enough to live on his own in the mansion in Hellerup.

Vuk thought of all this as he took the train from the Central Station out to Hellerup. He had made this journey so many times before. He could still picture the house. Built in the twenties, on three floors, with a basement and masses of rooms. It sat down by the Sound, so close that you could walk from the lawn straight into the water. Mikael hadn't sounded surprised when he called. Half-asleep, but not really surprised. He had told Vuk to come whenever he liked. He had the house to himself. He did not seem to find it strange that Vuk should call him after all these years: it sounded as if he was living in a world of his own, without any normal sense of time.

Vuk was wearing his leather jacket, with his homemade garrotte in the pocket. He was the only person to get off at Hellerup station. The sun was shining from a clear blue sky as he walked down to Mikael's house. The bad dream from the night before was only a faint murmur at the back of his mind. He thought of Mikael and of Peter, who had had his heart set on being a journalist even back then and was now a reporter on the Danish news. But what about Mikael? There was only one thing he was interested in: computers. In his inside pocket Vuk had the disk from the Carlsens' apartment, he was hoping that Mikael would be able to crack the password and open the document for him.

Vuk pushed open the garden gate. The hedge was thick and overgrown, it screened a rank lawn covered in leaves, moss and seeded dandelions. Weeds peeped out of the four or five neglected flowerbeds. The house lay at the far end of the ground sloping down to the Sound. It was a white house and very beautiful, despite the flaking paint on the window frames. It had not been particularly well looked after, but with such a location it must nonetheless be worth a fortune.

Vuk pressed the bell and heard it ring out inside the house. It still had the same crisp, old-fashioned chime and brought back memories of boyhood games in the big garden and sailing on the Sound in the rowboat and dinghy. And later, high-school parties in this open hospitable home, where there was only one rule: everything had to be cleaned up before Mikael's parents got back. They, on the other hand, never showed up unannounced. They always gave the kids a chance to get things back to normal, at least to the point where the cleaner did not have undue cause for complaint.

Vuk heard footsteps approaching, and the door was opened.

They looked at one another. Mikael saw a tall, well-built man with lifeless blue eyes. He looked as though he hadn't shaved for a day or so because his face was covered with a short blond stubble. He saw a chum from his childhood and youth who hadn't changed a bit and yet was not the same person at all. The difference lay mainly in his eyes. They no longer looked as if laughter came easily to them.

Vuk saw a scrawny little guy who was already going thin on top. The eyes behind his thick glasses were lively and intelligent, and he had not lost his old habit of tugging his earlobe when excited or nervous. He wore a pair of battered jeans and a green shirt over a white T-shirt. He looked like the nerd he was, the clown of the trio, the boy with the big house.

'Hi, Mikael,' said Vuk.

Mikael tugged at his earlobe. He looked both pleased and bashful.

'Janos, you old *Gastarbeiter*! Long time, no see! Come on in. I've got the place all to myself.'

'Yeah, so you said on the phone,' Vuk said. Twice now, within the past couple of hours, he had heard his old name, his real name spoken out loud. He had used it himself when he called Mikael. 'Mikael. It's Janos,' he had said. But the name was alien to him, it belonged to someone else, not the person he was today. His family and his friends in Denmark had called him Janos, but Janos had died in the living hell of Bosnia, and out of the ashes had come Vuk, who might resemble Janos on the outside but not on the inside. Janos was dead. Vuk inhabited his body. The name Janos was as foreign to him as Carsten, the name by which Ole Carlsen knew him.

As usual, Mikael talked non-stop. The house looked exactly the same, with the large hall and the stairs up to the first floor. The spacious kitchen was littered with newspapers and computer magazines; in one corner MTV was running with the sound turned down. The sink was full of dirty dishes, despite the presence of a dishwasher under the kitchen worktop. Vuk glanced through the window at yet another lawn, which ended where the Sound began. Mikael was saying how good it was to see Janos again. They had had such good times together. And had Janos seen that Peter had become a big star on the television news? His rise had been pretty meteoric, taking him more or less straight from the College of Journalism to presenting the evening news. For his own part, well…he'd gone to the Technical University for a couple of years, but when it came right down to it he couldn't really be bothered. He was going to inherit all this lot anyway, and he had that trust fund in Switzerland. His parents spent their time playing golf in Spain or on an island in the Caribbean. They seldom came home. One of his brothers was in Los Angeles, the other in Switzerland. Mikael lived here alone. Only went out to stock up on frozen dinners and ready-made meals for the microwave. He never saw anyone, and that suited him just fine. He had his computers, his music and his books. What more could he ask for?

While he was talking, Mikael took a large bottle of cola from the fridge, produced a couple of glasses and filled them. They sat down at the kitchen table. There was a brief silence and Mikael tugged at his earlobe again.

'Jeez, it's great to see you, Janos. You old *Gastarbeiter*. You and Peter were the only guys I ever liked. The rest were all such frigging morons. When did you get back to Denmark?'

'A couple of days ago.'

'From down there?'

'From down there, yeah.'

'Okay,' said Mikael and took a drink of his cola.

'It's good to see you too, Mikael,' Vuk said. 'This house takes me back to when I was a kid. Those were great days. I always think of that as being the only normal time in my life.'

Vuk hadn't really intended to say that: it just came out, but he meant it.

'Why did you leave Denmark?'

'My parents wanted to go home.'

'And you just tagged along?'

'It's how I was brought up.'

Mikael leaned across the table, his face growing grave. That too, Vuk remembered about him. He was always playing the fool, but sometimes, when he saw pictures of war and suffering on the television, he would suddenly grow very serious and be plunged into something akin to depression. They used to kid him about it: he was too sensitive for this world, they said. He was the thinker of the three of them, the one who was most preoccupied with the big issues in life. He was always looking for answers to impossible questions and had once

185

astonished an irate teacher, who had demanded to know what weighty matters he was pondering when he should be paying attention in class, by replying 'the riddle of life' He had been eleven at the time, and the whole class had collapsed in fits of laughter. To begin with, Mikael had been surprised and hurt, but eventually he too had started to laugh. He had a habit of saying exactly what was in his mind at the oddest moments, and you never knew whether he was being sarcastic or serious. Whether he was making fun of himself or of others.

'Janos. It's great to see you. Don't get me wrong,' Mikael said. 'You're very welcome here. It's not that. But I don't really see anybody anymore. Apart from Peter, once in a while. I just don't like people, Janos. I can never figure out how they tick. How their programmes are put together. I crash when I'm with other people. So I keep myself to myself. I stay here. At night I sit at the computer and surf the Net. And sometimes I take a run up and down the Sound in my dinghy. Know what?'

Vuk shook his head and waited for Mikael to continue:

'I never see a soul. And yet I'm in touch with thousands of people around the world. From Sydney to Moscow. That way there are no problems. It's too much of a hassle meeting folk face to face. It's much easier to do it through a modem. Out in cyberspace.'

He gave a rather sheepish grin, plucked at his ear and went on:

'Now if I could just get laid via the modem, I'd never have to see another human being for the rest of my life. I could live happily in cyberspace.'

Vuk couldn't help laughing. That had been Mikael's special gift: he could make people laugh. Vuk almost felt fond of him again, as Janos had done.

'You always were a crazy bastard, Mikael,' he said, as Janos would have said it.

Mikael grinned happily back at him. The slight awkwardness between them had been dispelled, and it almost felt like the old days.

'Maybe. But what does that matter when your parents are loaded?' he said.

Mikael poured more cola for them both.

'How're your mum and dad doing? Things are pretty bad down there, eh?'

'They're dead. Murdered, along with Katarina,' Vuk said flatly.

'Aw, Christ man! Vuk and Lea are dead? And Katarina? Fucking hell. Jesus, I'm sorry, Janos. What did I say? Stay well away from other people.'

'Yeah, Mikael. That's what you said.'

There was that awkwardness again. Mikael plucked at his ear and fiddled with the label on the cola bottle. Through the half-open kitchen window they could hear the sound of the sea and a neighbour starting up a hedge-clipper or something.

'Can you still crack a computer programme the way you used to do?' Vuk asked.

Mikael brightened up. He was saved from having to listen to more about the horrors in Bosnia.

'I'm better than ever.'

Vuk drew the disk from his inside pocket.

'What's on it?'

'The key to success,' Vuk said with a smile. Mikael smiled back, and the ugliness that had hovered in the air between them was gone.

'Let's go up to the den,' Mikael said.

Although Mikael now had the run of the whole house, Vuk saw that he had retained his big old room. With the same stripy wallpaper and the same unmade bed. The wall was still plastered with pictures of dinosaurs, but there was also one new photo – of Microsoft's Bill Gates, who appeared to be Mikael's only idol. There was the same leather armchair, a confirmation present from his parents, and in the corner stood his old desk. The room was awash with computing magazines, CD-ROMs, wires and disks, but Vuk detected a certain order in the chaos. There were two desktop computers, each sitting on its own brand-new computer table, as well as a laptop on another small table. There were several printers, a mass of cables and heaps of manuals. There were two telephones, a scanner, and on an old desk sat a colour TV, tuned to CNN with the sound turned down. The swivel chairs were on castors and looked brand-new and very comfortable. The window was ajar, and the breeze wafted the scent of sea and seaweed into the room.

CNN was showing scenes from Bosnia. They saw a man poking the earth with a long pole. He had a scarf wrapped round the bottom half of his face. The next shot showed him with a skull in his hand. Mikael looked away from the screen and pointed to the leather armchair. Vuk swept off a couple of computing mags and took a seat. Mikael sat down at one of the computer tables. Swivelled the chair around so that he was facing the computer screen with his back to Vuk. He clicked on the mouse, and a low hum announced that the computer had awoken from its slumber.

'I do try to keep up with what's going on in the world,' Mikael said. 'How did it happen? What can I do for you?'

'Which question shall I answer first?' Vuk asked.

Mikael ran the mouse back and forth across the pad. He seemed nervous and awkward again, Vuk noticed. He didn't like talking about what had happened to Vuk's parents and little Katarina, who had been six years younger than them, but he felt that he ought to ask about them. He was like so many other people. They didn't really want to know, and they were tired of hearing about some obscure war.

'Christ, I don't know. The first one, and in the meantime I can work on this,' he said.

Vuk got up and handed him the disk. Mikael took it from him with an inquiring look.

'There's a document on it. It's password protected. Can you get into it?'

'Do you know what type of document it is?' Mikael asked, relaxing. He was on home ground here.

'Word Perfect 5.1.'

Mikael swung his chair around so that he had his back to Vuk again and popped the disk into the disk drive.

'Piece of cake,' he said and started tapping away at the keyboard. Vuk stood at his shoulder, watching as letters and numbers began to dance across the screen.

'What are you anyway, Janos? Serbian? Or Croatian?' Mikael went on, while his fingers flew. 'I mean, in the old days you were all just Yugoslavian, weren't you?'

'No, that's not how it was, not even in the old days. You simply didn't know any better.'

Mikael hummed to himself while, with a few quick taps, he proceeded to crack the password and open the document.

'Won't be long now. My little baby's on the scent,' he said.

'The sun was shining when the Muslims came,' Vuk murmured. He was standing right behind Mikael, speaking to the back of his head. Mikael did not look round, concentrated instead on the keys and the screen.

'I designed this programme myself,' he said, trying to get Vuk to change the subject. He had only asked out of politeness, but he didn't really want to know what had happened. 'It unlocks all known text files. I could make a bloody fortune from it. If I wanted to,' he said, addressing the screen.

'Spring had just begun, Mikael. It comes early in Bosnia, to the valleys around Banja Luka. We lived in a mixed area – this was before the ethnic purges, before everyone started organizing themselves. But my father didn't want to join the Serbian militia. My father believed in Tito and Yugoslavia. In a single state. One beautiful spring day, four men came to call. Not much older than you and me. They tied my father to a chair. Roughed him up a little. But not enough to knock him out...'

'Right, we're almost there now,' Mikael muttered, still refusing to look round. He tried to block out the words coming from behind his back, but still they got through to him and hurt him so much that he wanted to put his hands over his ears.

'You see they wanted him to witness what they did to my mother and sister. They took it in turns to rape them. In front of my father. He howled like an animal, so they cut out his tongue.'

'For fuck's sake, Janos. I don't want to...'

Mikael kept his eyes fixed on the dancing figures and letters, as if they could shield him from the words falling tonelessly and monotonously on his ears:

'Before he choked on his own blood they cut off his dick, Mikael. They stuffed it into my mother's mouth before they killed her. Then they strangled my sister. And once they'd done all that those fucking Muslims set fire to our house. Do you hear me, Mikael? That is how Vuk and Lea and Katarina died.'

Mikael turned round and stared at him with fear-filled eyes. He was white as a sheet as he whispered:

'And people think I'm crazy. Just because I keep myself to myself. Just because I can't stand other people. Just because I like having a modem and a screen between them and me.'

He turned back to the screen.

'A-ha. Now my little baby's onto something,' he cried. 'Come on, baby!'

He looked round again, as if meaning to meet Vuk's eye. But it was not on his face that he fixed his gaze when he asked:

'Where were you? How do you know what happened?'

'I was in Belgrade.'

'So how did you find out about it?'

'I tracked them down. It wasn't hard. They lived only two houses down from us. I'd spent many a summer holiday running about with them, playing football with them. They were my friends. They had bragged to their mates about what they had done. They weren't hard to find, and then they told me.'

'Just like that?'

'I persuaded them. One after another. It took a while, but they told me everything. In detail, before…'

Vuk could tell from the look on Mikael's face that he already knew the answer but couldn't stop himself from asking anyway:

'Before what, Janos?'

'Before I killed them, of course.'

For a second Mikael looked him in the eye, then he turned back to the screen just as the computer gave a little beep. It was a relief to have it demanding his attention.

'That's it, baby,' he said. 'We've got it! What the fuck? It's just a timetable for some visit or other. Why the hell would anybody want to protect that with a password?'

'Can you print it out?'

'No problem,' Mikael said and pressed two keys. In a corner of the room a laser printer began to thrum as it warmed up. Mikael leaned back in his chair but kept his face turned to the screen.

'What is all this? Simba, Flakfortet, Press Conference, Airport, Safe House, dates and times. Weird. Ah, well. It's not my problem. Anything else I can do for you, Janos?'

Vuk pulled the garrotte out of his jacket pocket and curled his fingers round the two wooden handles. With one swift, fluid movement he flicked the length of strong, slender steel wire around Mikael's throat and yanked, stepping backwards at the same time. The chair toppled over, and the weight of Mikael's body dragged him down and left him dangling from the garrotte.

'Not a thing, Mikael. You've done your bit,' Vuk said, hauling back on the wire to cut through the larynx and stifle an incipient gargled scream just as the laser printer gently discharged a white A4 sheet containing the final schedule for author Sara Santanda's visit to Copenhagen.

Chapter 18

Vuk studied the sheet of paper that the printer had neatly deposited in the tray while he was strangling Mikael, who now lay on the floor with dead bulging eyes and a long bloody gash in his throat. Vuk paid him no heed, intent as he was on the schedule. What really intrigued him was Flakfortet. Even in Denmark, not the most security-conscious of countries, the airport was too well guarded and too hazardous, although the hit could conceivably be carried out in the arrivals hall when Santanda came through customs. Or as she left the arrivals hall on her way to the waiting car. It would be possible to slip away amid all the confusion but very risky. And for all he knew they might bypass customs with the Target. He would have to assume that they would. They would give her the VIP treatment, and he didn't have the time or the wherewithal to obtain the relevant details. Iran might be prepared to use its intelligence network if it could be done in such a way that their involvement would be masked, but he didn't want to ask the Iranians for help, even if they could get him the information he needed. The safe house would be under close surveillance. The only chance he would have there would be when the Target was entering or leaving the place, at that vulnerable moment between the house and the car door: a shot with a rifle from a spot above the street and the car, but could he gain access to a neighbouring apartment? The press conference seemed the obvious choice, but he wasn't exactly sure what Flakfortet would entail. There would be a lot of people at the press conference, which meant he would be able to mingle freely. The Target would be exposed, sitting behind her microphone, and when arriving and leaving. The problem was how to smuggle a gun in, but that he would figure out. But Flakfortet was a worry. He vaguely recalled the existence of some disused sea forts in the approaches to Copenhagen harbour, but he couldn't picture them. The police knew that the Target would be a sitting duck during the press conference. That may have been why they had chosen to hold it offshore, where it was easier to keep tabs on the reporters and photographers who would be attending. They could only get there by boat. And it wouldn't take too much in the way of resources to secure the area. He would have to take a trip out there as soon as possible, to reconnoitre. The main thing was to find out whether Flakfortet was open to the public or whether it was a restricted military area, which would make things more difficult, though not impossible. Killing a person was never impossible. There were only varying degrees of difficulty. But every contract boiled down to the same essentials: get close to the Target, hit the Target and make your getaway. That was the contract. Everything else was pure logistics.

Vuk was feeling quite pleased. He had a programme, a schedule, a deadline. For the rest, it was all a matter of planning and execution, as well as the modicum of luck which was always needed and which he did not believe he had used up yet, even if he did have the sense in his dreams that his account was almost empty. But he still had one big advantage: he had the schedule, and they didn't know that he had it. Five days from now he would know whether it was possible for him to start a new life with Emma or not. If anything were to go wrong this time, there would be no more jobs. He pushed this thought away as soon as it entered his mind. Failure was not an option. He couldn't see the Iranians simply letting it pass. He knew too much, another contract would be issued, this time with his name on it. It was now or never.

Vuk folded the sheet of paper carefully and rudely shut off the computer at the plug before removing the disk. He left it next to the computer. He would format it later, to delete the document containing the schedule. He lifted Mikael's body with ease and carried him down the stairs to the hall. He remembered that there were more stairs leading down to the basement. The door to the basement was behind the kitchen. He laid Mikael on the floor, opened the door and located the light switch on the wall just inside. The dry dusty odour of the cellar rose to meet him. He grabbed Mikael under the arms and dragged him down the stairs. The basement consisted of a long passageway with rooms running off it on either side. These had once done service as coalhouse, larder, washhouse and drying room. In the old washhouse two large tubs still stood against the wall, but the old copper was gone. In its place were a modern washing machine and tumble dryer. In another corner, on a trestle table sat what looked like a well-maintained outboard motor, and from the ceiling hung a black rubber dinghy. Vuk tipped Mikael into one of the tubs, folding him in half to make him fit into it. He took a look around and found a tarpaulin lying neatly folded in a corner. He spread this over the tub. Mikael might have been a slob as far as the house was concerned, but he had kept the basement spick and span. Maybe he hadn't come down here very often. The house certainly didn't look as though anyone came in regularly to clean. Mikael had been a loner, a bit of an oddball.

Vuk examined the dinghy, which was suspended from four hooks in the ceiling. It was a standard, black naval model. It was in need of a bit of air, but there was a foot-pump lying alongside the outboard motor. Vuk explored the other basement rooms. One was crammed with old suitcases, furniture and books. Another held bikes, an old scooter, sledges and skis. In a third, gardening implements were lined up like soldiers on parade, and in the last an orderly array of saws, hammers, drills and other tools hung on the wall above a workbench and lathe. The basement contained everything he needed. He would make the house in Hellerup the final crucial base from which to launch his attack.

He went upstairs to the kitchen. He couldn't stand the mess, he was itching to tidy the place up, but first he walked through to the sitting room. A fine layer of dust covered the old-fashioned furniture. This was not where Mikael had spent most of his time. Three connecting rooms looked out onto the back garden, enjoying a beautiful view of the Sound. On a sideboard in one of the rooms stood a range of bottles. From the fine grey film that had also settled over these, Vuk deduced that alcohol had not been one of Mikael's vices. He had stuck to cola and coffee. From the hall, a door led to a utility room, and from there to a locked garage. There were no cars. He had not expected there to be. In the garage were a motor mower, a wheelbarrow and a small trailer with rubber wheels, which he guessed Mikael must have used to run the dinghy down to the water. The garage smelt musty, as if some small trace of summer had been preserved in this sealed-off space.

Vuk returned to the kitchen and found the telephone directories under a pile of freesheets on a stool under the wall telephone. He looked up Flakfortet in the phone book but found only a restaurant by that name. After a moment's thought he picked up the Yellow Pages and turned to ferry services. There was an ad for a company called Spar Shipping. He gave them a call, introduced himself as Kaj Petersen from Viborg and said that he had heard that it was possible to take a boat out to Flakfortet. A cheery female voice assured him that this was indeed the case. One could make a group booking, but there were also daily sailings from Nyhavn in the centre of Copenhagen at 12.00 noon, 2.00 pm and 4.00 pm from the first of May to the first of October. It was just a matter of showing up. 'If I wanted to charter a boat, for a group of business colleagues, for example, could I do that?' Vuk asked.

'Certainly. We often cater for private parties. That way you have the boat to yourselves,' the woman said.

'We're organizing a company outing. Not a big affair, there would be about twenty of us, I would guess,' Vuk said.

'We could easily arrange that for you. And we could also book a table at the restaurant for you, if you would like. A lot of companies do that. Mostly in the summer, of course, but even now, in September. We can guarantee you a great trip, although we can't, of course, guarantee good weather.'

She laughed, and Vuk laughed with her.

'I know it's kind of short notice, but the date we had in mind was the twentieth of September.'

'Just a moment.'

Vuk waited, then the woman came back on the line:

'No, I'm sorry we can't do the twentieth. Another party has booked the fort for the whole day. Is there some other date we could try?'

'I'll have to check with the others,' Vuk said. 'Then I'll get back to you.'

'You'll be most welcome.'

Vuk thanked her. He stood for a second, considering. The kitchen would have to wait. He could clear it up this evening. The time was now half-past twelve. He could catch the two o'clock boat; he would have to check out of his hotel afterwards. He glanced round about. The door key was hanging on a board next to the telephone. He took a look in the fridge. There wasn't much in it except cola and an old pack of butter, but in the freezer cabinet underneath the fridge was a pile of ready-made meals. All he needed to buy was some bread, cheese and salami and a fresh pat of butter. He took the key and left his new lodgings.

A couple of hours later he was standing on the foredeck of the large converted fishing cutter, the *M/S Langø* which, after years of working the waters off the Norwegian coast and round the Faeroes, now sailed between Nyhavn and Flakfortet. Vuk stood there, along with a couple of fathers and their school-age children, three elderly ladies and a young couple, and watched Flakfortet come into view, a hillock in the middle of the Sound. The fortifications ran the entire length of the islet. The grey blocks of stone were overgrown with grass and bushes and on the very top of the fort were the remains of the gun emplacements. Attached to the restaurant was a glass pavilion with a soaring white roof. As they headed into the harbour Vuk spotted two entrances into the fort itself. Three yachts bobbed gently alongside the jetty, and a small group of tourists were waiting to sail back to Copenhagen on the *M/S Langø*. The cutter had a saloon where beer, water and coffee were sold from a little hatch and an upper-deck with seating in the shape of some benches under a green canopy. It was a mild grey day with a hint of rain in the light wind blowing from the west. Vuk wore a sweater under his leather jacket; a distinct, blond five-day growth covered his chin. Despite the clouds, he was wearing sunglasses. Over his shoulder he carried a leather bag.

Outside the restaurant were signs advertising the day's specialities: lobscouse and fried eel. He picked up a brochure in the little shop next door. On the front was a picture of Flakfortet, on the back a map showing its position. Vuk read about the history of the fort: Built between 1910 and 1916 as a sea fort designed to defend the Danish capital against bombardment. One of the largest of its kind, at its peak it had a garrison of 550 troops. It sat on a sand bar and covered an area of seven and a half acres. The manmade island measured seventy-five feet in height, read Vuk, who also learned that the fort buildings were on two levels, with passageways linking ammunition stores, sleeping quarters, machine shop and barrack rooms. It had been manned and fully operational during the German occupation from 1940 to 1945. In 1968 the Danish army vacated

Flakfortet, and for seven years it lay forsaken and neglected. It was still owned by the Ministry of Defence, but managed by the Flakfortet Society. During the summer months it was visited by a great many day trippers and sailing enthusiasts and could also be hired for private and business functions.

Vuk read all of this while walking down a long, well-kept, brightly lit passage under the fort, referred to in the brochure as Fortgaden. There were new brown doors in the cement walls and signs for public toilets. A flight of cement steps ran up to the old fortifications right at the very top, where cannon and anti-aircraft guns had once defended the narrow strait between Sweden and Denmark. Other steps led down into the bowels of the fort. Some of the corridors were clean and well lit. Others had not yet been renovated and were still shrouded in gloom. It was chilly down in the nethermost passages, probably no more than ten degrees Celsius. Vuk explored every inch of the fort, memorizing the general layout and every turn of its maze of passageways. He turned down one of the unlit corridors, ignoring the sign on the wall saying 'No Admittance' He took a torch from his bag. Its powerful beam revealed damp grey walls and rusting steel doors hung with ancient notices that told him he was down in the old ammunition and powder stores. He heard a squeak and in the cone of light saw a rat scurry along the foot of the wall and disappear into a gap between the steel door and the crumbling concrete. The doors were securely fastened with heavy padlocks. Vuk examined one of the padlocks by the light of his torch. It would be a simple matter to pick it. That had been one of many useful skills taught at the Special Forces school. He could make himself a lock-pick on the lathe at the house in Hellerup. Vuk began to discern the outlines of a plan. It would involve taking some huge risks, but he had to work on the assumption that Denmark was not geared up for hostage situations. He had to bank on having five minutes of utter confusion when his ruthlessness would afford him the head start he needed. Santanda would arrive by boat, Of that he was sure, although they might also opt for a helicopter, but he was betting on a boat: a pretty speedy craft, on which he would make his getaway. If they had a helicopter circling overhead he was done for. But he didn't think they would. They might have one on stand-by, though, and that was okay. They didn't know that he knew every step of their schedule inside out. That was his ace in the hole, his trump card.

Vuk made his way back along the passageway. He heard voices, switched off the torch and stood stock-still, blind in the darkness. All he could see was the light at the end of the tunnel, and the sound of the guide's voice reached his ears as if through a funnel:

'This part of the fort is closed off. We still don't have the money necessary for the renovation of the casemates. Flakfortet suffered from a lot of vandalism over the years when it was lying empty. Now if we go down here...'

Vuk heard the footsteps of the little group moving away. He slipped the torch back into his bag and returned to the main entrance and the new doors. One of the doors swung open, and a young man in chef's whites came out. He eyed Vuk uncertainly, obviously wondering what he was doing in the staff quarters.

'I was looking for the toilets,' Vuk said.

The chef pointed to the bottom of the passage.

'They're just down there,' he said.

Vuk gave him a big smile.

'Thanks.'

'You're welcome.' The chef couldn't help smiling back. Vuk's smile was so infectious.

'You must be the man who's doing the food for us.'

'Yep. How does fried eel sound?'

'Mmm. Great.'

'Well, you've still got time. See ya.'

'Yeah, bye.'

The chef nipped past him, and Vuk followed him down to the signs to the toilets. He committed the number of the chef's room to memory. It might come in handy later.

Vuk walked up onto the top of the fort. He looked across to Sweden and then to Denmark. The Swedish coast appeared close and inviting. He gazed back at Saltholm and watched the boats out on the water while he smoked a cigarette and mulled over his plan. He spied a Russian coaster sailing northwards through the Sound. It gave a short blast on its whistle as it passed a flat-bottomed barge heading south. The Russian tricolour flew from the stern of the barge, and an idea began to take shape in Vuk's mind. Again, it was very risky, but the odds were not impossible. If his luck held, it would definitely be worth a try.

In the restaurant, Vuk had fried eel washed down with a small draught beer and coffee while he turned things over in his mind. He was alone in the restaurant apart from the three elderly ladies, who were sitting over coffee, pastries and cheroots. The eel tasted odd rather than good, and the boiled potatoes had an unwonted floury texture. They brought back memories of childhood dinners with Mikael's aunt who had made what she called proper Danish food; he could almost taste the hamburger steaks with fried onions, the pork sausages and red cabbage, meatballs and roast pork with parsley sauce, and recall the scent of her tiny kitchen. She must be dead now, otherwise Mikael would surely have mentioned her. He grew a little sentimental and allowed himself to lapse into nostalgia. A lot of things in his life could have been different if he had made other choices. But maybe the fact was that the choices had been made beforehand.

He was shaken out of his reverie by the sight of the chef emerging from the kitchen. He was puffing on a cigarette, and when he spotted Vuk he came over to his table.

'Well, how was it?' he asked.

'Good. Like you said,' Vuk replied.

The chef nodded.

'So I guess you'll be taking the boat home now too?'

'God, no. I won't be going home until Saturday. We're out here from Tuesday to Saturday.'

'That must be pretty tough, isn't it?'

'Oh, it's amazing what you can get used to,' the chef remarked.

'I suppose so,' Vuk said and got ready to pay his bill.

He went back to the hotel, changed into his smarter trousers and jacket and put on a tie before packing the guns and the rest of his things. His luggage was still untouched. No one had tampered with it. He bound the sheath containing the doubled-edged blade around his ankle and made a thorough check of the room before calling reception to say that he had to leave, but that he would of course pay for the next night, since he was checking out at such short notice. He would be down in ten minutes and would be paying cash.

Then he called Ole Carlsen, who answered after one ring, as if he had been waiting by the phone.

'Hi, it's Carsten,' Vuk said.

'Oh, it's you,' Ole muttered. He sounded disappointed, as though he had hoped it would be Lise.

'I just wanted to say thanks for a great evening,' Vuk said.

'Aah, it wasn't the best really,' Ole said.

'No, I don't suppose it was.'

'I don't know where the hell she is.'

'It's all my fault, Ole. I'm sorry.'

'No, don't blame yourself. It wasn't your fault.'

'I wanted to ask if you could me a favour.'

'Sure. I mean, it's not as if I've got anything else to do.'

'I've managed to rent the first floor of a house in Hellerup...'

'Hey, that sounds great. Are you moving to Copenhagen?'

'Nah, but I'm back and forth so often these days, I wouldn't mind having a place of my own. I'm sick of hotels.'

'Very sensible, if you ask me.'

'I was thinking...you've got a car...and what with my cases and everything, I was wondering whether you...?'

'But of course. Where are you now?'

'Could you be at the corner of Istedgade and Reventlowsgade in half an hour?'

'No problem. It's the least I can do. I'll leave a note to let Lise know.'

'Does she deserve that?'

Ole laughed mirthlessly:

'No, not really.'

They drove in silence. Ole reeked faintly of booze but seemed steady enough behind the wheel, and his speech was clear and coherent.

Sad though he was, he seemed to have come to terms with things. As if he knew it was over. It would be just like the thing for them to track him down because Ole got arrested for drunk driving. The evening was dark and cold, and the tarmac glistened with moisture. The trees bent in the wind, which had freshened.

Vuk gave directions to the house, and when they got there Ole parked outside the front gate. Vuk had put his luggage in the boot. He let Ole take the one suitcase while he carried the locked Samsonite case and the holdall. An old lady walked past on the other side of the street with her little dog on a leash. She turned in at the gate of the house opposite, looking back at the two men as she did so.

'What a lovely house,' Ole said. 'You've struck it lucky here, all right.'

Vuk made no reply, merely went ahead of Ole up the short flight of steps to the front door. He set down the case and the holdall and unlocked the door. He switched on the light, stepped aside and let Ole walk in first.

'Have you got the whole of the first floor?'

'Yeah, I've got the lot,' Vuk said. Something in his voice must have warned Ole, because he turned and stared at Vuk in bewilderment, but far too late. Vuk punched him hard in the throat and with a gurgle Ole went flying back, slammed into the jamb of the door behind him and collapsed in a heap. In his eyes shone the unspoken question: why?

'You know me, you fool!' Vuk hissed and dealt him another blow: short, sharp and precise. All the light vanished from Ole Carlsen's eyes.

Vuk dragged Ole's body through the chaotic kitchen to the basement stairs. He gave it a push that sent it rolling down the stairs with him following behind. He removed the car keys from the dead man's jacket pocket before lugging him through to the washtubs, folding him into the second tub, next to Mikael's body, and covering both bodies with the tarpaulin.

Vuk spent the next hour clearing up the kitchen. He emptied the rubbish bins, piled up the old newspapers in a corner, filled the dishwasher and switched it on and when all that was done popped a frozen pizza into the oven. He fetched the bottle of whisky from the sitting room, sat down at the kitchen table and studied the map of Copenhagen Harbour, which showed Flakfortet, Saltholm, the two coastlines and the shipping lanes hugging the land on either side. Between the one, known as Dutchman's Deep, and the other, King's Deep, was a marked-off section of the Sound shaped rather like Greenland. This was Middelgrund, the Dirty Sea. Vuk could see that the water here was very shallow.

He picked up the phone in the kitchen and called the mobile number he had been given by Kravtjov in Berlin. He preferred to use telephone boxes, but the likelihood of the police bugging Mikael's phone was so slight that he had no hesitation in taking the chance.

The phone was answered immediately. A man's voice said simply: 'Yes.'

'This is Vuk,' Vuk said in his halting Russian.

'*Ich verstehe nicht,*' the man's voice said. He spoke German with a Slavic accent.

'Kravtjov,' Vuk said.

In the silence that followed, the phone hissed in his ear, although the line was perfectly clear.

'*Haben Sie ein Nummer?*'

'*Moment,*' he said. He leafed through the phone book and sure enough, there was Mikael's father's name. He read out the number, first in Russian, then in German. The other man hung up.

Vuk had eaten most of his pizza by the time the telephone rang. He hadn't expected Kravtjov to be carrying that mobile phone himself. It would be in a safe house somewhere, manned by a succession of henchmen. Vuk was the only person to have been given that number. Once the job was done it would be deleted. The mobile phone was a wonderful invention: the phones themselves were easy to carry around and easily concealed, numbers were easily acquired and just as easily cancelled. It had made life a lot simpler.

'Yes,' said a new voice in English.

'Where's Kravtjov?' Vuk asked, also in English.

'I know who you are,' the voice said.

'Where's Kravtjov?'

'They got to him. He's dead.'

Vuk was silent for a moment, stunned. His mind was racing. His first instinct was just to drop the phone and run, get out of the country. The man in Berlin had possibly been in the field himself at one time. At any rate he seemed to know what Vuk was thinking.

'It was his old colleagues. But it doesn't appear to have had anything to do with that other matter,' the even voice said.

'What did he tell them?'

'According to our sources, not very much. Nothing of importance. His heart was weak. It gave out.'

'The contract?'

'It stands,' the voice said. 'The same terms. There's been a reshuffle at our end. The client still intends to honour the agreement.'

'I'm going to need transport home,' Vuk said.

'So the contract will be fulfilled?'

'Yes.'

'Tell me what you need,' the voice said.

'A Russian coaster or one of the barges I've seen here. From Volga–Nefti or Volga–Balt.'

'I know the ones. We have good contact with a number of them.'

'It has to be at a certain spot on the twentieth.'

'That doesn't give us much time.'

'Can it be done?'

'For a price.'

'The price is immaterial.'

'We'll arrange to have one in the vicinity from now on.'

'You'll get the exact coordinates just before.'

'Fine,' the voice said.

Vuk paused for a moment, then said:

'Have the competition got wind of the contract?'

'Yes.'

Again Vuk had the feeling that he ought to make himself scarce as fast as possible. All the signs were there: the warning tingle down his spine, the quickening of his heartbeat and the film of moisture on his palms. It was the adrenalin, he knew, but these were also danger signals.

'Are they ahead of us?' he asked.

'No. They're fumbling in the dark. They're not as far ahead as us.'

'Okay,' Vuk said. 'We proceed.'

'Okay,' said the voice in Berlin.

Vuk poured himself another small whisky and drank it in the kitchen. He had tuned into CNN on the television in the corner. There was still nothing but bad news from Bosnia. CNN switched to a new item. Vuk saw the Tibetan leader, the Dalai Lama, come out of a door and walk towards the waiting press. The Dalai Lama was surrounded by people who were crowding in on him while his aides did their best to shield him. Vuk saw a couple of uniformed police officers struggling to keep the reporters, press photographers and television cameramen at bay, but they just went on jostling to get close to the monk, who looked so small and defenceless in his orange robes. They jabbed their microphones into his face like long lances. Vuk observed the scene with some interest. He did not understand the reporters and all their pushing and shoving and shouting. But their impatience and their lack of consideration gave him an idea, one which he considered that same night as he drove Ole's car back and parked it, with the doors locked, outside the apartment in Østerbro. He threw the car keys down a drain and took the train back to the house in Hellerup.

He went upstairs and switched on the computer. He could see from the little envelope in the email icon that there were some messages for Mikael. He went into the programme. There were eight new mails. Vuk read one of them. It was from Australia and had something to do with a programming tool unknown to Vuk. All of the other electronic mail also had to do with computers and programmes. None of them required an immediate answer, but from the list of mails Vuk could tell that Mikael had been corresponding with people all over the world. He exited the email programme, formatted the disk from Lise's apartment and stuck it into a pile of fresh disks lying on the desk.

He collected the whisky bottle and a glass from the sitting room and went back upstairs. There were numerous rooms on the first floor, among them Mikael's parents' bedroom overlooking the Sound, a room that appeared to do duty as a lumber-room, a large bathroom and a guest room with a bed already made up and covered with a patterned bedspread. Vuk drew the curtains and lay down on the bed with the bottle of whisky. He had to down two large ones before he felt sleep stealing over him. He dreaded sleep and the way it robbed his subconscious of all control, but he slept peacefully and dreamlessly. He had two full days in which to make the final preparations. All the pieces of his plan had now fallen into place; he knew exactly what he had to do.

Chapter 19

Lise Carlsen stood on the veranda of Per Toftlund's apartment, smoking a cigarette. She couldn't sleep and had gone out onto the veranda to have a ciggie. Not that Per hadn't told her she was welcome to smoke in his apartment, but she didn't like to. He was so tidy it was uncanny. She didn't feel right in these almost stringently masculine surroundings. She thought of Ole. She had stormed out of the apartment in high dudgeon the night before and had more or less told herself that she wasn't going back until he was out of there, but she supposed that wasn't really feasible. They had bought the apartment together and they would have to sell it together. She would need to start looking around for something else once Sara's visit was out of the way. She couldn't stay at Per's place. It was too small, too much his own, and they would soon start to get on one another's nerves, once they stopped spending most of their time in bed. Could she afford to go on living in that big apartment on just one income? Probably not, but she would have to do her sums. There always seemed to be something she had to do. And no matter what, tomorrow she would have to go home for some fresh clothes. Or today, rather. She was wearing Per's thick bathrobe and nothing else, and the night air was cold. She shivered; her eye was drawn to the dark shadow of Vestskoven and the flashing lights in the distance. Somewhere out there, she thought to herself, an assassin was waiting. If what they had been told was right. The police had been asking around on the street, as Per put it. They had checked out scores of hotels, put their snouts to work and asked the mobile units to make a few inquiries when called out anyway to incidents in the Copenhagen underworld. But no luck. She thought of the hired killer, assassin, hit man, or whatever one was supposed to call the nameless, Danish-speaking foreigner who might be lying in wait out there, somewhere in the city. She tossed her cigarette over the rail of the veranda, her conscience pricking her, but this place was simply too neat and clean. She tried to concentrate on the thought that had been just about to surface: a sense of something important that had come to her at that point between waking and the beginnings of sleep, when they were snuggled up together, spoonwise, after making love. But she couldn't remember what it was that had struck her, and now she was thinking of Per and his strong agile body.

She heard the veranda door being pushed back, and Per put his arms around her. He was naked. He slid his bed-warm hands inside the bathrobe and placed them gently over her breasts. Kissed the nape of her neck.

'Come to bed,' he said.

'I can't sleep,' she said, leaning back against him. He caressed her, and it felt so good.

'Who said anything about sleep?'

'Again?'

'Hmm.' She felt his lips on her neck. The bristles on his chin prickled slightly.

'I was thinking about something.'

'So was I,' he said, running his hands over her belly and down to her crotch.

'That's so nice,' she said.

'So are you.'

He turned her round and kissed her while his hands slid down her back under the robe and cupped around her buttocks. His penis brushed against her, she wrapped her fingers around it lightly and felt it grow. It was wonderful to be wanted. Maybe that was the whole secret of love: to be the object of such great desire. He stopped kissing her, picked her up and carried her back to the bedroom. Afterwards she fell asleep without that elusive thought returning.

It came to her, however, the next morning when they were having breakfast together in Per's little kitchen. He had been out for a four-mile run in Vestskoven, made coffee and gone down to the baker's for bread and was now sitting reading *Politiken*, clad in what she described as his uniform: jeans, button-down shirt and tie – to which, later, would be added the gun at his belt. She still hadn't got used to that. She had slept an hour longer than him and felt fit and rested.

'Per,' she said. 'Why is he so hard to find, this hit man?'

'Because he works alone.'

He put down the paper and poured himself another cup of his strong black coffee.

'We're keeping a close eye on all anarchist groups, extreme left-wingers, Nazis, nutcases and diplomats from certain countries. That sort have a tendency to blab, some might be persuaded to turn informer; they operate in groups, within organizations. They find it hard to keep their mouths shut. Most of them, anyway. If he were one of them, we would have him in no time. But he speaks Danish like a native and works alone. It's going to take luck to track down someone like that.'

'I was thinking…' she said.

She could see that he was about to make one of his cheeky remarks, but when he realized that she was serious he buttoned his lip and allowed her to continue:

'If this hit man speaks Danish well, so well that he can pass for a Dane, then he must have lived here a long time, right?'

Per nodded, and she went on:

'You can't really learn to speak the language – properly, I mean – unless you're born and brought up here. You can always tell as soon as someone opens their mouth whether they're Danish or not. It's the little things that give it away, right?'

'Go on,' Per said.

'The Danes are a tribe. We take a person to be a Dane if he or she speaks the language without an accent. If you can't speak the language you stick out like a sore thumb in this little tribal society of ours. Prince Henrik doesn't speak Danish well, so we've never thought of him as a real Dane. Everybody loved Princess Alexandra because she had hardly been in the country any time before she was speaking Danish beautifully. There are so few of us. We're afraid of being swallowed up by the big world outside. Our language is our shield. That's why it matters so much to us.'

'Yes, teacher,' he chipped in with a grin.

She tutted impatiently:

'No, listen. Just let me pursue this idea for a minute, will you?'

'Okay, go on.'

'Our killer, right? I think we have to take a gamble. He must have been born in Copenhagen around 1969. That's the year the Russians mentioned, isn't it? And he must have attended school for at least nine or ten years. He might even have gone to high school. There can't be that many Yugoslavian boys in Denmark who've managed that. And every school keeps copies of the class pictures for each year. Somewhere in a school in Copenhagen is a picture of the man you're looking for. Of your killer.'

Per eyed her appreciatively.

'*Muy bien, guappa*,' he said, reaching for his mobile phone. He keyed in a number, beaming at her as he did so and making her feel as proud as a schoolgirl being praised by her teacher.

'John, it's Per,' he said. 'Get a couple of people to start ringing round the churches, get them to check their registries. I want the names of male children born to Yugoslavian immigrant workers here in 1968, '69 and '70. Once we've got the names, we'll get on to the National Register Office and double-check whether they're still resident here and in which school district they grew up. Have you got that?'

He listened, then broke in:

'I know damn well that 25,000 Yugoslavians came to Denmark to work in the sixties and seventies, but we're only talking about three particular years here, so it shouldn't be that hard a job, and the longer you go on blethering to me, the longer it will take. I'll be there in half an hour…'

Per drove Lise back to her place. Ole's car was parked outside, which meant he must be home, unless he had taken a taxi to work because he'd been drinking the night before and didn't want to drive. Per gave her a quick kiss.

'I'll call you,' he said.

'I'll be at the office later.'

She watched him drive off, missing him already. She walked through the main door and up the stairs, dragging her heels. She couldn't stand the thought of another confrontation, so she decided to act huffy and just get changed, then bike in to work. Lise was one of those rare individuals who had never learned to drive. She had never had any notion to do so. She let herself in to the apartment. It had a shuttered unoccupied feel to it. She called out tentatively, but there was no reply. Ole had tidied up the living room and run the dishwasher but hadn't done any shopping. The light on the answering machine was flashing. It was Ole's secretary, asking Ole to give her a call please, was he sick or something, and should she cancel his appointments for the next couple of days?

Lise called the secretary, who didn't know where Ole could have got to. He had not shown up for work, nor phoned to say that he wouldn't be in. Lise told her it would probably be best to cancel his appointments for that day and promised to call her back. The secretary sounded worried but also grateful to have someone else make a decision. Lise rang the newspaper office and asked if Ole had called, but he had not.

She sat down in the kitchen with a glass of juice:

'Where the hell are you, you stupid bugger?' she sighed. She was worried; it wasn't like Ole to simply go off without a word to anyone. And it certainly wasn't like him to let down his clients, whatever problems he himself might have.

She got changed and went to work, where she got her pieces on Sara Santanda's visit ready to go to press. She had written a profile of the author and a summary of the Iranian government's fatwa on her, but as agreed with Tagesen, she had not put it out on *Politiken*'s online newspaper for everyone to read. She would not do that until the evening before Sara's arrival on the morning flight from London, so that it would appear in the paper on the day of the press conference itself. It was going to be the most fantastic scoop, and Per had not been able to talk them out of it. He would have preferred to eschew all publicity, but he had no say in this matter. *Politiken* wanted the story on the front page. For once the newspaper would have the jump on the TV and radio. They would hold the press conference, and afterwards Lise would conduct an exclusive interview with Sara at the safe house. They would be one step ahead of all their rivals.

Lise tried calling home several times and rang Ole's secretary twice, but she hadn't heard from him either.

Per called, and she expressed her concern to him, but he made light of it. As if he saw nothing unusual in the fact that her husband had simply vanished into thin air. Or at least was not getting in touch. But how was he to know that they had always told one another where they would be? They had always felt it was important to check in with one another at least once a day. Even when out travelling, although it was usually her who was away somewhere, they had made a point of calling one another every day, if it was at all possible. Lately, she had to admit, this had tended to be a pretty one-sided arrangement, but at least she had always known where Ole was. Or had she? Per, on the other hand, was the sort of person who divulged only as much as was absolutely necessary about his activities. It wasn't like Ole not to get in touch. Again she found herself missing the old day-to-day routine. Just to have the time to read a good book again…

'Wasn't it you who left him, Lise?' Per asked rather coolly. Stung by this comment, she told him she was too busy to talk and put down the phone. But she was happy when he called a couple of hours later and asked if he should pick her up at eight. She felt restless. There was nothing else to do now but wait and hope that Per's and John's investigation would bear fruit. But that was not her department.

Per picked her up, and they drove back to his place. She wanted him so badly. They took a shower together and ended up in bed, where she forgot all about Ole and Sara and hired killers and gave herself up to a passion she had not thought she possessed. And afterwards, when she was lying there still, and he brought her a glass of red wine, her cigarettes and an ashtray, she thought her heart would burst.

'It must be love,' she said.

'Just give me time. I'll wean you off them eventually,' he said. 'Pasta and salad?'

'Sounds divine,' she said, stretching and feeling warm all over and so happy to be alive at this moment.

He had set the table in the living room; she sat there, swathed in his big bathrobe and ate, while he filled her in on the investigation. In order to narrow the field, they had chosen to concentrate on sons of Yugoslavian guest workers in state schools who had sat the school-leavers' examination in either ninth or tenth grade. They had had five people working on this all day. It was a long laborious process. There had been no such thing as databases back then, so the people they called had to look up books and registers, but they had narrowed it down to 109 Yugoslavian boys who had taken their school-leavers' certificate. The team had now started cross-checking these names with the National Register Office, police records and the Motor Vehicle Registration Department, to find out how many of them were still in the country or if any of them had died. It was basic police work – tedious but necessary. Tomorrow he would be able to go round the schools with a list of perhaps twenty names and try to match them with faces in the class photographs kept by the schools. If they were lucky, they might come up with a name and a face for the police artists to work on. A computer-generated Identikit picture could then be distributed to the security officers involved in the visit. And they would be able to check whether Interpol had any record of the man: fingerprints, police record, whether he was wanted for anything.

'It's a simple process of elimination,' he said.

'And what if that doesn't pay off either?'

'Then we're back to square one. Our best bet still is that we can manage to keep the schedule a secret. Word leaked out that Simba was coming here, but that was all, no details.'

'This is delicious,' she said.

He took a sip of his wine:

'What are you doing tomorrow?'

'Nothing in particular. Waiting. Looking forward to basking in the admiration of my colleagues when they read my articles,' she said dryly, although she did in fact mean it.

'Why don't you join me, then?'

'I'd love to,' she said.

'John will be allocating each of us some schools to visit. We'll call them in the morning and go round them in the afternoon.'

'Okay,' she said, but then he saw her face fall.

'You're thinking about Ole, aren't you?'

She nodded.

'I don't understand what can have happened to him.'

'Don't worry, he'll turn up tomorrow, you'll see.'

'Yeah, you're probably right,' she said, although she didn't really believe it. She didn't know why, but she had the feeling that something was very wrong.

By lunchtime the next day they had whittled the list down to twenty-one names, all sons of Yugoslavian guest workers who fulfilled both of their two criteria: they had sat their school-leavers' examination in the mid-eighties, and they were no longer resident in Denmark. Eight people had worked right through the night on this, and Per didn't dare think about the overtime chits he would be asked to sign later. His boss would nod approvingly if his gamble paid off and give him a bawling-out for lack of judgement if it turned out to be a wild-goose chase. Per could not help feeling a little guilty that he had not been there to help, but it was routine work and he was really going to have to be on the ball over the next forty-eight hours. Besides which, he had to admit that he hated the thought of missing a night with Lise. Not that he didn't feel pretty sure of her, but that didn't stop him from being afraid that she might walk out of his life as suddenly as she had entered it. She was worried about her husband. A laudable trait in a human being, perhaps, but it also told him that she still had feelings for Ole, and it wouldn't be the first time he had seen an errant wife return to the safety of the nest. Which had been fine with him, on those other occasions, but he was not so certain that it would be so this time. This was developing into something more than an affair.

She seemed agitated when they set out to visit the three schools they had picked out. He knew she had spent the morning calling friends and family, but no one had seen Ole. She did not want to report him missing just yet; she would give it another day. He hadn't taken anything from the apartment. The car was parked at the kerb, but she couldn't find the car keys. Only the spare set, which was hanging on a hook in the kitchen. It was like the story of the man who went out to buy cigarettes and never came back. She borrowed Per's mobile and called home, but every time she tried she got the answering machine.

At the first school they drew a blank. They looked at the class pictures, and the school had a list of the pupils' names for them, but there had been only two Yugoslavian boys in the class, and their profiles didn't fit. One was still living in the area and had a Danish wife. The other had been killed in a car crash only four years previously. None of the other pupils at the school matched up with any of the twenty-one names on the list given to Per by the officers who had done the spadework. The second school lay in Nørrebro, in an old redbrick building. Here, in the late afternoon, it was empty and quiet, with no children or teachers around. An elderly man was standing just inside the door, waiting for them. He looked as though he had been there for some time. He was impeccably turned out in an old-fashioned tweed jacket complete with waistcoat and tie and grey flannels with a knife-edge crease. His hair was snowy white but still thick and bushy. The skin of his face had a pinkish cast to it, as if he had given himself an extra close shave that day. Lise gauged him to be at least seventy, possibly more. He was the very image of a venerable old schoolmaster, the last of a dying breed. He had about him a whiff of schooldays long gone, but the word Lise would have used to describe him was 'distinguished'. He stepped forward and shook their hands:

'Gustav Hansen, senior teacher, retired.'

'Lise Carlsen, Danish PEN and *Politiken*.'

'Detective-Inspector Toftlund.'

'Excellent,' said Gustav Hansen. His hand was dry and cool. He spoke slowly and very distinctly in a deep baritone. He pointed down the corridor and up a stairway and walked ahead of them with a firm, if slow stride, talking as he went: 'I know you are pressed for time, and I have been thoroughly briefed regarding the purpose of your investigation, so I gathered together all the material I believe to be relevant while awaiting your arrival. The headmistress has been of great help with everything and has even given us the use of her office.'

He opened the door of the headmistress's office. The headmistress herself was a small, slightly built woman in her forties who greeted them politely then left, saying that they were in the best possible hands with Gustav Hansen.

Mr Hansen laid nine class photos out on the desk, as if he were dealing cards, explaining as he did so in his distinct didactic tones:

'Here they are. These are the photographs of the final-year classes of 1984, '85, '86 and '87. Difficult classes but good. Still bearing the marks of a rather too liberal upbringing; victims, if you like, of all the confusion of the seventies, but they were bright those children. That they were. That they were.'

The photographs were in colour and were all pretty much identical. The young people were arranged in rows and looking straight at the camera. The length of the boys' hair was the only indication of the passage of time. Each year it was a little shorter than the year before.

'Do you also happen to have the class registers, sir?' Per asked as he examined the pictures.

'Why would you need those, Detective-Inspector?'

'Because we would like to be able to put names to some of these faces.'

Gustav Hansen straightened his shoulders and eyed Per squarely.

'I was a teacher for fifty years,' he said. 'I remember every single child I ever taught. I do not need registers. I even took part in a so-called quiz programme on television once, where they tried to catch me out. I am proud to say that not even on television could they do that. I would also like to point out…'

'Sorry, no offence meant,' Per interjected. Lise caught the note of impatience in his voice, but she found the old teacher charming and quite fascinating. She thought she would like to write a piece about him at some point. What they had here was a small piece of bygone Denmark. It would make a nice little human-interest story.

'How many of these kids are Yugoslavian?' Per asked.

Gustav Hansen regarded the pictures with what might have been wistfulness, or love even, Lise thought, before he said:

'We had quite a few of them at that time. Thirteen children, in all, from Yugoslavian homes. Six of them were girls. Quiet, but very bright. That they were. Oh yes, that they were. It's terrible what's happening down there now. There was never any trouble between them during my time here. Seven boys…although we couldn't have said whether they were Croatian or…'

Now it was Lise's turn to interrupt:

'Can you remember which of them went on to high school?'

'From these years? Let me see now. A handful. There was Janos, and Jaumin. Apart from them…no. Oh, yes, there was one girl. A bit weak in physics, but otherwise…let me see…they were really starting to make progress. With their Danish. The ones who were born here. A command of the language really is so important.'

Hansen stood there, sunk in thought. They seemed to have lost him to his memories.

'Were any of the boys fair-haired and blue-eyed?' Lise asked.

Gustav Hansen's face lit up once more and he was back with them again.

'How extraordinary that you should ask that,' he said. 'You know, I was just thinking about him. In fact I mentioned him only a moment ago. Janos?'

He picked up one of the class photographs and pointed to a very young version of Vuk. Standing among the other teenagers, grinning broadly at the camera. The boy on his left was Mikael, and to the right of him stood another boy whose face seemed familiar to Lise. She took the picture. There was something about the young, fair-haired Yugoslavian whom Gustav Hansen had pointed out that stirred something in her memory, but it was the boy to the right whom she recognized.

'What is it?' Per asked.

'Isn't that Peter Sørensen from the evening news?' she said, looking at Gustav Hansen.

'That's right.'

'Janos?' said Per.

'Janos Milosovic. An extraordinarily gifted boy. I wonder what became of him,' Hansen said.

'That's something we'd like to know too,' Per commented, running his eye down his list. The name was there.

'Well, for heaven's sake, why don't you ask his old friend?' Hansen said, sighing impatiently as if he were talking to two rather inattentive children. 'He might know. I have to say I am rather proud to have had him as a pupil. One cannot help feeling that one has had a hand in his success. Those first years are so crucial, you know. The moulding of these young characters.'

'I'm sorry, I'm not with you.' Per said, no longer able to conceal his irritation.

'Peter Sørensen, the foreign correspondent, of course. From the evening news. Miss Carlsen mentioned him herself. He lived next door to Janos. They were very good friends.'

Per thought for a moment. Then:

'Lise, do you happen to know offhand the number for the Danmarks Radio news desk?' he asked, pulling out his mobile.

Peter Sørensen was out on a shoot, but they were given a mobile number at which they could reach him. He said he would be back in the office around seven, but then he had the story to edit so he was going to be really busy. If they could come around eight-thirty, though, that would be okay. Per explained what it was they wanted to talk to him about, and he sounded very interested, but that didn't alter the fact that he had a story to edit first.

They called in at the last school on their list, but it did not furnish them with any likely candidates. Then they found a restaurant in Nørreport and had dinner together, eating mostly in silence. Sara Santanda was arriving the next day, and in three days' time she would be travelling on to Sweden. Lise wondered whether things would be different between them once they were no longer working together. She didn't know. Her usual healthy appetite had deserted her, and she merely picked at her food. To save Per knowing that she was calling home again, she used the payphone next to the toilets but still got only her own answering machine. She also rang the paper and spoke to the sub-editor, who told her that her pieces were fantastic and would be given all the space they needed. Normally this would have given her a tremendous boost, but somehow she couldn't get worked up about it at all. She was scared and did not know exactly why, although she realized it was probably because she was so worried about Ole. Where could he have got to?

At 8.00 pm they drove out to the Danmarks Radio studios. The breeze had stiffened, and it had started to rain, but Lise knew that the forecast for the next day was for a clearer, brighter morning with the possibility of showers in the afternoon. Just at that moment, in the dark and the rain, the idea of a press conference at Flakfortet did not seem such a brilliant idea.

Peter Sørensen came down to meet them at the security desk and led them up to his office. He shook Per's hand formally and introduced himself, then turned to Lise, shook her hand too, with a 'Hi, how are you doing?' His office was tiny and chaotic, but he pushed a pile of newspapers off one chair, fetched another from the corridor and got them settled. He took his own seat behind his overloaded desk. On his computer screen, in white characters on a blue background, was a wire story from Reuters about the situation in Bosnia. He gave them coffee in plastic cups, and Per showed him the class picture.

'Yeah, sure. That's Janos. And muggins there, that's me. Where the hell did you dig up this old picture?'

'So you know him?' Per said.

'I should think so. Janos went back to Yugoslavia at the end of our second year in high school. It was a bloody shame. He was so fucking bright, that guy. I actually tried to trace him when I was down there for DR. My sources tell me he's one of the Serbs' top hit men. They say he kills people as casually as you would squash a fly.'

Per's eyes were fixed on him. Lise thought he looked like a hunter or a wild beast – a puma – that has caught wind of its prey.

'Did you find him?' Lise asked.

'No. I heard something down there about the Muslims having massacred his whole family. I tried to trace them too. I really liked his parents, and he had the sweetest little sister, but there was just no way, what with the war and all.' He turned to Per and added: 'But why are the police asking questions about him? Has it to do with Bosnia? Or…has it something to do with Scheer?'

'What makes you think that?' Toftlund said.

'Well, Lise here has called a press conference with Scheer for tomorrow afternoon. And they're out to get him in Germany. I'll be covering the event for the evening news.'

'I'm afraid I can't comment on that,' Per replied stiffly.

'No, I don't suppose you can. But what do you want with Janos?'

'To talk to him.'

Peter Sørensen sipped his coffee. His curiosity was piqued, Lise could tell. The newshound in him scented a story here. He guessed that there was more to this than met the eye, although obviously he couldn't know what. Ten to one he would be on the phone to her later, when the police weren't around, trying to pump her for information.

'I lost touch with him. But have you spoken to Mikael?'

He could tell by their faces that they had no idea who he was talking about, so he continued:

'He was Janos's other friend. We three hung out together a lot.' He lifted the class photograph and pointed to Mikael as he went on talking: 'Mikael's a real screwball, computer mad. He's become a bit of a hermit, you might say. Lives alone in his parents' old house in Hellerup. They're rolling in money and spend most of the year in Spain. They were doing that even when we were kids. So Mikael lived with his aunt and grew up along with the rest of us lads in

Nørrebro. They wanted to send him to boarding school, but Mikael kept running away, so he ended up staying with his aunt. Have you spoken to Mikael?'

'Do you have a number for him?' Per asked.

Sørensen fished a little notebook out of the clutter on the table, leafed through it and wrote down a telephone number and an address in Hellerup on a pad, tore off the sheet and handed it to Toftlund.

'He can't always be depended on to answer the phone. He's kind of special. But listen, what's this all about? Is Janos in Denmark? You're not from PET are you?'

'Thanks for your help,' Per said.

'Is Janos in Denmark?'

'That's what we're trying to find out,' Lise said, disregarding a warning glance from Per.

Toftlund called PET headquarters on his mobile from the DR car park. He said that he was bringing in an old photograph. He was going to need a photo technician, an artist and an Identikit expert. He had a face and a name. Then he called Mikael's number. He let the phone ring and ring, then eventually shook his head and flicked the mobile shut.

'Now what?' Lise asked.

'I'm going to run you home.'

'And then?'

'Then I'm going to pay a call on Mikael. He might be in.'

'Shouldn't you have backup for something like this?'

'Why?'

'Well, what if this guy Janos is somewhere around?'

'Yeah, maybe.'

'But you don't want help?' she said.

'No, not yet.'

He put the car into gear and drove off.

'I'm coming with you,' Lise said.

'Why? What for?'

'So we can hold hands and neck like a couple of American teenagers.'

He laughed.

'All right then.'

The house in Hellerup lay hushed and still behind its hedge, but there was a light burning in the kitchen and in one of the upstairs rooms. Lise waited in the car while Per rang the doorbell, then took a walk around the house. It was almost 11.00 pm, and all was quiet in the streets round about. The grass was long and damp under his feet. It looked as though something had been dragged across the grass and down to the water. The Sound stretched out, black and rain-drenched, at his feet. He noticed a couple of flashing lights out on the water, but visibility was very poor in the driving rain. He peered through the French windows, but the rooms were in darkness. He tried the door. It was locked. He walked back to the car. There was a light on upstairs in the house opposite, and he was conscious of someone tweaking a curtain aside and peering down at him. They keep close tabs on one another around here, he thought to himself.

He climbed into the car beside Lise. He smelled of rain, and the windows steamed up.

'Right, let's go home. I don't know whether he's in there, or whether he'll be back later, but I'll organize a search warrant tomorrow morning. I'm pretty certain I can get one if he isn't answering the door or the phone.'

'Do you think there's something wrong?'

'It's just a feeling. But yes, I think there's something wrong.' He placed a hand on his stomach. 'Gut instinct. That's all it is,' he said.

'Intuition.'

'That's another word for it.'

'And what happens after tomorrow?' she asked.

'Well, we have a couple of days' more of her, and then Simba is no longer our problem but our Swedish colleagues'. And by then everyone will know that she's on the move. They're going to have their work cut out for them over there, but they'll probably have more resources to draw on too.'

'And after that?'

'I've got a whole lot of time off owing to me,' he said.

'So have I,' she said, keeping her eyes front. Raindrops coursed down the windscreen.

'Maybe we could go to Spain,' he said softly, but Lise thought that even so she heard a hidden prayer there, a new uncertainty, which said he did not take her for granted.

'That sounds wonderful, Per. Only…'

'It's your husband, isn't it?'

'Yes. Ole. As long as he's missing I don't see how I can…'

'It's okay. We'll find him. And then we'll go.'

She turned her face to his, and they kissed, and at that same moment the car was flooded by a light from the rear that made the raindrops on the windows sparkle like tiny crystals. A patrol car had pulled up behind them, and as they watched one of the officers got out. His partner remained behind the wheel, already in the process of keying Per's registration number into the car's computer.

Toftlund got out:

'Good evening,' he said.

'Good evening,' the policeman said.

Toftlund slipped his hand slowly into his jacket pocket and pulled out his ID card.

'Toftlund. G division,' he said.

The policeman behind the wheel opened his door a little way and shouted:

'It's okay, Niels. He's one of us.'

'Christensen,' the uniformed cop said and offered his hand. The rain had slackened to little more than a drizzle, veiling houses and hedges and enveloping the lampposts in a lovely soft glow.

'The lady across the road gave us a call,' the policeman continued. He wasn't very old, and like so many other young policemen, he spoke with a pronounced Jutland accent. He sported a neatly trimmed moustache and most likely dreamed of a couple of years of working undercover before landing a plum job somewhere in Jutland. 'She thought you two looked a little suspicious. There are a lot of embassies in this area, you know, so we keep an eye out.'

'That's perfectly all right,' Toftlund said.

'It's not the first time she's called. She's an old lady, we know her. She hasn't seen the owner of this house for some days. But she has seen another young man coming and going, which she thought was a bit strange. And then suddenly there was this car parked here, so she called us.'

Toftlund thought for a moment. Then:

'Tell your partner that you and I are going in,' he said.

'But we can't just go breaking into people's houses,' the officer protested.

'I'll take responsibility. Have your gun at the ready.'

'What's going on?'

'Maybe nothing. But it may have to do with a man we're looking for,' Toftlund said, already moving towards the garden gate. Whatever way you looked at it, Toftlund was a superior officer, so the uniformed cop glanced back at his partner, pointed to Toftlund, then followed after him.

'What about your partner?' the young policeman asked.

'She's a civilian. She stays where she is.'

Toftlund rang the bell again but there was still no answer. He pulled his gun and saw the young policeman do the same. There were beads of sweat on his brow, even though the evening was chilly, and Toftlund could see that he was nervous. It could be that he was still just a probationer. They stole round to the back garden. The inky waters of the Sound lapped gently, and the grass felt wet and clammy against their shoes. Per crept up to the French windows, which consisted of lots of small panes of glass set into a white wooden frame flaking slightly along the seams. He turned to Constable Christensen.

'Now, Christensen. You watch what I do, and you listen to what I say, and then you write it all down in your report. I am about to force entry to this residence because I have reasonable grounds for believing that a person possibly wanted by the police may be on the premises. Is that understood?'

'Yes, sir,' said Christensen.

Per Toftlund turned his gun around and used the butt to smash the pane next to the keyhole. He poked a hand inside and found the key in the lock. People just never learned. They made it so easy for burglars to get in and so easy for them to get away again with their loot. He opened the door, cocked his gun and stepped inside, followed by the young policeman who – prompted by the tense set of Toftlund's body – cocked his own pistol before entering the dark gloomy house.

Chapter 20

But the man who called himself Vuk was gone. At that precise moment he was approaching Flakfortet, which lay shrouded in the mist of rain. Using a short double-bladed paddle he manoeuvred the black rubber raft alongside the outer face of the breakwater on the north side of the man-made island. With slow but efficient strokes he skirted the breakwater. He was dressed in black from head to toe and almost impossible to make out in the rain-dark sea. Lashed securely to the bottom of the dinghy was a black waterproof sack the size of a sailor's duffle bag. A few lights still burned on Flakfortet, but the last guests had sailed back to Copenhagen long ago; the crew on the two pleasure boats were asleep, and the restaurant staff were either flopped in front of some TV programme or had gone to bed. They had had a visit from the police, who had checked their ID, gone over the whole place with dogs and informed the yacht owners, whose identities had also been confirmed, that they would have to leave the harbour early the next morning, since the fort would be closed for a fire drill between the hours of 10.00 am and 5.00 pm.

Vuk had been busy.

Early in the morning two days before, he had rented a middle-range car at Avis's main office in Copenhagen. He had used his British passport and driving licence and his British Eurocard/Mastercard, given an address in south London and said that he would need the car for seven days. He would deliver it in Stockholm, where he would be checking in to the SAS hotel. He had phoned ahead to book the car, so within a mere ten minutes he was able to drive away. His Eurocard number was checked and found to be in order.

Vuk drove first to Østerbro where earlier he had passed a sports shop specializing in diving equipment. He was served by a muscly young man with a toothpaste-ad smile, who turned out, nonetheless, to be competent enough and knowledgeable when it came to scuba diving. It took Vuk an hour to choose his equipment. He spoke English to the young man. Explained very briefly that he was from the Czech Republic, and that it was far better and cheaper for him to buy his gear in Denmark, since he could get the tax refunded at the border. The assistant couldn't have cared less. He received a commission on everything he sold, and he soon found out that Vuk knew what he was talking about, so he helped him to select and try on a wetsuit, explaining as he did so, quite unnecessarily, how the wetsuit worked by allowing the water to seep through it and form a very thin layer between the suit and the skin, thus insulating the body against the cold of the surrounding water. Vuk also bought a mask and snorkel, flippers, a lead-weight belt and a full oxygen tank complete with harness, as well as a small buoy for tying to one's belt or fixing to an anchor, to warn passing ships of the presence of a diver in the water. To all of this he also added a powerful torch specially designed for use both above and below the water and a little waterproof pouch for hanging around the neck. He paid cash.

In another water sports shop Vuk bought a detailed chart of the waters between Copenhagen, Saltholm, Flakfortet and Sweden, along with an anchor and anchor chain. He deposited his purchases in the boot of the rented car and made his way down to a shop near Nørreport station specializing in all manner of outdoor gear. Here he bought a lightweight sleeping bag, a sleeping mat and a waterproof rucksack, a battery-driven camping lamp and a waterproof wrist-compass with a luminous dial of a sort used frequently by divers. Again he paid in cash. In the hunting supplies shop Hunter's House he found a large waterproof bag with a zipper and a drawstring neck for sealing it shut. His last stop was at the Magasin department store, known so well from his childhood and youth. Here he bought a black woollen pull-on hat and a pair of black deck shoes. In the food hall he purchased a pack of sliced bread, salami and cheese. And finally, in the cosmetics department, he picked up some black hair dye.

He dumped the lot on the floor of the kitchen in Hellerup and made a round of the house to make sure that everything was as it should be. There were no signs that anyone had been inside; there was nothing in the ordinary mailbox except advertising bumph, but in the computer's mailbox lay messages from all over the world. He did a quick scan of them. They were all for Mikael and all perfectly innocent.

He drove up to Helsingør on the north coast and took the ferry across to Helsingborg in Sweden. There was no queue; he was able to drive straight on. He had his Danish passport ready, but there was no control when he drove ashore. He drove south, past Malmö and parked the car close to Limhamn harbour, in a quiet residential street with no parking restrictions. Then he took the ferry back across from Limhamn to Dragør on the island suburb of Amager. He ate a steak with onions on board and read the Danish newspapers. There were only a few passengers on the ferry, mostly pensioners returning from a shopping expedition to Sweden.

Vuk took the bus into the city centre, then the train out to Hellerup. Twilight was falling on the villa, but another tour of the house told him that everything was as normal. He poured himself a vodka from the bar in the sitting room and carried the glass through to the kitchen where he switched on the television to watch the early evening news at 6.30. The news was mainly Danish. It didn't mean much to him. Minor disputes that were blown up into great dramas simply because things were, by and large, so peaceful here, he thought to himself. There was no news from Bosnia and nothing about Sara Santanda. Normality reigned. He popped a frozen pizza into the oven, got out the sea chart and proceeded to study it. The distance from Copenhagen to Flakfortet was approximately five miles, and about half that from Flakfortet to Saltholm. What interested him most were the international shipping lanes on either side of the patch of Dirty Sea. On the city side there would be markers around the outskirts of the Dirty Sea He remembered how the *M/S Langø* had sailed in a wide arc from the mouth of Copenhagen Harbour to Flakfortet, instead of heading for the man-made island in a straight line. A quick look at the key map in the Copenhagen A-Z was enough to show him why, but the sea chart gave a very clear picture of the way in which Middelgrund and the Dirty Sea lay like a barrier, a kind of minefield, between the two shipping channels. He assumed that in the shallows of the Dirty Sea lay an old rubbish dump or ships' graveyard.

He turned his attention to the weather forecast that followed the news. The weatherman said there would be rain that evening, but that this would clear away during the night. The weather the next day would be cloudy but generally dry, with the possibility of showers later in the evening; but these too would give way to brighter weather, and on the day itself the nice man on the TV promised that the morning would be sunny with scattered clouds, a moderate wind from the east and temperatures a little above normal for the time of year. In the afternoon rain and strong winds would move in across the country from the east. The weather forecast pleased Vuk. Rain and poor visibility at night was exactly what he wanted.

He picked up the remote control, switched to CNN and turned down the sound. He went on scanning the chart while he ate his pizza, making quite certain of the coordinates he would give to Berlin. They, in turn, would see to it that these were passed on to the captain of the Russian barge, which, with any luck, was already laid up somewhere close by with supposed engine trouble – probably in some small harbour not far from Copenhagen. He called Berlin and had to wait fifteen minutes for them to call him back. He read out the coordinates from the sea chart, first in English and then, to be on the safe side, in German. Between 14:00 hours and 16:00 hours, Thursday. He had his specifications read back to him over the clear line, then said:

'Any problems with the competition?'

'Negative.'

'Okay.'

'This office will close once the deal has been completed,' the voice in Berlin said.

'Understood,' Vuk said. 'I'll need a note of the new address.'

'We prefer email.'

'Fine.'

Vuk took down the email address. Now he would be able to get in touch with his employers via any computer with an Internet connection, without anyone knowing what he was writing to them about. This he could do from an Internet café or a library, for example, in Vienna or Belgrade; and they would have no idea of his actual whereabouts. He would head back to Serbia, he had decided. From the news reports he knew that NATO forces in the Balkans now appeared to be actively hunting down and arresting those whom enemies of the Serbs called war criminals. He would get in touch with Emma, and together they would lie low until all the fuss died down. They would never be able to find him on his own home ground. That was the safest place for someone like him right now while the plan of pinning the blame on some fanatical Muslim was given time to work.

He plotted his course on the sea chart, marking the vital reference points. He would be able to take his bearings from the Nordre Røse lighthouse, Saltholm, Flakfortet, the spires of Copenhagen, and in daylight he would be able to see the innocent-looking buoy he would be dropping on the border between the Dirty Sea and Dutchman's Deep.

He packed his diving gear into the rucksack and drew it closed. Into the waterproof bag he stuffed the sleeping bag, the mat and the torch. There was still plenty of room. He laid his black, rubber-soled Ecco shoes on top of the mat. He neatly folded his smart tweed jacket, grey flannels and a light-blue shirt and placed these too in the bag. To these he added a discreetly patterned tie, a pair of dark socks and a small mirror he had found in the bathroom. And lastly he packed in the black jeans, polo-neck and a thick cotton undershirt. He tamped the whole lot down firmly by cramming a large bath towel on top.

Down in the basement he lifted the black rubber dinghy off its hooks. He did not so much as glance at the bodies of Mikael and Ole under their tarpaulin. His mind was on the dinghy. It was in good nick, if a little soft, looked like it hadn't been used in a while. In the bottom of the raft lay two short canoe oars and a stubby, double-bladed kayak paddle. He fetched the foot-pump from the corner, pumped up the dinghy with ease. It was a four-man craft, a navy model: a real beauty. He inspected the outboard motor. It seemed well cared-for and relatively new. What luck for him that one of Mikael's few hobbies, apart from computers, had been to chug up and down the Sound looking at ships. Vuk found an old petrol can in the workroom and filled the motor's tank. He was beginning to feel tired after having to stay so focused all day. When shopping in town he had been constantly on the lookout for possible tails, or simply for people he knew, who might recognize him.

Vuk spent the rest of that evening and a good part of the night at the workbench in the basement, making two lock-picks on the well-equipped lathe. That done, he had another glass of vodka and turned in for the night. He slept peacefully, with no worries about nightmares. He knew himself well enough to be aware that both his conscious mind and his subconscious would now be concentrated on the job in hand, allowing no room for anything else. After the successful completion of the job, the demons would return, but right now they were leaving him in peace. He felt perfectly safe in this house. No one knew he was in the country, and no one knew that he had the schedule for the condemned writer's movements during her stay in Denmark.

Vuk woke early, but well rested the next morning. The weatherman had been right, he saw, when he looked out of the window. The clouds hung low and looked heavy with rain, but it stayed dry. He made coffee and watched CNN while he had breakfast. After that, he cleared the kitchen table and got out his weapons. He dismantled the rifle and put it back in the case. He would not be using the rifle. They would have police snipers positioned up on the old gun emplacements, of that he was sure. For his escape plan to work he would need to create utter chaos during those few crucial minutes.

He lifted the pistol. He had checked it and seen that it was okay, but you could never check too often! It could have been bought or stolen. It was a very common model, so in all likelihood it had been obtained legally. It was an Italian gun, a black Beretta 92F, the pistol that had come out on top in field trials carried out by the American military to find a new service pistol. It had replaced the old Colt 45, to which it bore a great similarity. But it was more stable and safer to use. Vuk actually preferred revolvers to pistols. They were more robust and could take a lot more punishment than the more complex pistols, which had a tendency to jam at the most inconvenient moments, but his revolver of choice, the Smith & Wesson, could only take five cartridges, which was too few when there was an element of uncertainty attached to his escape. And the Beretta was a good gun that he knew well. It would give him fifteen bullets in the magazine in its butt plus one in the chamber, and that was all-important. He loaded fifteen 9 mm bullets into the magazine and smacked it up into the butt. Having made sure that the safety was on, he raised the pistol into the firing position, holding it with both hands. The two pounds or so of steel was nicely balanced. Vuk knew that a bullet would leave the barrel at a speed of almost 1,300 feet per second and at the distance at which he planned to use it would go right through the Target and wreak appalling damage on the human body on the way out. He would be able to plant three bullets in the Target in a second or two. Vuk also assumed that the gun had been tested, but he needed to discover for himself how it reacted and which way it pulled. He wasn't happy about this. Denmark was a small country, no one here was ever very far from anyone else, and hence it was hard to find a place where he could try it out, but he had to. It would have been easier in Sweden, but he wasn't stupid enough to try carrying a pistol across an international boundary. It was too risky. The odds on getting caught were too high.

Vuk took the train to Hillerød then switched to the little private line, nicknamed 'Grisen' – the Pig – that carried him through the largest forest on Zealand, Grib Skov. He was the only passenger on the train apart from two high school kids conducting a *sotto voce* discussion about classmates and teachers. Vuk got off at Gribsø and struck off into the forest. He walked for twenty minutes, until he was sure that he was far enough off the beaten track. He had a dense thicket of pines to one side of him and old beech woods to the other. The trees would deaden the sound. The clearing in which he stood measured about two hundred square feet. He picked up three large pine cones and arranged them four inches apart at head height in a hollow in an ancient tree that had been gashed by lightning. He walked back ten paces, cocked the pistol and fired. The gun pulled a little to the right. The bang had not been particularly loud, but it had still sent a bird flapping, screeching, into the air. The bullet had hit home just above the right-hand pine cone. He steadied the Beretta with both hands, aimed along his outstretched arms and fired again. The pine cone disappeared in a cloud of dust. He took two paces forward, at the same time pressing the trigger four times in rapid succession. The other two cones shattered. He walked up to the tree: four bullet holes all in a row. He slipped the gun back into the satchel in which he had transported it. It was of blue canvas, indistinguishable from so many others. He left the forest quickly, going in the opposite direction to that by which he had come and found his way to the station, where he had to wait half an hour for a train. He didn't meet a single person and had the train to himself for most of the way back to Hillerød.

Back at the villa he cleaned the pistol and refilled the magazine. He loaded bullets into the reserve magazine, then made himself some tea with lots of sugar and a dash of rum, and a cheese and salami sandwich. He wrapped the sandwich in foil and popped it, along with the thermos of tea and a bottle of water, into the waterproof bag, which he carefully sealed. He packed the pistol and the reserve magazine into a plastic bag and placed this in his satchel, along with the notebook and a ballpoint pen. There would be room here too for his toothbrush and toothpaste, an extra comb and toilet paper. He put what cash he had left, the passport and credit card into the small waterproof bag that he would wear around his neck.

In the bathroom he coloured his hair and his beard – which, though short, now covered the lower half of his face well – black with the hair dye. He washed the sink thoroughly afterwards and threw the dye tube into the rubbish bin outside the house before climbing into the wet suit. It had a hood, but he pulled on the woollen hat instead. He slipped his bare feet into the black deck shoes.

Vuk had to push the dinghy onto its side to get it through the basement door and up into the back garden. The rain pelted him in the face as he stepped out onto the sodden grass and dragged the dinghy down to the bottom of the garden and the dark choppy waters of the Sound. He returned to the basement for the outboard motor and mounted it on the dinghy, then lashed the rucksack and the waterproof bag securely to the bottom. He made the buoy fast to the rucksack with the anchor line, in such a way that the anchor was fixed to the rucksack itself.

He was ready.

Vuk went back to the house. The rain was getting heavier, and his fingers and toes were a bit cold, but they would soon warm up again. Suddenly he started. The phone was ringing. He stood where he was for a moment, waited till it stopped, then locked the basement door and left the house by the front door, which he could simply slam shut. He went round to the back garden, pushed the rubber raft out into the Sound and used the kayak paddle to row away from the shore before trying to start the outboard motor. It roared into life at the fourth attempt, but the sound was soon swallowed up by the murky Sound. He checked the luminous dial of his compass and the sea chart, which he had wrapped in thin plastic. The raft skimmed smoothly and steadily over the choppy waves as he headed down the coast towards the edge of the Dirty Sea, which he knew the dinghy, with its shallow draught, could cross without any problem. It was pitch-dark on the Sound, but he could make out the lamps of several boats in the shipping lanes, and the bright lights of ferries on which passengers would be sitting snug and warm over a coffee or the last beer of the night. On reaching the outskirts of the Dirty Sea he put the motor into its lowest gear and glided over the treacherous reef until he reached his position. He checked the compass and, half-standing in the boat, found his reference points. Then he lowered the rucksack, with the anchor attached to it, into the water. Weighted by the anchor and the lead belt it sank swiftly to the bottom, in what was, by his calculations, about eight feet of water – which meant he was on the right side of whatever there was of railway sleepers or concrete blocks and other old junk down there. Once he had felt the rucksack settle on the bottom he paid out another six feet of rope before taking the knife bound to his shin, cutting the line and tying the end to the buoy. He looked at the compass, then over to the shore and down to the right towards Nordre Røse. He could see the Lynneten sewage plant and the lights atop Copenhagen's spires. He took his bearings, feeling certain that he could find this spot again without much trouble. They had practised this sort of thing hundreds of times during their frogman training at the Special Forces School: infiltration and sabotage, getting in and out again unseen. As it is practised by Special Forces the world over.

Again Vuk checked his compass. His fingers and toes were chilled, but nothing serious, not badly enough to hinder him in his task. The wetsuit protected him against the water that occasionally slopped in over the dinghy when it hit a rogue wave. He set course for Flakfortet, all the while keeping an eye on other vessels in the Sound. He knew they could not see him. Just before he reached the fort he switched off the outboard motor. Giving the harbour entrance a wide berth, he rowed round the island, following the breakwater that encircled it, and brought the raft to rest on the seaward side of the breakwater.

He clambered up onto the stones of the breakwater, hauled the watertight bag up after him. Had there been anyone out in the rain and the dark, it's unlikely they would have seen him, even if they had been standing only six feet away inside Flakfortet itself. Nonetheless, he hunkered down and listened intently. All he could hear was the rain on the stones, and the sea. The Swedish and

Danish coastlines were lost in the drizzle. Flakfortet was deserted. Vuk climbed back into the raft, hoicked up the outboard and pricked a tiny hole in the rubber with his knife under the water level, before pushing the dinghy out into the current. In less than thirty minutes it would have sunk to the bottom.

He bound the shoulder straps of the waterproof bag around his waist and with his right hand holding the satchel out of the water slipped into the strip of water that separated the fort from the breakwater and shielded it from the sea's constant assaults. Three kicks of his legs took him to the other side, and he crawled ashore.

Vuk peeled off the wetsuit, feeling exposed, naked and white in the darkness, but he did not want to leave a trail of water when making his way through the fort's passageways. He opened the bag, took out the towel and rubbed himself dry before slipping into the black jeans, the undershirt and the black polo-neck, socks and shoes. He tossed the wet deck shoes into the water and watched them drift away. He rolled the wetsuit up in the big towel and tucked it into the top of the bag, which he drew shut again before shouldering his gear and entering the fort's benighted maze. His night vision was perfect, but the darkness of the passageways was absolute. He switched on his torch, after first straining his ears for any sound in the night. He located the concrete steps and climbed deep down into the bowels of the fort. The temperature in the casemates was only ten degrees Celsius, and he began to shiver slightly with cold.

He found the padlocked door to the old ammunition store. He pulled out his pick and set to work on the lock. It was a very basic one, and he sprang it without any trouble. The other, more sophisticated lock-pick he would need tomorrow. He removed the chain and opened the door into the cold dark room, to be met by a wave of rank musty air. He stood quite still and listened, could hear nothing but his own breathing. He laid the bag, the satchel and the lighted torch inside the room and closed the door. No light showed. He retrieved the torch, returned to the main entrance, got down on his knees and swept the dust on the cement floor carefully with the palm of his hand, erasing his footprints. He worked his way back to the ammunition store and obliterated all tracks outside it before pulling the heavy steel door closed and padlocking it on the inside.

He switched on the camping lamp, which gave him enough light to make out the dry livid walls of the low-ceilinged room. There was a sudden movement in a corner where the concrete was crumbling away around what might have been an air vent or sewage outlet. The rat eyed him, as if wondering who could have penetrated its domain after all these years. Vuk's hand slid down to his shin and curled around the knife, then it shot out. The tip of the knife caught the rat in the side as it tried to scuttle off down the side of the room. It emitted a short squeal as it was run through. Vuk pricked it in the throat and stomach, opened the steel door and chucked it out. It looked like a victim of one of the fierce territorial battles in which rats engaged. Its blood trickled slowly out.

He unrolled the sleeping mat and laid the sleeping bag on top. He spread the wetsuit out to dry and sat with the sleeping bag wrapped around him, massaging his cold feet. He was exhausted from all his physical exertions and the mental strain. He was dying for a cigarette, but smoke could be smelled a long way off, and he didn't know what sort of ventilation there was from the casemates. So instead he poured tea into the thermos cup and ate his sandwich, while he waited for morning.

Chapter 21

Per Toftlund whirled around as he heard Lise scream. He had dragged the tarpaulin off the two tubs and was staring down at the bodies of Ole and Mikael. Her first shrill shrieks subsided into gasping grating sobs. Rigor mortis had set in and passed. The corpses were a ghastly white, with livid patches where the blood had drained down and coagulated, the eyes sunken and blank.

Per held Lise and let her weep onto his shoulder. He stroked her hair, caressed her cheek, which felt cold and clammy. The uniformed policeman stood riveted to the spot, his eyes flicking back and forth between them and the bodies. He had seen dead people before. You didn't have to have been a policeman in Copenhagen for very long before you saw your first body. Usually, though, they were suicides or old folk who had died alone and neglected. He had never seen a corpse lying doubled-up in an old-fashioned washtub with its throat gouged by steel wire.

'Get onto the murder squad, man!' Per snapped, his arms still wrapped tightly around Lise, who seemed to be teetering on the brink of shock. 'Use the phone. Not the radio,' he added. He knew the tabloid crime desks listened in on the police wavelength. Their scanners were as good, if not better than the police's own. He wanted to keep the lid on this for the next twenty-four hours at least.

'It's Ole. It's my husband,' Lise cried for the third time. 'What's he doing here? Why didn't I take care of him?'

'Lise, Lise, Lise. It's not your fault,' Per said as her sobs increased again.

He took her upstairs, sat her down in the kitchen and poured her a glass of water, which she gulped down. Her eyes were red and swollen, but her tears had abated. She had hiccups from drinking the water so fast, but she emptied the glass, and he filled it again from the tap.

She looked up at Per.

'I remember him,' she whispered.

'Who?'

'The boy in the school photograph. The one they call Janos.'

'What do you mean?'

'He was at our apartment. He said his name was Carsten.'

'When was this?'

'The other day. He was this new friend of Ole's.'

Her voice broke again at the mention of Ole's name, but then she seemed to Per to get a grip on herself. Or was she stronger than he thought?

'All of a sudden, when I saw Ole there, I made the connection between the photograph and the man who was at our place. Why didn't I think of it before? Why Per? If I had, none of this would have happened.'

'The memory can play tricks on us. Sometimes it needs to be jogged,' he essayed.

'It wouldn't have happened!' she cried, dissolving into tears once more.

Per left her to sit for a while. The patrol cars would be here any minute, closely followed by the murder squad and the forensic team with all its equipment. This was no longer his case. This was murder, and there were others with far greater expertise in that field than him. They would take over, start their investigation, issue a description of the man they wished to interview, the usual stuff. His eye fell on the rifle in the open suitcase on the floor. Janos had gone off without his gun. He must be long gone by now. Something must have scared him off. Sara Santanda was actually safer now. Not that that was any comfort to Lise, but it did take some of the pressure off him. Nevertheless, he asked:

'How much did your husband know?'

She looked at him. Her eyes swam with tears, and his heart went out to her. Why hadn't she stayed in the car? Blasted reporters, they never could resist poking their bloody noses in.

'He was my husband. Obviously I told him things…'

He considered her.

'Oh, what the hell. Janos is miles away by now. Something must have gone wrong with his plans.'

'I want to go home,' she said softly.

'Is there someone who could keep you company? I have to…'

'I have a good friend. She can probably come over.'

'Good.'

He could tell by looking at her that the full force of what had happened had not quite hit her yet. She could still break down completely.

'I want to go home,' she said.

'What could Ole have told him?' Per asked. He couldn't stop himself, even though he saw the pain return to her face.

'Nothing. Ole knew none of the details. I want to go home, Per.'

But Per went on, talking more to himself than to her:

'He's no kamikaze, this guy. He's a pro. Simba will be safer now. He didn't take his rifle. Did Ole know about Flakfortet?'

'Per, didn't you hear what I said? I want to go home.'

'Did he?'

'No, he did not.'

'I'll get one of the patrol cars to run you home.' He handed her his mobile. 'Here, call your friend and take a sleeping pill when you get home.'

'No thanks. I've got a long day ahead of me tomorrow. I mean today.'

'You're surely not thinking of going through with this tomorrow, Lise? No one would ask or expect you to go ahead as planned, not after what's happened.'

'If I don't work, I'll crack up,' she said, keying in the number.

She was sick of people telling her to go to bed. Her friend had kept urging her to, when they were sitting in Lise's kitchen, drinking wine and smoking cigarettes; Tagesen had called early this morning to say the same thing and had said it again while they were standing together in the outermost finger at Copenhagen Airport. Didn't they understand that the only way to stop herself from falling apart, the only way to keep her feelings of guilt and grief at bay, was by concentrating on her work? She knew she was going to feel awful when the visit was over and the police – after due examination and a post-mortem – released Ole's body; when she would have to think about a funeral, lawyers, her future. When that time came she would want to be alone with her grief and her guilt, but she would be the one to say when she was ready to go off and hide from the world for a while.

She was standing with Per, John and Tagesen, waiting for the arrival of the plane from London. She had put on a skirt and a smart blouse, with a jacket on top. She was very carefully and somewhat more heavily made-up than usual, but even this could not disguise her pallor or the strain in her face. She had slept for a couple of hours, curled up next to her friend and clutching her hand. In a deviation from standard procedure, the police were keeping the whole business completely under wraps for the time being. Not to shield her from the attentions of her fellow reporters but solely to save Janos from learning that they had found his hideout – just in case he hadn't, as they believed, done a runner. Per was in his usual jeans and windbreaker, but Tagesen had donned a suit for the occasion. Per had been informed that Sara's British Airways flight had landed. She would be allowed to leave the plane first.

Tagesen laid a paternal arm briefly around Lise's shoulders.

'You don't need to do this, you know, Lise. There's nothing to stop you going home,' he told her yet again.

She shrugged his arm away.

'I'd rather be at work. I'd go spare with nothing to do.'

'You're not to blame, you know.'

'I'd just rather be doing something, okay?'

'Here comes Simba,' Per said and sent a quick message over his walkie-talkie to the two cars waiting on the tarmac at the foot of the finger.

Sara Santanda looked exactly like her photograph, except that she was not clad in the traditional Iranian women's costume, as she was in one of the most renowned pictures of her. Instead she wore a long skirt with a jacket and a shirt underneath. And those now famous gold earrings. Over her arm she carried a small handbag, which, in some absurd way, made her look a little like a young Margaret Thatcher. But Lise recognized her soft smile as she advanced to meet Tagesen, who greeted her effusively while Per muttered into his walkie-talkie. All of this Lise saw through a sort of a fog; somehow, though, she managed to collect herself enough to shake hands with the author, to wish her welcome and tell her what a brave woman she was. And Sara very sweetly said how nice it was to see her again.

Per shepherded them out of the finger, through the emergency exit and into the Volvo saloon with smoked-glass windows that was waiting outside. Tagesen got into the back along with Sara Santanda, and Lise and Per climbed into the front alongside the driver. At the wheel of the other car was John, with the female member of the team, Bente, in the passenger seat. Within a matter of seconds both cars were on the move. If she hadn't felt that she was viewing the whole thing through cotton wool, Lise would have been impressed by the efficiency of the exercise.

Tagesen chatted to Sara in the elegant Queen's English he had picked up when doing his PhD at Cambridge, while Lise gazed out of the window at the disaster area from which, at some point, a bridge to Sweden would rise. At the moment the area looked as though it had been hit by a minor earthquake.

'You have had a war here?' Sara Santanda asked in her light, dry Iranian English.

'They're building a bridge to Sweden. Just as you are building a bridge between cultures with your courage,' Tagesen explained with that characteristic intensity which normally made Lise feel proud to be working for him but which today made her toes curl. For the first time she felt happy with the programme for the day. Tagesen would be taking Sara to a brunch with her publisher and a select gathering of writers and intellectuals at his apartment in Copenhagen, while Lise got everything ready for the press conference at Flakfortet. She was sailing out to the island with the members of the press. John was going straight to Flakfortet with the six officers allocated to Per. He had asked for twice that, but Vuldom had cut back on the numbers when he reported that the hit man appeared to have fled. He had, however, kept the dog teams, which he would get to comb Flakfortet one more time. Himself, he would come out on the *White Whale* with Sara and Tagesen. He had a helicopter standing by at Værløse Air Force Base, only ten minutes' flight time from Flakfortet. Lise could tell that he hadn't slept a wink the night before. His face was pale, but his eyes burned in it. He looked as though he was running solely on his last reserves of adrenalin.

Lise heard Tagesen apologizing for the fact that no government minister or prominent member of the opposition had so far agreed to meet Ms Santanda. The politicians were, unfortunately, staying well away, for fear of damaging relations with Iran. It was *realpolitik* at its very worst.

Sara gazed out of the window:

'It doesn't surprise me,' she said. 'Follow the money, and you'll never be surprised by what people will do, especially people in power. And the Danes are no different, I'm sure.'

'I know, but still…' Tagesen said, fiddling with his tie.

'Anyway, it's nice to be out and about,' Sara Santanda said with a smile, as the cars sped through Copenhagen. Lise felt a faint flutter of excitement at the thought of interviewing this woman later, even if she did still feel in constant danger of sinking into that fog where all she could see was Ole's dead, empty eyes. Under normal circumstances she would have been exulting over this day and the fact that her articles dominated that morning's paper, but instead she merely felt empty inside, as if her body were consumed by darkness.

The darkness was still there a couple of hours later when she stood on the quay outside the Hotel Nyhavn. It was a lovely day, and a few people were sitting outside with their beers at the restaurants along the harbourside. Everything seemed so normal that it made her want to scream. How could they sit there like that, quite normally, as if nothing had happened? Didn't they realize that the world was full of horror and guilt? Sailboats lay quietly alongside the quay. The scents of tar and salt water mingled with cooking smells from the restaurants. A young couple with glasses of beer in their hands sat with their legs dangling lazily over the edge of the quay. The drone of traffic filtered down from Kongens Nytorv, and passers-by gawped at the thirty-odd strong press contingent milling around the foot of the gangplank. Lise gave herself a shake. She had put on some more make-up in an attempt to conceal the ravages of the night, but as she watched the last of her press colleagues arrive on foot or by taxi, she felt naked and transparent and did not trust her own smile. The *M/S Langø* was moored at the quayside, the skipper peering out of the wheelhouse at the members of the press. Among them were reporters from five television stations, including one from Germany and a Reuters crew who, along with a few others, had soon put two and two together and realized that they were here not for Scheer but for Sara Santanda. She recognized cameramen from TV2 and Danmarks Radio, as well as the new guy from TV3 and most of the newspaper crowd, but there were also some faces that were new to her. She could see from her list that quite a few foreign journalists had also been accredited. Scheer's name had, as expected, proved a big draw, and a number of journalists whom she knew personally had called her, having twigged what this was really about, and had their names added to the list at the last minute. She nodded and smiled mechanically to those she knew. Two plain-clothes policemen were standing by the gangplank, checking people's press cards against the names on her list before allowing them on board. Everyone took it in good part. They all knew the routine.

Lise caught sight of Peter Sørensen standing in the queue at the gangplank with his cameraman.

'Hi, Lise. Where are we going? Is it Flakfortet?'

'Briefing on board, Peter,' she said, forcing a smile.

The last stragglers filed on board. A steady breeze was blowing, but the weather was quite mild with only a light scattering of cloud, so she gathered the press corps under the canopy on the upper deck of the old fishing boat, where pots of coffee and tea had been set out, along with bottles of Gammel Dansk, beer and soft drinks. Lise climbed onto a bench and faced the assembled company.

'Okay. Quiet please,' she called out and was surprised by how calm and assured her voice sounded. 'I'm Lise Carlsen, chair of Danish PEN. For the benefit of our colleagues from abroad I'm going to do this in English.'

She paused. They fell silent; all eyes were on her.

'Thank you,' she said and was filled with the quiet composure that comes from simply pulling oneself together and getting on with things. 'We're on our way to Flakfortet, in the middle of the Sound, where we will meet the writer Sara Santanda. She arrived in Copenhagen this morning.'

She heard their voices rise up to meet her and proceeded to answer their questions.

Vuk fell asleep in spite of himself but woke before six in the morning. The camping lamp was still burning. He ate his last sandwich, drank the rest of the tea and water. He got out the little mirror and inspected his face. The hair dye was holding up fine. He mopped his face with the towel and combed his hair neatly before removing his clothes and climbing into the wetsuit. It was still slightly damp and clammy. He hung the little bag containing his money and papers around his neck then pulled his shirt and trousers on over the wetsuit. He knotted the tie and donned the tweed jacket. He studied his face and as much of his body as he could see in the mirror. His clothes were possibly bulging a little, but no more than to make him look like a man who had put on weight and was filling out his clothes a little too well, but had not yet resigned himself to going up a size. He bound the knife in its sheath to his shin under his trouser leg, checked the pistol and its magazine and kept it in his hand, sitting there on his sleeping bag. Then he extinguished the camping lamp and sat in the darkness, concentrating on keeping himself awake and alert to any sound.

Not until around 10.00 am did he hear footsteps and voices outside in the passageways. They were making their last round. He could hear that they had a dog with them It was well trained and did not bark, but it had scented something. He could hear it whining on the other side of the door. He had been needing to relieve himself for ages, but had held it in: he didn't want a dog picking up his scent.

'There's nothing here,' a voice said. 'King! Come here! It's just a dead rat.'

'What about that door?' another voice asked.

'Just a minute.'

Vuk cocked the pistol. They were rattling the door.

'There's not a blind thing here. Some rats have been fighting, that's all. Real bloody rat-catcher is King. They drive him wild. Foxes and rats, they drive dogs crazy.'

He heard them walk off, gave them half an hour. He was guessing that once they had made a thorough search of the casemates they would position themselves on the roof of Flakfortet, from where they could see any boat approaching the island. The restaurant staff would be inside, preparing lunch. The other police officers would be deployed on the grass between the restaurant and the harbour to receive the press and, later, the Target herself. That, at any rate, was what he had gathered from the schedule. He hoped they were sticking to this arrangement and that he had read their intentions all right.

Vuk opened the door onto total darkness. Only a faint strip of light was visible at the far end, by the steps. Very quietly he eased the heavy steel door shut and fastened it with the chain and padlock. With the pistol in one hand and the torch in the other, he crept warily along the passage. He knew the layout of the place, he didn't need a light, but he wanted to be ready to dazzle any possible opponent. One floor up it became easier for him to see. Light filtered down into the casemates from above. He leaned against the wall and waited. There was no movement, and no sound except for a constant hum, which had to come from the generator that provided the fort with electricity. He carried on up to the main corridor, into which light fell from the open doors at either end. Again he stood for a while with his back to the wall, but still saw no sign of movement, heard no sound. He stole quickly along the passage in his rubber-soled shoes and down to the staff quarters. He pulled his lock-pick from his pocket. It took him only a minute to pick the simple Ruko lock on the door of the chef's room.

As he had expected, the room was empty: the chef would be getting the lunch organized. It was not much more than a shoebox containing a bed, a washbasin, a television, a large ghetto blaster, a little table and a high-backed chair. On the wall hung a picture of Denmark's European Cup-winning team and two Playboy centrefolds. On the table stood a photograph of a buxom young woman – the chef's girlfriend, he presumed. With a bit of a struggle he pulled his trousers down and the wetsuit fly to one side, peed into the washbasin with a sigh of relief then rinsed it carefully. It was awkward, and he felt very vulnerable, standing like that with his trousers round his ankles and his back to the door.

He adjusted his dress and sat down on the chair, facing the door; he removed a cigarette and lighter from the waterproof bag, lit up and took a long drag, biding his time until the press corps showed up. His plan was to go upstairs and mingle with them when they were wandering around the fort, waiting for Sara Santanda to arrive. According to the schedule, they were supposed to get to the fort half an hour before the Target. One journalist more or less would never be noticed by the police. Their eyes would not be on the press. They were expecting the threat to come from outside. They would be looking outwards, not inwards. And that would be their big mistake.

The dog patrol reported back to John. They had searched every inch of the place and had found nothing untoward. He glanced up at the ramparts and the four police snipers whom he had posted there. The pleasure boats had left the harbour. The only craft lying there was the harbour police's own speedboat, which had brought them across. Another two armed policemen were stationed down by the quayside. Along with Bente, who was in constant touch with the control room. Everything that could be done had been done. He called Per on his mobile. Per didn't trust radios. He preferred mobile phones: the press could not monitor calls on them, or not yet, at least.

'Per? It's John. Everything's secured. You can bring the Subject in.'

'Great, John. The press are on their way. We're on schedule.'

The restaurateur came out to join him in front of the pavilion.

'Well, what's the story?'

'Your customers will be here in half an hour. Press conference in an hour.'

'We're all ready for them. Would you like a cup of coffee while we're waiting?'

'I'd love one, thanks,' John said.

Per was to transport the Subject in the car with the smoked-glass windows from the brunch meeting into the city centre, to the quay fronting the old converted warehouse that was now home to the Ministry of Foreign Affairs. Here Jon and his deckhand would be waiting with the *White Whale*. John looked at his watch. Per would then help the Subject into the boat and down to the cabin, where the door would be locked and the curtains drawn. Tagesen would follow them on board, and they would set sail for Flakfortet. He would receive a call once they were on their way. There was time for a cup of coffee. Everything was going according to plan. Even the weather was on their side: scattered cloud and a watery sun, although he had also noticed black clouds building up on the horizon over Sweden.

There would be rain later in the afternoon, as forecast, and the wind would freshen, but by then this hurdle, at least, would have been cleared.

The *M/S Langø* sailed into Flakfortet's harbour. The TV cameramen had been filming like mad for some time. It was a brilliant set-up, with Flakfortet looming larger and larger in the Sound as they drew closer. And then, as they sailed into the harbour, great shots of the armed police on top of the fort, against the dramatic backdrop of the sky. The big black clouds on the horizon, Flakfortet's grassy slopes and the rough fieldstone of its solid walls – they couldn't have asked for better pictures.

Peter Sørensen turned to Lise:

'It makes great television, Lise. Is all this just for us?'

'No, it's also a secure location,' she said. She had had to answer countless questions, not least about the history of Flakfortet. The foreign journalists were particularly interested in this, so she had not had time to dwell on her grief or had at any rate pushed it down into some deep recess of her mind. It was there, she knew. It would rise to the surface again, but she would not fall apart.

'Is Janos connected to this in some way?' Peter asked.

'Why do you ask that?'

'Come on, Lise, give me something to go on, at least.'

'I can't think why you should ask that,' she retorted, aware of a slight quaver in her voice, as the thought of Janos brought those ghastly images back into her mind.

She was saved by the reporter from Reuters, who wanted to know who owned the old military fortress and whether it had ever seen battle. She began to tell him about it but could still feel Peter's sceptical eyes boring into the back of her head. They docked, streamed ashore. Reporters and photographers scattered in all directions, and she took the chance to get well away from him. Some of the press people went up to the restaurant for a beer; others were taking cover shots while they waited. John observed them. There was nothing to be done about it. Their credentials had been checked, and he knew it was a waste of time asking them to stay where they were. But that was one of the other good things about Flakfortet. They knew who was on the island, and no one could get on to it unremarked.

Vuk heard people in the passageway outside the chef's room and got to his feet. He took his notebook from his bag, left the room and made his way to the toilet. He locked himself in there until he heard a voice crying:

'She's coming. Her boat's on its way in now.'

He heard running feet out in the passageway, left the toilet and followed three men and a woman who were dashing on ahead of him. He emerged from one of the main entrances to see reporters and photographers flocking round the quayside, jostling for the best position. They came hurrying out of the restaurant, down from the ramparts and out of the shop where they had been killing time by browsing through brochures. The craft that slid smoothly through the harbour entrance was a lovely, low-hulled, wooden motorboat, whose skipper stood up on the quarterdeck surveying the scene before him on the grassy quayside. Vuk saw the Target emerge from the cabin to stand between two men. The one in the windcheater looked like a bodyguard. The other was in a suit and had to be one of the organizers. Vuk's mouth was slightly dry, and his heart was beating a little faster. But that was all right. That rush of adrenalin was essential. He was ready.

Chapter 22

Tagesen stood on the quarterdeck of the *White Whale*. He was gratified to see such a large press turnout, although somewhat less happy that the proceedings had to be conducted under the protection of armed police. Most of all, though, he was proud that he and his newspaper had made this meeting in the middle of the sea – one which he looked forward to describing in a forthcoming leader – a reality. Should it, though, have been Lise standing here alongside Sara Santanda? Had he stolen too much of the limelight? Well, he had to think about the paper and himself. He was the activist editor of an activist newspaper. Danish PEN did some sterling work, but it would have to take second place on this day when his paper made history. Somewhere along the line Lise understood that too, he was sure. Although she might well have objected, if tragedy had not struck. She was a tough cookie; she never gave up. But, all things considered, the division of responsibilities they had arrived at was probably the right one. In any case she was employed by the newspaper, and it was mainly thanks to *Politiken* that Sara Santanda was here at all. And hence it was only because Lise worked for *Politiken* that Danish PEN was able to take some of the credit, Tagesen reasoned smugly.

He looked at Sara Santanda and from her to the pointing camera lenses, the flashes, the eager faces and jostling bodies. Sometimes he found himself wondering about the profession which he had chosen and which he represented. This lot were like a pack of wolves scenting their prey. Even the most level-headed journalists forgot all about politeness and good manners when faced with a good story; when all that mattered was to be in the front row.

'I'm sorry it's such an out-of-the-way place,' he said in English.

She gave him the soft, friendly smile that he had come to cherish during the few hours they had spent in each other's company. He couldn't understand how this charming, mild-mannered middle-aged woman could have sent the clerics in Teheran into such blind paroxysms of fury. He found it incomprehensible, but, irrational though it was, it made him happy to think that literature could have such an effect. That the written word mattered so much. Had so much power. He had said this in today's leader. And he was looking forward, tomorrow, to lambasting those spineless Danish politicians who hadn't dared to put in an appearance here, so worried were they about export figures. *Follow the money.* He could make that the headline.

'That's all right,' Sara said, waving to the reporters. 'It's perfectly all right. And I love the sea. Just the smell of it. I think this is great. And it's only the beginning. The first step. Like a little child, I'm taking my first steps into the open.'

The reporters were all shouting at once. How did she feel? Was she afraid? When had she arrived? And photographers cursed one another as lenses were blocked by other camera-wielding hands and arms.

'Easy,' Tagesen shouted. 'Take it easy, now. Let Sara Santanda get ashore and into the restaurant, then you'll have plenty of opportunity to put your questions to her. And Sara has agreed to give separate interviews to the television stations after the press conference. So let's just take it easy, ladies and gentlemen.'

Per Toftlund beheld the spectacle. He had never understood the members of the Fourth Estate, to him they were a right royal pain in the ass and so totally self-centred; their behaviour now only confirmed his low opinion of them. He came ashore first, taking the four strides onto the quayside and waiting there for Sara Santanda, holding the journalists at bay with his broad back. He took the writer's hand and helped her out of the low wooden vessel and up onto the grassy wharf. The reporters and photographers kept pushing and shoving. Per motioned to John, who elbowed his way through to him, and together they succeeded in creating a little space around the slightly-built writer, who was smiling and waving and looking as if she were enjoying all the attention, though with a growing unease over the disorderly crowd flickering in her eyes.

'Please, ladies and gentlemen. Please. Let's be civilized,' she said, and her quiet voice seemed to have a calming effect. At any rate she was given a bit more room as they all drew back a pace or two, forming a circle around her. Peter Sørensen was at the very front with his microphone in his hand and his cameraman right behind him. The cameraman nudged Per aside, obscuring his view. He cursed the man but couldn't bring himself to push the camera away. Relations between the police and the press were not exactly great as it was.

'How are you, Ms Santanda?' Peter Sørensen asked.

'I'm very well, young man, and very happy to be here,' she replied.

All eyes were on Sara Santanda. No one noticed Vuk, who had made his way from the main entrance of the fort to the fringes of the crowd of press people encircling the tiny writer. In his right hand he held a notepad and a pen. He let these fall to the ground, slid his hand across his stomach and into his satchel, drew out the pistol, cocked it and held it straight down alongside his leg. He pushed the man in front of him so hard in the back that he stumbled forward, dragging another reporter with him. Like ninepins they teetered but did not go down. Voices were raised in complaint, but it gave him the room he needed. Vuk was now only three feet away from the Target, who had her back to him, speaking into a microphone. Becoming aware of ructions in the ranks, the television reporter looked up, straight into Vuk's eyes. Even with the beard and the dark hair he knew him.

'Janos!' Sørensen cried.

Vuk's arm was on its way up, but for a second, recognizing his old friend and staring him in the face, he froze.

Lise was standing on the edge of the crowd, but Vuk's shove had created an opening in the mass of bodies, and suddenly there he was, as if he had risen out of the ground itself.

'Carsten!' she screamed.

Vuk's arm was moving upwards again, but Toftlund had spotted the movement. He launched himself into a flying tackle, which spun the TV cameraman round on his heel as the policeman shot past him, and rammed into Sara Santanda, all thirteen and a half stone of him, sending both her and himself crashing to the ground, which she hit first with a dull thud. Per heard the wind being knocked out of her lungs and the snap of an arm breaking or a shoulder dislocating. She groaned, but he flattened his broad frame over hers, twisting round as he did so to look up at Vuk.

Per heard a shot and felt the gust of air as the bullet whizzed over the back of his head. He heard another ring out. Vuk's first shot hit the television cameraman in the throat, went straight through and into the shoulder of the man standing next to him. His next shot pierced the upper arm of a female reporter and carried on into the calf of a press photographer. Both started to scream, and the panic spread. Some people threw themselves to the ground. Others tried to run away. Still others stood transfixed.

Out of the corner of his eye, Vuk saw a man in plain clothes pull a pistol from a holster at his belt. Vuk whirled about, gripped the Beretta with both hands and shot John twice in the chest, then he flung an arm round the throat of the woman standing closest to him, Lise, and held her in front of him, with the barrel of the pistol pressed against her neck.

Lise gasped but did not give way to tears. She was filled with a mixture of fear, anger and despair.

The two wounded were moaning. John lay lifeless on the ground, blood trickling from his chest and from under his back, where the bullet had exited. Bente stood with her arms outstretched, mouth gaping in a mute shriek. The cameraman lay on his stomach with blood gushing from his throat. The other press people had drawn back a little and stood silently staring, or lay on the grass, gaping in horror. A number were in tears. Others, ashen-faced, were in the first stages of shock. Peter Sørensen kneeled down next to his cameraman. Sara Santanda writhed in agony under Per's weight. He had covered her completely with his body and had pulled out his gun.

'Stay down,' he hissed at the prone form beneath him.

'You've broken my shoulder and several ribs,' she hissed back with something that might almost have been a laugh in her pain-wracked voice. 'Is that what you call saving me?'

'Stay down!' he said again. This woman was something else.

Vuk raised his pistol and aimed it at Per.

'Move. I have no quarrel with you,' he said.

Per yelled:

'If he shoots just one more, take him out. Hostage or no hostage. That's an order.'

The two uniformed policemen had kept their heads. They had cocked their machine guns and moved one pace to the side, so that they had Vuk and Lise in their line of sight. Per knew them from previous security assignments.

They were good solid men, not easily panicked.

Lise felt Vuk's hold on her neck tighten. It suddenly struck her what Per had said.

'Per,' she tried, but the pressure on her throat was so hard that she couldn't get the word out. She could see it in Per's eyes. He had made his choice. She gazed at him imploringly, but his eyes left her to focus instead on the man with the pistol.

With his gun trained on Vuk, Per said:

'Janos. You can't have her. If you shoot again, you're a dead man. You're not getting her. You know that. We will not relinquish the Target.'

Vuk shot a swift glance to right and left. The two uniformed officers had assumed the standing firing position, their guns pointing steadily at him. He knew there were snipers up on the ramparts. It was time to admit defeat and put his escape plan into action. Vuk, with Lise as a human shield, kept his pistol trained on Per, who was covering Sara Santanda with his body.

'Okay,' Vuk said coolly and began to back slowly towards the quay. There were stirrings in the crowd, and the policemen took a step closer.

'Stop!' Vuk bellowed. 'Nobody move. I've got nothing to lose. This one'll go first, then Santanda and then a couple more. I will not be taken. Is that understood?'

'Understood,' Per said. He could hear Santanda's laboured wheezing, she was crying softly now. He only hoped she hadn't punctured a lung. 'Stay down,' he breathed, then said out loud:

'Name your terms.'

Vuk shot a quick glance behind him. Skipper Jon was standing on the bridge of his boat along with his deckhand, staring in stunned disbelief at the scene. The whole thing had taken less than a minute.

'He's to take me away from here. The deckhand leaves the boat. She's coming with me. If any boat leaves Flakfortet or if a boat puts out from Copenhagen to intercept me, they both die.'

'You don't stand a chance. Give yourself up,' Per argued. He was white as a sheet, but the hand holding the gun was steady as a rock, and his eyes were locked on Vuk's own.

'Fuck you,' Vuk said.

Per glanced over at John's lifeless body, knowing that others had also been hit. The main thing right now was to help the wounded and get Janos out of here. They would get this guy later, one way or another.

'What about the wounded?' he said. 'They need help.'

'If any boat leaves the harbour within the next half-hour, they die,' Vuk said in his clear expressionless voice.

Per gripped his pistol more firmly, as if wondering whether to risk it. Lise was terrified out of her wits by now. Not just because of the man who was gripping her so tightly round the neck, but also because the man who had been her lover now seemed like someone who was prepared to sacrifice her.

'Don't try it,' Vuk said, and she silently thanked him.

'It's a deal,' Per said.

'Per,' Lise ventured again, but the stranglehold on her neck tightened even further as Vuk dragged her backwards, still holding her as a shield.

'Out!' Vuk barked at the deckhand, who bounded the four steps onto the quayside and scrambled away.

Vuk sidled down to the boat, still with his arm locked around Lise's neck. She was conscious of how strong he was, but his arm felt odd, as if he were wearing something rubbery under his jacket. There was a split-second when he almost tripped, and the grip on her throat slackened, but he neatly regained his balance and resumed the agonizing stranglehold.

'Cast off!' Vuk shouted to Jon, deathly-pale on his bridge.

He had edged behind the *White Whale*'s skipper so that he was now screened by both Lise and Jon. He didn't trust the policemen on the fort ramparts. One of them might just try to play the hero.

With his hand on the ignition key, Jon looked to Toftlund.

'Cast off!' Vuk said.

Toftlund still lay spread-eagled across Sara.

'Cast off,' Vuk repeated, adding: 'I've got nothing against dying. I come from a country where death is commonplace. But you'll go first. Then her, and probably one or two others as well. So cast off!'

Toftlund nodded, and the deckhand on the quayside slipped the moorings. The *White Whale's* carefully maintained engine sprang smoothly to life, and Jon manoeuvred her away from the quay. When the boat reached the harbour entrance, and the frothing water round the propeller indicated that Jon had opened the throttle, Per jumped up.

'Værløse, helicopter now!' he roared at Bente, who fumbled with her radio, but kept a cool head and steadily proceeded to make a brief report. Most of the reporters and photographers were still on the ground, as if they had not yet grasped exactly what had happened, but others were getting slowly to their feet.

Toftlund looked back at the *White Whale*, which was now heading out of the harbour at full speed.

He turned to Bente:

'Find the restaurant first-aid box and take charge here!'

He pressed the transmit button on his radio and proceeded to outline the situation, emphasizing the fact that the fleeing hostage-taker was extremely dangerous and that no one was to go near the *White Whale*. He wanted a helicopter dispatched to Flakfortet with a medical team. Then he walked over to John and kneeled down beside him. No doctor could help him. Rage and desperation welled up inside Per as it finally dawned on him that it was Lise on that boat. She had been the hostage who had to be sacrificed to protect the Target. But now she was no longer simply a hostage, she was Lise. His eyes went to Sara Santanda who was being helped into a sitting position by Tagesen. She was weeping and holding her side with her right arm while her left arm dangled limply at an odd angle. That she was alive was the only bright spot in a situation that could have turned out a lot worse. He watched the low, sleek wooden boat with Lise on board drawing further and further away.

The *White Whale* could do up to seventeen knots. Vuk ordered Jon to push the engine to its limits. Flakfortet dropped away astern, and when Vuk was sure that they were out of range of the snipers he pushed Lise over to Jon. He, for his part, moved all the way back to the sternpost, from where he had a clear shot at them both. He had his back to the cylindrical white canister containing the inflatable life raft. Jon was standing at the old ship's wheel. Lise was now almost demented with fear. Vuk, Carsten, Janos, or whatever his name was, was uncannily calm. Only the beads of sweat on the bridge of his nose betrayed, perhaps, the strain he was under. Jon's hands were shaking so much that he had to clench the wheel hard. The *White Whale* pitched and plunged in the low swell whipped up by a wind which felt as though it was bringing rain with it. The sun had vanished, and the black clouds that had hung over Sweden were moving over the Sound. Lise looked at the vessels in the channel: the ferry to Limhamn, sailboats hugging the shore, a tanker gliding majestically down toward the Baltic. A plane was turning in over Saltholm. A coaster flying the Russian flag was leaving Copenhagen harbour; and some way ahead of them one of those ugly river barges which reminded her of holidays in France appeared to be struggling against the current, it was chugging along so slowly.

'Do you smoke?' Vuk asked.

She nodded.

'Light me a cigarette!'

She had lost her handbag, so she stood there staring at him in fear and bewilderment.

'Skipper?' he said.

Jon stuck his hand into his jacket and pulled out a packet of Prince, handed them to Lise, along with a lighter. With trembling fingers she lit the cigarette and held it out to Vuk at arm's length. He took it with a steady left hand, the right one still pointing the pistol at them.

'Have one yourselves,' he said, as if they were exchanging polite chitchat at a cocktail party.

They lit up, although the wind made it difficult.

'Where to?' Jon asked after taking a long drag.

'Set course due west towards the harbour.'

'I can't do that. I'll run straight into the Dirty Sea. The *White Whale* is all I've got.'

'Don't fuck with me, mister,' Vuk growled.

'We'll rip the bottom out of her.'

Vuk raised the gun, and Lise huddled against Jon.

'Do as I say. Immediately before we reach the Dirty Sea you'll receive a new order, to head south into Dutchman's Deep,' Vuk said.

'They'll catch you when you go ashore,' Jon said.

Vuk did not reply, only puffed on his cigarette.

'How could you do it? Who are you?' Lise sobbed. She was trembling from top to toe and shivering with cold in her thin clothing. 'Why Ole? Why? What had he ever done to you?'

'Shut up!' Vuk broke her off.

The radiophone rang. Vuk raised the pistol, motioning to them not to touch it.

He looked at the sky. It couldn't be too long before the helicopter showed up.

'Skipper! Where do you keep the lifejackets?' he asked.

Jon pointed to one of the chests along the bulwark that served as benches on the small quarterdeck. The *White Whale* was making good headway now, bucking through the waves, and the first raindrops were falling onto the gleaming planks.

'Take out two!' Vuk commanded Lise.

Jon eyed him. Some of his fear seemed to have dissipated, possibly because he was now in his proper element, at the wheel of his boat.

'You're expecting a ship. Is that it? You've got a ship waiting for you.'

'Shut up!' Vuk snapped.

Jon turned the wheel slightly, and the *White Whale* slowly altered course.

'What are you doing?' Vuk asked.

'She draws six feet. I've got to keep to the bloody sea-lane. Look at that buoy dead ahead of us!'

But Vuk's eyes remained fixed on him and on Lise, who had got the chest open and was peering down at the orange lifejackets.

'Stay on course and get those on. Both of you,' Vuk rapped, tossing the last of his cigarette over the rail.

'What are you up to?' Jon asked.

'It's your decision,' Vuk said. 'Either with or without. But this is where you get off, so move it!'

Vuk removed a split pin, pulled the release and the white canister flew over the stern into the foaming grey water. He tugged on the cord, and the circular life raft began to inflate behind them.

'What are you doing?' Jon yelled.

'Get a move on!' Vuk barked.

Lise drew the lifejacket over her head and tried to tie it but got into a tangle with the strings. Keeping one hand on the wheel, with the other Jon assisted her. In turn, she pulled a lifejacket over his head, and he knotted it with deft efficiency. Vuk heard the helicopter before he saw it. There were two of them. One big air-sea rescue machine and a smaller one, the sort normally used for monitoring traffic. They flew out from the coast at a fair height. The big Sikorsky stayed on course for Flakfortet, the smaller one passed over the life raft, banked and whirred down towards the *White Whale*.

'Okay, jump – now!' Vuk shouted, raising the pistol. But they simply stood there, benumbed. The sea was grey and streaked by the rain that was falling harder and harder, and to Lise the boat seemed to be travelling appallingly fast. The helicopter drew closer, dipped over the *White Whale*. Vuk pressed the trigger twice in rapid succession, shattering the glass next to Jon's head and sending splinters showering down into the wheelhouse. They must have had binoculars trained on him, because the helicopter swung off to the right and rose steeply, as if to say it would be sure to keep its distance.

'I said *now!*'

Vuk raised the gun again and aimed it right between Jon's eyes. Jon took his hands off the wheel, stepped up onto the rail and threw himself as far out from the side as possible. Vuk turned the gun on Lise. She was shaking uncontrollably, didn't know how she was to get up onto that rail and make herself jump. She only knew that she was more afraid of staying on the boat than of being in the cold grey sea. She saw Jon bobbing up and down in the waves behind the *White Whale*, and then she sprang, gasping as she ducked under the chilly water. She was seized by panic and swallowed water, but the life-vest turned her right side up and brought her to the surface, where she lay on her back, staring up at the big black clouds. She trod water and watched the *White Whale* speeding away from her. She was, in fact, a very good swimmer, and although the water was cold, after the long hot summer the temperature still hovered around twelve to fourteen degrees. And she was relieved to be free of that cool, calm man who never smiled. She waved to Jon and they backstroked towards one another. The helicopter flew down and circled around them. They waved up at it; it rose, turned and came back. Something square and yellow was dropped from the side of the helicopter; it landed on the sea between Jon and her and automatically began to inflate into a life raft. Lise started to swim towards it. She reached it at the same time as Jon and clung to it, at once laughing and crying. Jon clambered into the raft and pulled her in after him. Once there she threw up and cried and cried until she thought she would never stop.

Jon kneeled beside her. He gazed after the *White Whale*, took his bearings from the coastline. The motorboat skimmed across Dutchman's Deep, but instead of turning either south or north it carried straight on.

'You bastard!' he roared, shaking his fist at the *White Whale*. 'You mean, fucking, murderous, destructive bastard!'

Seconds later the *White Whale* exploded in a flash of red and yellow as Vuk steered her full throttle into the Dirty Sea, where an old railway sleeper tore a hole in her bottom and checked her speed with such force that the diesel tank burst. Diesel oil mingled with the gas from the flask in the galley and was ignited by the red-hot steel of the engine.

The observer in the helicopter had been keeping an eye on the two people in the sea, to make certain that they got themselves into the life raft, so he could not substantiate Jon's claim that he had seen a black-clad figure leave the *White Whale* seconds before she ploughed full tilt into the Dirty Sea. Nor could the observer say for sure whether the motorboat had been manned or not, for he had only managed to get his binoculars focused on her just at the moment when she exploded.

The helicopter flew low over the area, searching the waves. They spied a buoy drifting outwards on the current, otherwise no sign of life down there. Two sailboats had changed course and were heading towards the site of the explosion, but the captains knew all about the Dirty Sea and maintained a respectful distance. A Russian river barge and other, larger vessels in the vicinity also reduced speed – as required by maritime law in the event of a shipwreck. The shipping wavebands crackled with inquiries in a host of languages. All shipping was told to stay on course. Navigation conditions were difficult, and help was on the way.

But by the time the first pleasure boats reached the vicinity of the wreck, the man who had sailed the *White Whale* into the Dirty Sea was gone. The only trace of him was his tweed jacket, found drifting not far from his right shoe, a thousand feet away from the wreck. His clothing had presumably been ripped off him when he was hurled into the water by the explosion.

Visibility was rapidly deteriorating as the easterly storm from Sweden swept across Zealand, bringing high winds and driving rain. At nightfall the search was called off.

The Russian barge which had been battling with engine trouble at a less than felicitous spot in the sea lane just off the Dirty Sea managed to get its tired old turbine turning again and ponderously proceeded on its scheduled passage to Limhamn in Sweden, where it discharged a load of ground soya, and the captain was given a right bawling-out for sailing the Sound in bad weather with such poor engine power, especially when he had been laid up for two days because of trouble with that self-same engine, which wasn't powerful enough to drive a bloody Skoda. The captain explained in broken English that what with all the upheaval in his own country he had to go where the money was. And if his freight rates were lower than some others, well, he thought that was all part of the market economy to which he obviously had to adapt. The harbour-master at Limhamn informed him that he would never again be allowed to enter a Swedish port and that that went for all his fellow Russians and their leaky old tubs as well. Sweden had already banned his sister ships, the oil-carrying Volga-Neftis, from docking at Swedish ports.

The Russian captain couldn't have cared less. He could retire now anyway. The young man had asked for nothing except clean clothes, vodka, coffee and cigarettes. Despite the wetsuit, he had been chilled to the bone when he climbed over the low rail an hour after some weekend sailor had rammed what had actually been a very pretty motorboat smack into the biggest underwater rubbish dump outside of any busy commercial harbour. The taciturn young man had hauled himself over the rail south of Saltholm just after they had begun their approach to Limhamn in the dark and the pouring rain. The captain's four drunken crew members had been advised that they had suddenly been struck blind and deaf, as can happen to anyone who has been given a bribe or too much too drink, or a combination of both.

So only the captain had seen the young man.

And the captain asked no questions. Some things were none of his business. He knew the guys who had contacted him and paid him: you didn't fool with them. And he had known other lads like the silent youth who had climbed over his rail, from his time as a submariner in the Soviet navy. Many's the time when he had set lads like that ashore on one or other of these low-water coastlines. Set them ashore and picked them up again without the imperialists noticing a bloody thing. In the dear old country these boys were called *spetznats*, and they had climbed and swam as though they had had goats' hooves and gills. Back then, he had been fired by patriotism. This time round he had been paid twenty-five thousand dollars for being at a specific spot at a specific time. He had had no trouble spotting the buoy and the black figure which had dived overboard in those perilous few seconds before the explosion and come up again just once, nostrils breaking the water on the lee side of the blazing wreck before it disappeared again, and the buoy could be seen starting to drift. The diver had swum into the submarine forest of twisted, algae-coated metal, concrete and crumbling brick, that devil's reef. The captain knew the story. It would have taken him only a second or so to get the mouthpiece working, and then the rest of his equipment, before bearing towards his old river lass who, for such a sum, would happily pull him quite a way, hanging onto the ring attached to her hull for that very purpose. The captain drank another glass of vodka, thinking fleetingly that he might almost have done it for nothing. Simply to savour once more that old thrill he remembered from his youth.

But only almost, he thought to himself, watching the young man disappear across the deserted wharf, while he hollered at his lazy drunken sailors to get their fingers out and set course for Kaliningrad before the police came around asking stupid questions, as only the police – in every country and under every regime – can do.

Chapter 23

Lise and Per sat, their bodies not touching, on the sofa in her apartment, watching the nine o'clock news. In front of them they each had a glass of red wine and the remains of an almost uneaten Chinese takeaway that Per had picked up. They were on the second bottle of red wine, but the wine had really only left them feeling even more listless and drowsy. Lise had lost weight since the 'incident', as she chose to call it, and it did not suit her, but he thought nonetheless that a little colour was returning to her cheeks. Or maybe it was just the wine. She held herself at a distance from him that he could not seem to cross; it was as if a barrier had dropped between them. He knew why, of course, but as yet neither of them had wished to put it into words or talk about it. And maybe there were some things it was better not to talk about. For his own part, he was just so tired. Tired of meetings, tired of statements, tired of bosses, tired of the press's conjecturing, tired of the thought that he would be made the scapegoat. Filled with anger and grief at John's death and his inability to do anything for his partner's wife and children. Tired of the whole damn business, which had left nothing but broken lives in its wake.

He wasn't listening to the news. Instead his eyes rested on Lise again. He cared so much about her, but it was as though that first wild infatuation had burned out before it could blossom into full flame. The spark had been extinguished. Maybe it was nerves. Maybe it would be reignited when they made love properly again. The one time when they had tried she had wept as if her heart would break, only afterwards to say that she loved him for not leaving her but would he please sleep on the sofa or maybe it would actually be best if he went home. Or stay if he wanted. As long as she could be by herself, but not alone.

So now he was half preparing to go back to his own apartment. That had been the pattern over the past few days. They saw one another in the evenings, groped blindly for one another but never made contact, never talked, and then he left with not an angry word spoken, or any other words, for that matter, other than a banal 'Hi' and 'Bye' and 'See you tomorrow'. She didn't want to be alone, but she no longer wanted to sleep with him either. He was supposed to both stay and go away. He felt miserable and exhausted and confused and didn't know what to do, but still he spun out the time, knowing that soon he would have to say goodnight and go home to his own empty apartment, where his thoughts and feelings of guilt darted around the rooms like demons.

Lise was watching the news through drooping eyelids, but she straightened up when Peter Sørensen appeared, standing outside the door of the prime minister's office, and a little 'live' logo started flashing in the bottom left-hand corner of the screen.

Speaking to camera, Sørensen said that Prime Minister Carl Bang was now back in Copenhagen after his tour of the Jutland constituencies. It was because of this tour that the prime minister had been unable to spare the time to meet the Iranian-born writer Sara Santanda, who had been the subject of an assassination attempt on Flakfortet in the waters off Copenhagen.

Then came the pictures from Flakfortet they had seen so many times: Vuk's cold face, which was hard to make out because of the light and the black beard and hair. You could see the pistol on the edge of the shot of Per launching into his flying tackle of Sara, before the picture tipped as the cameraman was hit. John's body, the body of the television cameraman, the blood and the pale, horror-stricken faces. Per glanced at Lise, but she just went on watching. Maybe she had now seen these sequences so many times that it no longer hurt in quite the same way. The events of that day had been examined from every angle in all the papers and had already been dubbed 'the Flakfortet massacre'. The same shots had been shown again and again on every channel, on the normal news broadcasts and in one special edition after another.

Peter Sørensen was saying that Sara Santanda had gone to ground again and was being treated at a secret location in the United Kingdom for shock and for the injuries she sustained when Detective Inspector Per Toftlund all but killed her instead of protecting her life, as was his job. Toftlund, who had been responsible for the security surrounding Santanda's visit, had declined to comment on the matter, the reporter said.

'Arsehole,' Per muttered.

'Ssh…' Lise said as the camera zoomed out to show Prime Minister Carl Bang stepping through the glass door of his office and presenting himself for interview. Carl Bang chose his interviews carefully and always preferred to speak live on the television news so that his words could not be edited. In this case he had issued only a brief statement to the press and left his minister of justice to carry the can. That was often how he worked where matters of policy were concerned. He let his lieutenants spy out the land, debate, argue and get lambasted by the media and then, once a line became clear, he would step in with a couple of fatherly words. He never appeared on television unless he himself had chosen the time and the place. As now, when it had been decided to set up a board of inquiry to look into the whole Flakfortet affair and assign responsibility.

'Prime Minister, you haven't wanted to make a statement before now,' Peter Sørensen began, 'but the minister of justice has said that someone will be held accountable for the fact that things went so terribly wrong at Flakfortet. Is that also how you see it?'

Carl Bang wanted to look straight at the camera but remembered from his media training course that this made a bad impression on viewers. So instead he looked gravely at Peter Sørensen and answered him in what he himself believed to be an avuncular, authoritative and responsible voice, although others found it preachy and annoyingly didactic:

'First, I would like to say that this was, of course, a highly regrettable and deeply tragic incident. And that it should happen on Danish soil is quite unheard of and totally unacceptable. That cannot be emphasized strongly enough. But at the same time we must be grateful that Ms Santanda survived. We are now in the process of checking whether the relevant authorities had taken adequate security measures to protect this great writer who was visiting our country. And we will find out who is to blame for the fact that this terrorist managed to escape. If that is what happened. Because there seem to be conflicting reports on this point. If there has been any dereliction of duty, those responsible will be called…how can I put it?…to account. Naturally. Nothing will be swept under the rug. Senseless terrorism has now made its presence felt in Denmark. This is something to which we must now adjust.'

'What about Iran? Will this have any effect on Denmark's relations with the state of Iran?' Peter Sørensen asked.

'Well, it would appear, from the investigations so far, that the hit man was acting alone. That he was a crazed fanatic, so we ought not to jump to any hasty conclusions about other sovereign nations. We will have to wait for the inquiry to ascertain the exact sequence of events. Everything points to the terrorist having drowned while making his escape. All of this will be looked into, and only once we are in possession of all the relevant facts and have considered them very carefully will we decide whether there are grounds for further deliberation.'

Peter Sørensen was about to break in, but the prime minister carried on undaunted:

'I would also like to take this opportunity to extend my condolences to the families of those members of the press who died in the course of their work and the police officer who was killed in the line of duty. All honour to their memory!' He paused for a moment, looked straight at the camera, then turned his head away again: 'This was a tragic event and, fortunately, a very rare one in our otherwise very safe country. I feel for all the families, both those of the people killed at Flakfortet and those whose loved ones died elsewhere at the hands of this barbaric terrorist. Thank you.'

Carl Bang made to leave, but Peter Sørensen said quickly:

'Do you regret not having had the time to meet Sara Santanda?'

Carl Bang permitted himself a weary little smile:

'Of course. I'm sorry my schedule did not allow it. It would have been a great thrill to meet such a great writer. What more can I say? I hope there will be another opportunity.'

'Do you really think she would want to come back to Denmark?' Sørensen asked, but Carl Bang had turned on his heel and retreated through the glass door to the safety of his office.

'Hypocrites! God, they make me sick!' Lise exclaimed.

'They'll fob all the blame off on us as usual,' Per said.

'On you personally?'

'Yep. I'll probably wind up taking the rap,' he remarked matter-of-factly.

'That's not fair.'

'Fairness doesn't come in to it.'

They sat for a while watching the television, although their minds weren't really on it.

'But what happened to him?' she asked.

Per shrugged.

'*Quien sabe?*' he said in Spanish. 'Who knows?'

'I have a feeling he got away,' Lise said.

'I don't think so.'

'Then why haven't you found his body? And why did two Russian ships just happen to be in the area? They could have been owned by the Mafia. Why was his rented car found at the Stockholm-Helsinki ferry terminal? Did it drive itself to Stockholm? Did it swim across the Sound, maybe? Answer me that!'

Most of this he had heard before. It was the press's favourite sport: painting scenarios, speculating, conjecturing. Per couldn't take it anymore, not least because he simply did not understand how Vuk had got away, *if* he had got away. But he would find out, that was for sure. If he was allowed to. He thought about what Lise had just said. Swim across the Sound maybe? Was there a lead there? Might Vuk have trained as a frogman? If he had, then that opened up a whole new channel of investigation. Because he would be able to do things that ordinary mortals could not do. Things one could only learn at the Special Forces Schools around the world, skills Per himself had been taught. But in order to find out they would need the Serbs in Belgrade to give them some information, and that could only be achieved by dint of diplomatic pressure, so the Ministry of Foreign Affairs would have to get to work on the Germans, the Russians and the Americans. What if they could get hold of his service papers? Well, if nothing else, he could start by ringing round the diving shops in Copenhagen. He brightened up a little. There were avenues here that could be explored – assuming, that is, that he could get the go-ahead. Which wasn't likely. Ten seconds ago he had been sick of the whole business, now his head was buzzing with ideas again. Although it was probably a big waste of time. He fully expected to be suspended for the duration of the inquiry.

But all he said was:

'He's in the water, trapped under a sleeper. His bones are being picked clean by those big fat eels down there. They're going be particularly tasty this year.'

She dug her elbow into his side, snorting in disgust. It made him so happy. It was the first time she had been able to joke with him just a little.

'Ugh, you're horrible,' she said, but he could tell by her voice that she didn't mean it.

'If he did get away – and I say *if* – then we'll get him eventually. We have his name, pictures of him and masses of fingerprints. He's on wanted lists all over the world, and one of these days he's going to get caught, you can bet your life on it. If the bloody Iranians don't knock him off themselves for not fulfilling the contract. He'll have to spend the rest of his life on the run. He'll never be able to go to bed at night without looking over his shoulder. He'll have to watch his every step, spend all his money on protecting himself. He won't be able to trust a soul. He'll have to stay on the move all the time. It'll drive him out of his mind. He'll make mistakes. And in the end he'll die, if we don't catch him first. If he's alive.'

'I wonder who he really was. Or is. Vuk, or Janos, or Carsten or whatever the hell he's called.'

'The product of a new world order,' Per sighed, and she heard the note of weariness in his voice. They were both very far down, but perhaps they could help each other to climb up to the surface again. Did she have that much more to lose? Could she ever hope to find love again? Wasn't she surrounded, day in day out, by lonely people who scanned the lonely-hearts ads on the sly? What did she have to lose?

Per leaned back in the sofa. Lise turned down the sound with the remote control, took his hand and snuggled up against him. She felt the surprise with which his body welcomed hers.

'You scared the hell out of me, Per,' she whispered.

'I know I did.'

'I felt so betrayed, so abandoned.'

'I know.'

'I was scared shitless.'

'I know.'

'I don't think I'll ever really forget it.'

'I know.'

'No matter what happens.'

'I realize that.'

'But I'm willing to try,' she said, turning her face up to his. He stroked her cheek as if she were a little child.

'I'll probably be suspended,' he said, placing a finger on her lips as he added: 'I might go to Spain for a while…'

'I'd like to come with you, if you'll have me. And after that we'll just have to see what happens.'

'I can't ask for more than that. As long as I don't lose you,' he said.

'Oh, I don't think that's liable to happen any time soon,' she said and closed her eyes.